# BENEATH THE SECRETS

PART ONE

SHANDI BOYES

# DEDICATION

*For my crazy family.*
*Chris, Haidyn, Clayton, CJ, Mason & Mackenzie*
*Thanks for putting up with me.*

## WANT TO STAY IN TOUCH?

Facebook: facebook.com/authorshandi

Instagram: instagram.com/authorshandi

Email: authorshandi@gmail.com

Reader's Group: bit.ly/ShandiBookBabes

Website: authorshandi.com

Newsletter: http://eepurl.com/cyEzNv

# ALSO BY SHANDI BOYES

### **Perception Series:**

Saving Noah

Fighting Jacob

Taming Nick

Redeeming Slater

Saving Emily (*Novella*)

Wrapped up with Rise Up (*Novella - should be read after Bound*)

### **Enigma:**

Enigma of Life

Unraveling an Enigma

Enigma: The Mystery Unmasked

Enigma: The Final Chapter

Beneath the Secrets

Beneath the Sheets

Spy Thy Neighbor

The Opposite Effect

I Married a Mob Boss

Second Shot

The Way We Are

The Way We Were

Sugar and Spice

Lady in Waiting

Man in Queue

Couple on Hold

Enigma: The Wedding

Silent Vigilante

**Bound Series:**

Chains

Links

Bound

Restrained

Psycho

**Russian Mob Chronicles:**

Nikolai: A Mafia Prince Romance

Nikolai: Taking Back What's Mine

Nikolai: What's Left of Me

Nikolai: Mine to Protect

Asher: My Russian Revenge

Nikolai: Through the Devil's Eyes

**RomCom Standalones:**

Just Playin'

The Drop Zone

Ain't Happenin'

Christmas Trio

Falling for a Stranger

## **Coming Soon:**

Skitzo

Trey

*Dear reader,*

I know you have fallen in love with Hugo from the Enigma series and that you know and love him as he is now - but Hugo didn't become the man he was overnight. Certain events and people in his life influenced the man he has become today. So, in saying that, I feel it's important to show you how Hugo became the man he is. To do that, we need to go back to the very beginning. Only by showing you who he was in his past will you truly understand why he made the mistakes he has made, and the consequences that followed his massive decision.

Are you ready? Because it's time to dive beneath the sheets and learn about the real Hugo. The Hugo Marshall only those closest to him know.

I hope you enjoy his story.

Cheers

**Shandi xx**

# From the Beginning...

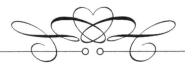

# ONE

# HUGO

I loosen my tie in the mirror, ignoring the roach devouring the crust of a sandwich on the cracked vanity in front of me. With my failure at securing a job today, I may very well be scavenging for food alongside him next week. My desperation to find a job had me arriving for an interview at a piece of shit club on the outskirts of New York City.

Calling this establishment sleazy would be an understatement. Its walls haven't seen a coat of paint since the day I first breathed air; the bathroom is more outdated than my grandma's petticoat she wore on her wedding day, and that roach isn't the first one I've seen, but I'm so desperate to add a few more digits to my scarce bank balance that I'm open to *any* opportunities available. When your options are limited, you take what you can get.

Unfortunately for me, even a crack dime bar in the middle of whoop whoop is too dignified for an ex Air Force sniper. After a brief five-minute chat with a guy who looks like he stars in seventies pornos, I was told there were no suitable positions available for a "person like me." I drove over an hour to be blown off in five minutes. Even my brother would have lasted longer than that.

Laughing off the fact I've been rejected by a Ron Jeremy wannabe, I amble out of the bathroom. My black wingtip boots click along the cracked, uneven floor as I make my way across the room. I throw my jacket onto the counter and sit down on the grime-covered barstool for a beer. I may as well down a cold beer and wait for the peak hour traffic to lessen before heading home. The bartender with a sleeve of home-botched tattoos on his left arm nods at my request for a Bud Light as he sets a scotch on the rocks down in front of the gentleman next to me.

"Leave the bottle," my nameless companion requests. The bartender doesn't blink an eye at his demanding tone.

I toss back half the bottle of beer placed in front of me before lifting my eyes to the grainy image on the small TV hanging from the ceiling. The picture is so blurry, I can't tell if it's the LA Dodgers or the Chicago Cubs playing.

Deciding the eye strain isn't worth the hassle to know the score, I shift my gaze to the dance floor. Although the bathrooms are severely outdated, and the beer isn't as cold as it could be, there are still at few dozen patrons crammed onto the four-sizes-too-small dance space.

After tipping my beer in greeting to a trio of girls at the side of the dance floor, batting their eyelashes excessively, I turn my eyes back to the TV screen. Even dolled up in pretty dresses and wearing more makeup than Prince wears on stage, their demeanor screams stage five clinger.

Since I do not want and am not looking for *any* type of relationship right now, bed companions who are reluctant to leave in the morning are not on my radar. My prime focus is on securing a job. Once I achieve that, my motivation will return to washing away the two years of hell that still plague my dreams every night.

"Are you a regular?"

A brief chuckle escapes my lips. "Normally, you wouldn't catch me dead in a shit hole like this."

I swing my eyes to where the voice is coming from. The more my gaze roams over my drinking comrade, the more my brows join.

"You?" I ask, even though I already know the answer to my question.

It's not just the expensive *Hugo Boss* suit, polished dress shoes, and one-hundred-dollar haircut that gives away the fact he's a fly-in visitor. It's the expensive watch on his wrist that's the biggest indication. That piece, no doubt, costs more than I made my entire time serving in the Air Force.

Shaking his head, Mr. Trust Fund throws back a three-finger serving of scotch before pouring himself another generous helping. When he lifts his eyes to mine, the uniqueness of their coloring gathers my interest, but it's the shroud of secrets hidden in their darkness that holds my attention.

"I was considering buying this place."

"Why?" My tone is blunt and straight to the point. "If you want to throw your trust fund into an empty pit, toss it this way."

He smirks against the rim of his dirty glass before downing another nip. After running the edge of his hand along his mouth, he says, "Unless you look past the surface, you'll never find the diamond hidden beneath the rubble."

"Hey, I'm all for finding a diamond in the rough, but this place isn't it. Even if you throw a bucket load of money into this project and had her sparkling like Mariah Carey in a sequined mini dress, you'll still be throwing money away."

He places his glass onto the countertop and angles his body to the side. "Why?"

"For one, the demographic is all wrong. The average age in this region is twenty-five to forty-seven. Even if they haven't been tied down with the standard two point five kids most people in this county have, they're either unemployed or financially strangled by the housing market. Before the stock market crashed, house prices in this area were astronomical. People went nuts, buying any partial of land they could get their mitts on. Once the market crashed, so did the land value. You may get people walking through the doors, wanting to escape the misery of life for a few hours, but they'll be the patrons who arrive already drunk, and leave once the buzz wears off."

I wave my hand around the space. Even with fifty plus people on the dance floor, including me and the mystery stranger, only four people are gathered around the bar, ordering drinks.

"This place will never be anything more than a money pit. In my opinion, you'd be better off investing in another fancy watch than this dump."

My scotch-drinking comrade gathers his suit jacket hanging on the back of his chair, and places a hundred-dollar bill onto the counter before turning his eyes to me.

"Do you have any plans tonight?"

I grin before taking a swig out of my bottle of beer. "I'm sorry, but you're not my type."

I nudge my head to the ensemble of girls formed at the side of us. Their lips pucker when they noticed they've secured our attention.

"I'm sure walking up with one of them on your arm would still give your mommy dearest the shock factor you're after."

My focus is pulled from the pretty brunette in the middle of the group when a low chuckle rumbles out of my drinking companion's lips. "I'm not gay, but I can assure you if I were, your long-haired, *Mills and Boons* romance book cover appearance you're *trying* to pull off isn't tickling my fancy."

My mouth gapes, surprised by Mr. Trust Fund's witty comeback. I knew there was something hidden in his eyes, I just had no clue it was a personality.

He puts on his suit jacket and adjusts the gold links on the cuffs before his gray eyes lock with mine. "So what do you say, Fabio, five hundred dollars for an hour of your time?"

I leap off the barstool. "Hell, if you'd mentioned the five hundred dollars at the start, I wouldn't have even made you buy me a drink first."

Winking farewell to the gathering of women floundering around the bar, I follow the smirking stranger out to an awaiting black town car idling at the curb.

"Corner of 57th and Welsh," he instructs the driver as he gestures for me to slide into the backseat before him.

Forty minutes later, we're pulling into another nightclub on the other side of the city. Since Mr. Trust Fund isn't the talkative type, preferring to interact with his cell phone instead of the real-life person sitting next to him, the entire trip was made in silence.

"Go inside and have a look around; I'll meet you in there in a few minutes," he instructs.

I nod, acknowledging I heard him before exiting the vehicle. My eyes lift from the cracked white pavement. Although not as rundown as our previous establishment, this club has still seen better days. After the driver of the town car has a quiet word with the rake-thin gentleman standing at the door, I'm ushered inside the building, forgoing the moderate size line waiting to enter.

My lips purse as my eyes absorb the space. With the poor lighting, dark furnishings and black carpeted floors, it feels like I'm entering a seedy strip club more than a dance club. Although the floor space surrounding the bar is crowded, the dance floor is nearly empty. It's only once the jukebox music alters from a slow, lazy song to a club thumping beat do partygoers emerge from the dark corners of the room like vampires coming out after sunset.

After using the clean but stark bathroom facilities, I make my way to the bar. On my way, I spot Mr. Trust Fund sitting in a stool at the very end. His suit jacket has been removed, the sleeves on his light blue business shirt have been rolled up, and he has a 25-year-old bottle of Cragganmore scotch sitting in front of him.

He raises his brows in silent questioning as I approach him.

"Is this another potential purchase?"

He lifts a crystal glass to his lips while curtly nodding.

My eyes drift around the space. "It's better than your last selection. What's your aim? More profit or better clientele?"

He hides his smirk beneath the rim of his glass. "You tell me?"

"Approximately eighty percent of the crowd here tonight are college-aged students. College kids are ideal for a nightclub, but they're cheap drunks, rarely spending over ten dollars a night on drinks. This club could benefit from charging an entry fee. That way you get the ten dollars out of them before they walk in the door, easily doubling your profits, because they will still spend their stingy ten on drinks once they enter. At this age, their focus is on the head in their pants, not whether they will have enough money to pay the heat bill."

Mr. Trust Fund leans over the counter and snags a glass from the wire rack. Remaining quiet, he pours a generous helping of scotch in the new glass before sliding it across the counter. Expensive whiskey spills over the rim and lands on the faded wooden countertop.

I dip my head in thanks before lifting the shot and downing the significant serving in one hit. A fire of warmth slides down my throat and settles in my gut, but even knowing they charge in excess of $35 a nip for Cragganmore, my taste buds can't tell the difference between its high price tag and a standard old bottle of scotch.

"If I were to charge an entry fee, what would the impact to the clientele be?"

I shrug. "I'd say maybe sixty-five percent would continue to come here even if a cover was charged, but you'll easily gain back the lost clientele within months. At the moment, the ratio of females to males is sitting at around forty, sixty. If you get rid of the cheap drunk males, the female ratio will increase, which in turn will bring back the more reputable male clientele. Girls expect guys to buy their drinks, not spill their drinks on them or puke on their shoes."

Mr. Trust Fund's smirk forms into a full smile. "Business major?"

I chuckle. "Nope," I say with a shake of my head. "I just frequented these types of places a bit during my college days." *And now,* but I keep that snippet of information to myself.

Nodding, Mr. Trust Fund stands from his chair and produces a leather wallet from the back pocket of his trousers. After removing two business cards, he hands one to the pretty blonde waitress, completely oblivious to the fact she's making kissy gaga faces at him.

"Have the owner contact me. I want to purchase this club," he instructs her, his tone firm and direct.

The bartender's teeth munch on her bottom lip as she nods her head. Ignoring the sex kitten who wants to purr at his feet, Mr. Trust Fund turns his eyes to me. While tucking a business card into the pocket of the long-sleeve dress shirt I rummaged from the back of my closest this morning, he says, "Call me tomorrow morning. I want you to join my empire."

With that, he pivots on his heels and stalks out of the building without a backward glance. Removing his card from my pocket, I discover his name is Isaac Holt, entrepreneur and founder of Holt Enterprises. It's only when I notice his business address is for a bum hick town over two hundred miles away does it suddenly dawn on me that I'm stranded in the city with no ride back to my truck.

*Fuck!*

Mumbling incoherently under my breath, I make my way outside while logging into my internet banking, praying I'll have enough in my account to pay for a taxi ride back to my truck. My brows furrow when I step onto the sidewalk and notice my truck parked at the curb. Seeing my shocked expression, a gentleman with a thick silver moustache pushes off the back-quarter panel of my truck and ambles toward me. Even though his pistol is hidden, I can tell he's carrying a weapon just from the way he walks. He has the recognizable swagger of a police officer.

"Hugo," he greets me.

I nod, masking my surprise that he knows who I am.

"Mr. Holt requested for me to give you this." He smiles while handing me a sealed white envelope. I don't need to open it to know what's inside. My nose can sniff out freshly printed Benjamin Franklins from a mile away.

"I look forward to working with you," states the unnamed

gentleman before he enters the passenger seat of a black town car idled at the side.

The black Lexus pulls into traffic just as slowly as the back passenger side window glides into place, concealing the curious gaze of Mr. Isaac Holt, A.K.A. Mr. Trust Fund.

In that instant, I knew my life was about to change. I just had no idea it would be so fucking mammoth.

## TWO

## HUGO

SIX WEEKS LATER...

"Are you sure you don't just want to go and purchase a new one?"

My sister Jorgie's cornflower blue eyes shift from gazing outside to me. Her top lip forms into a snarl, bearing her teeth before she turns her gaze back to the storm forming outside. For a majority of the day, the scattering of dark clouds in the sky pummeled the dry land with much-needed moisture.

Although the wind that intensified during the day has dispersed the clouds to the horizon, the threat of rain is still paramount. The pouring rain has turned the humid air in our hometown crisp with a cooling freshness I'm relishing after spending months living in the unbearable conditions of a hot dessert.

Jorgie is a year younger than me, and the youngest member of my family, which earns her the coveted title of *Baby Girl*. Her real name is Marjorie, but just like every member of our family, she hates her christened name, so we call her Jorgie. Although she's tall for a girl, standing a little over six feet tall, she's a little stick of dynamite, feisty and full of life. Her hair is as dark as the clouds in the sky, which makes her blue eyes stand out even more on her beige skin.

For years, she rebelled against everything and everyone who tried to get in the way of her plans to escape the clutches of Rochdale and living her life how she envisioned. She didn't want a nine-to-five job or a little house with a white picket fence. She wanted freedom; she craved adventure; she wanted to live.

All her big plans came to a halt the instant I introduced her to Hawke, my roommate from college. We were both members of the Kappa Sigma Phi fraternity. Even with our difference in age, we became blood brothers from the moment we met. Girls, partying, and hitting the club scene were how we spent the first two years of our newly founded kinship.

Watching the sparks fly between Jorgie and Hawke was like watching fireworks in a pitch-black sky. It was explosive, but I wasn't having it. For one, Hawke was two years older than Jorgie. He played the field nearly as much as I did, and he also had every intention of leaving Rochdale in the wake of his dust. And as much as Jorgie wanted to escape the stranglehold of her dreary existence in Rochdale, Rochdale is her home; she was born and raised here. Although our parents were strict and never let us get out of line when we were younger, they're the glue that ensures we remain a close-knit family.

Jorgie just rebelled more as she not only had mom and dad's stringent set of rules to adhere to, she also had Chase's. Chase is five years older than me and is the eldest sibling of my family. If you thought my aversion to Jorgie and Hawke dating was harsh, you should have seen some of the elaborate ruses Chase pulled.

Not many men can make Hawke nervous, but one wry look from Chase, and Hawke quivered in his boots like the earth was shaking beneath his feet, but Jorgie is as stubborn as a mule, and when she wants something, she never gives up. She fought tooth and nail for Hawke, and in the end, she won.

Now, I can't comprehend what my original objection was about. Jorgie is glowing and the happiest I've ever seen her. She lives in a cute little house on a street nearly smack bang in the middle of

Rochdale. She has a steady job as a bank teller, and she and Hawke are getting married in three weeks' time. He balanced out her rebellion by instilling the discipline she fought so hard against in her teens. My mom has always predicted that one day the right man would swoop in and calm the raging storm of Jorgie. Hawke was that man. He's her serene.

I slide out from beneath the motor of Jorgie's beloved 1969 Chevrolet Chevelle SS. It's a piece of shit rust bucket she purchased over eight years ago, but she loves it like it's her own child. After nagging me relentlessly for the past three years to assist her in restoring it, I managed to squeeze in a couple of hours this afternoon to replace the carburetor.

My time has become a little more flexible since I returned from my second tour in Afghanistan. Since I'm unemployed and unable to sleep, I have more hours in the day than ever before. Sleep has never been a close friend of mine, and when I joined the Air Force, it became an even more distant acquaintance.

"By replacing the faulty carby, it should be drivable again, but you have a whole heap of other issues you need to have a mechanic look at before you can even consider getting behind the wheel," I inform her, wiping chunks of black grease from my hands with an old rag hanging over the radio antenna. "Does Hawke know you're trying to get *baby* back on the road?"

Jorgie stops peering at the gathering of storm clouds on the horizon and stares at me. Her little button nose is screwed up tightly, and her lips are pursed, but she remains as quiet as a mouse. My lips tug high when I see in the guilt marring her eyes.

"You know Hawke doesn't want you driving this around, Jorgie. It isn't safe for you or your little bun in the oven," I chide, poking my index finger into the round curve of her pregnant stomach.

"Ouch." She rubs the area I poked, feigning injury. Her blue eyes lift to mine. They're glistening with the usual mischievousness that always sparks them. "He never complained about me driving it when we used to take it up to the Mt. Louis lookout during summer break."

I inwardly gag. The last image I want in my head is my little sister making out in the backseat of a car with my best mate. Some images you can never wash from your memories. When she notices my scrunched-up face, her small giggles bounce around the dingy garage.

"You do know there's only one way this baby got inside my belly, don't you, Hugo?" she jests, her tone thickly drenched with cheekiness.

"Yeah, I'm fully aware." I roll my eyes. "But that doesn't mean I want to hear all the explicit details coming out of your dirty little mouth."

Her giggles increase as she bounces on her heels. Jorgie and I are close, and I don't mean by our difference in age. We're two peas in a pod, both rebels cruising through life one adventure at a time. Although she found her Achilles heel and is expecting her first baby in a few months' time, her cheeky antics and playful disposition keep Hawke on his toes, even when he's on the other side of the world.

Hawke is currently deployed to Iraq. He's on his second and final tour as part of the First Battalion. With all troops being pulled from Iraq by the end of the year, it's the perfect time for him to leave the service.

My suspicions became piqued when Jorgie scratches her brow. It's a nervous trait she does every time she's either in trouble or is creating trouble. I cock my head to the side and arch my brow. The corners of her mouth lift as she tries to conceal a smirk.

"What are you up to, Jorgie?" I release the latch on the hood of her car. The loud crack of heavy steel clanking back into place rumbles through the quietness of the late afternoon.

Jorgie's teeth gnaw on the side of her lip as her hand fiddles the oversized button on her shirt. "You don't have any plans tonight, right?"

Even though she's asking a question, she continues talking, not waiting for a response.

"Because I'm cooking that chicken dish you love, with a side of ribs, mashed potatoes, green beans--"

"What are you up to, Jorgie?" I ask again, overemphasizing her name in a thick drawl that relays I'm not buying her bullshit offer of cooking me a free meal. Jorgie only ever cooks when she's scheming a plan or sucking up after her last failed scheme.

Her already large eyes widen, making them stand out even more than normal. "Ava is coming over for dinner."

I cringe. "That's nice; I'm sure you'll enjoy the company." I move to the corrosion-riddled driver's side door to crank the engine.

A grin carves on my mouth when the motor kicks over on the first turn of the ignition. I've never studied to be a mechanic, but I picked up some useful skills during my wild ride from rebellious teen to even more insubordinate man. I rev the engine, trying to quell Jorgie's ramblings, but I still manage to catch portions of the same pleas she has declared a minimum of once a day since I returned from my tour in Afghanistan.

"She's the perfect match for you, Hugo. She has a well-paying, stable job, owns a three-bedroom apartment in that fancy new building on the river. I went there last month; the views are too die for. Mom and Dad already know and love her, and even Helen's given her approval. And you know Helen; you have to be valedictorian four years in a row to get the smallest smidgen of attention from Helen," she jests.

I rev the engine more. It's not a requirement to check the capabilities of the motor, but it does successfully drown out Jorgie's incessant blubbering. Everything she's saying I've heard a million times before. Ever since Ava moved back to town, Jorgie has made it her mission to force Ava and me together. She gathers since she's marrying my best mate, I should marry hers. In her head, it makes perfect sense. She just failed to get the memo that I'm not interested in dating anyone right now, let alone getting married.

Once Jorgie finally stops jabbering long enough to inhale a much-needed breath, I release the heavy compression of my foot on the accelerator.

Jorgie crosses her arms in front of her chest and glares at me.

"Deny it all you want, Hugo, but you can't fight fate. One day, you and Ava will be together, and you'll have me to thank for it."

A lewd grin curls on my lips. Jorgie's favorite quote since the day she met Hawke has been "You can't fight fate." I'll admit they did meet in unusual circumstances. Most saw it as luck; Jorgie saw it as fate.

"What have you got against Ava anyway?" She paces closer to me. "You were close when you were younger."

What Jorgie is saying is true. Back in our teen days, Ava and I were close. It was a weird hidden kinship only a handful of people were aware of, but circumstances change. People change. I've changed. I'm no longer a teenage boy who can't control his cock around a beautiful girl. I'm a grown man, a man whose skins crawls when anyone mentions the dreaded M and C words: marriage and commitment.

Cranking my head to the side, I catch Jorgie's murderous glare staring at me, demanding an answer to her question.

I smirk. "For one, Ava's a dentist. You know I hate dentists." I give her the same excuse I've given the past two months.

Jorgie scoffs and rolls her eyes, not buying my pitiful excuse. "You'll never have a cavity again," she remarks, her tone smug.

I angle my head and cock my brow. "Two, she probably *smells* like a dentist."

Jorgie's bottom lip tucks into the corner as she tries in vain to stifle a smile, but she doesn't refute my claim, as she knows as well as I do Ava most likely smells like every child's worst nightmare: the dentist's office. Ava's last two weeks of high school saw her interning at a fancy dental practice downtown. I swear to god, a week after her visit, I was still smelling that ghastly dentist surgery smell.

Jorgie pledges Ava only smelled like that because her employer made her spend a week sterilizing all the equipment at the local training hospital for being insubordinate, but I'm not convinced. Ava never bent from her strong stance on following the rules to the most stringent detail, so I can't comprehend why she'd suddenly rebel against anyone, much less someone as important as her employer.

"And third, but not at all least, she's too... *innocent*," I say, my tone lowering when I say the last word.

Now don't construe this the wrong way, the last time I saw Ava, six years ago, she was no doubt attractive. Although she has always been a little nerdy, and her head never left the inside of a book during her entire academic career, she could garner the attention of any hot-blooded male she feigned an interest in – myself included.

Ava was the very first and only girl I've ever lusted over. One flash of her killer smile, and I wanted to drop to my knees and kiss her fucking feet. My infatuation with her only ended when she left for college. Unlike Jorgie and me, Ava chose to attend a university on the other side of the country. Although we kept in contact the first two years, all contact stopped when I joined the Air Force. The last time I saw Ava in person, she was walking into the airport with a flood of tears streaming down her face.

An eerie silence encroaches the garage as the first splatters of rain fall from the sky. Big drops of water sizzling on a sun-heated steel roof makes Jorgie's silence even more paramount. The only time Jorgie is quiet is when she's telepathically communicating with Hawke or fuming in anger. Placing the dirty rag onto the rickety wooden shelving at the side of the garage, I pivot on my heels.

Jorgie has her hands on her expanded hips and her brows knitted tightly. "You're seriously condemning Ava because she kept her legs closed during high school?"

Even with a pleasant breeze blowing in from outside, the room is roasting from the furious heat pumping out of Jorgie.

"Would you prefer she opened her legs for any man who feigned an interest in her?" Her lips purse as she screws up her nose. "Perhaps like Victoria Avenke." Spit flies out of her mouth when she sneers Victoria's name.

I smirk. I should have known Jorgie would have heard about my *arrangement* with Victoria. Vicky and I have been on a handful of dates. By dates, I mean casual hook ups. No strings attached. No false promises. Just two consenting adults happily sticking to the no commitments requirement of our agreement.

"Vicky knows what she's getting."

Jorgie huffs. "Yeah, with you and at least another ten guys."

"Cattiness doesn't suit you, Jorgie."

Her eyes snap to mine. "It's not being catty when it's true. Vicky puts out more rides per year than the Ferris wheel at the State Fair."

I try to hold in my laughter, but my chuckle rumbles through my gaped mouth when I spot the repulsed mask slipping over Jorgie's face. Jorgie has always attracted men, ever since she passed the awkward puberty stage. When she was younger, her legs were too long, and her body was as straight as a board. It was only once she filled out did mine and Chase's big brother protective mode kick up a gear.

Vicky was the equivalent of Jorgie's schoolyard bully in a nasty prom queen bitch way. Vicky was one of those girls who gained the devoted attention of every guy in school, including the male teaching staff. Even back in the day, when Vicky and I first messed around as seniors, Jorgie was disgusted.

It's safe to say, no matter how much time passes, Jorgie and Vicky will never be classed as casual acquaintances, let alone friends. Jorgie still holds a grudge against Vicky from when she called her a giraffe in junior high. As much as Vicky's taunting words hurt Jorgie, it was true. In her pre-teen years, Jorgie was tall, lanky and had the hugest pair of wobbly knees. She was the very definition of a giraffe.

"You won't be laughing when you catch something off her," Jorgie mumbles, her snarky tone barely audible from the heavy pelts of rain hammering the steel roof.

"Very mature," I remark.

She screws up her nose and sticks out her tongue. I pace to the side of the garage to pack away the tools I used. A grin carves on my mouth at the anal cleanliness of Hawke's garage. He's so meticulous about his man cave, each tool has its own rightful spot. Like Jorgie,

Hawke also collects vintage cars, but unlike Jorgie, his are actually valuable.

One of his beauties is a 1969 Chevrolet Camaro Z-28 SS Coupe. I've known Hawke for seven years, and I've only driven his Camaro once. That was only because he was too drunk to drive and refused to leave it at the college dorm where we were attending a party. My eyes drift to the other side of the garage. Even hidden under a protective car cover, I can recall its shimmering dark blue paint with thick white stripes and fat-rimmed tires. Just the thought of its 500 horsepower aluminum V-8 engine rumbling through my ears as I cruise down the highway has my pulse quickening and my palms sweating.

Noticing my appreciative glance, Jorgie stands next to me. "Stay for dinner, and I'll show you were Hawke hides the keys." Her voice is barely a whisper, like she's afraid Hawke will hear her all the way in Iraq.

My eyes rocket to hers. "You're that desperate for me to stay for dinner?"

A vast grin stretches across her face as she nods her head.

"Deal," I say, thrusting my hand out in offering.

I balk as bile forms in the back of my throat when Jorgie spits on her hand and wraps it around mine before I have the chance to protest her disgusting and childish prank.

"You've always said 'a deal means nothing unless it's been sealed with a spit shake or a pinkie promise.'"

"I haven't said that since I was ten, and if I knew I had a choice, I would've chosen the pinkie promise," I reply, running my spit-sticky hand down my jean-covered thigh.

Jorgie's giggles resonate over the heavy downpour of rain as she makes her way into the three-bedroom weatherboard house with me following closely behind. She has a smug grin etched on her face, clearly looking victorious. Little does she know I would have agreed to date Ava exclusively for a month if it meant getting behind the wheel of Hawke's baby again. Hell, I may have even agreed to marry her. Oh, who am I kidding? That would *never* happen.

"Have I got enough time to shower before Ava arrives?" I peer down at my grease-stained jeans. It isn't that I'm trying to impress Ava, but I don't want her looking at me as an unemployed grease monkey. Even if that's what I technically am right now.

Jorgie's eyes flick to the large grandfather clock in her small but well-decorated living room. "Oh, yeah, plenty of time. Ava won't be here for at least an hour."

My brows scrunch from the evasiveness in her tone. Spotting my expression, the biggest grin stretches across Jorgie's face.

"I'll be out in ten," I advise, snubbing the gleam in her eyes that displays she's in the process of planning a mischievous scheme.

I've only been in the shower for a matter of minutes, crooning to an old classic, "Footloose" by Kenny Loggins, when a door creaking open resonates into the room. I twist the volume dial down on the water-clogged radio shower and prick my ears.

"Jorgie?"

I hear a breathless snicker before, "I have to pop down the street. I'll be back in a few minutes; I forgot the ribs... and the chicken for dinner."

I roll my eyes, unsurprised by Jorgie's forgetfulness. She has a memory like a sieve, full of holes.

"I've thrown your dirty clothes into the wash, so grab some clean ones out of Hawke's closet."

"Alright," I reply as I massage Jorgie's strawberry-scented shampoo into my scalp.

"I'm going to smell like strawberry fucking shortcake," I mumble under my breath.

My brow arches when Jorgie's chuckle bellows through the now closed bathroom door. My shoulders lift into a shrug. *Maybe she heard my quiet declaration?*

Once the smell of sweat and grease has been replaced with strawberries and soap, I turn off the shower and step out of the bath, being extra attentive not to slip ass-over-tit on the glossy tiles since the bathmat I put down before climbing into the shower has been removed. My teeth grit when I notice the towel rack I replenished with a large fluffy towel is also void of any water-drying apparatus.

"Jorgie!" I yell. "Bring me a goddamn towel."

The last time she pulled this prank, she at least left the bathmat, which adequately covered me as I made the ten-second walk from the main bathroom to the master suite on the other side of the house. My naked dash had me strolling straight past Jorgie's co-workers, who were getting ready to leave for a colleague's bachelorette party.

When they spotted me sauntering by, totally saturated and practically naked, they assumed Jorgie hired me for pre-party entertainment. The spark in Jorgie's eyes dampened when she learned two valuable lessons that night. One, I'm not ashamed of my body, and two, her co-workers are a bunch of deviant housewives whose husbands lack in the art of seduction. Within ten minutes, I walked out of the living area two hundred dollars richer, and one point higher on mine and Jorgie's record-breaking prank tally.

After running my hands over my body to remove the excess droplets of water, I crank open the bathroom door. The house is eerily quiet; the only sound I hear is the grandfather clock's pendulum swinging. I strut down the hall, not bothering to cover my junk. My hips are jutted, my cock is swinging, and the biggest, leering grin is stretched across my face. If Jorgie wants to pull this type of prank, she can suffer the consequences of her actions.

I take a detour into the square-shaped kitchen at the end of the hall, expecting to find a grinning Jorgie. My steps are eager as the excitement of watching her prank backfire in her face gains momentum with every stride I take. My eagerness is dampened and my smirk fades when I discover the kitchen is empty. *Maybe she did need to go the grocery store?*

Deciding to make good use of my detour, I help myself to a bottle of beer. Thankfully, beer is the one thing that remains unchanged in this house when Hawke is deployed. Strawberry-scented bath products, hand-knitted teapot covers, and hideous floral cushions emerge from the attic within days of his deployment. When Hawke returns home, he'll spend a minimum of two weeks returning his house to its pre-Jorgie days, as there's no way a man like Hawke would be caught dead with strawberry shortcake-scented hair.

Pivoting on my heels, the condensation-covered bottle of beer slips from my wet grasp and plummets onto the floor. I grimace when it clangs against the linoleum floor but remarkably stays in one piece. Following the natural flow of the old weatherboard house, the thankfully still-capped bottle rolls away from me, only coming to a stop when it hits a black high heel-wearing foot.

My brow arches and my heart rate kicks up a gear. It isn't just the height of the heel that makes me aware these shoes aren't being worn by a pregnant Jorgie, it's the fact they're holding up one of the most stellar pairs of luscious, caramel-colored legs I've ever seen in my life that's the biggest giveaway.

Women's legs are my weakness. The longer they are, the better. This black pump shoe-wearing female has one of the longest, smoothest, and sexiest pairs of legs I've ever laid my eyes on. That might have something to do with the fact only mere inches of her thighs are covered by a super small scrap of white material called a pair of teeny, tiny mini shorts.

Prying my eyes away from the dick-twitching skin of her inner thighs, I continue with my perusal. I chew on my lip when my eyes run over the itty-bitty curve of a seductive set of hips and an even more generous swell of a pair of curvy breasts barely contained in a super thin skin-colored sweater. My head angles to the side, and my eyes widen when they finalize their journey at the captivating beauty's hypnotic face.

"Ava?" I ask in disbelief.

For the love of god, someone please tell me this stunner isn't the geeky wannabe dentist, Ava. One rake of my eyes over her beguiling body and gorgeous face has my dick turning to stone. I could barely suppress the urge to have her beneath me when she had braces on her teeth and a big mess of black ringlet curls on the top of her head. Now, I don't stand a fucking chance.

"Hey, Hugo," she greets me, confirming my suspicion.

Even rattled with nerves, her voice is a soft, husky purr that makes my cock even harder. When her perfectly straight pearly white teeth become exposed in a dimple-baring smile, my cock jumps.

*Holy shit, call an ambulance. We have a man down.*

# THREE

## AVA

My eyes don't know where to look. I try to pry them away from the core-clenching visual displayed in front of me, but no matter how much my brain signals for my eyes to shift their focus to something less stimulating, they refuse to budge.

Every inch of Hugo's glistening, panty-drenching body is on display, and by every inch, I mean every goddamn rock-hard inch. Other than an Air Force squadron tattoo on the lower half of his left arm, the remainder of his skin is untouched, wet, and completely exposed to my overeager eyes.

Ripples of muscles, throbbing veins, and a small trail of hair that flows down the middle of his stomach to join the trimmed patch of dark hair displayed above his... I gulp as the temperature in the room turns roasting.

My focus from his impressively sized erect cock diverts to his face when, "Ava," sounds from his apprehensive voice.

He tilts his head to the side as his eyes bulge. He appears utterly surprised to see me. *Did Jorgie not tell him I was coming?* On numerous occasions the past few months, I informed Jorgie my childish crush on Hugo matured and moved on, but no matter how confident my declaration was, she continued to plead for us to get together. Last week, I succumbed to her hormonal pleas.

"Hey, Hugo." I internally battle not to squirm from his avid gaze.

I've grown up a lot since my eyes last absorbed the hunk of a man in front of me, but his piercing blue eyes and well-carved face still sets my pulse racing. Hugo was my very first childhood crush, but since he was the epitome of every girl's walking fantasy, my high school crush never amounted to anything more than awkward glances, drunken kisses, and the occasional embarrassing attempts at flirting with the corny one-liners I picked up from the Cosmo magazines I sneakily read while my mother purchased groceries at our local supermarket. No matter how often I batted my eyelashes or pursed my lips in that duck face pose only the Kardashians can make look sexy, Hugo only ever saw me as a friend... unless he was drunk.

But from the thickness of his cock standing tall and proud, and the rugged smirk etched on his mouth, I'd say he has noticed a few changes I've made the past few years. *It's a pity his craved attention is years too late.*

Releasing shallow breaths to cool my overheated body, I bob down to gather the bottle of beer resting at my feet. The slickness of sweat misting my body thickens when my quick movements in my ridiculously high stilettos cause me to tumble. My eyes bulge when I land on my knees and come face to face with Hugo's crotch. One inch closer and I would have lost an eye.

*Great position, Ava. Two minutes in his presence and you're already on your knees in a begging pose. Can anyone say "Loser?"*

Swallowing the meteor lodged in my throat, I lift my mortified eyes to Hugo. A confident smirk is carved on his ruggedly handsome face, his eyes blazing with mischief. My breathing deepens to a ragged gasp when I catch sight of his cock twitching in the corner of my eye. His penis is beautiful. Thick, long, heavily veined, and cut. *Perfect!*

Suddenly, like the sun peering out from a dark cloud, lucidity forms in Hugo's gleaming eyes.

"Shit, sorry," he mumbles as his eyes bounce around the kitchen, looking for something he can use to cover himself.

When his avid gaze comes up empty, he lowers his hands down in front of his crotch, only just concealing the salivating view from my sight. With both of his hands occupied vainly maintaining his dignity, I scramble off the floor.

Blowing a wayward strand of wavy hair from the front of my eye, I attempt to hand the froth-topped bottle of beer to Hugo. A snarl curls on my lips when he doesn't attempt to remove the bottle from my clasp.

He bites on his bottom lip as his eyes lock with mine. "Unless you want another visual of my," he coughs, clearing his throat, "cock, I can't accept it."

The brash grin on his mouth lifts higher when I hesitate for only the slightest second before placing the beer on the kitchen countertop at my side. I can't help it. I've never been quick-witted, and my brain is barely functioning after absorbing the awe-inspiring visual in front of me.

Just as quickly as the temperature in the room rose, awkward tension invades the air between us. We stand across from each other, staring but not speaking. It's the quietest we've ever been in each other's presence. During high school, Hugo and I were as opposite as they came in the popularity rankings, but I still classed him as a friend.

The gaucheness plaguing our small gathering gets a moment of reprieve when a car honking wails through the kitchen, closely followed by Jorgie's soft voice. "Hugo, come and help me with the bags."

I shift my eyes to glance out the kitchen window. Jorgie is waddling away from the driver's side door of her beat-up old Honda to the trunk. She's huddled under a lopsided yellow umbrella that's miserably failing at keeping her dry from the downpour of rain.

Drifting my eyes back to Hugo, I say. "I'll go and help Jorgie?"

My tone makes my statement come out more as a question than a confirmation.

"Alright." His voice is tempting. "You do that, and I'll go and get dressed."

I hunch my shoulders. "If you want to; you know, whatever suits you," I reply, trying to pretend I'm not affected by his nakedness.

His heavy, hooded gaze rakes my body before it lifts to settle on my eyes. "Seeing naked men a regular occurrence for you now, Ava?"

I purse my lips and return his stare. "I am a doctor."

*Sheesh! Here comes the stupid one-liners. I'm a dentist. The only thing I'm stripping naked is a tooth cavity, not hot-blooded men.*

Lifting my hand, I shelter my face from the smile that morphs onto Hugo's face.

"Well, in that case." He grabs the beer off the counter with one hand and uses his spare hand to crack it open, leaving himself exposed.

My pupils enlarge to the size of saucers as my saliva glands work overtime, but I somehow manage to maintain his eye contact. Although, the internal battle not to drop my eyes is the hardest fight I've ever endured. My chin quivers when our combat merges onto a dangerous battlefield riddled with landmines when the contents of his beer fizz over the neck of the bottle.

When he lifts the beer to his mouth, droplets of the overflowing liquid dribble down the side of his hand, dripping onto his smooth pectoral muscle. My eyes follow every slither the envious droplets make down the impressive ridges of his torso, bumped abs in his stomach, and formidable V muscle before it's absorbed by the dark patch of hair above his...

"Oh my god, Hugo! Go and put on some clothes," squeals Jorgie.

I jump from her thunderous roar bouncing around the kitchen before diverting my eyes to the window.

"You're so disgusting! We eat in here! Your nephew is going to eat in here!"

My shoulders shake when gagging noises escape Jorgie's mouth, closely followed by the profound rumble of Hugo's laughter. This type of jeering is nothing new for Jorgie and Hugo. They have one of the longest running prank tallies in the history of sibling rivalry.

Their mom, Edie, said it started before Jorgie even escaped the womb. When Edie was heavily pregnant with Jorgie, any time Hugo would climb onto her lap, begging for attention, Jorgie would kick up a storm. Mrs. Marshall said the aim of Jorgie's monstrous size foot was always firmly rapt on Hugo.

My eyes return front and center when bare feet stomping on the wooden floorboards in the living room resonates through my ears. A grin tugs on my mouth when I spot Jorgie's narrowed gaze planted on a retreating Hugo. Unlike mine, her eyes are shooting daggers at the back of his head. I'm happily implanting the visual of his naked derriere into my memory for future use. Hugo has always had a spectacular backside, but just like every other muscle in his body, it seems to have improved with age.

Jorgie's gaze swings to peer at me. Her brows are scrunched, and her beige skin is whiter than normal. *"That* gets you all hot and bothered?" She hooks her thumb over her shoulder.

"Used to," I correct. My tone is confident even though my stomach is riddled with the fluttering of butterflies mid-flight.

Jorgie rolls her eyes before digging her hand into the drenched paper bag. She has never understood my crush on Hugo, and in all honesty, it would be a little weird if she did. I playfully bump her with my hip before assisting in unpacking the groceries. My brows furrow when I notice the bag is full of non-perishable food supplies most people generally have stacked in their pantries on a regular basis. My suspicion piques when I notice the glass canister of cracked pepper is half empty.

"Jorgie..." My tone is low and crammed with suspicion.

"What?" She moves to the fridge to pull out the pre-prepared marinated chicken and ribs.

I pace closer to her. "You didn't really go to the grocery store, did you?"

Her right shoulder lifts into a shrug, but she remains quiet. She may be conniving and sneaky in her endeavors to force Hugo and me together, but she can't lie straight in bed. Even when she tells a little fib to get herself out of trouble, her deceitfulness only lasts a matter of minutes before the truth blurts out of her mouth.

"Oh fine," she huffs. "I didn't go to the store. There, are you happy?" Overdramatically, she throws her arms into the air.

*See, proof she can't lie.*

She puts the chicken in the oven before pivoting around to face me. I guess my first clue she didn't forget the most vital ingredients for dinner was that the oven was sitting on a pre-warming setting, but in all honesty, even with the room being heated by the 390-degree setting, it wasn't the oven creating the sweat-forming hotness in the room. That honor solely belonged to Hugo.

"Didn't you learn after your last shower prank that Hugo doesn't fluster over his nakedness being on display?" My pulse quickens when I refer to his naked body.

Jorgie's face pales. "But you missed out on all the fun that night."

"So you thought you'd try again?"

She smiles and nods her head.

"Jorgie, I told you."

"I know, I know," she interjects. "You no longer have a crush on Hugo."

My heart ceases beating when a rumbling, smug tone sounds through my ears. "You had a crush on me?"

My mortified eyes glare at Jorgie before I shift them to Hugo. Although his body is covered with a lot more clothing than it was, I'm still imagining him naked.

"Yeah, *had*, but that was years ago," I respond, acting like it's no big deal. "That was way before I knew who you did…umm, what you did… umm, who you really are."

*For crying out loud, Ava, shut your mouth!*

I prop my hip on the counter and snag the bottle of beer resting on the top of it. While shifting my eyes between Jorgie and Hugo, I take a large mouth-filling gulp of the luke-warm beer. I don't care whose beer it is; I just need something to clog the word vomit dribbling out of my mouth. Hugo helps himself to a cold beer as Jorgie excuses herself to use the restroom. Once he cracks open the fresh bottle, he hands it to me.

"Thanks," I mumble, placing the half-empty bottle back onto the counter.

When he collects the bottle, I assume he's going to put it into the trash. So you can imagine my surprise when he lifts the bottle to his mouth and consumes the liquid inside, not the slightest bit concerned that my dark plum-covered lips were just pressed against the rim his lips are now sealed over. *I wonder if he can taste the flavor of my lip gloss?*

We stand across from each other with nothing beer being swallowed between us. I fight to keep the repulsed expression off my face when I swig on the malted liquid. Even though beer has never been my drink of choice, the coolness of the beverage is helping to dampen the cluster of spasms twinging my womb.

Hugo's jean-covered hip is propped against the counter, replicating my position. He doesn't speak, but I can feel his gaze on me. I keep my eyes on anything but him. I don't want to run the risk of the visual of him fully clothed replacing the more stimulating images of him naked in my mind. *Oh my god, did I just say that?* What I meant to say was, *I don't need to see any more of him than I already have....*

*Yeah, don't worry, I'm not buying my pathetic excuse either.*

As the minutes tick by, the silence between us becomes unbearable. We were never like this when we were younger. We may have been complete opposites on paper, but when we were alone, away from prying eyes, we were friends. I push off the counter to go in search of Jorgie. Interrupting a pregnant lady in the bathroom would have to be more entertaining than being stuck in the awkwardness plaguing this small eat-in kitchen.

Just as I'm about to exit the room, Hugo questions, "So are you a fully qualified dentist now?"

"Yes," I reply with a little too much dramatic flair, but talking about dentistry comes easy to me as it's one of my greatest passions. "Well, kind of, I'm halfway through two years of clinical training. I work at a surgery downtown and assist in the free clinic every Thursday morning at Rochdale Village. I've already been offered a partnership at the surgery office once my practical training is over."

I lean my hip back against the counter. "In the main practice, I only work with children, but at the clinic I also work with adult patients. It's a demanding job, not like a surgeon at a major hospital or anything dramatic like that, but it's still an important industry. I really enjoy it," I babble.

Hugo's nose scrunches up as a grin tugs his lips high.

"What?"

He shrugs. "Nothing."

"Oh come on, Hugo, spit it out," I jest, dying to know what has caused the odd expression on his face.

He chuckles and takes another sip of his beer. My eyes zoom in on his mouth when his tongue delves out to gather a small smear of beer glistening on his lips.

"I just find it amusing that you enjoy torturing little children for a living."

My eyes snap from his mouth to his gleaming blue eyes. "I don't torture kids."

His brow cocks. "Yeah, you do; you're the equivalent of every child's worst nightmare."

I balk. "I am not," I reply with a stomp of my foot, chucking a childish tantrum like a five-year-old instead of the twenty-four-year-old woman I am. "My patients love me. I even get cute little paintings in the mail and thank you cards."

My heart flutters faster when a broad grin stretches across his face. "That probably say, 'thanks for not drilling my teeth today, Doc.'"

My immature tantrum stops, and a small grin tugs the corners of my mouth. "That's only in every second card," I retort, crossing my arms under my chest.

The heat in the kitchen is more noticeable when Hugo's hearty chuckle bellows throughout it. It was that very laugh that captured my attention well over ten years ago. It was also the laugh that made me realize my feelings for Hugo were more than just a small schoolyard crush.

Years ago, Jorgie and I were undertaking a bitch-fest on the queen of bitches herself, Victoria Avenke, completely oblivious to the fact Hugo was eavesdropping on our private conversation. When he impersonated my mimic of Victoria's pompous hair flick, I sneered at him through my brace-covered teeth before I dove over the sofa and tackled him to the ground.

When I straddled his hips and commenced a tickling onslaught on his stomach, that also became the first time a tingling of excitement dashed through my body and clustered in my womb. Mortified with embarrassment from the husky moan that spilled from my lips and unable to comprehend why my body was reacting the way it was, I scrambled off Hugo and bolted out the front door without a backward glance.

I don't know whether Hugo sensed my body's reaction to him or if I was just paranoid, but things were different between us from that day. Then as the years went on, Hugo's presence in my life became less and less, but even with him dating a range of beautiful ladies, attending college parties, and being the cool guy on campus, I still saw him at least five to six times a year. The past six years have been the longest we've gone without physically seeing each other in nearly fifteen years.

When Hugo's laughter dies down, his tear-glistening eyes lift and lock with mine. "What about in your personal life, Ava; any changes there the past few years?"

It may just be my overactive imagination or the fact I feel like I've time-warped back to my teenage years, but I swear there's a whole heap of sexual innuendo laced in his simple question.

I uncross my arms and pick at the plum polish on my thumbnail. "Yeah, a few changes," I mumble with a small shrug.

I hate talking about my private life. My parents are extremely strict and Catholic, and I'm also an only child. By the time Jorgie came into my life, I'd become so accustomed to keeping my feelings locked away that I've never openly expressed them.

I lift my eyes to glance at Hugo. He's watching me with a spark in his eyes I've never witnessed before. When he catches my curious glance, the unidentifiable glimmer is replaced with his usual cheeky blaze that regularly fires his vibrant blue eyes. He smirks against the rim of his beer before taking another mouth-filling gulp.

"What about you? How are things with Vicky?"

## FOUR

## HUGO

It takes all my strength to swallow the beer and not spray it over Ava's beautiful face. Ava has always been attractive, in a librarian, geeky type of way; but like a bottle of fine wine, she keeps getting better with age. The last time I saw her, she had a crazy mess of ringlet curls on the top of her head and was wearing the most hideous pair of baggy jeans and a bulky sweater that covered every inch of her skin, but today, she's captivatingly beautiful. Not just in her clothes, but her skin as well.

Her hair is cut to sit just below her shoulders in a wispy curl design that frames her face perfectly. She has finally grown into her dark eyes that always seemed too large for the small features of her face, and the years of her wearing braces has paid off with her now bearing a perfect smile. Her allure is so impressive, she made me forget I was standing in front of her stark naked. If that wasn't bad enough, I also had a raging hard-on like a thirteen-year-old boy who can't control his cock.

One rake of her body and I was straight back to the sixteen-year-old boy she tackled to the ground years ago. That day was the first time I realized Ava was more inexperienced sexually than most teenage girls her age. I'm not saying the girls at my high school were easy, but they had no hesitations in hooking up under the bleachers after a football game or at Mt. Louis lookout, where Ava acted like she'd never kissed a guy before. When I bucked my hips against the warmth her panties failed to conceal, her face paled, her eyes widened, and she bolted out of the house without a backward glance, not giving me the reaction I was aiming for.

It was that night I decided inexperienced girls weren't for me. Virginity snatching is too much of a commitment for any guy to make. It wouldn't matter if you were the worst lay they ever had, girls remember the guy they gave their virginity to. That's not a stigma I want attached to my name. *He was a great lay. The best sex I've ever had. He had the largest cock I've ever seen.* They're titles I'll happily accept. *Virgin snatcher?* Nope, not happening.

My focus returns to the present when a hand waves in front of my face. Turning my gaze, I catch the amused eyes of Jorgie glaring at me. After absorbing the expression on my face, she dramatically huffs before strolling to the cupboards under the wall oven. Even with the clanging of the pots and pans rattling through my ears, I hear her murmur, "Probably daydreaming about Vicky's fake double-D breasts."

From the grimace that crosses Ava's face, I assume she also heard Jorgie's quiet ramblings.

"Vicky and I aren't dating," I blurt out, suddenly having the urge to ensure Ava is aware that Vicky and I are not a couple.

"Oh." Ava takes a swig of her beer, hiding her smile behind the neck of the bottle.

"They aren't a couple," Jorgie confirms, reinforcing my statement.

The smile curling Ava's lips enlarges.

"They just fuck each other," Jorgie adds on.

My eyes snap to Jorgie at record speed as a splattering cough sounds from Ava's mouth.

"What?" Jorgie feigns innocence. "It's true, isn't it?"

Once Ava regains the ability to breathe through the beer now in her lungs instead of her stomach, she places the bottle on the countertop and moves to stand between Jorgie and me. Wetting a dishcloth in the sink, she uses it to remove the spittle of beer from her bone-colored short-sleeved knit top. My hand scraping along the three-day old stubble on my jaw is the only noise heard when my eyes zoom in on the budded peaks of her nipples straining against her thin shirt.

My nostrils flare and my eyes narrow as an oven mitt smacks me upside my head. My teeth grinding together sounds just above the doorbell ringing when Jorgie mouths, *"That's what real boobs look like,"* as though I've never seen a real pair before. Yes, Vicky now has a large set of fake breasts, but I've seen plenty of real ones, including Vicky's before she had the augmentation done.

My brow cocks when Ava declares, "I'll get the door." Her appearance has gone from calm and kicked back, to a woman who looks like the grim reaper is knocking at her door.

With a flash of a smirk, she bolts out of the kitchen. I wait until I hear the clicking of her heels on the tiles in the entranceway before I turn my gaze back to Jorgie.

"What the hell did you do to Ava?"

Jorgie smiles broadly. "That wasn't me." She raises her eyes to me. "That was all Ava's doing. Don't act surprised though, Hugo; you've always known what she was hiding under those hideous baggy clothes she wore."

Yeah, I knew, but I preferred being the only guy who did.

When I take a step closer to Jorgie, my stomach grumbles as the smell of marinated chicken filters through my nostrils.

"Is Ava still *innocent*?" I blurt out.

Fuck, that didn't come out how I'd envisioned.

I know this makes me a chauvinistic ass, but no red-blooded man could run their eyes over Ava's enticing body and not be interested in finding out *exactly* what she looks like under those teeny tiny shorts. Jorgie's mouth gapes open, and for the first time in her entire twenty-four years on this planet, she's rendered speechless. The temperature in the room turns excruciating when she crosses her arms, squeezing them between the minimal space left between her stomach and her chest.

"That's an extremely personal question, Hugo."

"I know. Why do you think I asked you instead of Ava?" I smirk to hide my grimace.

Jorgie's eyes narrow into tiny slits, unimpressed by my attempt to defuse the insensitivity of my question with humor.

"Would you prefer I asked Ava?"

*Thankfully, even with all the blood from my body rushing to the head of my cock, I was smart enough not to do that.*

"Ask me what?" queries Ava, walking back into the kitchen.

Jorgie's roughish eyes shift from me to Ava. "Hugo wants to know if you're a v--,"

My hand shoots up to cover Jorgie's mouth before she can ask her bold question. She waggles her brows as a fiery ember ignites her eyes, believing she's secured a vault full of ammunition in our long-running prank game.

The victory in her eyes dampens when I mutter, "Do you recall where my hands were earlier?" in a smug tone.

Jorgie appears gaunt like it did the first three months of her pregnancy. After giving her a few moments to absorb the scandalousness of my prank, I grandly wink before removing my hands from her mouth. Air escapes my lips in a hurry when she ribs me with her elbow and knees me in the backside. She sneers at me as her hands dart out to grasp a glass of sparkling apple cider that she guzzles down at breakneck speed.

"It's alcohol-free, Jorgie; it ain't going to burn away my cooties," I jest, my tone full of cheekiness.

"I can pretend," she garbles between mouthfuls.

My neck cranks faster than a missile being fired from a jet when a male snickering filters through my ears. The muscles in my stomach tense when I see Ava being clasped around the waist by an African American man. My brows scrunch as my eyes roam over a face I've seen many times before. Even though seven years has passed since I last laid my eyes on him, he still has the same clipped close-to-the-scalp afro, prominent nose, dark green eyes, mocha skin coloring, and arrogant grin he's always had.

"Marvin," I greet, holding my tongue from calling him his infamous nickname.

Marvin was adeptly given the nickname of "pencil dick" during our final year of high school. It was because... Hold on, does a title like that need an explanation? It's pretty self-explanatory. Alright, for those of you who are a little slow on the uptake, it means his dick is long and skinny – like a pencil.

"Hugo," he greets me, removing one of his hands from Ava's waist to offer a shake.

I suffocate a growl rumbling up my chest before accepting his handshake. It isn't that I want to possessively stake a claim to Ava, but Marvin is a dawg, and he knows it. Even with his less-than-impressive male appendage, he's one of the biggest bed hoppers in our hometown. It was the whole reason his nickname spread like an out-of-control wildfire during summer break before our final year of high school.

It's also the reason why he has had so many bed companions – they never want to return for round two. Ava was naïve in her younger years, but even if she has been living under a rock the past few years, she'd have to be aware of Marvin's reputation now.

"Hey, Marvin." Jorgie leans in to place a kiss on the side of his cheek. "Ava said she was bringing a friend to dinner; she just failed to mention it was a male."

Jorgie's surprise at Ava's *date* is clearly audible in her voice. With Ava's caramel skin coloring, it takes a lot to make her blush, but the slightest hue of pink adorns her cheeks from the stern glare Jorgie is directing at her. Ava's gaze flicks to me when Marvin hands Jorgie a bottle of Duckhorn Napa Valley Cabernet Sauvignon, gauging my reaction to her arriving with a date. The concern marring her face fades when I smirk and wink at her. In the past, I did have some *slight* jealousy issues when it came to men wanting to get close to Ava, but this time is different. I have *nothing* to be worried about. The guy has a pencil dick for crying out loud.

For the next three hours, things go surprisingly well. Marvin and I had a lot of mutual friends in school, so the conversation flowed nearly as freely as the alcohol in his wine glass did. I gave Marvin updates on the guys he'd lost contact with, and he rambled incessantly about himself. The only good thing that has come from his long-winded tirade is that I discovered why a woman like Ava would agree to go on a date with a man like Marvin. His dad owns the dentistry practice Ava has been offered a position at, and Marvin is already a partner at the same practice, even with him only finalizing his dentist credentials two months ago.

A small chuckle escapes my lips when Jorgie awakens from her latest powernap. As riveting as Marvin believes his conversation has been, I swear on at least three occasions, Jorgie has fallen asleep on the sofa. It's only when Ava nudges her with her elbow does she wake up. Jorgie's surprised eyes bounce between three sets of eyes staring at her. She appears utterly confused. My laughter becomes uncontainable when she wipes away a smattering of drool from the bottom of her chin.

"You might need to cut back on those apple ciders, Sis," I playfully quip.

In true Jorgie style, she screws up her nose and sticks out her tongue.

"We should probably get going anyway," Ava says, shifting her gaze to Marvin, who is eagerly nodding at her statement.

"Oh no, don't go," Jorgie pleads when Ava stands from the couch and gathers the beer bottles from the table. "It's only just hitting nine PM on a Saturday."

Ava's eyes drift between Marvin and Jorgie while she contemplates. Her brows are pulled together tightly, her lips pursed.

"I have that paperwork I need to do." Marvin glares at Ava, reprimanding her for wanting to stay out on a Saturday night.

"Okay," she whispers so faintly it's only just audible.

Jorgie huffs, and her shoulders sag when Ava turns to face her. She doesn't need to speak, Jorgie can see her decision marred all over her disappointed face.

"Party pooper," Jorgie mumbles when Marvin raises a cell phone to his ear to call a taxi.

Jorgie's gloomy mood continues the entire time we wait on the front porch for their taxi to arrive. Thankfully, since it's still early, it only takes five minutes for a yellow cab to pull into the driveway. Ava propels herself from the wicker chair when she spots the taxi, no doubt eager to get away from the thick stench of awkwardness plaguing our group. Jorgie's never had the ability to conceal her anger, and for the past five minutes, her obvious annoyance has been firmly rapt on Marvin.

A smirk etches on my mouth when Ava turns her dark brown eyes to me. "It was good seeing you again, Hugo," she whispers. The twinkle in her eyes relays the truth of her statement.

I lean in and wrap my arms around her shoulders before pulling her into my chest. My nostrils flare when they detect the aroma of the chocolate truffles she ate for dessert. She smells delicious. Almost good enough to eat. Chocolate and strawberries have always been a mouth-watering combination.

*Where the fuck did that notion come from?*

"Let's not have another six years pass by without some sort of contact," she murmurs in my ear before placing a kiss on my cheek.

A smirk curves on my lips when I see the furious glare Marvin is directing at me. His penetrating gaze is shooting daggers of fire. His blatant jealousy ensures my friendly cuddle with Ava lasts a little longer than would be classed as acceptable. My smirk turns into a full-toothed smile when his face reddens over my playful jibe.

*He should be worried,* my *nickname in high school was...*

"Why are there two cabs?" Jorgie asks, interrupting me from my private thoughts.

Her baffled eyes flick between Marvin and Ava.

"Ava lives by Hamilton. I live in an apartment building on Pinter," Marvin explains.

"Yeah, so." Jorgie's tone is full of bitchiness. "That's still within a few miles of each other."

"Marvin doesn't see the sense in sharing a taxi fare if you aren't going to the same location," Ava answers while slipping out of my embrace.

Her tone is pleasant, but her eyes expose her real opinion on Marvin's logic. She thinks he's just as stingy as the rest of us.

"Then why do you need to leave?" Jorgie glances at Ava. "Marvin is the one who has to work. You obviously aren't going home together, so why can't you stay and hang out with us?"

She wraps her arm around the crook of my elbow, enticing Ava to join the fun crowd. It's like we're in high school all over again. Jorgie's squeeze on my arm tightens the longer Ava contemplates her request.

A quiet squeal of excitement omits from Jorgie's lips when Ava shifts her gaze to Marvin and says, "You wouldn't mind if I hang out with Jorgie a little longer, would you?"

My jaw ticks over the fact Ava is required to seek permission to stay at her friend's house. The tick ramps up to a full spasm when Marvin crosses his arms in front of his chest and glares at her. "I've already requested the taxi. If you refuse their service, they may not come back and collect you later this evening."

"Oh," Ava mumbles.

"I'll drive you home, Ava," I offer, not giving Marvin the opportunity to guilt-trip her into going home early when she clearly wants to stay.

Marvin's eyes slit even more from my suggestion. From the stern glare he's directing at me, anyone would swear I was bending down on my knee and proposing to Ava instead of offering her a lift home.

"I don't think that would be wise."

"Why not?" Jorgie interrupts.

It's times like this I love that she has no filter.

"Because Hugo has been drinking," Marvin's stern tone makes him sound older than his twenty-five years.

I shake my head. "I've only had two beers. One when Ava first arrived."

Ava's widened eyes lower to her hand clasping her small black bag. A broad grin stretches across my face. *Obviously, my naked display is still in the forefront of her mind, hours after the incident.*

"And the second beer I had was during dinner. So I'm perfectly capable of driving Ava home – if she wants me to," I continue, shifting my gaze to Ava.

Ava was bullied her entire childhood, but it wasn't by who you're thinking. Yes, kids in the schoolyard can be cruel, but Ava wasn't subjected to bullying from them. It was by the man whose idea of a perfect child was one who was seen but never heard. Ava never rebelled during her teenage years, because she was scared of the extreme reprimand she would have faced if she dared to step out of line. Ava's father isn't just strict; he's a verbally abusive tyrant of a man who doesn't deserve the right to claim Ava as his daughter. By the time my parents found out about Ava's family predicament, she was already in her first week of college, so it was too late for them to get her out of his clutches.

Ava's father is the sole reason she shouldn't be with a man who'll give her ultimatums and rules to live by. If she wanted that type of lifestyle, she would have stayed living under her father's roof.

"What do you want to do, Ava?" I keep my tone low even though I'm close to ripping Marvin's head off from the furious scowl he's directing at Ava.

Jorgie's breathing ceases as Ava's eyes drift between the three of us. I can hear her silent prayers, hoping Ava will throw a little rebellion into the night. Marvin's eyes slit even more, and I remain quiet. Ava doesn't need any more people influencing her decisions.

"You have work--"

"On Monday," Jorgie interrupts, staring at Marvin with the same amount of intensity he's glaring at Ava.

My teeth gnawing on the inside of my cheek fails to hide the growl that emits from my lips when Ava turns to Jorgie and says, "I'll call you tomorrow."

The gleam in Jorgie's eyes is doused as she nods her head. I can't hear what Ava whispers in Jorgie's ear when she bids her farewell, but a vast grin stretches across Jorgie's face, and her hearty chuckle sounds through the quiet night. She laughs even more boisterously when she pulls away from Ava and runs her index finger under her nose. *Weirdos.*

After a quick smirk, Ava dashes to the awaiting taxi. I clench my fists at my side when a victorious grin stretches across Marvin's face. He waits until Ava's cab is nothing but a blur of taillights in the distance before entering his taxi, ensuring Ava leaves as instructed. I grit my teeth, internally battling not to raise my middle finger into the air over the pompous smirk etched on his face.

The instant Marvin's taxi exits Jorgie's street, I turn to face her. "Why is Ava dating Pencil Dick?"

Jorgie doesn't balk at my statement, indicating she's aware of Marvin's nickname and why he has it.

"Your guess would be as good as mine," she huffs, throwing her arms up in the air.

She plops into the empty wicker chair on her patio. "You know Ava, Hugo; she craves security. Dick Weed can give her that."

I stifle a chuckle. "Dick Weed?".

She smiles and nods her head. "Our grade called Marvin 'Dick Weed,'" she informs me. "You know, because his dick is like a weed in a garden, all wilted and shriveled up."

No longer able to hold in my laughter, my loud, hearty chuckle echoes through the quiet night. My laughter is so thunderous, it startles Ms. Mable next door. She flicks on her security light, blinding both Jorgie and me since its bright rays are pointing at Jorgie's patio.

"It's just Hugo," Jorgie shouts to ensure Ms. Mable can hear her since she's half-deaf.

My lips curve into a grin when Ms. Mable shrieks back, "Okay, dear."

Once the bright light is switched off, I turn my eyes back to Jorgie. An array of dancing lights obscure my vision for the next several seconds, but they don't hinder my sight long enough to miss the yawn Jorgie tries to suppress.

"Aren't you sleeping?"

Her face grimaces. "You know I can't sleep when Hawke is over there."

I nod. Hawke joined the military two months before he and Jorgie officially became a couple. He has often stated if he knew Jorgie was going to come into his life, he would've never enlisted. It's taken a bit of adjustment for Jorgie to get used to being a military wife, but she's handling it better than any of us expected.

"Only two more months and you'll be begging for me to get him out of your hair," I jest.

My heart warms when her little giggle sounds through my ears. "I can't wait for that day."

I noogie her head, because I know how much she hates it. "I'll drop by tomorrow afternoon after my meeting and put a few more hours into *baby*."

Her eyes spark as a broad grin stretches across her face, making her appear like a kid waking up Christmas morning.

"But until Hawke gives *baby* the all clear, you can't drive her."

Her bottom lip drops into a pout. "Party pooper."

After a final noogie on her head, I make my way to my truck. Once Jorgie is inside and the front door is dead-bolted, I pull my truck away from the curb. A grin curves on my lips when I spot the silhouette of Ms. Mable standing behind the sheer curtain in her living room. I lift my chin in greeting and smile, silently relaying my thanks for the vigilant eye she keeps on Jorgie.

Rochdale is a large, hard-working lower- to middle-class community, but it is, and will always be my hometown.

# FIVE

# AVA

I switch off the water in the shower and crank my head to the side. My ears are pricked, straining to work out where the banging noise echoing through my master bathroom is coming from. This is the only downfall about living in an apartment building. More times than I can count, I swear I hear people knocking on my front door. Only after begrudgingly scampering to my entranceway do I realize the knocks were for my neighbors; or a handful of times, they've been for the apartment at the end of the hall.

My debate between continuing to shave my legs or go in search of what the banging noise is ramps up when the rumble of a male voice closely follows three rigid taps of what I'm assuming are knuckles on a wooden door. My breathing becomes difficult when my strained ears recognize the rugged drawl of the masculine voice. Now, there's no doubt in my mind that the bangs bellowing through my apartment is someone knocking, or should I say, banging down my door.

I twist a towel around my drenched locks and secure another one around my body before ambling to the door. My heart thrashes wildly against my ribs, panicked at what has caused this impromptu visitor to arrive at my apartment at eleven PM on a Saturday night.

After ensuring the towel is adequately covering my private parts, I swing open the front door. My breath hitches when the delightful view of Hugo in a pair of low-hanging jeans and a short-sleeve fitted shirt swamps my vision. My brows furrow when the gleam in his eyes alters to the same unrecognized spark he had earlier tonight.

"Is everything okay?" My words come out shaky due to the quickening of my pulse from his avid stare.

He leans his broad shoulder against the doorjamb as one corner of his plump lips tug higher. "It is now," he croons.

Breathing is a thing of the past when his eyes scorch my skin as he rakes them over my body.

"Go out with me, Ava," he says, returning his eyes to mine.

"W-w-what?" I stammer, certain the words I've wanted to hear seep from his mouth for years didn't just occur on my doorstep while I'm wearing a skimpy towel, not one ounce of make-up, and with only one leg shaven.

He smirks. "Come out with me. Tonight," he clarifies.

*Ouch.* A slap to the face would have hurt less than that.

Suddenly, a notion hits me. "Are you drunk?"

That would be a very plausible reason as to why he has suddenly arrived at my door.

The flutter of my heart increases when his lips lift higher. "Maybe a little."

A rueful grin stretches across my face. Tonight isn't the first time I've had to handle an inebriated Hugo. The very first time was at his eighteenth birthday party...

*"Sugar," I mumble as my eyes leap around the desolate walls of a coatroom, seeking anything but the visual of a female with cascading blonde hair on her knees in front of a pair of trouser-clad thighs.*

*Even with the light from the entranceway beaming into the small closest space, the female's slurping sucks and frantic movements don't falter a bit as she continues with her mission to unravel the man whose rough pants of ecstasy have my cheeks warming and pulse hastening.*

*I spin on my heels, preparing to give the couple a small moment of* privacy in a house overrun by out-of-control, frantic teens. I freeze, half out of the coatroom, when "Yeah, Vicky, baby, just like that," sounds from a voice I've heard many times before.

My brain signals for my legs to move, but instead of pacing away from the train wreck that will inevitably shred my heart into a million pieces, my head cranks and my eyes roam over a well-splayed pair of thighs, a half-tucked-in disheveled shirt, and the ecstasy-riddled face of Hugo. His head is flopped back, his eyes are snapped shut, and his mouth is gaped open. He's the exact visual I'd conjured of him many times before.

The twisting of my stomach amplifies when he fists Vicky's hair to increase her pace, forcing a muffled gag to sound from her throat. Hugo's eyes snap open when a vile grunt tears from my throat. His pupils widen as his eyes absorb the repulsed expression on my face.

"Sorry," I mumble, scrambling.

Mortified that he busted me ogling him during a sexual activity, I throw my red coat onto the floor, slam the door shut and dash toward the dense crowd gathered in the sunken living room. Since I had to wait for my parents to go to bed, I've arrived to the party fashionably late. Blaring music, hot sweaty bodies, and half of the school population has congregated in the Marshall residence this Friday night.

When Chase, Hugo's older brother, discovered Jorgie and Hugo were going to be left unattended, he decided to throw an early eighteenth birthday party for Hugo. I don't normally attend these types of events, but since it is a significant milestone in Hugo's life, I chose to bend the normally unbreakable rein my father has gripped tightly around my neck. By scaling down the thorn-riddled latticework on the side of my house, I've arrived at Hugo's birthday party a little after eleven PM.

Barging my way through a mass of bodies grooving to the latest club beat, I continue with my pursuit of the even more crowded backyard. Even with it being overpopulated with drunken teens, I need fresh air, and I need it pronto. A blast of brisk night air relieves my *overheated skin when I yank open the glass sliding door that leads to the wooden deck.*

My heart stops beating when, "Ava," is shouted across the room from a deep rumbling voice that invades my dreams every single night.

In the reflection of the glass, I spot Hugo standing in the entranceway, adjusting his shirt to a more dignified configuration. Once his clothing is back in place, his eyes shift in all directions, no doubt seeking me amongst the crowd. I cowardly hide. Due to Hugo's large size, he spots me across the vast span of the living area within a matter of seconds. I dart out the door when he commences striding through the sea of partygoers. My urgent dash to evade Hugo is aided by the numerous party attendees who stop dancing to pat him on the back in greeting when they spot him striding by.

I rush down the short flight of stairs that lead to the fire pit and take a sharp left. When I reach the edge of the paved fire pit, my elbow is seized. I don't need to look up to know who is grasping me. My body's reaction is all the indication I need to know that Hugo's long strides have finally caught up with me. Sucking in a big breath, I neutralize the expression on my face before pivoting on my heels. I smile sweetly, vainly pretending I didn't witness what just happened. The longer Hugo's glassy eyes roam over my face, the more his brows furrow.

"Damn, Ava, I'm sorry you had to see that." The repentance in his eyes adds strength to his apology. "Did you not see the scarf wrapped around the door handle?" Due to his closeness, his whiskey-laced breath flutters my lips.

"The what?"

The tautness on his face firms. "The scarf around the handle," he repeats.

I return his stare before timidly shaking my head. Blood rushes through my veins, flaming my skin with heat when his eyes bore into mine, calling bullshit on my false statement. I did see the scarf, but I had no clue why it was there. I assumed it was lost property, but from the glimmer in Hugo's eyes, and the scowl on his face, I guess my assumption was wrong.

"Happy birthday," I say, thrusting the gift I'm clutching into his chest, praying for a moment of reprieve from the awkwardness suffocating the air surrounding us.

"Ava." His tone lowers as his gaze drops to the black gift box in my hand. "I thought we said no gifts this year." The purr of his words causes goose bumps to prickle on my arms.

I push my thick-rimmed glasses up my nose and hunch my shoulders. "It's nothing major."

A boyish grin stretches across his face as he accepts the gift. I inwardly sigh, relieved that the awkwardness between us has been dodged. I cross my arms in front of my chest, hiding my body's reaction to the sexy-as-hell grin etched on his face as he pries at a piece of cello tape on the side seam.

For as long as I've known Hugo, he has always taken his time unwrapping presents. He has said on numerous occasions he likes to savor the moment, to bask in the glory of being the center of attention. It's the perfect antidote for the poor, neglected middle child.

Just as the side flap has been carefully opened, the swarm of people milling around the pool realize the birthday man has emerged amongst them. Within a matter of seconds, Hugo is inundated by well-wishers wanting to bestow their birthday felicitations.

As the rowdy crowd congresses around him, I get elbowed and barged out of the way until I'm once again on the outer circle of the popularity contest that always launches when Hugo is in the vicinity. The stabbing pain piercing my heart lessens when Hugo's gorgeous face pokes out from the heavy crowd. When he spots me standing to the side he grins a heart-flattering smile.

"Thank you," he says, staring straight at me.

"You're welcome," I mouth back, smiling.

When his grinning face becomes nothing but an ambiguous blur in the crowd, I spin on my heels. Quietly, I sit in a vacant chair next to

Jorgie, not wanting to interrupt her game of tonsil hockey with her on and off again boyfriend, Blake.

Snubbing the sucking-face noises neighboring me, I spend the next several minutes immersed in the fascinating world of people watching. Even though everyone in eyesight knows Hugo in some way, the gathering of people is diverse. You have your school jocks and Barbie doll cheerleaders gathered in a large group near the edge of the pool. The dark, moody, artsy crowd is milling around the fire pit, and even though they remain hidden in the shadows, I spotted a handful of members from the computer club gathered at the side of the house when I first dashed into the backyard. And then there are the people like me. The awkward anti-social crowd who scatters themselves throughout the groups, hoping one day to work out exactly which faction we belong to.

My people gawking is interrupted when a red plastic cup full to the brim with bubbling soda is shoved under my nose. Lifting my eyes, I absorb an older, although not any more mature version of Hugo. Hugo and Chase are two men cut from the same cloth – their father's. Same dark, thick shaggy hair hanging loosely on the top of their heads, large round piercing blue eyes, and well-carved facial features that make my pulse and other parts of my body flutter faster.

"Hey, Chase," I greet him, accepting the cup he's jutting toward me.

"Ava," he croons in his deep, throaty tone. "Make sure you only accept drinks from Hugo or me tonight," he instructs, his tone firm.

His inched-high brows lower when I curtly nod. He grins, lessening the confused scowl before nudging Blake in the shoulder with his enclosed fist. Blake's heavy-lidded eyes snap open, furious that his heavy petting session with Jorgie has been interrupted. His angry gaze switches to panic when he realizes who has disturbed his above PG-rated make-out session.

"Beat it," Chase instructs, glaring at Blake.

"Chase," Blake drawls with a laugh, "help a brother out."

Any further slurred words preparing to escape Blake's mouth

become entombed when an angry growl rumbles through Chase's snapped-shut lips.

"You either leave voluntarily or I'll walk you out myself," Chase advises.

His stern tone causes an ice cold chill to run down my spine. Even with Chase attending college two towns over, his protective big brother stance hasn't eased when it comes to men getting close to his baby sister, but I must give credit where credit is due. Even after a vicious caution from Hugo and Chase, Blake continues to pursue Jorgie with just as much vigor as he did before he found out she was the Marshall Brothers' little sister. A lesser man would've run for the hills. Many men before him have done exactly that.

"I'll show you out," Jorgie says, swinging her gaze from glaring at Chase to a staggered Blake.

Jorgie places her hand on my shoulder and gives it a gentle squeeze. "I'll be back in a minute," she says with a waggle of her brows.

I smile and nod. That was one of our secret friends' code. Saying she'll be back in a minute while waggling her brows means she'll be no less than thirty minutes. I run my index finger under my nose, acknowledging I understand her statement and that I'm fine being left unattended. After one last glare at Chase, Jorgie heads toward the house with a broad grin stretched across her face and Blake shadowing closely behind.

Not long later after Jorgie has left, a roaring chant of laughter drags my attention from picking the polish on my nails. A smile gleams across my face when I spot six members of the rowing team hoisting Hugo off the ground and charging toward the vacant pool. Even though Hugo appears to be struggling against their hold, I can tell he isn't putting in a real effort.

On the boisterous count of three, Hugo is thrown into the undoubtedly frigid water. Men hollering resonates over the roar of laughter when a trio from the cheerleading squad strips out of their clothing and dives into the water squealing, "Pool party!" at the top of their lungs.

A disdained grimace morphs on my face when the bra and panty-wearing troupe circles Hugo like a pack of sharks in heat. I gasp when Victoria Avenke's lips enclose over Hugo's and he doesn't pull away. I try to act brave and pretend I'm not affected, but in all honesty, it hurts. It hurts like a fucking bitch, but then I remember, they aren't seeing the real Hugo Marshall.

Tonight, he's the popular school jock who is friends with everyone. By Sunday, he'll be back to the real Hugo. The one only I get to see. The one who lounges around in his pajamas until midday every Sunday morning and hates when I beat him on Mario Kart. That is the real Hugo – the Hugo I have a mad crush on. Not the boy undertaking a course in the art of resuscitation in the pool.

"A pool party and a bonfire, quite the odd combination."

Lifting my eyes from the dancing embers of the fire, I'm met with a knock-your-socks-off smile. My eyes bug when they roam over Rhys Tagget, my childhood crush No. 2. Rhys screams bad boy with his clipped dark hair, tattooed arms, and impressive swagger. Even when he was a junior, the senior girls fawned over him. He graduated from our high school two summers ago. When he isn't attending university, studying to become a surgeon, he works at the local tattoo parlor, hence the vibrant collection of artwork on his body.

"Freeze in the pool, thaw by the fire," I reply, shyly smiling.

Rhys chuckles a hearty laugh. "For some strange reason, that kind of makes sense."

Goose bumps prickle my skin when he nudges my bare shoulder with a chilled bottle of beer. My eyes bounce between the clear bottle of beer with a wedge of lime crammed in the neck and the full cup of bland soda I'm grasping. When my eyes drift to the pool, and I spot Hugo still training to be a lifeguard, I place the soda on the ground and accept the bottle from Rhys. Leaning back in the chair, I take a generous swig of the frosted beverage. My face grimaces at the bitter flavor engulfing my taste buds. Rhys grins before dragging the chair Jorgie vacated closer to me. When he straddles it backward, his glistening hazel eyes turn from Hugo and his posse of female friends to me.

"You're best friends with Hugo's little sister Jorgie, aren't you?"

I nod before taking another swig of beer. I try to keep the repulsed expression off my face as I swallow the ghastly liquid. Even though it tastes disgusting, the coolness of the beverage is helping to lessen the furious rage burning a hole in my heart.

"Then why haven't I seen you at any of Hugo's parties before?"

My eyes snap to his. "Is this a regular occurrence?"

He smiles against the seam of his beer before nodding. "It isn't normally here, though. It's normally held at the lookout or down by the river."

"Oh," I mumble before taking another mouth-filling gulp of beer. "I've never been invited before."

Now, I'm guzzling the beer down so quickly, my taste buds don't get the chance to protest the abhorrent taste.

"These parties have an open invitation, sweetheart; you don't need to be invited." Rhys informs me.

My eyes burn as I fight to swallow the beer in my mouth instead of splattering it all over Rhys' face. I've never been called a term of endearment before, let alone one as endearing as sweetheart.

"Ah, now it makes sense."

My eyes shift back to his. "What makes sense?"

His worldly eyes absorb my face before they drop to my baggy boyfriend jeans and one shoulder knitted sweater. "You're fresh meat."

My cheeks get a rush of blood forming beneath them. "Excuse me?" My words quiver. I may be naïve, but even I know what that saying means.

"I didn't mean to embarrass you, Ava. It just makes sense why I've never seen you at these types of functions before. They're not suitable for--" His eyes say the word his mouth fails to produce.

Dying from embarrassment, I lose the ability to maintain eye contact. Lifting the beer to my mouth, I guzzle the remaining smidgen. Noticing my beer is empty, Rhys opens the lid of a cooler at his side and cracks open another bottle. After squeezing a lime into the neck, he hands it to me.

"You need to slow down your guzzling if you're not used to drinking, Ava. That's not soda in that bottle."

I smile a thanks before drifting my eyes to the gathering of people milling near the pool. I freeze with the seam of the bottle pressed against my lips when I catch the murderous glare of Hugo. His head is angled to the side, and his brow is arched high. His stern gaze follows the beer when I lower it from my mouth and rest it on my shaking thigh. I sink deeper into the chair, moving away from the fire since Hugo's glare is roasting my skin. I timidly shake my head when Hugo motions for me to join him in the pool. His narrowed eyes slit even more before his angry gaze shifts between Rhys and me. The furious scowl on his face doesn't lessen when I playfully screw up my nose and stick out my tongue.

My heart rate quickens when the lean muscles in Hugo's arm flex as he lifts himself out of the pool. Even with the blare of music pumping through the crisp night air, I don't miss the disdained gasps of the cheerleaders devastated by his brisk departure. I roll my eyes when a flurry of girls congregate around him to offer him a towel or a birthday kiss. Inwardly gagging from their desperateness, I turn my gaze back to Rhys.

His eyes shift between Hugo and me. "I didn't realize you had an older brother," he mumbles against the rim of his bottle.

"I don't," I reply through clenched teeth.

"Boyfriend?" Rhys probes, staring into my eyes. In the moonlight, the brown flicks in his eyes are more prominent, making them dazzle ever brighter.

A heartwarming smirk curls on his lips when I shake my head. Rhys takes a sip of his beer as his eyes turn back to the pool. His small smirk morphs into an amused smile.

"Prepare yourself, Ava," he warns.

I'm so immersed in unearthing what's ignited the spark in Rhys' eyes that I don't notice the prowler sneaking up on me until it too late.

*With a rough yank on my wrist, I'm thrusted from my chair and hoisted over a broad shoulder. A chill runs through my body when freezing droplets of water are absorbed by my bland red sweater. Not having anywhere else to grasp, my hands shoot down to secure a deathly tight grip on a pair of drenching wet black cotton boxer shorts.*

"Put me down, Hugo," *I wail when his familiar smell invades my senses.*

*I kick as hard as possible, aiming for the one part of his anatomy I know will slow him down. My squirms come to an immediate halt when his open palm slaps my backside. The sting of both pleasure and pain rushes through to my core, making me ache with desire.*

"Time for a swim, Ava."

*I dig my nails into the rock-hard muscles of his lower back when the marble tiles surrounding the edge of the pool come into vision.*

"Don't you dare throw me in the po--"

*Before the entire sentence can escape my mouth, my glasses are knocked off my face, my jeans become the weight of concrete, and my nipples turn rigid. They're so firm, they could cut through diamonds. My screams of protest trap in my throat when the sub-zero water steals my ability to breathe. Even peering through the blur of rippling water, I can't miss the smug look smeared on Hugo's face as he stares at me under the water. Fuming with anger, I kick him in the shins before swimming to the surface. Numerous mumbled curse words escape my lips as I attempt to flop my body over the edge of the pool. I grit my teeth when Hugo exits the pool with ease. The heaviness of my soaked jeans and sweater double my weight, impeding my efforts. Through gritted teeth, I accept the hand Hugo offers. He adeptly pulls me out of the pool before gathering me in close to his chest. I place my palms on his drenched pecs and push away from him. The sloshing of water in my boots sounds over the pulse ringing in my ears.*

"Why did you do that?!" *I squeal, glaring at his smug face.*

*He crosses his arms in front of his chest, strengthening his pose.* "You were told not to accept drinks from anyone but Chase or me. You didn't listen."

"It was a bottle of beer!" I yell.

"I don't care if it was a can of diet Pepsi, you don't accept drinks from men you don't know."

I glare at him while pulling off my black boots. His lips twitch, battling to hold in a smile when the contents of my boots create a puddle of water around his feet. Even being overheated with furious anger, a shiver jolts down my spine when cool air pelts my drenched chest. Air whizzes from Hugo's mouth when I thrust my boots into his chest.

"I'll have you know, Rhys isn't a stranger," I inform him, pulling my limp sweater over my head. "He and I go way back."

I grunt when the soaked material clings to my arms. The smile tugging Hugo's lips vanishes and a set of hard-edged lips ruefully take its place. I snarl at him while dumping my drenched sweater on top of my boots.

"Rhys used to tutor me," I enlighten him, undoing the button on the fly of my jeans.

"Ava."

"In French," I add on, noticing the conceited smirk on Hugo's face. "All things French. It is the language of love and many other things."

I overemphasize my brash statement, loving that my jibe is creating a quiver in Hugo's jaw.

"Ava," Hugo growls.

"It was the most fun I've ever had studying."

"Ava."

"Who knew being forced to learn a foreign language by my father would turn out to be such a riveting experience?" I continue to taunt while shimmying out of my jeans plastered on my thighs.

I nearly lose my footing when the left cuff of my jeans gets stuck on my ankle. Lifting my leg high into the air, I yank the rigid material off with one clean swoop. It's lucky I don't wear skin-tight jeans, or I would've never been able to remove them. After thrusting my jeans into Hugo's heaving chest, I grasp the hem of my white cami.

"Ava!" Hugo rumbles again.

"What?!" I yell, exasperatingly throwing my arms into the air. Is that the only word he knows today?

His livid eyes glare into mine. "You're stripping naked in front of half of the school population."

I freeze. "What?" I manage to squeak out before the reality of the situation crashes into me full pelt.

I swallow the rock in my throat before filtering my heavily dilated eyes around the dead quiet space. The walloping of my heat increases when I spot numerous party attendees staring at me, wide-eyed and open-mouthed. My anger at being dumped in the pool had made me lose sight of the bigger picture. My eyes shoot from the abundance of partygoers to my barely covered body. My horror increases when I notice my drenched cami is failing to conceal my homely black bra and red striped G-string bikini bottoms. Tears burn my eyes as I lift my gaze back to Hugo. The expression on his face is no longer laced with amusement. It is full to the brim with remorse and silent apologies. I yank my clothing out of his grasp and rush toward the house.

Cat calls, wolf whistles, and sexual propositions thud through my ears as I run through the gauntlet of partygoers gawking at me like I'm the night's free entertainment. I hold my sweater against my chest, futilely trying to maintain a small shred of modesty as I bolt up the roped-off stairwell. The first splash of tears hits my cheeks when I slam Jorgie's bedroom door shut and slide down it. The clanking of my backside hitting the blue carpeted floor swamps the sob that tears from my throat. After dumping my drenched clothes to the side of Jorgie's disheveled room, I wrap my arms around my legs and burrow my tear-stained face into my knees, hiding from the world. This is the exact reason why I avoid these types of functions. I'm awkward enough as it is, let alone trying to mingle with strangers.

My head lifts from resting on my knees when, "Ava, let me in," barrels through the door only minutes later by a voice I immediately recognize.

I freeze and attempt to lessen my sobs, not wanting Hugo to witness my immature tears.

"Come on, open up, I know you're in there," he whispers through the crack of the door. "I can hear you crying."

I snap my mouth shut, trying to mask my tears. The smallest whimper still escapes my lips. The sound of the locked door handle being twisted rattles over the thumping of my heart.

"If you don't open the door, Ava, I'll kick it in," Hugo warns.

"The only thing that needs kicking is my backside for trying to be sexy by wearing a stupid G-string," I mumble.

I snuck the red and white striped G-string into the shopping cart last week when my mom and I went to Walmart. I concealed its bland cotton material amongst the red sweater my mom picked out. The cashier's eyes lifted to mine when it tumbled out of the rumpled-up sweater and fell to her feet. Seeing my wide-eyed, panicked expression, she conspicuously gathered the scrap of material off the floor, scanned it and shoved it into the pocket of my one-size-too-large boyfriend jeans, leaving my mom none the wiser to my sneaky purchase. I mumbled my silent gratitude to the grinning cashier as I snagged the bags from the carousel and rushed out of the store. Although I never intended on anyone seeing it, it made me feel daring when I slipped the G-string up my freshly shaved legs tonight.

My head cranks to the side when the door handle stops rattling and Hugo's large shadow vanishes from beneath the door. I drag my bottom lip between my teeth, shocked that he gave up so easily. I shouldn't be surprised, though. It's not like I'm a princess trapped in a castle waiting for prince charming to rescue me.

The sinking of my heart stops when, "If you're sitting behind the door, Ava, I need you to move," vibrates through the door.

He wouldn't really kick down the door, would he? Jorgie would never forgive me if she had to live with no privacy until her door was repaired. Knowing how annoying her older brothers are, they'd take their sweet ass time replacing her busted door. They'd do anything if it lessened the chance of her having any "private" time.

"Have you moved, Ava? Please tell me you've moved. I don't want to hurt you." My heart clutches from the torment in his voice.

"Wait." I scamper off the floor.

The darkness shadowing the bottom of the door returns, closely followed by the big pants of Hugo's breath. I suck in a nerve-cleansing breath before sweeping open the door. The mixture of whiskey and a scent that belongs solely to Hugo filters through my senses when he steps into the room. The concern contorting his face amplifies when his eyes zoom in on my tear-stained cheeks. He smiles a wary smirk before pivoting on his heels to close the door.

"Ava, I'm sorr--"

"I'm not leaving this room," I interrupt, pacing to stand in the middle of it. Surprisingly, my reply is delivered stronger than I'm expecting. "I'm never leaving this room."

Not just because I don't want to face the roguish taunts of my peers, but because I'm petrified of what my father's reaction will be if he learns about my lewd strip. In the glimmer of the bedside lamp, my eyes catch sight of a photo on Jorgie's nightstand. It is a picture of Jorgie, Hugo, and me taken at Hugo's thirteenth birthday party. We were so young and carefree back then. Our only concern that day was who got the biggest slice of cake. Oh, how things have changed in five years.

"You don't have to go out right now, but eventually, you're going to have to leave this room," Hugo says, his tone sincere but with an edge of wittiness to it.

I stick out my lip and pout. "Why? Can't I just stay in here forever?"

A smirk tugs Hugo's lips higher as he paces closer to me, shaking his head. "You would soon grow tired of Jorgie's loud snoring," he jests playfully.

I roll my eyes. Jorgie may have a slight wheeze when she's sleeping, but it isn't loud enough to douse my enthusiasm for hiding in her room for the rest of eternity.

"And Jorgie doesn't have cable TV, so how will we spend our Sunday afternoons watching re-runs of 'Friends' if you're locked up in here?"

*My lips curl into a small smile. I love our Sunday afternoon ritual. Since Jorgie isn't a fan of "Friends," it is the only time I get Hugo all to myself. It may only be for an hour out of an entire week, but I cherish every single second of our alone time.*

*Sensing my determination to be a hermit in Jorgie's room is wavering,* Hugo continues. "There's also no kitchen in here, and goddamn it, girl, knowing your blueberry pancakes are waiting for me every Sunday morning when I wake is the only thing that keeps me going during the week."

*No longer able to hide my happiness, a broad grin spreads across my face. I swear I roll over like a dog begging for my tummy to be scratched when it comes to Hugo, but it isn't just his cheeky disposition that keeps me coming back for more. It is the fact he doesn't expect me to change from the dorky girl hiding behind a mask to what society deems acceptable that I love. Unlike Jorgie, Hugo doesn't care if I wear jeans that are a size too big or sweaters we could both fit into. He still greets me with the same amount of excitement no matter what hideous outfit I'm wearing.*

*Smirking, I lift my eyes and lock them with his. He paces closer to me and hands me my black thick-rimmed glasses.*

"Thank you, but I don't need them to see," *I mumble under my breath.*

*My heart skips a beat when he says,* "I know, but they're your protective shield that keeps you hidden from the strangers lurking in the dark."

*He places his hand under my chin and lifts my deflated head high into the air. Any leftover tears dry from the kindness radiating out of his eyes.* "You're like Clark Kent. You keep your superhero identity hidden from outsiders."

*My heart warms as a genuine smile tugs on my lips. I wouldn't say I'm a superhero. I'm more like a tortoise. I only emerge from my shell around Jorgie, Hugo, and their family. The instant I'm pushed back into society, the armor I wear to protect myself slips right back into place. Although I do need glasses to stop my eyes straining when* looking at a computer monitor, they're not a requirement for me to see clearly. My vision is so precise, I can see every small droplet of water clinging to Hugo's thick lashes.

A small stretch of silence crosses between us as Hugo gives me time to calm down from the debacle of my existence. Once my usual self-composed nature has returned, his glassy eyes shift between mine as he mutters, "Borrow some of Jorgie's clothes, and when you're ready, come back out and enjoy the party. If anyone says anything about what happened, they'll have me to deal with."

I smile, hiding the grimace trying to cross my face. The last thing I want in my life is the guy who invades my every waking thought taking on the role of big brother.

"Thanks for the offer, but I can't borrow Jorgie's clothes," I say, peering into his concerned eyes.

His face screws up. "Why not?" He stroll to Jorgie's bursting-at-the-seams closet.

My brows meet my hairline. "Because I'm five foot two and Jorgie is as tall as a gir--"

I stop talking, and my mouth gapes. Hugo's head cranks back quicker than a bullet being dislodged from a weapon.

"I wasn't going to say it," I squeak out when a huge grin stretches across his face.

"Oh, yeah you were. You were just about to call Jorgie a giraffe."

"I was not!" I retaliate as my eyes dart to the doorway, hoping to hell that Jorgie isn't within earshot. Jorgie never forgave Victoria for calling her a giraffe in middle school. Even though I'm her best friend, I'm not willing to test her forgiving nature.

"I was going to say she's as tall as a gir... gir... a girl!"

Hugo smiles a shit-eating grin. "You're so full of shit."

"I am not," I respond with a stomp of my feet.

"Oh, yeah you are," he says, lunging for me.

I squeal and dash across the room before his tortuous hands can get anywhere near my ribs. Air whooshes from my lips when he wraps his arm around my waist to tackle me to the ground. I squirm and giggle like an immature fifth grader when he straddles my hips and his fingers unleash a torrid of tickling on my upper stomach. I squirm and buck my hips, fighting against his cruel tickling onslaught. Within minutes, my face is red, I'm sweating profusely, and I can hardly breathe through the stream of tears seeping from my eyes.

"Okay, okay, I give up!" I squeal, still squirming. "Mercy! Mercy!" I scream at the top of my lungs, knowing it is the only word that will stop his tortuous hands.

Upon hearing my roaring pleas, he un-straddles my hips and flops onto his back beside me. His chest thrusts up and down, matching the rhythm of mine as we endeavor to refill our lungs with air.

I don't know why he's so exhausted. I'm the one who was subjected to torture.

Once I can breathe again, I roll onto my hip, crank my elbow, and rest my saturated mop of hair on my open palm. Hugo's eyes shift from staring at the ceiling to peer at me. His gaze looks complicated and uneasy. When he notices I've caught his odd expression, a roughish smirk etches on his sinful mouth. Oh no. I know that look. It's a look that means he's about to stir up trouble.

"If you tell Jorgie I nearly called her a giraffe, I'll kill you," I warn.

Panic scorches my veins when he waggles his brows before scampering off the floor. I freeze for all of two seconds before I dive at him. He hits the ground with an almighty thump when I scuttle across the carpet and wrap my arms around his ankles. His thunderous laugh booms through my chest when I hook my legs around his torso to hold him down.

He crawls across the carpet, not the slightest bit impeded by my monkey hold. When he stands from the ground, taking me with him, I leap from his back and dart for the door. I slam the door shut, plaster my back against it and lift my eyes to his.

"I'll do anything," I plea breathlessly. "Anything at all."

We're standing so close, our thrusting chests connect every time we take a breath. A small smile curves on my mouth when he loosens his grip of the door handle and runs his hand along his jaw. That's a sign he's considering my request. It's something Hugo always does when he's contemplating.

"Anything?" His tone drips with innuendo.

My tongue delves out to replenish my dry lips before I nod. My heartbeat kicks up when he presses his palms against the door on either side of my head and tilts his body closer to me, leaving even less space between us and trapping me between his imposing body and the thick wooden door.

"Alright," he breathes out heavily.

His alcohol-scented breath adds even more heat to my already flustered cheeks.

His gaze lifts from my parched mouth to my eyes. "You have to cook me breakfast."

I eagerly nod. I've done that exact thing every Sunday morning for the past two years so that will be a walk in the park.

The eager nod of my head lessens when he says, "I want the works. Bacon, eggs, pancakes. If it's associated with breakfast, I want it. And I want it tomorrow morning."

My nose scrunches. "Jeez, what happened to your last slave?" My tone is full of wit.

"Nothing... yet," he replies with a cheeky wink.

My O-formed mouth curves into a grin when he tugs on a strand of my curly hair that has sprung in front of my eye. As my wild mess of hair starts to dry, the super tight curls are beginning to sprout. I was never a fan of my ringlet curls growing up, but they've grown on me the past two years. I don't know if he realizes he's doing it, but when we watch re-runs of "Friends," Hugo twists my hair around his index finger the entire time. It is the meekest touch, but it sparks a surge of excitement in me every time he does it.

The room turns roasting when Hugo's eyes burn into mine and he says, "I want my breakfast served in my bed."

I swallow to relieve my parched throat. "Okay."

A bead of sweat rolls down my back when his gaze returns to my lips. "If its edible, and it's in my room, I'm going to taste it."

"Okay," I respond again since my brain has lost the ability to form intelligent words.

A small stretch of silence crosses between us as we undertake an intense, sweat-forming stare down. My breathing stills when he tilts his head toward me, bringing his lips to within mere millimeters of mine. A rush of excitement courses through my body as every fantasy I've ever conjured transpires before my eyes. Just as Hugo's lips brush against the edge of my mouth, a loud knock sounds on the door. The tap is so hard, it vibrates through my heaving chest.

"Ava, it's Jorgie. I just heard what happened. Let me in."

When she pushes the door open with her shoulder, my body lunges toward Hugo, smashing our faces together. If I were a few inches taller, my lips would have landed on his mouth, instead of his chin. Hugo's heavy-lidded eyes drift between mine for several heart clutching seconds before he lowers his arms and takes a step backward, unpinning me from my the door.

After giving myself a few seconds to regain control of the erratic beat of my heart, I push off the door and pace into the middle of the room. The instant I step away from the door, Jorgie charges into the room. Her eyes are wide; her cheeks are flushed, and excitement in beaming out of her. She looks nearly as flustered as I feel.

"You know how you didn't have a date for the summer fling?" Her words are barely audible in her breathless state.

I nod. My lack of date isn't because I can't find a dance partner for the night. It's just an excuse I've used so I don't have to tell Jorgie I'm not allowed to go to the senior dance. It's being held the same night my parents are going to Napa Valley for the weekend to celebrate their twentieth wedding anniversary.

My dad arranged for me to stay at my grandmother's house two towns over. When I requested to stay at Jorgie's for the weekend, my father said my desire to spend time with my grandmother should outweigh my need for social interaction. That was the beginning and end of our discussion.

Jorgie grips my arm as her gleaming eyes beam into mine. "You no longer have an excuse not to go. Because not only did I overhear Richie Santo asking Rhys for your digits, I also saw Chase dragging Robert Parker down the stairwell. Chase didn't say it, but I'm fairly certain Robert was up here looking for you."

Her neck cranks to the side when a thunderous growl emits from Hugo's lips. The skin around her nose scrunches when she discovers Hugo standing at my side. I don't know how she could miss a man with a frame as large as his?

"You're lucky your immature prank backfired or I would've told mom what you did to Ava," Jorgie says, her voice coming out snarkier than normal as her eyes shoot daggers at Hugo.

A grin tugs on my lips when a fretful mask slips over Hugo's face. I love Mrs. Marshall. She treats me as if I am her daughter, but I grew even fonder of her when I discovered she's the only person in the world Hugo fears. It isn't a quaking-in-your-boots type of fear. It is the worry he may one day disappoint his No. 1 fan that keeps him on the straight and narrow.

My eyes lift and lock with Hugo's. His jaw is set into a hard line; his fists are clenched at his side, and he's returning Jorgie's evil glare.

"I'll see you tomorrow?" I mouth, hoping our earlier agreement is still in effect.

His eyes shift from glaring at Jorgie to me. A smirk curves on his mouth before he rubs his stomach and winks. After I return his smile, he ambles to the door and exits without a backward glance, but we never got our breakfast the following day......

"So, are you going to get dressed, Ava, or do you want to go out like that?" Hugo asks, interrupting me from my reminiscing thoughts.

My pupils widen as my eyes dart down to the peach-colored, floral-printed towel wrapped around my body. Although it doesn't match the sleek design of my modern apartment, it was a house warming gift from Mrs. Marshall, so I couldn't part with it.

I lift my gaze and lock it with Hugo's twinkling baby blues. "I guess that will depend on where we're going? It's not like half the town hasn't already seen my naked derriere."

# SIX

## AVA

My sassiness is foiled when a panty-combusting smirk morphs on Hugo's face. Well, they would have combusted, if I were wearing any. A squeal escapes my parted lips and echoes down the hallway of my apartment building when Hugo suddenly launches for me and throws me over his shoulder.

A ragged gasp expels from my lips, and my hands shoot to the hem of the towel, wanting to ensure my neighbors don't get an eyeful of my *lady garden*. Once again, that is a metaphor. I can't technically call it a garden when it doesn't have any foliage. I've just always found the word "pussy" a little too risky if you aren't in the bedroom, and calling it a "vagina" is a huge no-no in my book.

A rush of excitement pelts my body when Hugo smacks one of my ass cheeks with his large open palm. "As riveting as it would be to take you out only wearing a towel, Jorgie would kill me. So you've got five minutes to get dressed, Ava," he instructs while placing me down onto my feet.

"It's eleven PM!" I declare, like there could be a possibility he's unaware of the time. "The only place I'm visiting is my bed."

His brow arches high into his thick, luxurious shaggy hair as an unscrupulous grin etches on his sinful mouth.

"Alone," I clarify. I'm surprised how confident my statement came out considering how fast my pulse is racing.

"How old are you, Ava?"

I cross my arms in front of my chest, hoisting my moderately sized bosoms higher into the air. "Exactly six months younger than you, remember?"

"Then stop acting like my mother and get your goddamn ass dressed."

My mouth pop opens over his audacity. Any word vomit preparing to exit my lips traps in my throat when I notice the direction of his heavy-lidded gaze. It is a well-known fact Hugo has a fascination with legs. Nearly every inch of my legs are on display since my strengthened stance has inched my towel higher on my thighs.

When I uncross my arms, my towel drops back to a more respectable level, and Hugo's heavily dilated eyes return to mine.

"If you aren't dressed in five minutes, Ava, you're going to leave your apartment in only your towel. The choice is yours."

With that, he saucily winks before sauntering out of the room. I stand motionless staring at the door he exited, utterly flabbergasted. I'm not just shocked by Hugo's sudden interest in me; I'm also surprised he knew the location of my bedroom. I'm not bragging, but my apartment is decent in size. I worked hard throughout college and saved every single penny I made so I could afford the down payment.

I was called naïve and stupid when I signed on the dotted line after only viewing the blueprint designs for this building. Even living all the way over the other side of the country, I knew one day I'd return to Rochdale. It wasn't a matter of if; it was a matter of when, but the only way I could afford an apartment in this area was by investing my money in the concept of an idea, not a physical building.

It was a risk, but it was one I was willing to take it. The taunts on my so-called stupidity continued when people discovered I was placing my hard-earned cash into the hands of a businessman who was younger than me. Now, nearly two years later, I'm the one laughing in their faces. Purchasing this apartment was the best financial decision I ever made. The value of the apartments in this building skyrocketed the instant the project was completed, meaning I'm now sitting on a very lucrative nest egg.

I dash to my wardrobe like a frantic woman when Hugo declares, "Three minutes."

"Can you at least tell me where we're going?" I yell, digging my hands deep into my closet, trying to find something suitable to wear.

"What does every twenty-five-year-old on the planet do on a Saturday night?"

"Shave their legs? Or is that just losers like me?"

My cheeky snickering is replaced with a gasp when Hugo strolls into my room unannounced.

"What if I were naked?"

His lengthy strides have him crossing the room in two heart-thrashing seconds. "It wouldn't be anything I haven't seen before."

My brows furrow. "You haven't seen me naked."

My pulse quickens when he stops rummaging through my vast collection of clothing and turns to stare at me. His eyes are glistening, but there's something more tangible beneath the devious spark that has my interests piqued.

My breathing returns when he says, "Camp Levitt, the lake house, and that time you vomited after we went trick or treating because you ate your candy as it was handed to you, instead of putting it into your pink powder-puff collection bag."

My jaw drops. Not just because he's seen me naked on at least three separate occasions, but because he remembered a bag I used for Halloween over fourteen years ago.

"Those times don't count. Nothing before puberty counts." Embarrassment places a stranglehold on my vocal cords.

"Like you can talk," I say, my tone having a whip of edginess to it when I catch sight of his pompous smirk. "I've seen you naked more times than I can count."

"Pfftt, name three times you've seen my junk."

"The morning of spring fling, that time you lost your board shorts surfing after Hurricane Claudette hammered the coastline in 2003, and the night Jorgie and I arrived at a party at your frat house in college," I respond, ticking off each item with my fingers. "Shall I continue? As I'm sure I have at least a dozen more memories I can recall."

That's a total lie. Including tonight, I've only seen him naked four times.

"You and Jorgie came to one of my frat parties?"

I roll my eyes before accepting the little black dress he's handing me from my extensive collection of LBD's. I shouldn't be surprised he doesn't remember my admission, because lo and behold, Hugo was drunk.

"Your five minutes is up, Ava," he says, pacing closer to me with a wicked grin etched on his mouth.

I freeze as my panicked eyes flick between the skimpy towel wrapped around my body and the beast of a man prowling stealthily toward me.

"I was waiting for you to turn around," I remark, blurting out the first excuse that pops into my head. "Even though you *may* have already seen me naked, there are no free peep shows happening here tonight."

My heart rate soars when his chuckle sounds through my ears. "Party pooper."

"Turn around." I wriggle my finger in a circular pattern to enhance my request.

When he does as solicited with a broad grin stretched across his face, I unlatch the side zipper of the black dress and step into the small opening. With a few tugs, a couple of rough yanks, and a handful of grunts, I manage to get the skin-tight dress onto my body without even needing to drop my towel.

"If you weren't going to remove you towel, why did I need to turn around?"

My brow cocks. *How did he know I didn't remove my towel?*

My mouth drops when I spot his grinning reflection leering at me in the full-length dressing mirror in the corner of the room. If I didn't take such over-the-top precautions, he would have had a full view of my entire body. My naked *post-pubescent* body.

I gulp.

The smirk etched on his rugged face falters when I throw the drenched towel from my hair over his head, concealing his view as I swiftly pull a pair of black panties up my quaking thighs. I only just get the hem of my dress to a respectable level when he yanks the towel off his head. I stick out my tongue at the playful wiggle of his brows before ambling to the vanity mirror to run my fingers through my freshly shampooed hair.

After adding a sheen of lip gloss to my naked lips, I place a splattering of mascara onto my already dark lashes. I'm uncapping a black eyeliner pencil and adding a dash of blush to my cheeks when Hugo wraps his broad arm around my waist and pulls me backward. A yearning of desire clusters low in my womb when the Woods of Windsor aftershave I bought him for his seventeenth birthday filters through my nose.

"Time's up," he declares, breathing heavily into my ear.

My breathing shallows when my backside brushes against his impressive crotch. I already knew from his nickname in high school that his manhood was impressive, but until I was awarded with a full frontal visual of it, I had no idea it was that remarkable. I remain quiet, silenced by embarrassment as he carries me to the front door. It is no hard feat for Hugo, considering he's a foot taller than me and a hundred pounds heavier.

"My purse," I beg, pointing to the black clutch bag hanging on the coat rack near the front door. "I'll need my ID."

Even though I'm nearly twenty-five, I get carded every time I order an alcoholic drink. Hugo's lengthy strides don't falter as he snags my clutch off the rack and a pair of black heels from the entranceway. He strides down the long hallway to the elevator banks located in the middle. The hotness of the blood pumping through my veins has a fine mist of sweat forming on my freshly cleaned skin. The night air is already suffocated with humidity from the downpour of rain earlier today, but in Hugo's firm clutch, the heat is even more pulverizing.

When the elevator doors snap shut, I wiggle, attempting to get out of his tight grasp.

"You can put me down now," I say when my squirming effort comes up fruitless.

Hugo shrugs as he grunts. I grit my teeth and suck in a big breath.

"I'm not a child," I reprimand him, even though I'm being carried like I am.

Because of my small height and petite frame, people often say I look like I'm still a teenager. You'd think that not aging the past seven years would be an invigorating experience I'd happily shout from the rooftops. It isn't. My colleagues don't take me seriously, as they think I'm the female equivalent of Dr. Howser from the television show "Doogie Howser M.D." Grown men assume I'm jailbait, so they won't touch me with a ten-foot pole, and for the past three years, my professor has called me one of the most ridiculous nicknames I've ever heard in my life.

*Baby face.*

That hideous nickname was the sole reason for my latest makeover. I worked hard throughout college, my nose rarely leaving the inside of a book. Now it's time for my dedication to pay off, but unless I can get my colleagues to take me seriously, I'm never going to attain the stellar reputation I need to remain viable in the thriving dental conglomerate. So with a hefty increase in my credit card limit and nothing but my pride at stake, I went a little crazy.

My naturally dark brown long afro curls were chemically straightened to wispy waves of shiny locks that now sit an inch past my shoulders. My wardrobe had every baggy pair of boyfriend jeans, sweatshirts, yoga pants, and soccer mom outfits confiscated and given to Goodwill. And my natural plane-jane makeup was replaced with a more daring and bold color palette.

Although I've been sporting this new look for six months, this is the first time Hugo has seen the spit-polished version of Ava, but with him once again wearing his infamous beer-googles, he probably still sees me as the braces and baggy jeans-wearing, pimpled-face teenage girl he recalls from years ago. To be honest, until I ran into the hot-blooded male version of Hugo this afternoon, I was still imagining him as the teenage boy who both tilted my axis and shattered it……

*Unless you have battled the wrath of a Jorgie Marshall storm, you'll not understand the next part of my story. An hour after I was planning on borrowing a dress from Jorgie's vast collection of clothing and tootling home to hide my embarrassment under my gaudy pink sheets, I'm walking into the converted den in the attic of the Marshall residence, preparing to team up with Jorgie in a game of pool against two graduating seniors who were, I quote, "dying for the chance to meet me," unquote.*

*Hugo's eyes, along with numerous others, gawk at Jorgie and me when we enter the den. This is nothing out of the ordinary. Jorgie has remarkable beauty, the type that draws the attention of every male in the room. Her big blue eyes are prominent against her pale skin, and her dark hair makes them blaze, giving her an alluring combination of both seduction and uniqueness.*

*I smile warily at Hugo, gauging his reaction to my decision not to go home. The corners of his lips tug into a core-clenching smile before they become hidden behind a glass when he lifts a schooner to his mouth and takes a generous gulp of the liquid inside. Even though I can't see his smile, I can feel his eyes on me as I continue shadowing Jorgie into the den.*

*Panic sets in when my attempts at concealing my face from prying spectators with my thick curly hair comes up fruitless. Before we left* her room, Jorgie pulled my unruly hair back into a tight ballet-style bun, fully exposing my face. My invisibility glasses have been dumped on the vanity of her shared bathroom with Hugo, and the lightest splattering of make-up has been applied to my face. I feel awkward, out of place, like I'm in the midst of an outer body experience. My dash for the door is thwarted when Jorgie strengthens her grip on my wrist.

"They aren't looking at you because you look weird," she affirms, her eyes drifting around the room. "That spark you see in their eyes is the spark of interest and intrigue. Trust me, Ava, you want to see that spark."

Inhaling a big breath, I endure with my shaky steps toward the blue felt-covered billiard table. After Jorgie scribbles our names onto a chalkboard, advising we're the next set of players for a game of pool, she pivots on her heels to face the mass gathering of partygoers crammed into the space.

A clap of her hands gains her the devotion of nearly every man in the room. My attention is diverted from Jorgie when the trio of cheerleaders from the impromptu pool party stalk their way to Hugo. Head cheerleader and No. 1 bitch of our school, Victoria, leads the pack of scantily clad women vying for his attention. Victoria is dressed in a bombshell, curve-hugging designer dress. Every hair on her head has been straightened and brushed to perfection, falling onto her shoulders in a gloss of blonde waves. Her face, although made-up, looks refreshing and not overly done.

My heart flips when Hugo angles his head to the side, brushing off Victoria's attempts at re-acquainting their lips. The pulse in my neck thrums when his dark, heavy-hooded eyes lock with mine. Even with Victoria jabbering in his ear and intimately touching his chest, his demanding eyes remain steadfast on me. His alluring gaze spears me in place and has my pulse quickening.

I clutch the hem of my dress, inwardly battling not to squirm from his piercing blue stare. I lose the ability to control my fidgeting when his glassy gaze lowers to absorb the dress Jorgie selected for me to wear.

The length of this skirt would be best described as indecent, but by adding a pair of heels, this dress became downright corrupt.

An idiotic smile forms on my face from Hugo's lengthened stare. Feeling brazen, I grasp the flare of my skirt and do a princess curtsy. A small giggle parts my lips when Hugo's eyes return to mine and he waves his hand pompously in the air like the paupers in the fairy-tale movies do when the princess saunters by. Our fire-sparking stare down is only interrupted when a pool cue is waved in front of my face. Shifting my focus back to the present, I am met with the charming smile of Rhys Tagget.

"We're going to play a game of doubles. Did you want to pair up with me or Jorgie?" His tone is friendly with a dash of sexiness.

"Umm." My eyes seek Jorgie. She grins a beaming smile and nods her head, encouraging me to accept Rhys' offer.

Before I can accept his invitation, a deep voice at my side says, "You pair up with Jorgie; I'll play with Ava."

My heart beats double time when I recognize the rugged drawl of Hugo. Jorgie's grinning face turns to repulsion.

"I don't want to play against you. Pool is about flirting and seduction, not embarrassing your brother in front of his little buddies," she declares.

Hugo's chuckle rumbles through my chest. "I'll be sure to let Blake know that the next time I see him."

Jorgie's eyes bug. "You wouldn't dare."

"Bring it on," Hugo mocks, waving for Jorgie to bring it. "You're just afraid I'm going to remind you whose name is written on that leader board," he adds, pointing to the Marshall Pool Champion Leader Board hanging proudly on a side wall. "Either bring it or wipe your name off the board and let another player take your spot."

"Oh, I'll bring it, then I'll bring it some more." Jorgie whips her head side to side in a matching pattern to her hips. "So be prepared, brother." She overemphasizes the word brother. "Because you're about to go down."

Their playful jibe gains the attention of the twenty-plus people still sober enough to focus on something other than the drink in their hand. Rhys smiles at me before graciously making his way to the other side of the table with Jorgie.

"I'm not very good at this game," I warn Hugo when he hands me a pool cue that has a new dusting of blue chalk on the tip. Any time I've played on the faded felt table at the Marshall residence, my skills were best described as woeful.

My jaw drops when he says, "I know. You suck."

He grins at my annoyed expression. "But that's okay, I'll teach you a few tricks," he says with a wink. His words come out with a thick slur, making me wonder how many drinks he downed the past few hours.

"Ava breaks," says Jorgie, fully knowing I can't hit the colored balls when they're an inch in front of the white ball, let alone all the way across the table.

When I sneer at her, she playfully puckers her lips. Sensing my apprehension, Hugo smashes down the last of the beverage in his glass, puts it on a table, and moves to stand in front of me. My brows furrow when he grasps my left hand in his and adds a sprinkling of white powder to the edge. A smile curves on my mouth when the freshness of baby powder filters into the air.

"It will stop the friction and make everything nice and smooth so the stick can glide through your hand with ease," he says, demonstrating what he means by gliding the pool cue between my hand. His voice is extra hoarse with a dash of seduction, and it sets my pulse racing.

Blocking out the curious stare of the spectators surrounding me, I arch over the table and prepare to take my shot.

"Lean your torso over the table more, and raise your ass higher in the air," Hugo instructs, placing his open palm on the middle of my back and pushing down.

Air rustles out of my lips when his spare hand smacks my backside. "Higher, Ava."

If I were still wearing my glasses, his playful tease would have had them steaming up, but it isn't just his frisky tease that has me perspiring like I'm sitting on a furnace; it's the burning glare from Hugo's posse of female friends snarling at me that makes me feel like a pig being roasted on the spit. Victoria's thin-slitted eyes shoot daggers at me as she prances to the chalkboard to rub out my name and replace it with her own. My throat becomes scratchy from the particles of chalk dust filtering into the air from her overdramatic dusting.

Ignoring the odd tension plaguing the large den, I adjust my position as per Hugo's advice. Several male eyes drop to the front of my dress when it tips dangerously low. I lean over the table and thrust my backside into the air as instructed. A shy smile tugs on my lips when I realize one of the handful of cleavage spectators is Rhys.

Snubbing the dropped eyes from across the table, I squint one eye and line up my shot, pretending I know what I'm doing. My eyes rocket back open when Hugo's hand grazes the skin high on my inner thigh as he leans over my shoulder.

"Don't aim for the middle of the ball; target slightly to one side, and it will give it a curve effect," he suggests, his warm breath fluttering my ear.

Unable to breathe, much less speak, I nod. The thrum of my pulse palpitates in my neck from Hugo's closeness. I glide the pool stick through the portion of skin between my thumb and index finger before giving it one final crack. Just before the tip of the cue hits the white ball, I close my eyes and exhale a large breath.

Time slows to a snail's pace, and the room plunges into such deathly quietness that the sound of the white ball rolling across the felt is the only noise resonating through my ears. My eyes pop open when a loud crack booms around the room. Colored balls roll in every direction from my powerful hit. Immaturely, I jump into the air as an excited squeal ripples from my mouth. Anyone would swear I'd just won the lotto.

My party for one halts when Victoria spits out, "Why are you excited? You just lost the game, you idiot."

My disbelieving eyes dart to Hugo. He doesn't need to confirm Victoria's testimony. The truth is written all over his face.

"How?"

He stares at me with amused eyes. "You sunk the black ball." His bloodshot gaze peers past my shoulder. "Rack them up again, Rhys," he requests before lowering his eyes back to mine. "Give it another shot; just don't use so much power this time," he says with a cheeky wink.

I smile at the playfulness in his tone before nodding.

"No, she had her shot; she lost. Now, we move onto the next person on the list," wails Victoria.

I roll my eyes before turning them to Vicky.

"Oh, look," she says, acting surprised while pointing her long index finger to the chalkboard. "That next person is me."

Her tone fuels my annoyance. A condescending smirk etches on her mouth as she lurks toward Hugo and me. I grit my teeth when she snatches the cue stick out of my hand and paces to stand next to Hugo. Jorgie's mouth opens, preparing to reply to Victoria's cattiness, but I stop any words spilling from her lips with a brief shake of my head.

"It's okay; I was thirsty anyway," I say, smiling to reassure Jorgie and Hugo that it wasn't a quiver they heard in my voice.

I hear Hugo's deep voice whispering, but I can't make out any words he's saying as I pace to a makeshift bar set up under the stairwell. Jorgie's pale light blue dress swishes against my wobbly thighs with every step I take.

A genuine smile curls on my mouth when Chase says, "I'm glad you decided to stay, Ava, but no more accepting drinks from anyone but Hugo and me."

He props his elbows on the bar, exposing the dancing gypsy tattoo on his arm when his short-sleeve shirt rides up high on his thick biceps. "We wouldn't want Hugo's feathers getting ruffled again," he adds on with a brash wink.

My brows hit my hairline. Chase mumbles incoherently under his breath as he pours orange juice into a champagne flute and hands it to me. I plop my backside onto the barstool and lift the glass to my mouth. My nose screws up when I take a sip of the grim-tasting beverage.

"I think your orange juice is out of date," I say, repressing a gag.

Chase chuckles and shakes his head. "So innocent," he mumbles.

"It's a mimosa," informs a cavernous voice to my side.

"A what?" I turn to Hugo.

"Mimosa. It's champagne and orange juice. The perfect drink to accompany the hearty breakfast you're making me tomorrow."

He removes the glass from my grasp and downs the generous serving in one large gulp. Luckily, I was only using my thirst as an excuse to evade an awkward situation. When Hugo's tongue delves out to lick a smidgen of orange pulp from his top lip, the need to quench my thirst is dire.

"Can I grab another?" I shift my gaze to Chase.

His eyes shoot down to the bar fridge under the counter. "Looks like you're shit out of luck," he replies after returning his eyes to me. "If you don't mind running to the kitchen, there's some more orange juice in the fridge upstairs."

"Alright." I jump off the barstool. "I'll be back in a minute."

Chase's devious eyes shift between Hugo and me. "Go and give her a hand, Hugo," he suggests, throwing a dishcloth at Hugo and gesturing his head to the stairs.

"It's okay. I know where to find everything," I inform him, my tone confident. "And Hugo is partnered in a game of pool with Vicky." I surprise myself when I manage to keep my tone friendly while saying Victoria's name because my thoughts are anything but.

I inhale a quick, sharp breath when I pivot on my heels and discover two new opponents versing the current tournament leaders, Jorgie and Rhys. Jorgie's lips are pressed together and her head occasionally nods at whatever strategy Rhys is whispering in her ear. Jorgie is highly competitive. It wouldn't matter if it was a game of pool or she was climbing Mount Everest. If there's a possibility of her winning, she gives it her all.

My skin prickles with bumps when Hugo mutters, "I guess you're not the only one colorblind," into my ear.

My jaw falls open. "Did you sink the black ball?" I glide my eyes to his.

I giggle when he nods his head.

"It wasn't as impressive as your stellar performance, though. I at least had two turns before the black ball found a home in the right corner pocket," he jests, following me into the hallway.

"Don't worry, you'll eventually get there. Being this perfect takes practice," I respond, smiling brightly.

A brief moment of silence stretches between us before he mutters, "That it does. That it does."

He remains quiet as we walk through the Marshall residence. Numerous partygoers stop dancing to greet Hugo when he strides by. The boys pat him on the back, and girls kiss him on the cheek. By the time we reach the kitchen, jealousy is hitting me fair in the guts, and Hugo's cheek is covered with lipstick smears. Ignoring the twisted pain in my heart, I move to the fridge. Hugo props his hip on the kitchen counter and swigs out of a bottle of beer I didn't realize he was holding until now.

Cool air blasts my face when I open the double door fridge to hunt for the orange juice. Mrs. Marshall's fridge has always been well-stocked with two young adults and two teens living under her roof, and today is no exception. When I fail to locate the OJ in the monstrous-sized fridge, I tilt my torso out and peer at Hugo.

"Does your mom keep the orange juice in the fridge or the pantry?"

He doesn't reply. His gaze remains arrested on something lower than my face. My pulse quickens when his hand scrapes along the edge of his jaw. My eyes dart down to his mouth when his tongue delves out to replenish the dryness impinging his top lip.

Once his lip is moistened, and his tongue is returned to his mouth, my eyes shoot down, eager to discover what he's staring at. A thin sheet of sweat beads my body when I spot the budded peaks of my nipples *standing erect in my thin cotton dress.* Is that what has attracted his attention?

When Jorgie initially handed me this dress, I placed a small cropped jacket over the top which she promptly removed, assuring me that we were not going outside, so a jacket was unnecessary. Now I'm delighted I didn't stick to my guns.

Hugo's eyes track mine as I lift them back to his face. The streak of desire in his eyes spears me in place and instigates a warm slickness between my legs.

"She keeps it in the fridge."

I stare at him, utterly confused as to what his statement refers. My mind is nothing but mush from his avid gaze. My grip on the fridge handle firms when he pushes off the counter and stealthily prowls toward me. Even standing in the coolness of the fridge, sweat slicks my skin more with every step he takes.

His large body towers over mine when he leans into the fridge to grab the carton of orange juice at the very back of the top shelf. The heat radiating off his body warms my already inflamed skin. When his woodsy smell permeates the air, I close my eyes and inhale deeply through my nose, drinking in his delicious scent. When my eyes flutter back open, I balk and take a step back. A blaze of amusement has warmed his eyes, undoubtedly proving he noticed my vigorous sniff of his tempting smell.

"Sor--," I attempt to say before his warm, beer-flavored lips press against mine, stealing my words.

My mouth opens to accept his kiss, but the remainder of my body freezes, unsure of how to react. His hand grips my bun as his tongue slips into my mouth to sample and taste every inch. A low groan simpers from his mouth when I unstiffen my clenched jaw and return his kiss by mimicking the slow sweeps of his tongue and the soft caresses of his lips.

He leans in until my back is splayed against the open fridge door. The coolness of the pickles and spreads stored in the door refreshes my *overheated skin. Our kiss builds in intensity when he wraps his spare hand around my waist and pulls me in close before ravishing my neck.*

*A surge of desire courses through my body when I feel the thickness straining against his trousers. His kiss is warm and wonderful. Mind-stealing. I rake my fingers through his long, shaggy hair when someone coughing clatters through my ears. A whimper leaks from my swollen lips when Hugo pulls away from our embrace and peers at the intruder interrupting our private time.*

*Following his gaze, I find the smirking face of Chase. "I take it you found something more appealing to drink than orange juice, Ava?"*

*His eyes are pointed down, peering at the dumped carton of juice on the floor. I was so entranced by Hugo's kiss, I didn't notice its cool and sticky contents had puddled around my borrowed shoes.*

*My eyes return to Hugo when he runs his thumb along my swollen top lip. He stares into my eyes for what feels like hours, but is only mere seconds before he stalks out of the room without a backward glance.....*

My focus returns to the present when Hugo leans down and takes a sizeable whiff of my hair. The wrinkles in my forehead extend to my nose when I catch the scent of his heavy pants of breath.

"Liar, liar, pants on fire," I squeal when I fail to detect the smallest smidgen of alcohol on his breath.

I grimace when my overly girly pitch bounces off the woodgrain walls of the elevator and shrieks through my eardrums. Unfortunately, no amount of make-up, fancy designer clothes or pretty new hairstyles can alter my immature voice.

My squeals turn into laughter when Hugo replies, "I don't care, I don't care, I can buy another pair."

Once my laughter dies down, I ask. "How'd you remember that?"

He chuckles a full-hearted laugh. "How could I forget it? You and Jorgie used to say it a million times a day."

Any refute I attempt to give is cut off when Hugo cocks his brow and bores his eyes into mine, daring me to deny his statement. I remain quiet, unable to negate his accusation, since it is accurate.

Jorgie used that statement numerous times a day from the age of ten until... last week. She breaks it out whenever she accuses me of denying my attraction to Hugo.

"You can run with a lie, but you can't hide from the truth. It will always catch up with you," Hugo says before placing me onto my feet.

I smile at his statement, but my heart isn't fully into it. Hugo's never been one to hide anything. Not his feelings, his mistakes, *his body*, so his brash comment is somewhat surprising for a man who has always been so forthright.

*Maybe it isn't just my life that's altered the past six years?*

# SEVEN

# AVA

A grin furls my lips when his chapped hand encloses around mine as the elevator door dings open. I nod in thanks to the doorman when he opens the glass door for Hugo and me. A blast of warm air hits my face when we merge onto the sidewalk. Even being late April, the night air has a nice amount of warmth to it since the heat from the day has been trapped by the clouds in the sky.

I crank my head to the left before shifting it to the right, seeking Hugo's truck. There are a still a decent number of people loitering on the sidewalks at this time of night, but Hugo's truck is nowhere in sight.

I stray my eyes to his. His lips are tugged high, his vibrant blue eyes peering at me, but he remains as quiet as a graveyard at midnight. A smile stretches across my face when a limousine pulls to the curb in front of us not even five seconds later. Excitement races through me, closely followed by confusion.

*Why would he rent a limo?*

"Come on," he says, dashing toward the limo.

We hustle through a throng of people, wanting to avoid the slight pelting of rain that has started falling from the sky. I can't contain my childish giggle as I jog to keep up with his long strides. His lazy steps are the equivalent of me undertaking a marathon stride.

My eyes shoot in every direction when we enter the cabin, eager to absorb the dark, moody interior. You'd think with the richness of the dark varnished wood, black leather seats, and the heaviness of the tint would give it a morose appearance, but it doesn't. It has the ambiance of seduction and intrigue deeply engrained in it.

"When did you win the lotto?" I turn my gaze to Hugo, who is watching me intently.

His chuckle booms around the cabin. "It's one of the perks of my soon-to-be new job."

"Are they still hiring?"

He laughs even louder. "You don't seem to be doing bad for yourself," he says, motioning his head to my building shrinking into the background as the limo merges into traffic.

I twist my neck to peer at the place I call home. It is a beautiful building designed to withstand the test of time. It is at the forefront of architectural design, being both elegant and masculine at the same time.

Other than the dream of one day owning my own dental practice, having a place to call my own has always been one of my greatest wishes. So passing that goal before I turned twenty-five was a remarkable accomplishment I'll happily praise myself for achieving.

I turn my gaze from peering out the back window to glance at Hugo. He appears to be watching the dense flow of traffic outside, but I'm not buying it. I can feel his scorching eyes peering at me.

"What really brought you to my apartment tonight?" I query, no longer able to assuage my curiosity for his spontaneous visit.

Before Hugo can reply, the driver advises that we've reached our destination.

"Wait here, I'll come around and get you."

I smile and nod at Hugo's request. As he darts around the car, my eyes absorb a long line of men and women wrapping half way down the block and around the corner. Hundreds of well-dressed patrons are huddled together under the shopfront awnings, vainly trying to keep dry from the sprinkling of rain falling from the sky.

A middle-aged gentleman with a thick silver mustache rushes out of a set of double doors. The umbrella in his hand shelters Hugo from the rain as he opens the door of the limousine and offers me his hand. I press my thighs together and slither out of the car, futilely attempting to maintain a sense of modesty in the super short skirt Hugo chose for me to wear.

"Good evening, Ma'am," greets the mustached gentleman.

"Hello," I reply shyly.

A roar of protest tears from the crowd when the large Maori-looking bouncer on the door of the club unlatches the red velvet rope and gestures for us to enter. My pulse increases with every step we take. Brushed metals; rich, dark woodgrain material; and hot, sweaty bodies writhing together to the latest club hits make a stimulating visual. As the heat in the room elevates, so does Hugo's grip on my hand.

Standing on the balls of his feet, he extends to his full height, allowing him to see over the dense crowd. His head cranks to the right before switching it to the left, like he's seeking someone amongst the sweat-drenched club goers. When his avid search fails to locate his target, he strides to the bar. Since he's still clutching my hand, I shadow closely behind.

A broad smile stretches across my face the closer we get to the polished wood bar. It's like the cast from *Coyote Ugly* and *Cocktail* danced beneath the sheets and had a baby. Beautiful, scantily clad women are performing a provocative dance routine on the bar top while equally attractive male bartenders flip and twist bottles of liquor into the air behind them.

Even though the scene could be construed as overly seductive, the beaming smiles on the bar staff's faces give it more a fun, playful vibe. Just watching the happiness projecting out of them forces a smile on my face.

When the performance is over, Hugo leans over the wooden

countertop and seeks the attention of a female bartender serving customers halfway down the bar. "Tammy, is he still here?"

The beautiful blonde turns her head to the side. "No, sorry. You missed him by ten minutes."

Hugo lifts his spare hand to his head and runs his fingers through his glorious, thick mane of hair, making my fingers twitch with jealousy. The blaring music pumping from the speakers hanging from the ceiling fails to drown out the swear word that seeps from Hugo's lips. My breathing halts when the bartender next to Tammy cranks his head to the side. *Rhys Tagget.*

Smiling, Rhys saunters toward us. Just like Hugo, age has been gracious to him. His body is lean with a splattering of muscles in all the right places. Just from the way he walks, you can tell he'd be extraordinary in bed, and he knows it. He brazenly winks before leaning over the counter so his eyes can rake my body. He studies me with just as much attention as I assessed him. Every inch of my skin is flushed with heat from his vivid perusal.

When his eyes return to my face, he croons. *"C'est un plaisir de vous revoir,* Ava." His voice is rich, like Marvin Gaye singing sweet serenades into my ear.

Masking my surprise that he remembers me, I accept the hand he offers in greeting.

"Nice to see you again, too, Rhys." I try to make my voice sultry and mature, but it still comes out a little girly.

I flick my eyes to Hugo when his grip on my hand tightens. His jaw flexes as he watches the exchange between Rhys and me.

"You remember Rhys; don't you, Hugo?"

A scornful smirk etches on Hugo's mouth. "How could I forget your French tutor?"

My heart gallops when I see a streak of possession in his vibrant blue eyes. I have no trouble recognizing that streak as I've worn it many times in the past when dealing with the troupe of women who always flounder around Hugo when he blesses them with his presence.

Even now, with Hugo's hand clasped tightly around mine, women are circling like a kettle of vultures, waiting for the prime opportunity to attack and devour their prey. Hugo's rugged looks attract a broad caliber of women, from prima donna Barbie doll-looking women to the geeky professor types.

My eyes revert from the skimpily dressed carcass-eaters when my name is spoken by a voice that still invades my dreams even after years of absence.

"Sorry, what did you say?"

Hugo flashes his photogenic smile that has the pack of vultures hovering in closer. "I've got to run a quick errand. Any drinks you want are on the house."

"Okay, thanks," I say with a shy smile.

Placing my clutch purse onto the countertop, I accept the cocktail menu from a smiling Rhys. Hugo paces one step away before he spins back around.

"Do I need to remind you of the non-fraternization policy of this club?" he questions with his vibrant blue eyes glaring at Rhys.

A broad grin morphs on Rhys's face before he raises his eyes to the crystal clock hanging above the glass shelving behind the bar, which displays it is 11:50 PM. "Nah, it's all good. In ten minutes my shift is over, so that won't be a problem anymore."

Hugo's fists ball as his face lines with anger. "I'll be back in five."

His eyes drift to mine for the briefest second before he pivots on his heels and struts through the crowd. Yes, I said strut, as Hugo Marshall has the perfect man strut. The right amount of swagger, a little bit of attitude, and a glimmer in his eyes that tells you he brings the kind of trouble your mother warns you about, but you can't help but want.

# EIGHT

# HUGO

Irrational jealousy weighs down my chest as I make my way through the horde of people grinding together on the dance floor. It is irrational, as I have no reason to be jealous.

Ava isn't mine.

She's never been mine.

She'll most likely never be mine.

But watching her go gaga over Rhys had the ugly green monster rearing his head, primed and ready to yank Rhys over the bar and pummel some sense into him. Maybe a good beat down will remind him that Primal, the first stop on my club-hopping adventure for the night, has a very strict non-fraternization policy between staff and patrons. Isaac, the clubs' owner, does not believe in the concept of mixing business with pleasure.

Until tonight, I never paid much attention to clause 23.1 in the employment contract I've been perusing the past two weeks. Although it is there printed in thick black ink, I never considered it set in stone. Now, I'll happily remind Rhys that any break in the terms of the contract he signed will make his employment with Holt Enterprises null and void.

*I'll use any tactics I can to keep his hazel eyes off Ava.*

Don't get me wrong, Rhys is a great guy. He's only working at Primal to occupy his time until he commences his internship as a surgeon at a local hospital in two weeks' time. He has the rare combination of both brains and good looks. If I was forced to pick a man for Ava to date, he'd be the first on my list, but even knowing that, my illogical jealousy built faster than Usain Bolt running the one hundred meter sprint.

*What does that mean? You tell me, as I don't have a fucking clue.*

By the time I make it through the mass of energetic partygoers grinding to the dub beats blaring out of the speakers, the back of my shirt is drenched in sweat and the five-minute timeframe I gave Rhys is already up. Racking my knuckles on the wooden door marked "Private" at the back of the club, I push down on the handle and sweep open the door. Isaac's head lifts from peering at a barrage of paperwork scattered on his desk. He motions for me to enter as he continues with his conversation on an old, outdated phone.

Isaac is a young entrepreneur who would rival the likes of well-respected nightclub owners Jeff Soffer and Noah Tepperberg. After our impromptu interview six weeks ago, I did a little snooping on Mr. Trust Fund. Even though Isaac is only twenty-two, he already owns a handful of nightclubs in the lower New York region.

His amassed fortune is rumored to be somewhere in the millions, but just like his personality, he keeps the actual value of his wealth a well-hidden secret. He's loaded and has looks that would make David Beckham pale in comparison, but what does Isaac lack that the others named above have? Some would say a heart.

Lucky for Isaac, I have a stellar knack for reading people. I can tell under his layers of darkness there's a good guy just waiting to be exposed. Since I've never been one to shy away from a challenge, I've made it my mission to unravel the mystery sitting in front of me. Once Isaac finishes his phone call, he puts his ancient cell in the breast pocket of his suit jacket and gestures for me to take a seat.

"You should consider updating your phone. Wearing a thousand-dollar suit just looks tacky when you're carrying a brick in your pocket."

He tries to hide it, but I see his lips tug a little higher from my playful jibe.

"Did you find Ava?"

Although Isaac is only twenty-two, his demeanor makes him appear a lot older than he is. He's well-respected amongst his peers and feared by his rivals.

I nod. "Yeah, but Tammy said Pencil Dick left ten minutes before we arrived."

This time, there's no doubt a smirk etched on Isaac's mouth.

After leaving Jorgie's house, I headed out for a night on the town. Drinking and escaping in the music were the only plans I had for the night. Isaac sweetened the pot in our ongoing negotiations by offering me the use of a chauffeured limousine from his private collection and unlimited drinks in any of his clubs.

The first thing my eyes zoomed in on when I stepped out of the limo was the long line of patrons vying to be admitted into Isaac's latest club. The second thing I spotted was the guy who drove the first half of my night into the abyss of boredom. Marvin failed to notice my furious glare burning a hole in the back of his head as his nose was buried deep into the neck of a girl who wasn't even half the woman Ava is.

I did initially consider interrupting Marvin and his date, but like all good books, the whole "show not tell" notion popped into my head. It was then I decided I was better off showing Ava that Marvin is a dawg rather than telling her. After a quick word to Isaac, requesting him to grant Marvin and his date access to his capacity-filled club, I headed back to Rochdale.

All my best laid intentions flew out the window when Ava opened her front door in nothing but a teeny tiny and completely hideous-looking bath towel. I didn't even attempt to put up a fight when my brain signaled for my eyes to run her barely covered body not once, but twice.

It was a battle I was never going to win, so why fight it? Ava was wet, exposed, and had a doe-eyed look of innocence that forced X-rated thoughts to run through my mind quicker than I could process them. After a stern reprimand to myself that Ava wasn't some tail I was chasing for the night, my initial game plan kicked back into gear. I may have selected the shortest dress Ava had in her wardrobe for her to wear, but that wasn't just for my benefit. That was to show Marvin exactly what he lost by fooling around.

I tried to keep my eyes off Ava's legs for the five-mile trip from her apartment to Primal, but they incessantly peered down to the generous portions of skin displayed on her smooth caramel thighs. I couldn't help it; I am a man, and Ava has a stellar pair of legs that would only look better if they were wrapped around my head.

I plop into the leather chair across from Isaac and rest my ankle on my opposite knee. "What's your surveillance like in this club?"

Isaac leans back in his chair. "Lacking. That's why I'm knee-deep in negotiations to secure a manager of operations. Once I get him to stop pussy-footing around and sign on the dotted line, I'll have him organize new state of the art surveillance to be installed in all six of my clubs."

My chuckle bounces off the walls of his well-designed office. That manager of operations he's referring to – that's me. The only reason I haven't "signed on the dotted line" is because the final negotiation of my salary has yet to be discussed.

Although Isaac has advised on numerous occasions that I'll be well compensated if I become a member of his empire, until I see a dollar amount written down, my signature will remain void on the one hundred plus page employee contract my advisor (aka Jorgie) is still combing through.

Isaac arches his brow. "Why, what were you after on the security tapes?"

"I figured since Ava missed the opportunity to see Marvin as the dawg he is in person, showing her on tape might be just as effective."

Isaac shakes his head. "I disagree. Seeing it for herself is one thing, but you forcing Ava to see it, that's just going to cause you trouble."

My brows meet my hairline. "I'm not the one who pretended I had to work and then went out to sharpen my pencil with another lady's sharpener. How could this cause me any trouble?"

My brows become lost in my hair when Isaac's chuckle bellows through my ears. This is the first time I've heard his true laugh.

"There are two people in the world, Hugo," Isaac says once his laughter dies down. "Healers and hurters. You, my friend, are a healer."

He runs his index finger across his brow when he spots the odd expression on my face. "When Ava discovers what Marvin is up to, you'll help her get back on her feet. Until then, you have to wait."

"What if she never finds out?"

Isaac's brow arches high into the air. "Give her some credit. She's a woman. They're very perceptive. For all you know, she could already be aware of his indiscretions."

My eyes follow Isaac as he stands from the chair. "Now, unless you're planning on signing on the dotted line, get the fuck out of my office. Some of us actually have to work for a living."

From the neutral expression on his face, I can't tell if he's being serious or not. Not wanting to push the boundaries of our newly developed bro-bond, I stand from my chair and make my way to the door. Just before I exit, I crank my neck to peer at Isaac. When he senses my presence, he stops ruffling through the papers on his desk and lifts his dark gray eyes to mine.

"Write a figure on a piece of paper. Any figure. I don't care how much it is. Just write it down and I'll sign the contract."

When someone hands you a golden ticket, you should grasp it with both hands, not make the ticket manufacturer jump through hoops to prove its authenticity.

Music blasts my eardrums when I exit Isaac's soundproof office. When I lift my gaze, the first thing I see is Ava's bright smile. My lips curl when her head flies back and laughter spills out.

Although I can't hear her laugh over the thumping music blaring out of the speakers, I can recall how angelic it sounds. Ava has a beautiful laugh, the type that shreds straight through to my soul. When I was younger, anytime I would hear it, my good intentions would waver. Tonight is no different.

I pop my head back into Isaac's office. "Can we change our meeting tomorrow morning to the afternoon?"

His brow arches high.

"She's just a friend," I say, my tone as unconvincing as the grin twitching my lips.

His gray eyes bore into mine. "Friends don't want to shred off other friend's panties."

"Who said I'd shred them? I'm more a pull them to the side type of guy," I reply with a saucy wink.

I just set a new record. I've made Isaac smirk more the past ten minutes than I have the entire time I've known him.

"Although no official documents have been signed, I'm happy to accept your verbal confirmation on joining my empire, but with me returning to Ravenshoe tomorrow morning, the finer details of our agreement will need to wait until I return."

Noting a slight pang of hesitation in his voice, I ask. "Everything alright?"

He nods. "Everything is fine."

Never the talkative type, his attention returns to the documents on his desk. Lifting my chin in farewell, I spin on my heels and pace out of his office. The battle to keep myself in check ramps up the closer I amble to Ava. All my good intentions are misplaced when my eyes zoom in on the strappy heels on her tiny feet.

When she crosses her legs, the scant hem of her dress edges closer to the pair of lace panties she sneakily slid on earlier. Dirty images of seeing her in *nothing* but those sexy heels and panties run rampantly through my mind. Shaking off my improper thoughts, I prop my hip on the counter next to her. She flashes me a quick smile before continuing with her conversation.

"So for nearly an hour you watched two guys on stage perform *genitalia* origami?"

Ava squeaks when she mentions the genitalia part of her sentence, and my brows shoot up into the air.

Rhys laughs a candid chuckle. "Yep. Seriously, it was the most hilarious thing I've ever seen."

Ava's pupils widen when Rhys adds on, "I also learned a few new party tricks that night too."

Although his tone fully alludes to cheekiness, an absurd rush of jealousy blackens my veins.

"Tucking your dick between your legs and pretending you have a vagina isn't a new party trick, Rhys. You've been pulling that move for years."

That's my half-assed attempt at keeping the conversation lighthearted and out of jealous territory. It is a futile attempt, but it's all I've got.

Rhys' riotous chuckle gains him the attention of a handful of women milling around the bar. "Hey, no breaking the locker room code. What happens in the locker room, stays in the--"

"Locker room," I fill in with a laugh as my eyes drift to Ava.

I can't help but smile at the flushed expression on her face. For a woman whose off-the-Richter-scale sexiness has instigated a stream of improper thoughts to flood my mind nonstop for years, it astounds me that she can also pull off the appearance of a virtuous saint at the same time.

"Let me get washed up, and then we'll get this show on the road," Rhys says with his gleaming eyes staring at Ava.

When Ava timidly nods, Rhys heads to the staff room located at the back of the bar.

"Are you going somewhere?" I ask Ava once Rhys is out of earshot.

My eyes shoot up to Jazzy, the bartender, when she places an ice-cold bottle of beer in front of me. After smiling a thanks for her service, I return my eyes to Ava.

Her tongue delves out to lick her top lip before she mumbles. "Umm... I've kind of agreed to participate in a dare." Her face grimaces as a fine layer of sweat beads her forehead.

I arch my brow but remain quiet, waiting for her to elaborate. When we were younger, I never backed away from a dare, no matter how crude it was, but Ava wouldn't lick a droplet of rain off a leaf, so I'm somewhat surprised she's decided to undertake a dare in the middle of a bustling nightclub. Perhaps it isn't just Ava's shell that's altered the past few years; maybe her insides got revamped as well?

Ava stares into my eyes and smiles a furtive grin. "If I win, I'll be living on easy street. Ten freshly printed one dollar bills will be lining my pockets."

I smirk and shake my head. "What happens if you lose?"

"Not a possibility," she blurts out.

Unable to maintain my eye contact, Ava's eyes drift around our surroundings. I swig on my cold beer with the hope of simmering the raging heat coursing through my body from watching her sexy-as-fuck lips wrap around the straw of her drink. Her lips are why fantasies were created. And I've fantasied about them in more ways than what could be classed as acceptable the past ten years. In case you're wondering, my thoughts have been anything but pure.

When Ava lowers her cocktail, I thrust my gigantic head into her peripheral vision.

"If you lose?" I ask again.

She mumbles something under her breath, but she's so quiet, I can't hear a word she's speaking.

I arch my brow. "What?"

"I have to go on a date with Rhys," she mumbles weakly.

"What?" I heard what she said, but the green-eyed monster missed it, and he's demanding for her to repeat it.

Her shoulders square as her chins lifts into the air. "I have to go on a date with Rhys," she says more forcefully.

Her eyes lift and lock with mine. "Do you have a problem with that?"

Loving the whip of feistiness in her voice, my lips twitch as I repress a smile. "Nope, no problem."

Her chin dips, then her shoulders sag. I angle my head to the side and peer into her downcast eyes.

"Why would there be a problem? You said there's no possibility of you losing. So unless you're going to recant your statement, I've got nothing to worry about."

She tries to hide her smile, but the whites of her teeth peek out the sides of her cocktail glass. Suddenly, she cringes and downs the remainder of her drink in quick succession. Following her fretful gaze, I spot Rhys sauntering toward us. His sole focus remains on Ava as he moves through a gathering of women vying for his attention. Jealousy places a stranglehold on my throat when I see the eagerness of his strides. He looks like a kid in a toy store who's told he can pick any toy he wants. His choice is a pretty little doll named Ava.

"You ready?" he questions, waggling his overly manicured brows at Ava.

Expelling a deep exhalation, Ava stands from her chair and runs her sweaty palms down the front of her dress. The frown on her face remains firm as she thrusts her clutch into my chest.

"Can you save my seat?"

Nodding, I sit in her barstool and swivel to face the crowd. My back molars grind together when Rhys and Ava walk toward the dance floor hand in hand. When they reach the edge of the wood-lined space, Rhys releases Ava's hand and paces to the DJ's booth at the side.

Maverick, the DJ, smiles a beaming grin when Rhys points to Ava fidgeting nervously on the edge of the dance floor. When *Scream and Shout* by Will.i.am and Britney Spears mellows, a new, very familiar beat beams out of the speakers. My eyes snap to Ava. Her appearance is fretful, her face pale. Releasing a big breath, she rolls her shoulders and loosens her toughened stance.

*No way, the old Ava would never be brave enough to do this.*

When Rhys moves toward her, bopping along to the beat of the music, a cock-twitching smile stretches across Ava's face. As the song progresses, the color in Ava's face returns. I spit my beer when the song hits the chorus and Ava starts ponying on the spot.

*Oh, yeah, she's going there.*

I slap my hand over my mouth, trying to conceal my chuckle when Ava lassos her arm in the air. The crowd surrounding the dance floor congregates closer to Ava when her "Gangnam Style" dance moves rapidly gain her the attention of everyone under the age of twenty-one. I stand from my chair, stretching to my full height when the crowd circling Ava blocks my view of her completely hideous but somehow arousing dance moves. Side-splitting laughter tears from my lips when she places her hand on her cocked hip and impersonates PSY's famous side-step to perfection. Mine and numerous other male eyes dart down to the globes of her ass when she bends over to flick her knee.

By the time her dance solo is finished, I have tears streaming down my face and a hard-on my trousers are unable to contain. I've also smiled more the past three minutes than I have the previous two years. *And I swear to god, I've never been so fucking hard.* Just imagine, if Ava has enough gall to get up in front of hundreds of people and dance like nobody is watching, what would she be like beneath the sheets? Bedding a woman who's not only confident in her skin but also willing to try new things would be a riveting experience. Just the thought of taking Ava out of her comfort zone has my cock twitching.

After curtseying to the wolf-whistling crowd, Ava gathers her ten one dollar bills from Rhys and paces toward me. Her face is flushed, her nape is dripping with sweat, and she has a knock-your-socks-off smile plastered across her face.

"I seriously didn't think you'd do it," say Rhys, jogging to catch up to Ava.

My teeth grit when he wraps his arm around her shoulders and pulls her in close to his side.

"I told you I knew all the moves."

Even though she's talking to Rhys, her eyes remain steadfast on mine.

"Yeah, but most girls are all talk. You followed through. That's a rare find these days."

*Nearly as rare as your teeth still being in your mouth*, I gabble to myself.

Rhys leans over the bar and signals for a bartender. "Tammy, another piña colada for Ava and I'll have a double of vodka."

Ava plops into the vacant barstool next to me. "I'm loaded." She fans the one dollar bills in the air like they have extra zeroes written on them.

"Tuck them into your pocket, cause you'll need them when I show you how real people dance."

She props her elbows on the bar and tilts to my side. "Is that a challenge I hear seeping from your lips, Mr. Marshall?"

Losing the ability to keep myself in check, I lean in intimately close to her side. I'm so close, her sugary sweet smell engulfs my senses, making my cock even stiffer.

"That's not a challenge, baby; that's a sure-fire promise."

# NINE

# AVA

The sweat slicking my body thickens when the deep richness of Hugo's voice as he taunts me. Normally, I'd never get up and shake my tushy in front of strangers, but the two piña coladas I downed while waiting for Hugo to run his errand made me a little bolder than normal.

In all honesty, when Rhys originally configured the bet, stating if I lost I had to go on a date with him, I had every intention of driving that bet straight off the bridge and into a freezing cold lake. Many women before me have invented far worse ruses to secure a date with him, but my best laid plans went to poop when Hugo sauntered back toward us.

Just like the past ten years of my life, every time I get a grasp on my childish crush, Hugo comes crashing back into my life with an almighty bang and throws a spanner into the works. Flirty one-liners, drunken kisses, and the hope that one day he'd see me as more than just his little sister's best friend kept me dangling on the line, waiting patiently for an opportunity to prove my worth.

Rhys' eyes drift between Hugo and me as he accepts the freshly prepared piña colada from Tammy. When his head slants to the side and his appearance becomes washed with confusion, I realize how intimately close Hugo and I are sitting. I scoot to the edge of my chair before accepting the cocktail glass from Rhys.

"Thank you," I say with a smile.

My heart stops beating when Hugo adjusts his position so the space between us is even more miniscule than it was before. The hairs on the nape of my neck spike when the blasts of his hot breath flutters my neckline.

Curtly nodding, Rhys' lips quirk as his eyes dart to the watch on his wrist. "Oh, shit, look at the time. I forgot I had a… umm… appointment tonight."

He downs his double of vodka before placing his glass on the countertop and turning to face me. "I'm sorry I have to dare and run, Ava, but I completely forgot about the… appointment."

"That's okay. It was great seeing you again." I lean in and place a friendly kiss on his cheek. "If you're ever after a dance-off partner, look me up."

Smiling, he wraps his arms around my shoulders and gives me a quick hug. "If things here cool down, I'll be sure to take you up on that offer," he whispers into my ear.

Turning his attention to Hugo, he says, "I guess I'll be seeing you around?" He seems hesitant, making me unsure if his statement is a question or an observation.

Hugo's eyes snap to mine when Rhys leans into his side and mutters something in his ear. After nodding, Hugo pats Rhys on the back and gives him a brief man hug. The fake smile burning my cheeks sags the instant Rhys scurries out the double doors of the club as quickly as his lean legs can take him. I flop into an empty barstool and chew on the straw in my drink.

"It was probably your Gangnam dance moves that scared him away," I grumble to myself.

My suspicions are confirmed when a broad grin stretches across Hugo's face. I huff before pulling the straw out of my drink to throw it at his mocking face. I smile when it hits its mark on his left cheek.

"Alright, let's just get this done and dusted, then we can move on. I'm an idiot. I made a fool out of myself to ensure I wasn't forced to go on a date with a man most women would give their left lung for." *All so I could continue on my non-date with a man who never gives me the time of day unless he's drunk.*

This, ladies and gentlemen is a prime example as to why I'm still single.

Hugo's brows scrunch. "Why did you give up the opportunity for a date with a guy most women would give their left lung for?"

Because he's not the one I want. He's not the one who dangles a carrot in front of my face and dares me not to touch it. He's not the one who makes me strive to turn my fantasies into reality. And he's also not the one who sets my pulse racing just from hearing his laugh. That honor has always solely belonged to Hugo.

Instead of saying what I really feel, I shrug my shoulders. "I'm not really looking for any companions right now," I fib.

Hugo's lips set into a hard line. "Because of Marvin?"

I try to hide the cringe crossing my face, but Hugo is very perceptive and notices it before I get the chance to fully suffocate it.

"Marvin and I aren't dating," I blurt out, mimicking his denial of dating Victoria earlier.

Hugo's lips twist and he eyes me with curiosity but remains quiet. Marvin and I have been on a handful of *dates*. I use the term *dates* lightly as they were *nothing* to call home about. It was like two work acquaintances decided to hold an informal meeting in a restaurant instead of a boardroom.

Our conversation never veered away from work, and one peck on the cheek is the closest contact we've had the past two weeks. He only came to Jorgie's house for dinner tonight because I accidentally let slip that Hugo was going to be there.

On that revelation, Marvin invited himself, rationalizing that he and Hugo were friends in high school and that it was a great opportunity for them to catch up. It was only after witnessing the testosterone-riddled stare down between Marvin and Hugo on Jorgie's porch did I realize three things.

1. Marvin and Hugo have *never* been friends.
2. Marvin wants to push our *friendship* to a level I'm not comfortable with.

And, last but not at all least:

3. Marvin has *way* too many similarities to my father.

Seeing the warning signs flash in front of my eyes, I leaned into Jorgie's ear and whispered that I was going to "weed the garden" the instant I got home. When she slid her index finger under her nose, signaling she understood my coded statement, I fled for the taxi without a backward glance.

I was still in the process of working out how I was going to inform Marvin of my decision when Hugo arrived on my doorstep. As much as Marvin *demanding* that I leave Jorgie's house irked me, I must tread carefully when it comes to him. I'm already struggling paying my mortgage payment as it is without adding exorbitant tuition fees into the mix.

When I agreed to become a partner at Gardner and Sons, part of my contract was that they were to pay for the last two years of my university fees. If that contract slips from my grasp before I officially take my position in a year's time, I'll be required to pay back any installments they paid on my behalf. Since that is a debt I cannot incur, I will tread cautiously when it comes to Marvin.

After a few moments of uncomfortable silence, I lift my eyes to Hugo. His lip twist as his panty-combusting eyes scorch every inch of my skin. His heavy-hooded gaze has my arousal surging through my veins and flooding my nether regions.

"Now that we have that out the way, can we continue with our night?" I squeak out, fighting the urge to squirm in my seat.

I lift my cocktail glass to my mouth, hiding my flushed cheeks. My eyes widen when Hugo places his hand on the base of the glass and tilts it higher. My nose hairs tingle when the freezing cold liquid slides down my throat to settle in my flipping stomach. Once all the scrumptious, but bitterly cold goodness is consumed, Hugo removes the glass from my grasp and places it on the countertop.

After a quiet word with a female bartender, he grips my hand in his and stalks toward the mass of people cavorting on the wooden dance floor. Halfway there, a sharp pain twinges my brain. I dig my heels into the plush carpet and lift my spare hand to my temple. Hugo angles his head to the side and eyes me curiously.

"Brain freeze," I cringe.

"Blow hot air on your nose," he instructs, his words muffled by a breathless chuckle.

Opening one of my squinted eyes, I glare at him. "What?"

Apparently, my ability to think straight around him doesn't just hamper my astuteness. It also affects my hearing.

He smirks a heart-fluttering smile. "Blow hot air onto your nose."

A small smile tugs on my lips when he demonstrates his instructions by puckering out his plump lips and fanning his nose with his breath. Deciding I can't look anymore ludicrous than I already have tonight, I blow hot air onto the tip of my nose. The more I blow, the more my brows lower.

"I can't believe that actually works," I say, once the pain of a knife digging into my skull vanishes. "How did you know that?"

Hugo grins. "You're not the only one with cool party tricks," he says with a bold wink.

"You thought my dancing was cool?"

"Not at all," he replies, his tone unapologetic.

My bottom lip drops into a pout. Heat blemishes my body from the tips of my toes to the top of my head when his index finger twangs my protruding lip.

Drawing my lip back in, he says, "It was a little dorky and *totally* uncool, but every person in this club under the age of 21 is looking at you like Beyoncé just graced them with her presence."

My nervous eyes peer around the space. Not quite everyone, but a large number of young adults with an under-21 illuminated band secured on their wrists are gawking at me. A few are smiling, a handful are laughing, and a group of males are winking while suggestively gyrating their hips. Their cheeky flirting halts the instant they cop the wrath of Hugo's firm glare.

My brain freeze turns into a rush of giddiness when Hugo yanks me in close to his body so my chest is flush against his. "Are you ready to learn one of my party tricks?"

Not giving me a chance to reply, he dips the top half of my body and rolls his hips. I stumble, unsteady on my feet, when he flips me back up and swings his hips in rhythm to the music thumping around us. Unlike many men before him, Hugo's dance moves aren't robotic and stiff. They're uninhibited and fluid. *Captivating*. He moves in a way that shows how well in tune he is with his own body.

Although we "hung out" a lot when we were younger, we've never danced like this. The vibe at a club has never failed to excite me. Tonight is no different, but it is even more energetic dancing with Hugo. I've dreamed of nights like this. I'm tempted to pinch myself just to make sure I'm not dreaming.

When Hugo pulls me in closer to his body, I grip his shoulders and get lost in the magic of dancing with a guy whose moves would rival the likes of Channing Tatum. In a haze of pussy tingles and shaky steps, we're quickly swamped by a mass of writhing bodies on the dance floor. The crowd mingling around us are thumping with bountiful energy, spurring a cluster of excitement to trickle through my veins. The intoxicating smell of sweat on heated skins filters through my nose.

When I lift my eyes, the music fades to a hushed buzz. With the combination of the seductive scent mingling in the air and Hugo's heavy-lidded eyes locking on mine, my libido hits a level I've never felt. Hugo encircles his arms around my waist, and we spend the next three songs dancing as if there are no clothes between us. The tension between us is static, like a storm brewing on the horizon, full of electric energy just waiting to combust.

When the music switches to a higher tempo beat, Hugo releases me from his grasp and takes a step backward. My body screams in protest from the loss of his contact, but my attention remains focused on him.

He dances like he's auditioning for the *Magic Mike* sequel. If it weren't for the smell of sweat lingering in the air from the mass of bodies dancing together, I would've sworn I'd ordered my own personal strip-a-gram. Except, unfortunately, this stripper keeps his clothing on.

Catching my lust-filled gaze, Hugo's eyes roam over my face before they scan my body. When his gaze returns to mine, my breath hitches. His pupils are wide, his eyes have darkened, and the undeniable look of lust is beaming from his heavy-lidded gaze.

Like they could get any more seducing, his dance moves become more provocative and entrancing. Pussy-thumping good. Fighting the urge to dig the dollar bills out of my pocket and tuck them into the waistband of his jeans, I close my eyes, lift my arms into the air, and let the music overtake me.

Over time, the air grows thick with humidity as the mass of bodies amalgamate. Sweat glistens my skin and my lips are parched even with downing fruity cocktails like they're cans of soda. For the past hour, the bar staff have kept mine and Hugo's supply of alcohol flowing like water from a tap.

Before my body can announce its thirst, a waitress arrives with a thirst-quenching drink. I feel like a celebrity attending a ritzy after party. My every whim is being taken care of without a single word needing to seep from my lips. Blood is teeming through my veins at a rapid pace, and my head is fuzzy with both the infusion of alcohol and adrenaline. Even with a horde of people bumping into me, I can't wipe the huge smile off my face. I'm loving every single moment of my new-found freedom.

A grin spreads across my face when my eyes open and lock with Hugo. His hair is messy and wet from the dampness suffocating the air; his eyes are snapped shut, his plump lips parted. It's a sexually gratifying visual that causes a slickness to form between my legs. As a crackling of energy sparks my womb, I'm unexpectedly grasped around the waist and yanked deeper into the dense crowd.

A warm body enveloping my back, and the roll of a man's hips has my eyes widening. Panicked over a stranger suddenly being plastered to my back, my body stiffens, and my pupils dilate. My fretful eyes arrow down when my dance partner's hands slither along my stomach before inching toward my erratically beating chest.

I clutch his wrists, securing them onto my hips before he has the chance to grope my breasts. The thickness of his alcohol-fueled breath hammers my senses when he slurs, "You're so fucking beautiful," into my ear.

"Th-th-thank you," I stutter while attempting to move out of his firm clutch.

Bile forms in the back of my throat when the sting of his fingers dig into my right hip as he strengthens his hold. Dizziness plagues my head when his erection pokes the curve of my backside, and his hand begins to wander back toward my chest. My stomach swirls from the excessive sways as he grinds against me. I stab my nails into his hands, clawing to get away from him. When my attack fails to stop his unwanted groping, my unnerved gaze lifts to seek assistance.

My breathing turns labored when I spot Hugo furiously sidestepping numerous club goers as he rushes toward me. His fists are clenched; his face is taut with anger and his steps, urgent. Relief engulfs me when one of his large hands pulls me into his chest while the other peels the unnamed dance partner off my back. His stealth movements have my feet leaving the ground and my assailant landing on his ass with an almighty thump.

The ear-splitting music blaring out of the speakers is unable to drown out the mad beat of Hugo's heart when he lays a boot into my accoster. The blood roaring through his body is so thick, the veins in his neck bulge as he steps over the man lying on the ground cradling his stomach.

Hugo's fast and furious steps don't falter until we reach a hidden nook between a mirrored wall and an office door at the side of the club. I lift my head off his chest, wanting to express my gratitude for his assistance. My words stay entombed in my throat. His gaze is predatory and full to the brim with silent rage.

My eyes rocket to the side when a manly voice asks, "Is she okay?"

My brows stitch as my eyes roam over the face of a man I swear I've seen before. Although he's not as built as Hugo, his impressive frame fills his tailored suit fittingly. His hair is dark and well-kept; his face is clean-shaven, and he has charmingly handsome good looks that would set most girls' hearts racing, but the angry scowl on his face and his unapproachable demeanor have my inside quaking more with fear than sexual interest.

"She will be." Hugo places me onto my feet. The strobing lights of the club flicker in his eyes as his narrowed gaze dances between mine. "Stay here. I'll be back in a minute."

Air whips the hair off my neck when he abruptly spins on his heels. Suddenly, the suit-clad gentleman's hand darts out to seize his elbow. Knuckles popping resonate in the eerie quietness of the alcove when Hugo clenches his fists. The veins on his exposed biceps throb when he turns to glare at the unnamed man.

"Look after her; I'll take out the trash." The suit-clad man's tone is stern and authoritative.

Not waiting for Hugo to reply, he relinquishes Hugo's elbow and ambles in the direction we just left. Sensing his unnerving composure, the crowd parts like the red sea. The last thing I see before my vision is filled with Hugo's fury-riddled face is the suit-wearing gentleman yanking my assailant off the ground by the scruff of his rumpled shirt.

Tucking a stray tress of my hair behind my ear, Hugo's eyes run over my face and body, vigorously assessing every inch of my sweat-slicked skin.

"Are you okay?"

I nod. "Yes, thank you."

My words come out breathless. My breathlessness isn't caused by my near attack, it's from having him standing so close to me. We're standing so close to each other, my breaths rebound off his stern mouth, blasting my lips with a fruity cocktail scent.

"Did he hurt you? Are you injured?" he questions.

I shake my head. "No. You got there before he had the chance."

"I should have gotten there faster."

My heart pains from the guilt clouding his eyes. The muscle in his jaw quivers when I run my thumb over the heavy groove indented in the middle of his eyes, futilely trying to smooth the regret dampening the spark of mischievousness that typically fires his vibrant eyes.

"I'm fine, Hugo; truly I am." I keep my tone spirited, desperately trying to lighten the mood.

I bunch his long-sleeve shirt in my hand. "I've never been better."

I stare into his eyes so he can see the openness being relayed by mine. Tonight is the first time I've ever truly let go. The awkward teenage girl who used to sit in the corner and watch everyone else have fun would have never gotten up and shook her tuchus in front of hundreds of people.

I've never danced like there would be no repercussion in the morning, because normally there would've been. Not from my peers, but from my father. It wouldn't matter if I forgot to say "thank you" after already saying "please" he would have heard about it, and I would've been reprimanded for it. Everything I did, no matter how minute, was monitored and reported back to him, but tonight – tonight I was free. I could finally fully extend my wings.

Noticing Hugo's demeanor slipping back into common ground, I continue with my ploy of easing his uncalled-for guilt. "I guess these are the consequences of impersonating your stripper moves."

His lips curve into an unsure grin. It isn't his usual large smile, but I'll take anything I can get.

"Stripper moves?"

"Yes," I say with a laugh. "I was waiting for the hidden cameras to jump out from behind the curtains and say 'surprise, you're on hidden stripper cam.'"

My eyes drift over Hugo's fetching face. The concern marring it is changing to a more relaxed expression.

My lips pucker as I eye him with fake curiosity. "Have you been harboring secrets from me?"

His brows furrow, and he swallows harshly.

"Because no white man should have moves like that."

Energy surges through my body when his chuckle booms through my ears. I smile, loving that I can still switch his mood from infuriating to playful in under thirty seconds. Once his laughter dies down, he takes a step closer to me, entrapping me in the tiny alcove with his impressive body. A whimper ripples from my lips when the coolness of the mirrored wall refreshes my inflamed skin.

All playfulness stops, and a new type of friskiness impinges the air when his hankering eyes lock with mine. "If I were a stripper, wouldn't that mean I should've been removing my clothes?"

My eyes remain locked with his, but I don't speak. *I can't*. I can barely breathe, much less articulate a response.

"Is that what you want, Ava?" He stares at me with wild eyes, his chest rising and falling with every breath he takes. "Do you want me to dance for you... *naked?*"

I stare into his lusty eyes. "I have the dollar bills for it."

My pupils widen as my mouth gapes, shocked by own audacity. Any apologies for my inappropriate remark are crammed back into my throat when the suit-wearing gentleman returns to stand next to us. My dropped jaw gains leverage when the mysterious stranger pulls a handkerchief from the breast pocket of his jacket and uses it to remove smears of blood from his swollen, red knuckles.

Once the evidence of a fight has been removed from his hands, his eyes lock with mine. "I hope the puerile actions of one doesn't deter you from visiting my clubs in the future. I can assure you that that type of foolhardiness will never be acceptable in any of my clubs."

I shrug my shoulders. "I guess it's part and parcel of spending your night out drinking and dancing."

He shakes his head. "Not in my establishments, it isn't." Even though his tone is stern, his eyes are relaying his genuine concern.

His dark eyes shift to Hugo. "Are we good?"

Hugo nods. "We're good."

"Good." He stuffs his hands into the pockets of his trousers before sauntering through a wooden door at the side of the mirrored wall.

When he enters the office, I turn my eyes to Hugo. "Who was that?"

He grins a full-toothed smile. "That's my new boss."

My head ricochets to the office door. "That's your *boss*?"

If I had to guess, I'd say the suit-clad gentleman would be only my age, if not a little younger. Although he looks impressive in his expensive designer threads, and his allure presents as fierce, his eyes give away his true self. Even guarded, they show that beyond his tough exterior is a young man trying to find his place in the world. How do I know this? Because Hugo's eyes have the exact same appearance.

My attention returns to Hugo when his fingertip brushes my cheekbone. Feverish heat follows the pattern of his index finger as it trails down the edge of my neck and along my collarbone before stopping at the swell of my breasts peeking out of my strapless dress. The tempo of my breaths quickens when his eyes lift and lock with mine. Even though he has been drinking, his gaze is vivid and clear. Almost readable.

I pull in a slow, shaky breath when he asks, "Do you want to get out of here?" The provocative tone in his words has butterflies fluttering in my stomach.

Stuck in a trance, I nod in agreement.

# TEN

# AVA

Smiling at my agreeing gesture, Hugo entwines his fingers with mine.

"C-can I use the bathroom first?" I stammer.

I manage to catch my eye roll halfway from the dimness displayed in my voice. All the work I've done the past six months transforming into an independent, strong woman becomes null and void with just once glance into Hugo's eyes.

Although I'm certain the throbbing between my legs is more associated with the gleam in Hugo's eyes than the fact I've downed half a dozen cocktails in quick succession, it's been engrained in me from a young age to use the restroom before traveling in any mode of transport. It wouldn't matter if we were driving to the corner store or halfway across the country, my father demanded I use the washroom before we left. He even went as far as to check the vanity sink was wet with water before I could exit the bathroom.

Remaining quiet, Hugo guides me out of the safety of our little alcove with his hand on the curve of my lower back. The earlier feeling of celebrity-ism catapults to a new level when Hugo's eyes dart in all directions, like a bodyguard protecting his target from any potential threats. His protective stance is so convincing, numerous cell phones lift to capture the "celebrity" amongst them. The blinding lights of camera flashes impede my vision as we work our way through the writhing bodies mingling around the vast space. The energy bouncing off the crowd is amazing, but it has nothing on the buzz of energy dashing through my body from Hugo's mildest touch. It is intense and electrifying.

My face scrunches when I notice the long line waiting to use the women's restroom. It is nearly as long as the queue outside of the club. My curiosity is intrigued when Hugo walks past the line and turns down a corridor on our left.

He opens a door to reveal a ladies' restroom. "Employee perks."

Snubbing the curious glare of two ladies washing their hands in the vanity, I hurry into a vacant stall, lift the seat, and sit down. I've only just finished my business when a rowdy group of women enter the washroom via the regular entrance.

"I can't believe her damsel in distress ploy actually worked. Some women are so desperate."

A volley of giggles bounce of the elegantly designed washroom walls.

"Help me! Help me! A naughty man wants to touch my body."

Curious as to whom they're talking about, I adjust my position and peer through the crack of the stall door. From this angle, I can only see the back of three women standing in front of a dark-framed mirror shackled to the wall: two blondes and one brunette.

"Did you see the hideous shoes she was wearing?" the blonde in the middle asks, suppressing a gag.

The blonde on the left leans toward the mirror to apply lipstick to her already heavily coated mouth. "The shoes have nothing on that revolting dress. She looks like she's going to a funeral. Blah and bland," she says before kissing the edge of the mirror.

When she pulls away from the mirror, now bearing her big red lipstick stain, I catch sight of her reflection in the mirror. Although

I'm certain I've seen her before, I have misplaced her name. "You can't buy style," she snickers.

"I thought she looked cute," squeaks out the brunette on the right.

My breath catches in my throat when the head of the blonde in the middle snaps to the side. I recognize that sneering profile. It is the Queen of Bitches herself: Victoria Avenke.

"Cute? You thought she looked cute?" Victoria sneers.

The brunette runs her hands down the front of her light blue pleated skirt before timidly nodding. "I don't think she's a threat to you, Vicky. They're most likely just here as friends."

"Of course they're here as friends! What else would they be here as?" Victoria's angry snarl reverberates off the walls.

The brunette swallows harshly when Victoria steps closer to her.

"Are you trying to say there's a possibility they could be more than friends?" Victoria queries.

The brunette shakes her head as the scent of fear permeates the air. "N-n-no. Of course they're only friends. J-j-just friends. She's his sister's best friend," she stutters.

Victoria's manicured brow arches high into the air. "Exactly. Tonight was nothing but a pity date to keep in his sister's good graces."

My heart plummets into my stomach when Victoria says, "It wouldn't matter how many drinks he has had. A man like Hugo would never be interested in a woman like Ava Westcott." Her lips form a snarl when she strangles out my name.

My eyes shoot down to my strappy heeled shoes. Although not as expensive as some pairs I've seen in fancy boutique stores, these shoes still cost me eighty dollars. That's a lot of money for one pair of shoes.

Even with eating ramen noodles for a week, they were worth the sacrifice. They're my favorite pair. With their wide heel and cushioned insoles, I can dance for hours and never get a blister. As for my bland and boring dress, you can't go wrong with a classic LBD.

Sophisticated, yet classy. Comfortable, yet sexy. *Well, I thought that was the case.*

My attention is pulled to the trio of women when a dark shadow fills the gap in the door. The pulse in my neck thrums when a pair of apologetic eyes peer at me through the crack. The only brunette in the trio offers me a contrite smile before following Victoria and the other blonde out of the washroom.

*Did she know I was here all along?*

After ensuring the coast is clear, I flush the toilet and pace to the vanity to wash my hands. Picking up a paper towel from the countertop, I wince when I look in the mirror. My hair is a damp, frizzy mess clinging to my sweat-drenched neck, my eyes are large and wide, and the small splattering of mascara I put on before leaving my apartment has oozed off my lashes and is now smeared under my eyes. Proof that what Victoria said is true reflects back at me.

After wetting the paper towel, I run it under my eyes while muttering personal insecurities to myself. Most follow the same tune: that there's no possibility a man with panty-wetting looks like Hugo would ever be interested in someone like me, but I could have sworn earlier there was a spark of attraction between us. The flirty banter, the suggestive dance moves, the streak of possession in his eyes. What was that all about if it was just a pity date?

Throwing the crumbling paper towel into the waste receptacle, I ignore the twisting pain in my heart and make my way out of the bathroom. When the door snaps shut behind me, I find Hugo standing at the side clutching my purse in his hand. His shoulder is propped against the wall, and he appears deep in thought. When he notices me approaching, the expression on his face changes from overwrought to easygoing. His eyes track my body as he pushes off the wall and strides toward me.

When he stops in front of me, he stares at me, wide-eyed and confused. The look of anxiousness in his eyes somehow calms me. The type of concern they're reflecting isn't something that can be manufactured on a whim. It is genuine and honest, making me realize, even if Hugo only ever classes me as a friend, it will be enough.

"Are you ready?" The smooth rasps of his question smothers any leftover unease jittering my stomach.

"Yes," I reply, nodding.

When he laces his fingers with mine, a jolt of energy surges up my arm. There's no way my brain is making this stuff up. That was electrifying! A gust of wind whips my hair off my neck and into my face when we exit the double doors of the club. Gathering my hair, I spot the limousine from earlier idling at the curb. The gentleman with the thick silver mustache greets me with a smile as he opens the back passenger door for me to enter.

"Thank you," I say graciously.

The skin on my thighs clings to the coolness of the leather material as I slide across the bench seat. On the drive back to my apartment, I catch sight of Hugo's impassive face in the tinted windows, but for the majority of the drive, his thoughts remain elsewhere.

"I could have taken a taxi if you wanted to stay," I say, no longer able to stand the frustrating silence between us.

His eyes turn from the darkened night to me. "It's fine, Ava; I want to make sure you get home safely."

"You can drop me off and head straight back out," I say with a shrug of my shoulders. "If you want to."

My suggestion is greeted with silence. I cross my arms in front of my chest and sink deeper into the leather seat. With Hugo's grim mood, anyone would swear it was his ego that copped a beating in the washroom – not mine.

Unable to comprehend the tension suffocating the air, I mumble, "Or you could just sit there and continue sulking like a five-year-old."

The flash of a smirk freezes my heart. "Really? I'm sulking like a five-year-old?"

"Uh huh," I say with a nod. "You have the same pouty-face look you had when the waiter wouldn't let you order blueberry pancakes as your main course at Jorgie's sixteenth birthday celebration."

He scoffs. "Name one restaurant that stops serving breakfast at 11 AM!"

"That one," I retort with a roll of my eyes.

My lips twitch as I try to hold in my smile from Hugo's shocked expression. Hugo has a fascination with breakfast foods. His love is so strong, he tried to order pancakes for dinner when we went to a fancy restaurant for Jorgie's sixteenth birthday.

He threw a tantrum like a kindergarten student when the male waiter told him the breakfast menu closed at eleven AM. The only thing that stopped his immature gripe was my suggestion that I could make him his own double batch of pancakes the following Sunday. When he agreed, I did exactly that – for the next two years.

During my high school days, every Sunday morning, my father begrudgingly dropped me off at the Marshall residence on our way home from church. Because we attended the dawn service, most of the Marshall family members were still sleeping when I arrived at eight AM. Everyone except Mrs. Marshall.

For the first few weeks, our talks were based on school and what happened at church that morning, but as the weeks went on, our conversations grew to a wide variety of topics, including Hugo's fascination with anything relating to breakfast. It was Mrs. Marshall who taught me how to make blueberry pancakes, homemade hash browns and Eggs Benedict. Although I've never told her, Sundays morning was the highlight of my week.

I turn my gaze to Hugo. The surly mood fettering his face has vanished and sparks of the old beloved Hugo have fired in his eyes.

"How long has it been since you've been home for Sunday brunch?"

He runs his hand down the side of his face. "Not since my first tour in Afghanistan."

"If you're not busy, you should come next weekend," I suggest. "Then you can test out Helen's rendition of scrambled eggs."

A chuckle escapes my lips when Hugo grimaces. Helen, Hugo's older sister, is brilliant at anything she does, except cooking. She's the spitting image of Hugo's mother with cascading blonde hair and vibrant green eyes, but that's as far as the similarities go. She didn't get Mrs. Marshall's cooking skills or nurturing nature.

"Are you going to be there?" Hugo questions.

Smiling, I nod. "Yes. I wouldn't miss it for the world."

My heart flips when he says, "Alright. If you promise to make me a double batch of your famous blueberry pancakes, I'll be there bright and early next Sunday."

Nodding, I bite the inside of my cheek, battling to keep my excitement from bursting out the seams. My eagerness intensifies when the limo pulls into the front of my building and Hugo rushes around the vehicle to open the door for me. I can't wipe the excitement off my face when he intertwines his fingers with mine and walks into my apartment building.

Patty, the seventy-three-year-old part-time night watchman of my building greets me with a dip of his hat and a broad grin. "Good morning, Ms. Westcott. No goodies today?"

I smile. "Morning, Patty. I think 3 AM is a little early for biscuits and gravy."

My cheeks inflame with heat when he replies, "It's never too early for a little bit of sweetness," as his glistening eyes dance between Hugo and me.

After entering the elevator, I spin on my heels and peer into Patty's worldly eyes. "I'll be here for our date at eleven, like I always am."

"Yes, ma'am," he replies with a smile just as the elevator doors snap shut.

When quiet snickering echoes in the elevator, I glance over to Hugo. He has his brow arched high in a sarcastic, jeering way.

"Hey, don't let that wrinkled skin fool you. In that seventy-three-year-old shell is a twenty-five-year-old man dying to recapture his youth. Wasn't it you who said dating someone with experience comes with its advantages?"

Ignoring the bitter taste in the back of my throat, I relish hearing

Hugo's hearty chuckle for the second time tonight. His laughter is so boisterous, it drowns out the ping of the elevator when it announces its arrival at my floor. I become lightheaded when he entangles his fingers with mine and we pace toward my apartment. Every step we take has my heart rate increasing and my palms sweating.

Reaching the front door of my apartment, I place the key into the lock before turning to face Hugo. "Did you want to come in?" I offer.

The most panty-drenching visual I've ever seen transpires when Hugo rubs the nape of his neck while biting on his lower lip. *There's nothing sexier in the world than a grown man biting his lip.* He shoves his hands into the pocket of his jeans as his eyes drift over my face for several heart-clutching seconds.

"I really should go. It's late and... I've got a thing in the morning... and you've got your *date* with Patty..." His ramblings simmer as he runs out of excuses to leave.

"Okay," I mumble.

Putting the feeling of rejection to the side, I say, "Thanks for everything. I had a lot of fun tonight."

Even though I still have no clue why he suddenly decided to hang out, I did enjoy our time together. It is like the past six years never happened. I'm once again a teenage girl fawning over the college quarterback.

Ignoring the tremor shaking my hands, I balance them on his chest and place a quick peck on the edge of his mouth. Dizziness clusters my head when his delicious woodsy scent engulfs my nostrils.

"Bye," I whisper faintly.

A grin tugs on his lips. "You don't say goodbye. You say, 'I'll see you later.'"

My heart squeezes painfully. That was exactly what he said to me when I said goodbye to him at the airport six year ago. His words were the only thing that managed to stop the flood of tears streaming down my face. I didn't truly believe so much time would pass between us until I saw him again. I hope I never have to experience that extent of absence again.

"I'll see you next week?"

"Without a doubt," I whisper, smiling.

After flashing a quick smirk, Hugo ambles toward the elevator banks. Halfway there, his hesitant steps stop, and he stands frozen in the middle of the blue carpeted corridor. My heart pounds fitfully when he turns around to face me. The streak of possession in his eyes has returned full pelt.

I stand frozen and quiet, my mind fritzed with confusion when he mutters, "Fuck it," under his breath before striding back to me, his steps agile and long.

Air whistles between my teeth when his lips brutally crash into mine. He kisses me with a sense of urgency, like a man worried I'm about to vanish. The brutal roughness of his kiss sparks a carnal desire in me. I grip his hair, pulling him closer, strengthening our kiss even more. My lips feel bruised, but it doesn't dull my eagerness. I've been dying for years to taste his cinnamon-flavored mouth again.

He cups the back of my thighs, encouraging my legs to wrap around his waist. A surge of desire streams through me when the thick crown of his cock brushes against the throbbing wetness between my legs. My breasts are aching with desire; my inner muscles are clenching, begging for attention. A growl from Hugo's lips rumbles through my propelling chest when I shamelessly grind against him, needing the friction to lessen the intense, tingling throb between my legs.

My pleasurable moans turn into a groan of frustration when he pulls his delicious lips away from my mouth and my feet are returned to the ground. He rests his sweat-beaded forehead against mine, keeping his eyes shut tight. My eyes drift over his beautiful face, categorizing every perfect detail into my memory. He looks so peaceful, like the teenage boy who stole my heart at the tender age of sixteen.

Opening his eyes, his alarmed gaze flicks between mine. "Tell me to leave." His throat is hoarse and dry. "Please, Ava, ask me to leave."

I peer up at him in shock, surprised he'd ever think those words could escape my mouth. His breath flurries my swollen lips when I shake my head, denying his pleas. Every fiber in my body is sparked as I precariously tread over the fine line that separates friends from bed partners.

I fist Hugo's shirt with one hand while pushing down on my front door handle with the other. The rise and fall of his chest amplifies when my apartment door opens with a slight creak. My heart hammers against my ribs as he shadows me into the entranceway of my apartment. My attention is sidetracked from staring into his lusty eyes when plastic crinkling crunches beneath my feet.

In sync, Hugo and my eyes dart down to the floor. When I discover what caused the noise, my eyes snap back to Hugo. A spasm plagues his jaw as he bends down to collect the clear cellophane-wrapped single red rose resting against the doorjamb. I eye him quietly as he reads the card attached to the side. The tension between us shifts from playful to uneasy when his eyes lift to mine. He stares at me, his mouth tugging into a phony smirk.

"I've got to go," he says, handing me the rose.

Not waiting for me to respond, he pivots on his heels and makes a beeline for the elevators. I remain speechless, staring at his impressively large frame as he stalks away, still dazed from his beguiling kiss. The muscles in his back flex when he elongates his finger and pushes the call button. The dashboard announces the elevator car is still in the lobby, causing a curse word to emit from his mouth. In a sense of urgency, he shoves open the fire door of the stairwell and exits my apartment building without a backward glance.

Blowing out a hot breath of frustration, I walk into my apartment. On the way to my bedroom, I detour into the kitchen and dump the red rose into the trash. Rambling under my breath, I kick off my heels and peel off my skintight dress.

After diving beneath the crisp pink sheets on my bed, I bury my head into the pillow and scream obscenities at the top of my lungs. A surge of anger pummels through me. I'm not just angry at Marvin and his stupidly-timed rose. I'm frustrated! And do you know what makes matters ten times worse? It's sexual frustration. There's no worse frustration in the world than sexual frustration.

That kiss... my God! That kiss was... panty-drenching... core-clenching... mind-blowingly good! But do you know what makes it worse? Hugo probably won't remember our kiss in the morning.

He hasn't previously, so why would today be any different?

## ELEVEN

## HUGO

I push open the fire exit door and sprint down the stairwell as if I have fire ants in my pants. Putting it bluntly: if I don't leave, I'd hunt down Marvin and shove his ass-kissing rose in a place where the sun does not shine, thorns and all.

Some may say it's all part of the game, and I should hate the game, not the player, but that's fucking bullshit. Yes, if it tickles your fancy, play the game, but play it fairly. Be open and honest. Surprisingly, most women appreciate when you're forthright and upfront. You may even get a few extra brownie points for the effort, but its guys like Marvin who fuck up the game and ruin it for the rest of us.

Even if it isn't written in the handbook, every guy knows you don't go out clubbing with one girl while sending another one a rose telling her how much you're missing her and that you can't wait to see her again. It's a dawg act, and it proves Marvin's tactics haven't changed since we left high school.

But in all honesty, even if I hadn't seen Marvin with his nose burrowed in the neck of another lady, I would have still reacted the same way. Even after years of absence, nothing has changed. Just one flash of Ava's killer smile, and I'm ready to drop to the ground and kiss her fucking feet.

I always thought the power of Ava's pull was because I was young and hadn't experienced life yet, but it isn't that. I've been through more the past two years than most men endure in a lifetime, aging and maturing me well beyond my twenty-five-years, but Ava's pull is just as magnetizing as it was when we were kids.

All the proof I needed was staring me right in the face earlier tonight. I didn't feel the slightest ping of jealousy when I spotted Victoria dancing with James Moreno. When Ava vanished into the crowd, my first reaction was jealousy. That quickly changed to fury when I saw the look of terror on her face as her dance partner's filthy hands slithered over her body.

Blinded by rage, I charged for Ava and her attacker. A barrage of memories pelted my brain when I yanked Ava to my chest and violently laid my boot into her accoster. It took all my restraint to walk away from her attacker, writhing on the floor, holding his stomach, but my desire to ensure Ava was unharmed was more vital than my need to pummel her attacker into the next century.

Even once Ava was safe and protected, standing directly in front of me, I couldn't stop the thoughts running through my head of what would have happened if I didn't get to her in time. *If I failed again.*

Those dreary deliberations had my mood souring quicker than the excitement of waking up Sunday morning and realizing it is Monday. Normally it would take a good dose of whiskey and a few hundred sit ups to drag me out of my woeful mood, but just like during our childhood, Ava pulled me out of the glum mood with nothing but her wit and a cheeky smile.

But even my morose mood couldn't dampen my desire to taste Ava's lips again. I fought the urge. I gave it my very best shot. I stepped away from her when we were dancing. I battled the yearning when we were in the hidden nook at the club and she was looking up at me, wide-eyed and eager.

I even made it halfway down her hallway before the little devil on my shoulder whispered wicked thoughts into my ear, but no matter what I did, nothing worked. I'm drawn to Ava like a magnet. I'm attracted to her, and I don't just mean her stellar looks. She's the entire package: sweet, kind-hearted, and off-the-Richter-scale sexy.

That kiss.... *my fucking God*. It had my cock breaking the zipper on my jeans, wrangling to get out and plunge into her ravenous pussy. Even through my jeans, I could feel how wet she was. She was the combination I like best: drenched and begging.

There are kisses and then there are *kisses*. Ava's are the latter. I've never been interested in a lengthy game of tonsil hockey, preferring to focus on the more needy regions of the female body. Kissing Ava forces an exception to that rule. I could kiss her for hours and never get enough.

Snubbing the erection I'm still sporting, I step onto the sidewalk outside of Ava's apartment building. I'm out of breath, wheezing for air, and sweating like a pig. *Karma's way of biting me on the ass for my impatience.*

Sucking in a big breath, I curl into the backseat of the limousine waiting on the curb. My heart hammers against my ribs when a mannish voice asks, "Is she as innocent as she seems?"

After gathering my heart off the limousine floor, I lift my eyes and meet the complacent smirk of Isaac.

Glancing into his smug eyes, I reply, "A gentleman never kisses and tells."

"Lucky for me, you aren't a gentleman."

Lewdly smirking, he places an empty crystal decanter into a concealed stainless steel minibar in the middle console between our seats. *I didn't even know that existed until now.* Once the leather seat is returned to its original position, his dark gray eyes lift to mine.

"Since my *business* dealings in Ravenshoe will take a little longer than originally planned, I decided to bring our meeting forward."

My brow curves over the unease in his voice, but I nod, acknowledging I've heard him.

Smirking at my agreeing gesture, his spare hand digs into the breast pocket of his suit jacket. "After seeing you defend Ava tonight, I know without a doubt you'll be a viable asset for my empire. You think quickly even when you're under pressure, and you didn't let prior events in your life influence your decision. So with that in mind, I decided to increase your initially devised salary."

He hands me the small folded up piece of paper he removed from his pocket. My eyes shift between him and the cream-colored document as I unfold it. A tickle scratches my throat when my eyes roam over the figure written in the payee amount of the bank check I'm now clutching for dear life.

Unable to grasp the reality of the situation, I lift my disbelieving eyes to his. "Are you pranking me? Cause this shit can't be real."

He raises his whiskey glass to his mouth and downs the entire overgenerous serving in one hit. After running the back of his hand across his mouth, his dark eyes bore into mine.

"The figure written down is correct."

The inside of the cabin becomes rife with muggy heat as my blood boils with excitement.

"On one condition," he adds on.

My eyes rocket to his. I'll do anything to cash this check into my dwindling bank account. Nothing is beneath me for this amount of money.

"You need to talk to someone about what happened in Afghanistan."

*Except that.*

My brows lower quicker than my heart plummeting into my stomach. "How do you know about that? Those files are meant to be sealed."

"With a little bit of money, even the stickiest glue comes unstuck." He stares at me, not the slightest bit concerned about what my reaction will be that he invaded my privacy.

"I didn't do what the file says I did," I sneer through gritted teeth.

"You don't think I know that? I would have never offered for you to join my empire if I believed a single thing in that file."

"Then what the fuck is wrong with you?" I interrupt breathlessly. "Only a lunatic would take the word of a stranger over an official government document!"

Isaac shakes his head. "I'm not taking anyone's word. I'm trusting my intuition. My intuition is telling me you aren't the man your file says you are. Until you prove me wrong, I'll continue to trust my intuition... and you."

After securing the middle button of his jacket, he slides out of the stationary vehicle. My eyes turn to his when he pops his head back in the car. "You start two weeks from Monday. The particulars of your employment are contained in the white envelope in the back of the seat," he advises, gesturing his head to the front passenger seat.

I wait all of two seconds for him to leave before delving my hand into the back pocket of the seat. Although I'm excited about securing employment, I'm also anxious about the stipulations he may have included in our agreement now that he's aware he's dealing with a criminal.

Emptying the contents of the envelope into my lap, the first thing my eyes zoom in on is a set of keys. The fake gold bullion keychain has four silver house keys and one black vehicle key dangling from it.

After dumping the keys back into the envelope, I collect a folded-up piece of paper with a four digit code scribbled on it. There are no other markings or indication as to what the code belongs to, just four digits: 3156. From the neatness of the handwriting, I'd say Mr. Trust Fund himself wrote the note. After storing the number in my memory, I place the piece of paper back into the envelope and gather a gold-embossed business card.

"Avery Clarke," I read off the card.

Air puffs from my nostrils when I read she specializes in psychology and the interpretation of dreams in real-life settings. I scrunch the card into a ball before dumping in onto the limo floor. The fourth and final contents of the envelope is a small, typed note on an official business letterhead. It reads:

> Your apartment:
> Apt No. 32
> River Vista Luxury Apartments
> 1324 Hamilton Way
> Rochdale

I double-read the address, just to make sure I'm seeing it right. Once I've assured all the numbers are in the right order, my eyes shift between the building on my right and the address on the piece of paper. *You've got to be kidding me. This can't be right.*

Unexpectedly, the back passenger door opens and the still unnamed gentleman with a thick silver mustache enters the frame.

My brows meet my hairline when he says, "Welcome home, Hugo," while gesturing his hand to Ava's apartment building.

## TWELVE

## AVA

"Are you okay, dear? You don't look very well." Mrs. Marshall's eyes roam over my face with concern. "You don't have that dreaded flu going around do you?"

Jorgie's mouth lifts when Mrs. Marshall places the back of her hand on my forehead, checking for a temperature.

"I'm fine. I just had a few late nights." *Fantasizing about your son.*

When Mrs. Marshall turns her back, I throw the dishcloth from my hand into Jorgie's grinning face. Biting the inside of my cheek, I fight hard to keep my laughter at bay when the drenched dishcloth slaps the side of Jorgie's face before comically drooping down the side of her cheek and plopping into her half-full mug of coffee.

"Still, you don't look very well. Perhaps you should go sit down and let me finish up here," Mrs. Marshall suggests, spinning around to face me and removing the spatula out of my hand.

"No, it's fine." I snatch the spatula back. "I've got this."

A broad smile stretches across my face when I flip the large blueberry pancake on the skillet and perfect golden coloring emerges. I've spent the last two hours making sure I've created the perfect batch of pancake batter. I kept the eggs at room temperature and floured each individual blueberry to ensure they didn't sink to the bottom of the batch. Now, I only have the last few remaining pancakes to fry and the double batch I promised Hugo last week will be ready for him when he arrives... *If he arrives.*

Mrs. Marshall's brows furrow, and her vibrant green eyes stare at me with uncertainty. "Okay, dear, but if you change your mind—"

"I'll let you know," I interrupt, smiling.

When Mrs. Marshall moves to the sink to peel potatoes, Jorgie props her hip onto the counter next to me. "I haven't seen you this eager to make blueberry pancakes since the day after my sixteenth birthday." Her eyes are full of suspicion.

While picking at an invisible piece of lint on her shirt, she adds on, "Hugo hasn't been to Sunday brunch in years, Ava, not since he went to Afghanistan. I don't see that changing anytime soon."

Ignoring the twisting pain in my stomach, I say. "I know, but today might be different."

"Because you went out with him last week?"

My confused eyes snap to hers.

"He had to get your address from someone," she explains to my bemused expression.

"Did anything... *happen?*" Her tone is low and crammed with unease.

My pupils widen and my throat dries. "Umm... no... we just went out... umm dancing," I reply before turning my attention back to the pancakes.

No longer able to ignore Jorgie's entreating gaze burning a hole in the side of my head, I sweep my eyes to her. The expression on her face has switched from anxious to playful in under two point five seconds.

"Dancing, hey?" she questions with a waggle of her brows. "What type of *dancing?*"

Blood rushes to the surface of my skin from the sexual innuendo laced in her voice.

Spotting my blemished cheeks, she squeals. "Ava Westcott, you dirty little hussy!"

"Shh," I request, panicked.

My eyes dart around the large eat-in kitchen of the Marshall residence. Once I'm satisfied no one is paying any attention to Jorgie and me, I return my eyes to her.

"Not that type of *dancing*," I inform her softly. "Dancing, dancing. Clothes left *on* dancing."

She cocks her brow high into the air. "What else happened?" she questions overdramatically. "You can act innocent until you're blue in the face, Ava, but I know something more happened. I can see it in your eyes. So come on, spill it. I want all the *raunchy* details."

*Is it just me or does that seem wrong coming out of the mouth of Hugo's baby sister?*

Seeing my repulsed expression, Jorgie says, "Hugo may be my brother, but you're my best friend. What kind of friend would I be if I didn't help my bestie wade her way through all the slimy frogs until she found her prince sitting on the edge of the pond?"

My brows furrow. Jorgie has never been a fairytales and Prince Charming romance-type of girl. Her idea of a true romance story is Romeo and Juliet. Obviously the pregnancy hormones running through her body have made her a little whacky.

"Pregnancy and wedding planning are making your insides all soft and squidgy," I joke, poking her rounded stomach.

Her mouth gapes open. "They're not!"

"Yeah, they are. You're turning into a marshmallow!"

"Whatever." She crosses her arms in front of her chest and rests them on her stomach, trying to fake annoyance, but the smile tugging her lips high displays her deceit. "You betta watch yourself; I get to choose who I'm friends with, but I'm stuck with Hugo. He's family."

I bump her with my hip. "Yet, you still love him."

She smiles. "Yes, I do, but I love you too, and I know this is something you've wanted for a long time."

Now it's my turn to huff and roll my eyes.

"Deny it all you want, Ava, you can't—"

"Fight fate," I interrupt.

"Exactly! Now spill the beans. This knocked-up, soon-to-be married marshmallow needs to live vicariously through you."

Grinning, I exhale a deep breath before my panic eyes nervously glide around the room. Happy no one is watching, I mumble, "We kissed."

My hand shoots out to cover Jorgie's mouth when her massive squeal gains us the attention of every Marshall in the kitchen and every dog within a five mile radius. Her eyes turn huge and unapologetic as she stares at me with nothing but glee. Her excitement intensifies when the screen door at the side of the kitchen squeaks open and the intoxicating physique of Hugo enters the room.

My heart beats double-time as my eyes roam over the man who kept me awake until the wee hours every night this week reminiscing about our kiss. I've scrutinized every detail of our night; every word he spoke, every look that crossed his face, and every time he touched me was studied in great depth, but even after an investigation Sherlock Holmes would have been proud of, I still went to bed just as confused as I was hours earlier.

Noticing the eerie quietness that has encroached the kitchen, my hands lower from Jorgie's mouth, and my eyes sweep the room. Helen and Chase are staring at Hugo like a stranger has entered their house uninvited. Mr. Marshall's eyes are twinkling with happiness, and Mrs. Marshall's hand is covering her mouth as her eyes well with tears. Their joy for the return of their beloved son is etched on both of their faces.

As a tear escapes Mrs. Marshall's eye, she rushes to her youngest son and throws her arms around his broad shoulders. Warmth blooms my chest when Hugo's voice soothing his mother breaks through the barrier of silence plaguing the small gathering.

After being greeted by Helen, Chase, and Mr. Marshall, Mrs. Marshall guides Hugo through the kitchen to the makeshift dining room on the outside deck. When Hugo ambles by Jorgie and me, his large hand darts out to rub Jorgie's rounded belly, and I'm greeted with a cheeky wink and a smile.

Once it is just Jorgie and me left in the kitchen, her glistening cornflower blue eyes turn to mine. "That must have been one hell of a kiss, Ava. Because you just got him to do something I've been begging him to do for years."

My nose tingles as fresh tears form in my eyes.

Jorgie places her ruined coffee on the counter and wraps her arms around my neck. "Imagine all the things you could get him to do when you dive beneath the sheets?"

My pupils widen as my throat turns hoarse. Just the thought of having nothing but sheets between Hugo and me has my pulse quickening and my lady garden throbbing. Spotting my flushed expression, Jorgie giggles before pacing out of the kitchen.

After pouring the final batch of pancakes onto the skillet, I let my mind wander. Images of Hugo and me dancing last week flash before my eyes. My visual isn't entirely accurate. It's a little more X-rated, since clothing is an optional requirement. My sweat-producing imagination only returns to the present when the smell of smoke filters through the air, closely followed by the smoke alarm.

*Oh, shit! The pancakes!*

A whimper erupts from my mouth when the scorching heat of the skillet burns my hand when I stupidly push it off the flame without using any protection. Peering down, my face cringes when I notice the first signs of a blister forming on the edge of my palm. The sting of the burn becomes non-existent when the back of my body is engulfed by another.

My breathing turns erratic as Hugo's woodsy smell invades my senses. He leans over my shoulder and uses an oven mitt to lift the skillet off the open-flamed cooktop. The thick, black smoke lingering in the room fades when he dumps the skillet into the sink and turns the tap on full pelt, dousing the now charcoal black pancakes with water.

The heat in the room fires up when portions of his formidable V muscle peek out beneath his shirt as he fans the smoke alarm with a tea towel. Once the smoke alarm stops announcing my failure to the world, Hugo's amused gaze turns to me.

"I thought my kitchen fire days were over once Helen realized she couldn't boil water."

The deep rasp of his voice makes the blemish on my cheeks turn from embarrassed to excited. His eyes drop to my wounded hand cradled by my uninjured hand as he moves to stand in front of me.

"Let me see," he requests, his tone low and full of concern.

"It's fine. It's nothing," I say, lowering my hands to the side of my body. My insides tense, but I give no outward appearance to the pain felt when the blister rubs against the hem of my skirt.

Hugo's eyes bore into mine as he gently clasps my hand and raises it to inspect. The hairs on the nape of my neck prickle when he runs his finger over the wound, being extra cautious not to touch the blister forming in the middle of the red welt.

Unable to control my breathing from his meekest touch, the heavy pants of my breath echo in the silence of the kitchen. Hearing my shameful response to his touch, Hugo's eyes lift to mine. Even with his eyes sparked with the same trepidation they had when he begged me to ask him to leave, the intensity of his blue eyes spear me in place.

My brain turns to mush when he lifts my wounded hand to his mouth and blows on the scalded skin. His breath makes the sting of the burn a forgotten memory. My breathing halts when his lips brush my palm.

From the sparks of sexual energy surging through my veins, anyone would swear he was blowing on other regions of my body and not the edge of my palm. Shamefully, a breathless moan whooshes out of my parted lips, and the heat in the room turns roasting.

Cringing with embarrassment, my eyes snap shut when, "If she has a blister, you better go and get the iodine out of the bathroom cupboard," sounds through my ears.

When Hugo's hands is replaced with a cooler one, I hesitantly flutter my eyes back open. Mrs. Marshall's translucent-skinned hand cups mine as she thoughtfully inspects the blister. The heat on my cheeks increases when I turn my eyes to the side of the kitchen and see Chase, Helen, Jorgie, and Mr. Marshall staring at me with a hint of intrigue in their eyes.

Lifting her eyes to Hugo, Mrs. Marshall says, "Grab the alcohol wipes and the needles from my sewing kit while you're getting the iodine."

My eyes bug at the mention of a needle. I hate needles. It isn't a small dislike. I hate *HATE* them. After shooing Hugo and the rest of the Marshall gang out of the kitchen, Mrs. Marshall pulls over a stool from underneath the counter in the corner of the room and gestures for me to sit. When I sit down, the feeling of being sent to the principal's office for reprimand overwhelms me.

"Umm... that wasn't what it looked like," I stammer, mortified that she busted me panting like a dog in heat in the middle of her kitchen.

Mrs. Marshall runs her hand down the front of her frilled apron before her green eyes lock with mine. "Do I look like I was born last century?"

Through a gaped mouth, I shake my head. Although Mrs. Marshall is in her mid-fifties, she has gorgeous long, cascading blonde hair, vibrant green eyes that show she hasn't hit her prime yet, and one of the most rocking bodies I've ever seen on a lady of her age. I'd be more than happy to look like her in my mid-thirties left alone fifties.

"Even being married for thirty years, I can recognize the sparks of attraction as well as the next person." She clasps my uninjured hand in hers. "This is something you've wanted for a long time, Ava."

My pupils widen. *Am I the only idiot who thought I did a good job of hiding my crush on Hugo?*

Mrs. Marshall's brow curves. "You wear your heart on your sleeve as clear as day for all to see, just like Hugo, but in saying that,

Hugo is not the boy you remember from high school. He has changed. The war changed him."

A stabbing pain inflicts my chest when I spot the tears pricking her eyes.

"What happened over there?"

Rumors ran rife through our hometown when Hugo was discharged from his position earlier than the remainder of his squadron. Speculations ranged from him being insubordinate to his superiors to a botched mission that caused casualties during friendly fire.

Never being one to believe rumors, I politely excused myself from the conversation whenever the topic of his dismissal came up. Over time, the rumors fizzled and the town gossips found something new to bitch about.

Mrs. Marshall's face scrunches. "Nobody knows exactly what happened because Hugo won't talk to anyone about it, but I know my boy. I can see in his eyes that he's suffering."

I blink several times in a row, hammering my eyes with flutters of air, praying it will stop my tears from falling. There's no greater love in the world than a mother's love for her child. That is exactly what is projected out of Mrs. Marshall's eyes when she talks about Hugo.

After running her index finger under her eyes to ensure her tears haven't spilled, Mrs. Marshall says, "Because you're like a daughter to me, Ava, I feel it is my responsibility to ensure you're not walking into this blindfolded."

My breath hitches from her calling me her daughter.

"Thank you, but I can assure you I'm not. My eyes are the most open they've ever been," I say, smiling.

Peering into my eyes, the concern in hers vanishes and a smile curls on her lips.

"I'm glad to hear that, Ava," she murmurs as Hugo saunters into the kitchen with a bottle of iodine in one hand and a sewing kit in the other.

Mrs. Marshall squeezes my hand before her eyes drift to Hugo.

"You look like you have this under control. Once you have Ava cleaned up, come and join everyone for brunch."

After a quick smile, she taps her hand on Hugo's forearm and bolts out of the kitchen like it was her backside set on fire instead of the pancakes.

## THIRTEEN

# HUGO

Ava's big doe eyes track me when I grab a stool from under the breakfast bar and drag it to sit in front of her. Even with her eyes plagued with dark circles and her skin a little more gaunt than it was last week, she looks beautiful.

*She always looks beautiful.*

When I entered the kitchen, I nearly spun on my heels and exited straight back out, knowing there was no way I could trust myself around Ava when I saw her clothing selection. She's wearing one of the shortest white pleated miniskirts I've ever seen in my life. If that isn't bad enough, she teamed it up with a pair of heels that make her legs go for days and days.

My attention was only diverted from her spellbinding legs when my mom threw her arms around my shoulders and wept into my neck. For as long as I can remember, the Marshall family has held a family brunch the first Sunday of the month.

Our get-togethers aren't exclusively for members of the Marshall clan, though. They're an open invitation, available to anyone who doesn't mind rolling up their sleeves and getting their hands dirty to prepare the food. Or in Helen's case – wash the dishes.

During high school, Sunday was my favorite day of the week. Not just because every breakfast food you could possibly imagine was displayed across the dining room table ready to be devoured once a month, but because every Sunday morning, Ava would greet me with a big braces-covered smile and the largest plate of blueberry pancakes I'd ever seen in my life.

*So much has changed since then.*

My mom's reaction when I walked in the door is one of the reasons I haven't been to brunch in nearly three years. After I returned from my first tour, any time she would peer into my eyes, hers would well with tears. She's always had a knack for knowing when her children are hurting, so she saw right through the covert ruse I dangled in front of her.

She's so in tune with me, when I was younger, she knew I'd skinned my knee before I even fell off my bike. Although I still visit my parents regularly, I prefer my mom's tears to be shed in private. The only way I could achieve that was by avoiding brunch, but last week, I told Ava I'd be here. Being a man who always keeps his promises – here I am.

This is hard for me to admit, but my mom has a legitimate reason for her tears. I've changed a lot the past few years. I'm no longer the little boy who used to beg her for an extra cookie with my glass of milk before I went to bed or the one who would agree to any dare Chase conjured up, no matter how crude it was.

Although a lot of people say my change was part of riding the crazy rollercoaster from adolescent teen to mature adult, for me, that wasn't the case. I changed because I joined an industry I should have never been a part of, an industry that nearly tore my life apart.

Afghanistan was nothing like I was expecting. Like every teen, I played *Medal of Honor* and *Call of Duty* from sun-up to sun-down every weekend. I held the number one spot in the rankings for over three months, completed every mission to the precise detail, collected every medal there was to achieve.

But it wasn't until I was over there, killing on demand did I realize it was *nothing* like the video games portray. You can't smell the scent of death through a TV monitor. You don't hear the cries of mothers when their babies are killed or the sounds of fathers on their knees begging for their sons to be returned home, safe and in one piece.

Here, once you've finished your mission, you switch off the TV, gallop down the stairs, and eat blueberry pancakes until you need to heave. There, it never switches off. The game never ends, but even more concerning than that was finding out the men I was playing the game with, my brothers who were supposed to have my back, were the biggest enemies of them all. When I was in the field, I was always on alert, seeking out potential threats. I should have been looking in my own backyard, because that is where the real danger laid.

My attention is pulled back into the present when a warm hand curls over my clenched fist. Lifting my gaze, I'm met with the Ava's wide, concerned eyes.

"Are you okay?" She stares into my eyes. "You're shivering. Are you cold?"

Not waiting for me to reply, she gathers my dad's wool-lined raincoat from the rack. A smile curls on my lips when she drapes it over my shoulders before retaking her seat across from me. I'm not smiling because of her thoughtfulness. I'm grinning because after Ava's little fire incident, the temperature in this kitchen is sitting well above 100 degrees Fahrenheit.

It's so hot, Ava's forehead has a layer of sweat beading across it. The shivers wracking my body have nothing to do with being cold, and everything to do with the hell I'm still trying to forget.

Shrugging off Dad's jacket, I place it on the island counter beside the items I gathered from the bathroom. Ava watches my every movement but remains as quiet as a church mouse.

After soaking a cotton ball with iodine, I remove a small needle from mom's sewing kit. Ava's tongue darts out to replenish her lips with moisture when I run the alcohol wipe over the needle to sterilize it. The fretful scowl marring her face amplifies when I scrunch up the alcohol wipe and throw it into a bin full of egg shells and empty blueberry containers under the counter.

"Are you ready?" I grasp her hand in mine.

The smile on my lips turns genuine when the hairs on her arms bristle from my meekest touch. When she nods her head, I move the needle toward the nasty looking blister on the side of her palm.

Just as the needle is about to pierce her skin, she screams, "Wait!"

When her eyes zoom in on the needle, her pupils widen.

"It won't hurt," I assure her.

"Says the guy who's about to jab me with a pointy object."

The fret marring her beautiful face fades when she hears my quiet snickering.

"Don't be rude; we're in your mother's kitchen," she reprimands, gazing over her shoulder to make sure our earlier spectators have left. She tries to keep her face serious, but the smile lifting her lips gives away her deceit.

"Trust me. That counter is the perfect height for fucking."

The smile on her face weakens, and her earlier gaunt appearance returns from my inaccurate tease. I may have been a little mischievous in my younger days, but our house was rarely empty, and I was too busy keeping the guys in my grade away from Ava that I've never had the opportunity to test out the theory.

"Here, I'll show you."

Ava's breathing quickens, and her eyes widen. Her chest rises and falls with every breath she takes.

"Not the counter height," I say with a chuckle. *Although if she keeps looking at me like that, I may not have the strength to fight her alluring pull any longer.* "That the needle won't hurt."

Before she can protest, I lift her uninjured hand and prick the end of her pinkie finger with the needle.

"Ouch," she whimpers as her eyes dart down to the bead of blood sitting on the tip of her finger.

Her cries of pain are muffled with a moan when I soothe the sting of the needle with the lash of my tongue. Heat scorches my veins when she squirms in her seat. Once the tangy taste of blood is gone, I drag her finger out of my mouth. A loud pop sounds from my mouth when her finger twangs my lip on the way by. Ava's pupils are heavily dilated, her lips parted, revealing she's aroused by my flirty tease.

Deciding to make good use of her being distracted, and needing to distract myself before I seal my mouth over her pouty lips and steal every little whimper that escapes them, I lift her injured hand and pop the blister before she can process what is happening. Once all the mucky ooze has seeped out of the small hole, I run the iodine-drenched cotton ball over the wound before covering it with a band aid.

"There you go, just like new."

She remains stunned, like a deer trapped in headlights.

"It's not how a trauma surgeon at a major hospital would have done it, but it gets the job done," I say jokingly, quoting some of the words she said last week.

Her bright white teeth are exposed in a full smile. "I guess I'm not the only one who enjoys torturing people for a living?"

"There's a *very* fine line between pleasure and pain."

I try to keep the sexual overtones out of my reply, but my words are still drenched in them. Smirking at Ava's wide-eyed expression, I lace my fingers with her uninjured hand and guide her out of the kitchen. Unsurprisingly, the large wooden deck in the backyard is packed with over three dozen people.

More than half are strangers to me. Spotting a section of empty chairs across from Jorgie and Chase, I place my hand on the small of Ava's back and direct her toward the makeshift dining table. Ignoring the snickering of Chase across the table, I pull out Ava's chair and gesture for her to sit.

For the first hour of brunch, the only audible noise is me shoveling Ava's blueberry pancakes into my mouth. I've never tasted anything more delicious in my life – except Ava's lips. They taste even sweeter than her world famous pancakes. Like she can hear my private thoughts, Ava's head shifts from talking to Chase to peer at me. Her eyes roam over my face before she flashes her killer smile. My cheek muscles twitch when she licks the tip of her thumb and runs it along the right-hand corner of my mouth.

"You had syrup on your lip."

Everything blurs when she pops her thumb into her mouth and sucks off the syrup with a little groan. Thoughts of her lips circling another part of my body rushes to the forefront of my mind, turning my dick to steel. It's only when I catch sight of Ava's lips twitching as she vainly tries to repress a smile do I realize what she's doing. She's returning my earlier tease with one of her own. *Who would have thought innocent little Ava would grow up to be a cock tease?*

Deciding I need to put some distance between us before I drag her onto the table and taste the syrup directly off her skin, I excuse myself and make my way inside. When I spot Jorgie washing dishes in the kitchen sink, I snag a tea towel off the bench and commence drying the mountain load of crockery stacked in the drying rack. Jorgie's lips tug into a thankful smirk, but she remains quiet, which is very unlike her.

Only once all the cooking dishes are clean and packed away do her cornflower blue eyes turn to me. "If you hurt Ava, I'll kill you."

I scoff. "I thought this was what you wanted." My reply relays my genuine confusion. She's nagged relentlessly for months for me to go out with Ava. Now, the instant things get a little interesting, she pulls out a yellow flag.

"No, this isn't what I wanted," Jorgie replies. "I wanted you to fall in love, have two point five children, and live in a house with a white picket fence. Not you look at Ava like you want to devour her on the kitchen counter."

I grin and waggle my brows. There's no use denying the accuracy of her statement. Even if I did, Jorgie knows me well enough to see straight through it.

Spotting my contemptuous face, Jorgie huffs and throws the damp tea towel at my head. "You're disgusting."

I stare at her. "Who are you and what happened to the real Jorgie

Marshall? The one who would take *Baby* up to the Mt. Louis lookout every weekend just to look at the *scenery*? The same Jorgie Marshall who danced on the tabletops at senior prom and went skinny dipping in the Hudson River because it was a full moon? The shackles aren't even locked on your ankles yet, and you're already acting like a middle-aged citizen."

Her nose screws up as she stomps her feet. "What is it with everyone giving me crap today? First Ava said I'm getting soft and squidgy and now you're saying I'm turning into our mother."

My wholehearted chuckle booms around the kitchen. Jorgie loves our mom, but no self-respecting twenty-four year old wants to be compared to their mother. My laughter dissipates when I see tears welling in the corners of her eyes. Jorgie's hormones have been all over the place the past few months, but this is the first time I've seen tears in her eyes in years.

I take a step closer to her and pull her into my chest. "What's going on, Jorgie?" The trembling of my heart is heard in my question.

"I'm scared."

My brows furrow. "Of what? What have you got to be scared about?"

She takes her time deliberating a response before she faintly answers, "That everything will change between Hawke and me when we become parents."

I'm taken back by her statement. I'm not kidding when I say Jorgie and Hawke are the strongest couple I've ever seen. Even when she's up to mischief, nothing but love beams out of Hawke's eyes when he looks at Jorgie.

Her head pops off my chest, and her glistening eyes lock with mine. "What if he doesn't find me attractive anymore?"

Like the sun rising over the horizon, clarity forms. Hawke was deployed when Jorgie was only a few months pregnant, so she wasn't showing yet. Tomorrow afternoon will be the first time Hawke will see Jorgie with a rounded stomach.

"He loves you, Jorgie," I assure her.

The smallest grin tugs on the corners of her mouth.

"Watermelon belly and all," I josh.

Her smile sags, and a frown ruefully takes its place. I pull her back into my chest and noogie the top of her head. She tries to fight me off, but she isn't putting in a real effort. As much as Jorgie acts like she hates being the baby of the family, on the inside, she loves every goddamn minute of it.

After a short time later, her grunts of annoyance turn into faint giggles, easing the heaviness weighing down my chest.

"Trust me, by tomorrow night you'll be wondering what all the worry was about. He never shuts up about you and the baby. You're his every want and desire. That isn't going to change because you shoved a basketball under your shirt."

I grit my teeth when she uses my shirt as if it is a tissue before nodding.

A short time later, she lifts her head off my chest and takes a step backward. "Pregnancy hormones suck."

"Tell me about it," I playfully jibe. "That's why I'm *never* having kids."

She snarls at me before moving to the back entrance of the kitchen to check her face in the mirror. Once she's happy her makeup is in its rightful place, she gathers a stack of Tupperware containers off the entranceway table. I aid her in placing all the leftover food from brunch into the containers.

"Are you heading straight home after this?"

She nods. "I have a few things to do before your housewarming party."

I cringe from the way she says *housewarming party*. To me, this afternoon's get together at my place is a few mates cracking some cold beers in celebration of my new apartment. Calling it a housewarming party sounds like a bunch of old ladies sitting around drinking tea out of china teacups.

"Have you asked Ava?" Jorgie questions.

"To the party?"

I place an overstuffed Tupperware container into a heated bag. Jorgie snickers and shakes her head. I arch my brow and stare into her amused eyes, soundlessly advising I have no clue what she's referring to.

"Asked her out... *out*." She overdramatizes the last word of her sentence.

I inwardly gag. "Am I twelve? That's not how things work these days."

Jorgie scoffs and rolls her eyes. "How is she supposed to know you like her if you don't ask her out?"

"Who said I liked her?"

Jorgie's brows hit her hairline. "Do I look like I was born last century?"

"No, but you do sound like our mother."

Air leaves my mouth in a huff when Jorgie punches me in the arm. "Deny it all you want, Hugo. You can't fight fate."

I chuckle and rub my arm, feigning injury.

Jorgie places her hand on her cocked hip. "Don't think I haven't notice the new look you're sporting. You've got that loved-up puppy dog look you had on your face years ago when I interrupted you in my room with Ava."

I roll my eyes but don't negate her statement. Any time I'm around Ava, I turn into the teenage boy who pinned her against the door, dying to taste her lips. If Jorgie hadn't interrupted us that night, I wouldn't have been able to fight Ava's alluring pull anymore.

Jorgie peers up at me while placing the final Tupperware container into a heat warming bag. "If you don't hurry up and snag her, someone else will," she warns.

My teeth grit as an absurd rush of heat surges through my veins. Before I can configure a reason for my insane reaction, Ava and my mom enter the kitchen, juggling large stacks of dirty dishes. An intangible string of emotions pummel me when Ava smiles.

It's hard to believe, but it truly feels like the past six years vanished with a snap of my fingers. I'm once again a teenage boy chasing after a beautiful girl. When Ava bends over to collect a tea towel from the ground, exposing inches of her smooth thighs, my desire to taste every inch of her turns rampant.

Jorgie cranks her head to the side. "Hey, Ava, did you need a lift home?" Her tone is super high, exposing her excitement.

Ava places a stack of white crockery plates onto the sink before shifting on her feet to face Jorgie. "Yeah, sure, that will be great. When are you leaving?"

"Now," Jorgie replies, loading my arms up with the Tupperware containers we just finished filling.

An adorable smile stretches across Ava's face. "Great. Let me grab my stuff."

Jorgie nods. "Hugo will meet you in his truck out front."

My eyes snap to Jorgie. She has a vast grin stretched across her face and is rocking on her heels, pleased at giving Ava and me one final push.

My eyes float to Ava when she asks, "Do you mind, Hugo?"

A grand smile stretches across my face when I shake my head, advising I have no objection to driving her home.

When Ava leaves the kitchen to gather her belongings, Jorgie turns to face me. "Grab her, Hugo, and don't let go."

The beaming smile on her face intensifies when I nod.

## FOURTEEN

## HUGO

"Did you want to play a game?"

I turn my gaze from the road to Ava, sitting quietly in the passenger seat of my truck. "What type of game?" I question.

Her grin stretches wider as she adjusts her position to face me. "Twenty questions."

I cringe. I've never been a guy who's had a problem stringing sentences together. I'll happily admit I'm a communicator, preferring to talk things out rather than let them sit and stew, but if I want to know something, I'll ask. If I want you to know something, I'll tell you. Being forced to share information – that makes me uncomfortable.

Ava's shoulders slump and she picks at the polish on her nail.

"You go first," I suggest.

I'll be subjected to any torture she wants to dish out if it swipes the frown off her beautiful face. My grip on the steering wheel tightens when a dimpled smile creeps across her face. Her lips twist as she considers a question.

"Sweet or sour?" she asks a short time later.

"Drrr, sweet." *Although I don't think I'll ever find anything sweeter than her lips.*

"You can't have one without the other." Ava snags her handbag from the floor of my truck and throws a packet of sour Skittles at my chest. She tucks her legs under her bottom and twists her torso to me, popping a handful of skittles in her mouth. "Your turn."

I arch my brow and stare into her eyes, pretending I'm stumped on finding an appropriate question. She cocks her brow, mimicking my expression. I snicker, loving that she can still read me so easily. She's the only woman who sees through my bullshit.

"Do you know how many fights I got into the night of my eighteenth birthday party, after I threw you into the pool?"

Ava coughs, splattering the cream leather dash of my truck with rainbow spit. Her hand clutches her throat as she works hard to swallow the remaining Skittle juice left in her mouth.

"Are you alright?" I shift my eyes between the road and her.

The faintest flush of color sneaks across her cheeks as she nods her head. Once she has recovered from a mini coughing fit, she turns to face me.

"How many?" she squeaks out.

"Three," I inform her.

"Who?"

"Richie Santo, Robert Parker, and Bryson Trapper."

She slants her head to the side and glances into my eyes. "Because you were protecting me like you always did with Jorgie?"

I shake my head. "No," I reply, truthfully. "I just hated the idea of any guy touching you."

She inhales a sharp breath, but remains as quiet as a monk on a vow of silence.

"I never meant to hurt you that night, Ava. I just had an irrepressible need to get you away from Rhys."

An adorable glint of excitement brightens her eyes. "I know."

"And while I'm being totally forthright, I fucking hate the 'Friends' sitcom."

Ava's beautiful laugh resonates over the quietness. "So do I!" Her words are barely audible through the barrage of laughter bellowing from her lips. "I only watched it because I thought you loved it."

My brow arches high. "What? You knew all the characters' names, job titles, even what their pets were called."

Ava laughs uncontrollably. "That's only because I studied their bios wanting to impress you."

I grimace. "God, how many hours did we waste watching a show we both hated?"

Ava laughs so hard, tears stream down her cheeks. "Too many to count," she says breathlessly between giggles.

She clutches at her stomach, easing the cramps from her thunderous laugh. Once her laughter settles down, she lifts her tear-stained face and peers at me. The flutter of the pulse in her neck quickens when I brush the back of my fingers across her heated cheeks, removing her tear stains. A smile curves on my lips when she leans into my hand.

The smile Ava wore the entire three-mile trip widens as we make our way into the foyer of our apartment building. The gentleman at the reception desk greets Ava with a smile before granting her access to a hidden office behind the impressively sized black and gray marbled reception area.

A security guard sporting a crisp black suit and a military haircut lifts his head when Ava saunters into the space. Noticing me shadowing Ava, his hand sweeps into his jacket, no doubt bracing the concealed gun holstered on his hip. He stares at me with both alarm and annoyance in his fiery eyes. His focus only returns to the bank of security monitors in front of him when Ava nudges her head to the Tupperware containers in my hand.

Although his attention appears to revert to monitoring the live feed, I can feel his eyes tracking me as I follow Ava into the manager's office at the back of the room.

Placing two Tupperware containers on the edge of the desk, Ava pivots on her heels and removes the four still-warm containers from my grasp. My eyes absorb the space as Ava paces to a wall-to-ceiling cupboard at our side.

Compared to other offices I've seen, this one is the size of a closet. The minimal floor space is taken up by a glass and chrome desk. There's a faded, cracked leather chair behind it and a black safe bolted to the ground on my left.

When Ava places cutlery and plates onto the desk, the office door swings open. A waft of Old Spice drifts into the room, closely followed by Patty. From the potent strength of his aftershave, I'd say he only put it on mere minutes ago.

"You're half an hour early today." Although his gruff tone could be construed as annoyed, his face does not give that allusion.

Ava smiles a beaming white smile as she greets Patty with a kiss on his cheek. A smile curls on my lips when Patty's stark white cheeks turn a shade of red. I can't blame him. Just the thought of having Ava's lips anywhere near my body sets my pulse racing, let alone other parts of my body.

"I'm a little early as Hugo was kind enough to offer me a lift," Ava informs him, gesturing to me.

Patty's head cranks to the side as he eyes me with caution. His stance is strong, primed and ready to shred me to pieces if needed.

"Patty, this is a... *friend* of mine, Hugo," Ava introduces. "Hugo, this is my dear friend, Patty."

The smile on my face broadens from the stumble she made introducing me.

"Nice to meet you," I say, accepting the handshake Patty offers.

My brow arches, surprised by how firm Patty's grip is for a man of his age. Maybe what Ava said last week is true. Maybe there is a twenty-five-year-old hiding in his body, dying to break free? Patty's grip on my hand tightens as his worldly eyes stare into mine, assessing my soul from the outside.

As I return his stare, my initial opinion on him alters. He isn't a man wanting to recapture his youth by parading around with a young trophy wife on his arm. He displays the qualities of a man trying to protect one of his most valued possessions. He cares for Ava. Not in a weird, dirty old man type of way. He truly cares for her like she's his family. Like she's his daughter.

*God, if I can read that just from looking into his eyes, what is he reading from mine?*

After a beat, he says, "I like you, Hugo." Nothing more. Nothing less.

Ava's excitement at his approval washes over her face. Seeing her excitement eases the tight knot in my stomach. Gushing, Ava directs Patty to take a seat in the leather chair on the other side of the desk. While giving him a full update on everything that transpired at the Marshall family brunch, she layers his plate with a selection of scrumptious goodies.

The twinkle in Patty's eyes illuminates when Ava opens the last container holding her blueberry pancakes. Even though I devoured enough pancakes to sustain me from eating for a year, my stomach still grumbles when their delicious smell filters through the air.

Patty's eyes lift from his overflowing plate to me. "Were those fighting words I heard?"

My brows meet my hairline, utterly confused by his statement. *I didn't say anything?* It's only when I see the possessive streak plaguing his eyes I was expecting earlier do I realize what his statement is referring to.

I rub my stomach. "It's all good, I'm stuffed."

Patty drags his plate across the table and guards it possessively. "Good, cause your mitts are not to go anywhere near *my* pancakes. All their sweetness belongs to me."

*I need to get fucking laid.* Even though Patty's statement is referring to food, my mind went straight to the gutter. Every improper thought that ran through my mind included Ava in some form of sexual activity. On her knees, in the shower, bent over the very desk Patty is eating his breakfast on.

My thoughts turn even more perverted when Ava pops her backside onto the desk and gestures for me to join her by patting the desk with her hand. Trying to act like a man, instead of the teenage boy Ava forces out of me every time I'm near her, I accept her offer.

Over the next forty five minutes, Patty eats his breakfast while updating me on his life history. He met his wife, Calista, when he was sixteen; they married six days after her eighteenth birthday. They had three children: two sons and one daughter. His wife passed away eight months ago, and since he was lonely, he decided to rejoin the workforce after being retired for over five years.

He was ecstatic when he secured his position as a night watchman in Ava's apartment building six months ago, but disappointed when he discovered his employer won't let him carry a gun like the rest of the security personnel.

"I've never failed an eye exam!" he exclaims, emphasizing his plea.

Ava leans across the table and taps Patty on his spot-blemished arm. I try to keep my eyes away from the delectable skin on her thighs. I fail miserably.

"They don't let you carry a gun to keep the staff moral up."

Patty stares at Ava with just as much confusion as I'm bestowing on her.

"They don't want you bruising the ego of the younger guards when you show them how a real man operates," she adds on.

Patty's chest puffs high, proud of Ava's compliment.

"Besides, what's that saying you quote all the time?" she questions, tapping her index finger on her lips. "A real man doesn't need to carry a weapon. His body is his weapon."

"Damn straight." Patty stands from his chair. His chin is higher than it was earlier and his shoulders more square. "Thank you for breakfast, Ava, but it's time for me to get back to showing these boys how it's really done." He places a kiss on Ava's cheek before ambling out of the room with a new-found spring in his step.

Ava's brows scrunch. "I think my little pep talk backfired."

"Why's that?" I query. "Patty walked out of here with his head held high. Isn't that the whole purpose of a pep talk?"

"But Patty works the graveyard shift. He's supposed to be going home to sleep, not showing the boys how it's done," she says with a little laugh.

I laugh before helping Ava clear away the Tupperware containers. By the time we walk out of the office, the worry fettering Ava's face fades. Patty is slouched in a grandpa rocking chair in the corner of the room, fast asleep. With a broad grin across her face, she bids farewell to the security officer still watching me cautiously with a wave of her hand before pacing out the heavy-weighted door.

When the elevator pings, announcing its arrival to the lobby, I guide Ava inside by placing my hand on the curve of her back. After pushing the button for her floor on the lift dashboard, I turn to face her.

"Do you have plans this afternoon?"

Smiling, she shakes her head.

"Did you want to come and christen my new pad?"

Her entire body blooms with heat.

I shake my head, trying to conceal the smile furling my lips. "I thought I was the only one in this elevator with the mind of a thirteen year old boy."

"I meant to say a housewarming party." I cringe at the thought of old ladies sitting in my sunken living area with china teacups in their hands.

All my good intentions for treating Ava like the woman she is crash into oblivion when she peers up at me, wide-eyed and eager. The hardness of my cock hasn't eased any since her little tease earlier this morning, and if she keeps looking at me like that, it will never quit.

My morals are left for dust when Ava's dark eyes peer up at me and she says, "I'd love to come christen your new apartment."

## FIFTEEN

## AVA

Even with my insides dancing like they're performing on *America's Got Talent*, I maintain a calm, rational façade. Although I tried to keep my tone laced with cheekiness, there was no denying the sexual undertone in my voice when I brazenly said I'd love to christen Hugo's new apartment. Ever since I issued my bold statement, the air in the elevator car became roasting, and the buzz of energy crackling between Hugo and me has my skin prickling with goosebumps.

In all honesty, half of me is jittering in excitement, and the other half is a shivering in terror. Although Hugo and I kissed last week, I have no clue what that means. Do friends kiss? Is this crazy sexual connection we have just the lust required for two people to be fuck buddies? And before I get ahead of myself, does he even want to be more than friends? I guess that's something I should've sought clarity on before I brazenly stated "I'd love to christen your apartment."

While I'm being totally forthright, even though I've never found the idea of casual relationships appealing, I'd consider entering one with Hugo if it means my years of fantasies may actually have a chance to transpire. I'd be willing to give up anything just to be with him for one night.

When the elevator car arrives at my floor, Hugo laces his fingers with mine and heads toward my apartment door. My struggle to secure enough air to fill my lungs ramps up more the further we pace down the hallway.

The air between us shifts when he releases my hand before I grasp my gold engraved door handle. My nipples bud when my eyes meet his rapacious gaze. After running his scorching eyes over my body, he licks his lips before returning his eyes front and center.

Pushing the key into the lock, I ask, "What time does your party start?"

His eyes shift from the door he had me pinned against last week to me. "Most people are arriving in around an hour, but whenever you're ready is fine," he answers.

"Okay, I'll be there in an hour," I say with a smile.

He smiles an uneasy grin. "Alright, I'll see you then."

"Bye," I say, placing a kiss on the corner of his mouth.

He arches his brow. "You don't say goodbye--"

"You say, I'll see you later," I interrupt. "And I will."

After placing a second peck on the edge of my mouth, Hugo ambles down the hall. While unlocking my front door, clarity forms in my mind, which always muddles when Hugo is in my vicinity.

Spinning on my heels, I shout, "I don't know your address!"

"Jorgie will pick you up."

My mouth gapes. "What if I had plans?"

He spins on his heels and walks backward. My heart flips when I see the boyish grin stretched across his face.

"I would've rocked up to your door, thrown you over my shoulder, and dragged your ass there myself."

Feeling cheeky, I reply, "I have plans!"

He graces me with a huge heart-fluttering grin and a cheeky wink before pivoting on his heels and increasing his brisk stride. Once his frame retreats into the elevator car, I enter my apartment. I have a ridiculous grin on my face and am feeling the most carefree I've ever felt.

Smiling like the cat that swallowed the canary, I throw my keys onto the entranceway table. My feet pad along the corkwood floors, eager for a quick refreshing shower to remove the stickiness from the sweat-producing heat in the elevator car. The sparks firing between Hugo and me were like watching a meteor shower in a dark sky. It was nerve-rattling and awe-inspiring. We've always had a weird, unexplainable connection when we were younger. Now isn't any different.

After a quick shower, a flurry of perfume, and a splattering of make-up, I rush to my apartment door. My plan to arrive at Hugo's party within an hour are foiled the instant Jorgie glances down at my denim jeans and long-sleeve printed top. With her brow cocked, she elongates her finger and demands for me to return to my room like she did every time we attended a party during our high school years. Stomping my feet like a child, I drop my bottom lip before doing as solicited.

Like always, our twenty minute mini makeover has two hours ticking by on the clock before we know it. Dressed in a curve hugging pale blue strapless dress and high altitude stilettos, I snag my purse off the nightstand and amble to the door feeling like a cast member from *Sex and the City*.

"What did Hugo say when you told him we were going to be late?" I use the mirrored elevator doors to dap a tissue on my over-sheened lips.

Placing the tissue into my black clutch purse, I secure a grip on the bottle of wine then turn to face Jorgie. Her eyes are riddled with guilt, and she has a crass smile etched on her face.

"You did text him to tell him we were going to be late? Didn't you?"

She doesn't need to answer my question, the guilt in her eyes in the only answer I need.

"Jorgie!" I reprimand as we walk into the elevator.

"It's a housewarming party, Ava. You won't get a tardy slip for being a few minutes late," she quips.

I gawk at her. "Two hours is a little more than a few minutes."

Shrugging off my reply, she moves to the dashboard of the elevator. My bewildered eyes shoot to hers when she presses the P button at the top and enters a four digit code into a security panel at the side.

Swallowing to clear the tumbleweeds lodged in my throat, I ask, "Where's Hugo's apartment located?"

A broad grin stretches across her face, and she rocks on her heels but remains as quiet as a church mouse. My heart pounds furiously against my chest with every floor the elevator glides past.

When it reaches the very top floor, Jorgie grasps my free hand in hers and strides out of the elevator. The wild beat of my heart kicks up as we pace toward a door at the end of the hall. My jaw drops when my vision is swamped by sharp edges of steel, crisp clean lines of gray linen, and a large gathering of people mingling in the vast space.

My ridiculously high stilettos shuffling on the marbled floors overtake the ringing of my pulse in my ears. "Hugo lives in *my* apartment building? In a penthouse?"

A rush of giddiness clusters in my head when Jorgie waggles her brows. Her grip on my hand firms when we step into the sunken living area. Plush, body-hugging dark gray sofas with giant red scattered cushions line the edges of an extremely large space. A colossal TV hangs above the open wood fireplace and a glass bar full to the brim with bottles of liquor sits in the corner.

"Did you want a drink?" Jorgie asks when she notices the direction of my gaze.

Even though my throat is parched, I shake my head.

"Maybe later?" I stumble out, my voice riddled with nerves. Even though I'm seeing it with my own eyes, my brain can't comprehend that Hugo lives in my apartment building. *This could be both an ingenious and foolhardy move.*

My eyes shoot in all directions, absorbing the space when Jorgie continues to move us through the extravagantly large apartment. *Calling this place an apartment seems a little understated.*

When we enter a well-decorated hallway, I notice three full-sized guest bedrooms painted in pastel colors on the right and a large set of black wooden doors halfway down the hall on the left. I stumble in my stilettos when Jorgie's fast pace has us reaching the doors in two heart-fluttering seconds.

After securing my grip on the wine bottle, I peer my eyes around the impressively sized den. A sleek, black full-size slate billiard table sitting in the middle of the room is surrounded by black round bar tables. An air hockey table is on my left and a pinball machine on the right. My face scrunches when I notice the five full-sized plasma televisions lining the back wall. *Why in the world would one room need five TVs?*

Even though my very first kiss I shared with Hugo was over seven years ago, the vibrancy in the room tonight makes it feel like I've step back in time. That night was full of playful teases, and sneaky feather-like touches before the night hit a climax with a once-in-a-lifetime kiss. I can only hope tonight follows a similar path.

My heart launches into an excited rhythm when Hugo enters the den from a second entrance on my left. He looks delicious in a dark t-shirt and a pair of jeans. His shaggy hair is wet and pulled back, exposing his breathtaking face. He's smokin' hot!

The nape of my neck prickles in excitement when his eyes drift around the room and he spots me standing at the side, gawking at him. The smile that morphs onto his face gives no indication of being annoyed at my tardy arrival. His eyes glide over my face before lowering down my body. When his eyes return to mine, I jingle the chilled bottle of wine.

"*Fridge?*" I mouth.

He holds up his index finger, requesting a minute. When I nod, he turns to speak to a blond-haired gentleman at his side. Once they've finished their brief conversation, he nudges his head to a door on the far right of the room.

"I'll be back in a minute," I say to Jorgie.

A childish giggle parts my lips when she rubs her index finger under her nose. After bumping her with my hip, I weave my way through the intimate crowd of people gathered in the den. Just like the last Marshall party I attended, the gathering of people is diverse. A shy grin twists on my lips when, from the corner of my eye, I spot Hugo making his way through the room. His long, efficient strides have him reaching the swinging door before me.

"Thank you," I say when he holds the door open for me.

I stare wide-eyed at the massive grandeur of the kitchen. "This is ten times bigger than the one in my apartment."

Hugo chuckles at my reaction while pacing to a large bank of cabinets in the middle of the ginormous space. My lips quirk when he opens a cherry oak door, revealing a large built-in fridge. Cool air blast my overheated face when I pace to the double-doored fridge to place my wine inside. A grin tugs on my lips when I see how well-stocked the fridge is. Mrs. Marshall's fridge was always packed to the brim with food. It seems Hugo is following in his mother's footsteps. My heart rate revs up when I notice a majority of the items in the fridge are breakfast foods.

"Are you expecting early morning guests?"

A large grin etches on my mouth when Hugo replies, "No harm in being prepared. One day you might decide to fulfill your debt."

My heart lurches forward when he unexpectedly leans forward and presses a kiss on the nape of my neck. I inhale deeply, dying to secure a full breath when his lips remain on my neck, peppering my skin with feather-soft kisses. I'm practically panting, the anticipation of his next move too much for me to bear.

I slant my head to the side, giving him full access to my neck. He ravishes every inch of my skin, biting and sucking it in a soft, playful kiss. The scratchiness of his five o'clock shadow intensifies the sensitivity of his kiss. I close my eyes, riveted beyond comprehension from his devotion. His hand slithers around my body, splaying across my lower stomach.

A husky moan parts my mouth when he pulls me backward, allowing me to feel the enormity of his excitement, proving I'm not the only one captivated and in a trance. He's just as spellbound as I am.

I spin on my heel, the desire to taste his lips again spurring my boldness. A knee-buckling groan rumbles from his lips when I seal my mouth over his. A low moan escapes my mouth as I run my tongue over his lips, absorbing his delicious cinnamon flavor before plunging it into his mouth.

I stroke my tongue along his, coaxing him to return my embrace. My heart leaps out of my chest when he fists my hair and tilts my head back, demanding control of my mouth. I give it to him. Giddiness overwhelms me from the demanding control of his kiss. I'm in complete awe.

My lips tingle when he pulls his mouth away. "You taste just as good as you did the first time I kissed you in a fridge."

I tilt my head back and peer into his eyes. Unlike our kiss last week, his eyes are clear, free of any encumbrance.

"You remember our first kiss?" My tone is high as a wave of emotions surges through me.

He looks at me, the shock in his eyes clearly apparent. "You thought I'd forgotten?"

I nod, a little overeager. "You were drunk. *Very* drunk."

An adolescent grin stretches across his face. "It wouldn't matter how may drinks I'd had. I'd never forget kissing you."

Hunger clenches my core with anticipation when he runs his index finger across my exposed collarbone, sending goosebumps to the surface of my skin.

"Is that why you didn't turn up for breakfast the following morning? You thought I'd forgotten?"

My brows lower as quickly as my heart rate. I stare into his vivid eyes before shaking my head. His eyes shift between mine, his concern building by the minute.

"What happened?" he asks after a short length of time.

I swallow the lump in my throat. "My dad saw my neck."

Hugo's brows scrunch, but he remains quiet.

"He saw the mark you left on my skin."

He sucks in a quick, sharp breath. "I gave you a hickey?"

I bite on my lip while nodding.

"And your dad saw it?" I hear his utter shock in his high tone.

My rapid head nod increases.

"Fuck! I'm so sorry, Ava," he states with penitence in his eyes.

"That's why I went to college on the other side of the country. My dad sent off an application that very morning," I disclose as emotions strangle my vocal cords.

Hugo's frame stiffens, his pupils widening as the reality of the situation dawns on him. My eyes prick with tears as memories of that day I left Rochdale filter through my brain. The Marshall family were the closest family members I'd had. Leaving them was the hardest thing I'd ever endured.

Hugo cups my jaw with his hand. "I'm so sorry, Ava. If I'd known--"

"I know," I interrupt, peering into his repentant eyes. "But there was nothing anyone could have done."

As much as moving to the other side of the country devastated me, it also saved me from the clutches of my father, so it was both a godsend and a tragedy.

Hugo's eyes dance between mine. "The past cannot be changed, forgotten, edited, or erased. It can only be accepted."

I smile and nod. "Accept the past, embrace the present and believe in the future."

A mesmerizingly dense stretch of time passes between us as we stand across from each other, staring but not speaking. Like always, the connection between us is intense and fired with lust, but there's something more forceful in his eyes infusing our fiery connection. It's so strong, I can feel his yearning in the core of my heart. If I could stay in this moment forever, I would.

Our emotion-packed stare down only ends when an ear-piercing squeal screeches through the room. The scream is so loud, the windows rattle, and my heart leaves my chest. Our eyes meet at the exact moment we realize the howl of pain came from Jorgie.

Panic scorches my veins as I push off the refrigerator and bolt toward the den, shadowing Hugo as he barges past anyone in his way. My heart is wildly beating, shaking my entire body with fear. When I reach the double doors of the den, my breath hitches and tears prick my eyes.

Decked out in his full military uniform is Hawke, standing in the den with a duffle bag in one hand and a bunch of flowers in the other. A tear escapes my eye and rolls down my cheek when Jorgie squeals again before rushing to her soon-to-be husband to throw her arms around his neck.

Hawke dumps his bag and flowers onto the ground and spins Jorgie around the room. Her excited squeals project over the jukebox playing in the corner of the room. When Hawke kneels down in front of Jorgie to caresses the curve of her belly, my heart painfully clenches. That is what I want. I want a relationship like Hawke and Jorgie's. I want a man who has no qualms in showing his affection even with a house full of spectators. A man devoted solely and entirely to me. That is what I want and crave. That is what I deserve.

I wipe my index finger across my face, flinging a tear off my cheek before turning me eyes to Hugo. He, along with numerous others, are watching the exchange between Hawke and Jorgie with broad grins on their faces. I stare at him while pondering will he be that man for me? Will he love me above all others? Will he cherish me as if I'm his most valued possession?

Like he can sense me watching him, his head shifts to the side, and he looks me straight in the eyes. He stares at me as if he's seeing me for the first time. My heart squeezes as the corners of his mouth carve into an illustrious and panty-clenching smile, adding potency to my every hope and dream that one day he'll be that man for me.

## SIXTEEN

## AVA

After paying an exorbitant fee, Jorgie and I amble into a bustling nightclub crammed to the brim with patrons out enjoying their Saturday night. Half-moon suede chairs line three of the outer walls of the club, leaving the entire core of the space devoted to a glass dance floor. A black steel and glass bar is suspended midair by thick twisted steel ropes on my right. A hallway leading to the bathrooms is on the left, and an area devoted to VIP clientele is on my right. The vibe at the club is invigorating, and the mood is sensual.

A gorgeous male host greets Jorgie and me with kisses on the cheek before he leads us to the roped-off VIP section of the club. A space with the ambience of intrigue and sexuality envelopes me. A broad grin stretches across my face, my excitement at spending the night dancing with my best friend clearly evident. I wobble in my stiletto heels when the hostess walks us to a black leather booth and my eyes connect with Hugo.

This is the first time I've seen him since our heartfelt connection in his kitchen last week. We live in the same apartment building, and our two best friends are marrying each other and I still haven't seen hide nor hair of him. Putting two and two together, I came to the assumption he was avoiding me.

Even annoyed from his lack of contact, my eyes can't help but drink in his deliciousness. As always, he looks deliriously handsome. The darkness of his black cotton dress shirt with printed cuffs makes his eyes even more effervescent and his boyish grin even more prominent. His hair has been recently trimmed, and his face is clean shaven. He looks both classy and roughish at the same time.

My heartbeat kicks up when his eyes drop to adsorb the Lovers + Friends Revolve Riviera strapless dress I purchased specifically because of the asymmetrical hem. The daring cut of the beautiful coral material means the dress rides extremely high on my left thigh. With a heart shape bustier and a high slit, I knew it would be the perfect cock-teasing ensemble for a man fascinated with legs.

My nipples tighten when Hugo's heavy-hooded gaze scorches every inch of my skin as his eyes run over my body. After he finishes his avid assessment, his eyes lift to mine.

The shift of air between us is so noticeable, the ground moves beneath my feet. Reaching out, I grab Jorgie's arm to steady myself before taking the final steps into the VIP section of the club. From the corner of my eye, I spot Hawke leaning against the bar, raking his eyes over his beautiful soon-to-be wife.

"Who invites their brother and husband-to-be to their bachelorette party?" My tone rattles with excitement.

Jorgie peers at me with impertinent eyes. "Did I forget to mention we were having joint bachelor and bachelorette parties?"

Her eyes soften as she tries to make her face appear innocent. It's a futile attempt.

She smiles broadly when I say, "Must be those pregnancy hormones playing up again."

After placing a kiss on Hawke's cheek and being introduced to three of Hawke's ex-frat brothers and two of Jorgie's work colleagues, I slide into the booth as instructed by Jorgie. By the time everyone takes a seat, I'm practically sitting on Hugo's lap.

"Ava," he greets me in his deep, rumbling drawl.

"Hi." I'm breathless from his closeness. I swing my eyes to his. "Did you know it was going to be a joint party?"

He shakes his head. "First I heard about it was when I saw Arthur and Martha walk in the club doors."

I gawk at him in surprise. "Who?"

He smirks against the rim of his whiskey glass before taking a large gulp. "Sorry, you probably know them as Kerri and Kirsty."

The light bulb switches on when he gestures his head to Jorgie's work companions. Although they appear similar in age and are wearing matching black and white polka dot dresses, I didn't realize they were related.

"Are they twins?" I question.

Hugo throws his head back and releases a boisterous chuckle. I stare at him, more confused than ever.

"No, they're not twins, but their racks are a good set of twin peaks," he chuckles.

Like a perfectly timed skit, Kerri leans over the table, and I cop an eye full of her more than generous twin peaks. My eyes dart in all directions, unsure of exactly where to look. Noticing my horror, Hugo chuckles even more wholeheartedly than he did earlier. His vivacious laugh makes my toes curl and my womb clench. Just hearing his laugh incites my own happiness.

Once his laughter dies down, I ask, "Does this bother you? Having me here?"

He adjusts his position so he can look me in the eyes. "As long as a group of strippers arriving when the clock strikes twelve doesn't bother you, we're all good."

I huff and cross my arms, embittered by his words.

"I'm joking, Ava." He takes a large gulp of the beverage in his hand. "Besides, I prefer my nuts attached to my body. I'm pretty sure Jorgie would castrate me if I took Hawke to a strip club."

He coughs, splattering whiskey all over the mahogany table when I rib him with my elbow, pretending to be offended by his comment.

In all honesty, I'm loving his playfulness. He's the most relaxed and carefree I've ever seen. His cheeky disposition has me doubting my initial reaction to his lack of contact. Maybe he hasn't been avoiding me. Maybe he's just been busy?

A waitress in a skin-tight black mini skirt, crisp white blouse and a top hat saunters to our group with a wide smile. "Hi guys, welcome to *The Chapel*. My name is Keke and I'll be your server today. Some platters will be arriving shortly, but how about we start you all with a few drinks?"

A loud cluster of hollering bellows through the air from the frat brothers. They bang their hands on the table, throw their heads back, and howl like wolves on a full moon night. My eyes snap to Hugo, expecting to see him undertaking the same ritual since he pledged at the same fraternity. I'm taken aback when I discover his eyes are focused on me instead of his rowdy frat brothers. His passionate gaze has my pulse quickening.

My focus returns to the rowdy crowd when Keke says, "I'm not even going to take your orders. I'm going to keep it a *big* surprise." After snatching the drinks menu off the black polished tabletop, she saunters to the private VIP bar.

"Ava is it?" asks the cute blond gentleman sitting next to me.

I believe Hawke introduced him as Aspen, but I've never been good at recalling names. Aspen has charmingly handsome good looks, a lean-built body, and wholesome eyes.

"Yes, nice to meet you," I say, offering him my hand.

"Is Ava short for anything or is it just Ava?" he queries, accepting my handshake.

"Just Ava."

I intertwine my fingers and rest them in my lap, inwardly battling not to squirm. The instant Aspen spoke, Hugo brushed his fingertips over the exposed skin on my back, sending a flurry of desire straight to my core.

"My dad didn't want me to have a nickname, so he picked a name that didn't have one." I smile, relieved my voice didn't give any indication to the hammering my heart is doing.

Aspen smiles and nods his head. "Well it's a beautiful name. Very fitting."

"Thank you," I reply softly.

Aspen scoots across the bench, filling the miniscule space between us. The refreshing smell of sand and coconuts filters through my nostrils. Any time I smell coconuts, it reminds me of weekends at the beach with Jorgie and Hugo.

"Can I buy you a drink, Ava?" Aspen overemphasizes my name by drawing out the last A in a long husky drawl.

Any reply I am about to give is cut off when Hugo abruptly places his whiskey glass onto the table. Its loud clang gains us the attention of everyone in the booth and those surrounding it.

"All drinks are on the house, Aspen, no one needs to buy Ava's drinks."

Aspen's eyes lift past my shoulder to peer at Hugo. They don't speak, but their silent conversation creates a misting of sweat shimmering on my skin.

"Then perhaps Ava will do me the honor of saving me the first dance?" Aspen suggests, returning his unique greenish-gray eyes to mine.

I nearly vault off my chair when Hugo places his hand on my knee and squeezes. At first, I take it as a silent warning to be attentive of my surroundings after what occurred the last time I went out dancing, but when his hand glides upwards, only stopping once it is high on my thigh, I realize it has nothing to do with being attentive, and everything to do with being possessive.

Not all women like jealous, possessive men, but I love them. Every book I devour is about hot possessive men claiming their women. Just the thought of being possessed by Hugo has my thighs pressing together and my stomach quivering with butterflies.

I drag my eyes to Aspen when he coughs, wordlessly demanding my attention. He stares at me, waiting for a reply to his question. I can hardly breathe, let alone formulate a response. I'm unable to focus on anything but Hugo's fingers tapping along to the beat of the music blasting out of the speakers. His simplest touch has my every nerve sparked and paying careful attention and my womb coiling tightly.

Aspen's head shifts to the side as he eyes me with curiosity.

"Maybe?" I squeak out with a shrug of my shoulders.

I try to keep my tone neutral, feigning that I'm not affected by Hugo's simple touch, but the smallest shudder is still heard in my voice, giving away my deceit. Happy with my response, Aspen grins and nods before turning his attention back to Hawke... and Hugo removes his hand from my thigh.

After gathering my dignity off the floor, I turn my eyes to Hugo. "What was that?"

"What?" he replies, acting innocent.

He can't fool me. The smugness is written all over his face.

"The hand on my thigh." I glare at him through squinted eyes.

My stomach muscles bunch after he tilts in close to my side and his delicious woodsy scent hits my senses. "Aspen is only twenty-six and already on wife number two."

*Oh.*

I turn my gaze in just enough time to catch Aspen sneakily slipping off his wedding ring and sliding it into his pocket. Even with having nothing to be ashamed of, guilt swamps me. I've never been that type of girl. I won't even socialize with married men at places like this; that's just asking for trouble.

I flick my humiliated eyes back to Hugo. "You couldn't have just whispered that in my ear?"

He brushes the back of his fingers over my inflamed cheek. "Nah. It wouldn't have been as much fun that way."

He can say that, but he isn't the one panting like a dog in heat.

Hugo adjusts his position, snagging my devotion when he leans in intimately close to my side. "Does it bother you? Having me here?" he questions, quoting me from earlier, his eyes smoldering.

"No." When a condescending smirk stretches across his face, I add on. "Unless you're planning on cock-blocking every guy who gets within a ten-mile radius of me."

He smiles, revealing his perfectly straight teeth. I blame Hugo for my career choice. A beautiful smile is one of the most captivating features a person can have. With a little bit of effort, everyone has the chance to achieve a smile nearly as alluring as Hugo's. Wanting to make people feel as good as I did when I was graced with Hugo's heart-fluttering smile, I chose to become a dentist. When I see the smile on my patients' mouths after orthodontics, it makes it worth enduring the less stellar parts of my job.

"And if I was planning on cock-blocking every guy?" His gaze slides over my face.

I shift my angle, leaning in to his side. We're now sitting so close, his warm breath dries my already parched lips.

"Then I have no problems with you being here," I answer truthfully.

There's only one man whose devotion I wish to secure. He's sitting right next to me. Sheepishly, I lift my eyes to Hugo, wanting to gauge his reaction to my boldness. His smile that greets me is crass and smug. A tingle races down my back, too turned on to control my body responding to his smile. I stick out my tongue before scooting across the bench seat. My excitement is evident when the skin on my thigh clings to the leather seat. I move far enough away from Hugo, my body gets a small moment of reprieve from his alluring pull, but not far enough that Aspen will misinterpret my closeness as an open invitation.

## SEVENTEEN

## HUGO

*Fuck me!* I nearly died when Ava strolled into the VIP section of the club. After spending my week wading my way through my new job, my mood was anything but pleasant. Add that on top of the guilt I felt knowing I was the cause of Ava's sudden decision to attend a university across the country, and my mood turned downright deadly.

I was riddled with guilt when I found out Ava was forced to leave her home town because of me and my foolishness. I did stupidly mark her skin, warning my competitors that Ava was taken, even when she wasn't. My jealousy was already hitting me fair in the guts from the number of men ogling her when she stripped out of her clothing after I threw her into the pool. My jealousy turned potent after I left Ava in Jorgie's room. What Jorgie said that night was true. Ava's seductive strip tease had guys crawling out of the woodwork, vying for her attention. None of them were worthy of Ava, and I was determined to make sure they were aware of that fact.

It was only after a night without a wink of sleep did I realize I can't change the past, but I can shape the future. I woke up the morning after my housewarming party more spirited than ever, determined never to be parted from Ava again. Little did I know at the time, my new job was going to do exactly that. For the past week, I've worked from when the sun set until it rose. Ava worked daylight hours. The realization of our situation had my mind scrambled and my mood souring.

My pitiful mood dissipated the instant I spotted Ava walking into the VIP section of the club. Just seeing her beautiful face told me she'd be worth weathering any storm for. The muscles in my thighs strained when my eyes raked over her delicious body. There's no hiding the fact I'm a legs man. My expertise in my field of choice is extremely high, meaning I've studied many pairs of beautiful legs.

But not one pair I've assessed has been as spellbinding as Ava's legs. Throw together a pair of ball-constricting legs, a captivating face, a seductive body, and a tight, strapless dress and what do you get? A drop-to-your-knees combination. I've never been more ready to fall to my knees and crawl to a pair of feet in my life as I was when Ava walked into the nightclub in a ravishing dress. No woman has ever beckoned me to drop to my knees the way she does.

When my eyes lifted from her captivating body to her face, a jolt of heaviness slammed into my chest, maiming my heart. It was in that instant, I realized, Ava is going to own me. Not slightly. Completely and utterly consume me. No doubts about it. For the past six years, I tried to act like I'd forgotten about the intense connection between us, but in reality, I just pushed it to the background of my mind, deciding that pursuing her was a fruitless endeavor. Now, I wish I'd been more stubborn and dug deeper as to why Ava chose to go to a university on the other side of the country, instead of just making assumptions.

Shaking off the thoughts that may have my foul mood returning, my ears prick, straining to hear the music blaring out of the speakers in the regular patrons' section of the nightclub. When I realize it is the song I thought it was, I nudge Aspen with the back of my hand, throwing a little extra power into my punch for his earlier flirting with Ava.

When he openly flirted with Ava, jealousy clawed at my chest, shredding my heart. I gripped my whiskey glass so tight, it nearly shattered. Jealousy has never been a curse of mine... until it comes to Ava. Then, it's blinding. As soon as a man shows a slight interest in her, I become a bull in a china shop. I charge first, ask questions later.

"Move out," I request when Aspen peers at me, looking confused.

Cozy booths seem like an ideal set-up for any club, but unless you're a couple looking to get intimate, they're more of a hindrance than an aid. Three people have to leave their seat just to let me out. Once I've been released from the booth, I band my arm around Ava's waist and hoist her into my chest. Her laugh is only just drowned out by Jorgie's excited squeal.

I hold Ava close to my chest while striding with urgency to the regular section of the club. My chest puffs high, proud that Ava doesn't put up an objection to my hold. When we enter the space, Ava's head shoots off my chest.

"No," she whispers with a shake of her head.

I waggle my brows and nod. "Time to dust of your *Gangnam Style* moves."

Being forthright, half of my mood is teasing, the other half is aroused. Visions of dancing with Ava weeks ago still occupy my dreams. Although I teased Ava last time she danced, she's a skilled dancer. She moves with grace and ease while also being innately sexual.

Watching her dance is like foreplay, teasing and stimulating while leaving you desiring for more. I've always found the club scene a provocative hot box of lust and desire. Dancing with Ava beats that tenfold.

By the time we reach the middle of the dancefloor, the song is halfway through. I place Ava onto her feet and circle my arms around her, protecting her from the mass of people surrounding us. I may have failed at protecting her last time, but that will never happen again.

Her chest expands with every breath she takes. She looks

worried. Staring into my wild, heavily dilated eyes, the concern on her face vanishes. The pounding of my heart increases when she flashes her killer smile before she starts ponying on the spot. Although she follows similar dance moves as she did last week, she adds an edge of seductiveness to it, sparking my dick to harden.

When it reaches the part of the song requiring her to bend over and flick her knee, she spins in my protective circle and attaches her backside firmly onto my crotch. Even with the hum of the vast gathering of people around us, and the blaring music, I don't miss the hiss that seeps from her lips when she brushes past the thickening of my cock. She braces her hands on my legs, digging her nails into my tense muscles as she bows forward and grinds herself against my crotch.

When she straightens her spine, her hair flicks my chin from my abrupt movements, engulfing me with her sweet smell. I find it amusing that someone who is a dentist smells so sweet. Ava's lips taste like candy apples, and her smell is even sweeter.

I grip the curve of her hips and swing mine, swaying to the beat of the new song playing. Ava dances around me, staying within the invisible safety bubble I've formed around us. Over time, the mass gathering of bodies in the small space soon has my body temp rising.

Sweat glistens on my skin, and my throat is parched from spending the past hour dancing. A new type of thirst awakens in me when Ava pivots around to face me. Her cheeks are flushed, and her nape is dripping with sweat, giving her the alluring look of someone who is sexually sated. She runs her tongue along the seam of her mouth as her smoky gaze lifts to mine.

No longer able to inhibit the desire of tasting her lips again, I tilt down and enclose my mouth over hers. Her husky moan fans my lips with the scent of strawberry lip gloss. I groan as her delicious flavor hits my taste buds. Her mouth has the intoxicating mix of the sweetness of candy mingled with the fruity cocktails she has been drinking.

I cup the curves of her ass, yanking her close to me, not leaving an ounce of air between us. Fisting her hair, I tilt her head back, demanding control of her mouth. A shuddering moan rumbles through my lips when she gives me complete control without a single protest.

I kiss her violently, stealing every moan whimpering from her mouth, and making up for the years we missed. For the past two years, my mom has regularly said, "One day the right woman will knock you on your ass." Little did she know, she already did.

Catcalls pelt through my ears when Ava curls her legs around my waist to rubs her pussy against the rock my jeans is failing to conceal. Taunts about "getting a room" and "give it to her" continue when I pace through the writhing bodies grooving on the dance floor with Ava still wrapped around my front.

When we enter the corridor, she inches back. Her eyes shift around the space, gathering her surroundings. Still striding, I pace to the office at the end of the hall. When we enter, Ava's eyes dance around the office with eagerness. Once she has absorbed the space, I place her onto her feet.

Pulling a strand of hair off her sweat-drenched neck, I tuck it behind her ear, ignoring the tremor of my hands. My heart is beating fitfully and my palms are sweaty. I'm the most nervous I've ever been.

I cough, clearing the frog in my throat. "Did you want to go out?"

*Fuck, that sounded nothing like I'd envisioned in my head.*

"To the movies or something?" I blurt out, trying to save myself from an embarrassing situation.

## EIGHTEEN

## AVA

When Hugo asks me out, my eyes zoom to his, certain I didn't hear him right. When he finalizes his question, I inwardly sigh. I thought my every dream was about to be fulfilled. Hugo curses under his breath while running his shaky hand over the top of his head. I remain quiet and study his posture.

A nervous twitch is hampering his jawline; his brows are furrowed, grooving a line between his eyes, and his posture is stiff. He's clearly nervous. I smile. I've never seen Hugo nervous before and I find it endearing that asking me out has made him this way. When he mumbles something about not listening to Jorgie's relationship advice, lucidity forms in my skewed brain.

"Are you asking me out on date, or to be your girlfriend?" I mask my excitement with a neutral tone.

His eyes missile to mine. When he spots the excitement I'm unable to contain, his eyes fire with his regular cheekiness. "I guess that'll depend on what your answer is going to be?"

"Is there a maybe box?" I'm pretending like I'm not in the midst of a panic attack. I swear if my heart keeps thrashing like it is, it will burst out of my chest cavity.

My insides clench when an angry growl rumbles from Hugo's chest. "You need time to consider?" Even though he's asked a question, his eyes say it's a statement.

I stand on my tippy toes so I can peer into his eyes. "No, but it's not entirely fair to give a girl a mind-blowing kiss and then expect her to answer a life-altering question."

He smiles a pussy-clenching smile. "Mind-blowing, hey?" His brows waggle, cockiness oozing out of him.

I shrug my shoulders. "It was okay," I lie.

That kiss was *way* beyond okay. Fireworks exploding in the sky, I'm going to have nothing but smut dreams for a week is what that kiss was. I can barely stand as my thighs are shaking so much. All playfulness vanishes, and a new type of friskiness develops when Hugo's fire-sparked eyes glance down at me.

My eyes dance over his face, drinking in every spectacular detail. He truly is a beautiful man. A straight, sculptured nose, plump lips that taste as delicious as they look, and dark, thick luxurious hair that frames his ruggedly handsome face perfectly. The intense pull I've always felt tugging between us strengthens, tethering my heart to him even more than it already is as we stand across from each other, staring but not speaking. He cups the edge of my jaw and stares into my longing eyes.

"I'm going to kiss you, Ava." He flattens his palm against my back to pull me nearer to him. "There are kisses and then there are *kisses*. Yours are the later. I could kiss you for hours and still not get enough."

*Holy mackerel!* Not wanting to give him a chance to recant his statement, I brazenly propel onto my tippy toes and seal my mouth over his. A rough groan tears from his throat when my tongue plunges into his mouth. He gently grabs my hips and guides me toward him. I can feel how hard he is. Hot, thick, and long. Unlike the last few times we kissed, this one is more controlled. Sweet and tender.

"Hugo," I whimper, needy when he pulls his sultry lips away from mine.

"I've been wanting to do that since the moment I saw you in that dress." He peppers my jawline with feathery kisses.

My skin prickles from the coolness of the glass washroom door when I lean against it, stabilizing myself from his breathtaking kiss. A spark of ardor surges through the air as he nibbles on the skin of my neck and collarbone before moving even lower. His lust-blazed eyes lift to mine as his index finger runs along the material of my dress sitting at the edge of my cleavage. When his eyes seek my permission, I brazenly nod.

My head flops back as a husky moan spills from my lips after he pulls down the damp material of my dress and encloses his warm mouth over my pebbled nipple. I exhale a shaky moan when a transfixing jolt gushes through my body and clusters in my core. My hand shoots out, seeking something to grab when his tongue teases my nipple into a tight, constricted bud. My search comes up empty-handed.

"You have beautiful nipples, Ava," he says breathlessly, staring at my taut buds.

Surprisingly, my nipples harden even more. He smiles, loving my body's reaction to his touch. He stares up at me as he gently bites on my nipple before sucking it into his mouth.

"Oh God," I cry out when the power of his suck overwhelms me.

I rake my fingers through his long, thick hair as he secures his mouth to my breast. The tension in my womb rapidly builds with every perfect flick of his tongue and tweak of his fingers.

"I-I—"

Any words about to spill from my parched lips become lodged in my throat when he slithers his spare hand down to squeeze the curve of my backside. His hand is so large, the tips of his fingers graze the uncontrollable throb between my legs. A moan I've never heard before rumbles through my lips as his fingers lightly brush my weeping folds.

He slips my panties to the side and glides his finger inside of me, causing my knees to buckle and my nails dig into his shoulder. The walls of my pussy squeeze and massage his digit with every thrust. Between his mouth teasing my nipples and his finger finding the spot many men can't, I shamefully moan like I'm starring in an adult film production.

"Please. I. Umm."

The ability to form an entire sentence is beyond me as a toe-curling sensation triggers a scattering of fireworks to form in front of my eyes. Sensing my silent requirement, the pad of his thumb rolls over the stiff bud of my clit. One, two, three strokes and I'm done. My knees buckle and Hugo's name tears from my throat in an ear-piercing scream, without the slightest bit of concern about the horde of people milling only mere feet from us.

He eases the pace of his thrusts, slowly guiding me down from the earth-shattering orgasm that just rocketed through my body. Once the tremors lessen, I glance down at him. Staring into my eyes, he removes his finger from my pulsating pussy. My breath hitches when he graces me with a heart-stopping smile before popping his finger into his mouth to remove the evidence of my arousal from his glistening digit.

He growls. "Your pussy tastes even sweeter than your mouth."

His teeth tugs on the erect peak of my nipple before he savors the skin on my neck and collarbone. I can taste my excitement on his mouth when he seals his lips over mine. Even just enduring a mind-hazing climax, a hot trickle of desire reforms in my womb. I comb my fingers through his hair, playfully tugging on the damp tips.

The thump of my heart increases when a throaty growl seeps from his mouth. I pull him closer, deepening our kiss at the same time a door being open clatters through my ears. A shameful whimper leaks from my swollen lips when Hugo briskly pulls away and shifts his head to the side. Thankfully, his large frame conceals me as I adjust the material of my dress back to a more respectable level.

"Is everything okay in here?" questions a male voice with a thick drawl.

"Everything is fine, Roger. We'll be out in a minute."

The ruggedness of Hugo's reply causes a tingling sensation to zap down my spine. After a beat, the office door closing sounds through the room. Hugo's gaze returns to me. His eyes float over my face, absorbing my flushed expression.

"What is it with us always being interrupted?" His tone is both playful and irritated.

I smile and shrug my shoulders. "Cursed?"

When his tongue delves out to lick his top lip, his eyes flare. "If Roger wasn't outside that door, waiting for us, I'd be feasting on your sweet-tasting pussy until the sun is hanging high in the sky."

The cotton material of my panties dampens, causing me to squeeze my legs together, futilely trying to lessen the intense throb of my clit begging for his attention. The rawness of the hunger in his eyes steals my ability to breathe. He smiles at my flushed cheeks before stepping away from me.

Engrossed by an active imagination, I'm vaguely aware of Hugo moving around me, gathering articles and rearranging my clothing. I'm too entranced by what just transpired for my brain to function. Once everything is back in order, Hugo encloses his hand over mind and we pace toward the door. The gentleman with a thick silver moustache I now know is called Roger greets us with a nod of his head and a set of straight-lined lips.

Hugo dips his head in greeting before briskly striding down the hallway. My feet scuttle across the tiled floor, scurrying to keep up with his large strides.

I swallow the dryness in my throat. "Was that Roger's office?"

Hugo smiles and shakes his head. "Nope." He guides me out of the corridor. "That was my office."

My mouth gapes nearly as wide as Jorgie's does when we enter the main section of the sweat- infused dance club and her eyes zoom on mine and Hugo's interlocked hands. I try to wipe the "I've just climaxed" look off my face, but Jorgie notices it before I can suffocate it.

Hugo's grip on my hand firms the closer we pace toward the group. It's only once we reach the booth do I realize why he's clutching my hand so tightly. It has nothing to do with Jorgie's shocked expression and everything to do with the look of contempt on Aspen's face. He looks like a kid whose candy bag was confiscated on Halloween night by his parents.

When we arrive at the booth, Hawke leans into Hugo's side and whispers something in his ear. Hugo nods before turning his eyes to me.

"Hawke's arranged to meet a few of the guys from his squadron at a club on the other side of town. Did you want to come with me or stay with Jorgie?"

My eyes shift to Jorgie in just enough time to catch the end of a large yawn.

"You guys go. I think Jorgie has had enough entertainment for one night," I say, turning my eyes back to Hugo.

Hugo chuckles. "All right. I'll see you tomorrow?"

Smiling broadly, I nod, my excitement beaming out of me. Jorgie and Hawke finally get married tomorrow afternoon.

My stomach quivers when Hugo dips his knees to place a kiss directly on my lips. A collection of sighs sounds around us, some gleeful, others disdained.

## NINETEEN
## HUGO

"I'll grab my suit and be right out."

I slam Hawke's car door shut and bolt up the stairs of my parents' home. With everything hammering my mind the past few weeks, I forgot to collect my suit from my mom's house earlier today. Since it's almost eleven PM, Hawke is refusing to come inside, claiming some shit about it being bad luck to see the bride the day of the wedding? I take the stairs two at a time.

Even with half a bottle of whiskey sitting in my gut, my steps are unimpeded. My eager strides down the hall slow when I notice a light creeping out of my childhood bedroom. An inane grin carves on my lips when I peer into my room and notice Ava walking around the space, absorbing the scene. I prop my shoulder onto the doorjamb and drink her in.

*Fuck, she's beautiful.*

The unique mix of innocence and seduction. Sharp, intelligent eyes, full curvy lips, little button nose, and a sexy tight body that molds against the hard ridges of my body like she was crafted especially for me. She's no doubt the sexiest woman alive.

There were a bevy of beautiful women as far as my eye could see at the strip club tonight, but I wasn't interested in a single one of them. Ava's husky moans, perfectly round chocolate nipples, and the way she tasted when I licked her sweetness off my finger kept my cock as hard as steel the entire night.

No matter how many propositions I received, my cock was only interested in filling one pussy - Ava's. I've never tasted a sweeter pussy in my life. If Roger hadn't interrupted us, I would've spent the rest of my night devouring it. I hadn't meant to be so crass when I told her I wanted to spend my night feasting on her pussy. The tactlessness of my statement became a forgotten memory when she stared up at me openmouthed and eager.

While I'm being forthright, our time together in the office was riveting, but I felt like a slack-jawed idiot when I attempted to ask her out. I don't know why I bothered adhering to Jorgie's advice. Not once in her life has she given solid relationship advice, but for some reason, this week I stupidly listened to her. I'll admit it, my attempts at wooing Ava were pitiful, worse than any fifth grader could have managed.

But in my defense, I do have a solid explanation for my lack of relationship skills. Before tonight, I'd never asked a girl out. Not once. Not to a school dance or a movie. Nothing. So just like Ava is my one and only crush, she's also the only girl I've asked out. Although, technically, Ava didn't respond to my question; her eyes relayed the answer I wanted to hear. I don't know where we go from here, but no matter what happens, I'm sure it will be one hell of a ride.

Hearing my bedroom door creak, Ava's neck cranks to the side, and she peers at me.

"Hey," she greets me, her lips curling into a lascivious smile.

"Hey." I try to keep my voice steady, but my attempts are borderline.

After placing a photo frame on my bedside table, she spins around to face me.

"What are you doing here?"

I nudge my head to a suit bag hanging on the bathroom door. "I forgot my suit,"

"Oh."

Even with disappointment shaking her vocal cords, I don't miss the slight slur of her words.

"Have you been drinking?" I take a step closer to her.

A husky laugh spills from her lips as she nods. "I played truth or dare with Kirsty and Kerri. Every question I refused to answer saw me taking a nip of vodka."

Her eyes lift from staring at the ground. My cock, now hard, strains against the zipper of my jeans when I see the hankering beaming from her rich eyes.

"Most of their questions were about you." She licks her lips as her eyes drop to my crotch. "And the accuracy of your nickname in high school."

When her eyes lift back to mine, it takes all my strength to remain glued to my spot. The savage smile on her face tells me she didn't miss the hardness in my jeans.

"It's true, isn't it?" She glances into my eyes.

"You'll have to wait to find out." The quiver in my words display how badly my restraint is wavering.

"When?" she asks, unashamed.

I peer into her candid eyes. "When you haven't been drinking."

The huff expelled from her lips makes me even harder. I amble to the door of the bathroom and collect my suit bag, no longer trusting myself around her. I spent half of my night with a throbbing cock, reminiscing about the taste of Ava's sweet pussy, imagining how invigorating it will be having her tightness wrapped around my cock.

Knowing I've never been able to restrain myself when Ava and I are alone, I need to leave before all my inhibitions gravely falter. I want her. I want her urgently. More than my next breath, but I don't want our first time together fueled by the alcohol lacing her veins.

My intentions on a quick getaway are foiled when Ava asks, "Can I ask a favor?"

Swallowing the brick in my throat, I nod, approving her request. I've never had the capacity to deny her.

The stiffness of my cock turns painful when she asks, "Can you unzip my dress? I can't reach the hook, and Jorgie is passed out in the middle of her bed."

I grin, stifling a chuckle before shuffling across the room to dump my suit bag on my bed. The closer I pace to Ava, the more her eyes widen. She stares at me with hankering eyes but remains completely silent. I would have assumed she'd passed out if it weren't for the occasional blink. Once I stop in front of her, she gathers her hair to one side before pivoting around, giving me access to the hidden zipper and hook resting beneath her shoulder blades.

It could be my overactive imagination, but I swear a soft moan escapes her lips when my hand brushes the bare skin on her back. Needing to know if my simple touch caused that type of reaction, I run my index finger along the edge of her right shoulder blade. What I heard the first time is accurate. There's no doubt in my mind a soft, lust-filled moan spilled from her lips.

My stiffened shaft digs into the fly of my trousers when I lower her zipper down her dress. Once the zipper is all the way down, stopping at the curve of her backside, she clasps her dress at the chest and spins to face me.

"Thank you," she whispers faintly, looking up at me with her beautifully unique eyes.

I smile, accepting her praise before taking a step backward. From the way she's staring at me, hungry-eyed and eager, I need distance between us, and I need it now.

My eyes bulge when Ava releases her grip on the dress. It plummets to the floor, crinkling around her stiletto-covered feet. Even though my brain is screaming at me to leave, my eyes rake her barely covered body, not once, but twice.

*Fuck me!*

There are two types of people in the world. The first are the ones who use clothing to accentuate their beauty, their garment selections purely made to enhance their god-gifted assets. Then there's the second group: a very small, carefully selected group of people who should wander the earth as naked as they day they were born just to give mere mortals the opportunity to witness pure perfection at least once in their lifetimes.

Ava belongs in that group.

Her beauty goes above and beyond what I could have ever envisioned when I was picturing her in nothing but a pair of heels and panties. She's... too perfect to ever formulate a word for. Go to a dictionary and look up the definition of beauty and perfection. Those are the words I'd use to describe Ava as she's standing before me now. A small gold cross sits between her pert, lush tits. Her frame is slender but seductive with curves in all the right places. From the sheer panties she's wearing, and from what I felt earlier tonight, her pussy is bare and erotically exposing her arousal. She's a fucking goddess.

My eyes rocket to hers when she takes a step closer to me. I shake my head, pleading with her to stay where she is. My inhibitions on making her mine are severely wavering.

"I want this," she mutters huskily, stepping closer to me. "I want you."

*Stick me with a fork. I am fucking done.*

# TWENTY

## AVA

Although my mind is hazy, it isn't the alcohol strumming through my veins causing my giddiness. It's Hugo. I've spent a majority of my night floating on cloud nine after nearly every desire, wish, and want I've ever craved was fulfilled beyond my greatest expectations. My every whim was satisfied – all except one. I plan on correcting that misconception now.

Anticipation buzzes through me as the indecisiveness hampering Hugo's eyes fades with every step I take toward him. The crackling of energy between us is electric, spurring on my desire to seduce him. The ache weighing down my breasts increases as I pace to him. His eyes are rapacious and firmly planted on me.

"I'm not drunk," I assure him, finalizing the last step.

My heart stops beating when an ostentatious smirk stretches across his face. Warmth floods my nether regions when he chews on his lip as his eyes rake my body. When his gaze returns to me, I swallow. Any apprehension in his eyes has completely vanished, replaced with a new fervent look.

I cup the edge of his twitching jaw with my hand. "Unless you count being drunk on you? If so, you better ship me off to rehab, as I haven't been sober in over ten years."

My breath snags when a greedy grin stretches across his mouth. Wetness puddles in my lower regions as his passionate eyes stare into mine. The yearning in his eyes sends heat sliding through my veins and my anticipation sitting on the edge of a very steep cliff.

"Hawke's outside—"

"We'll be quick."

My knees curve inward from the smirk carving on his mouth. Just from his smile alone, I can tell he doesn't know the meaning of a quickie.

"Are you sure you can handle this, Ava?" His coaxing tone makes me shudder with anticipation.

I nod. "I'll use two hands if I have to."

I smile, delighted my voice comes out in the husky rich purr I was aiming for. Hugo's chuckle rumbles through my body, clustering in my womb and making my pussy throb. I lean out, bracing my shaking hands on his thrusting chest. My womb tightens from the cajoling look in his eyes.

His gaze sweet-talks me without any words needing to leave his mouth. The heat in the room turns roasting when I lower my hand to grip his impressively sized erect cock. Air violently leaves his mouth when I squeeze him hard, kneading him through his jeans. My core clenches, loving the heaviness of his cock in my hand.

"The office was foreplay. Now it's time to finish what you started," I tease, staring into his vivacious eyes.

With a growl, he seals his lips over mine. My knees weaken when his tongue slips into my mouth. I sling my arms around his neck and return his kiss with brutal force. I gasp when he pushes me against the wall and turns his devotion to my aching-with-need breasts. I run my hands along the grooves of his tight pec muscles before lowering them to work on the buttons of his shirt.

My movements are frantic and hurried as every dream I've ever imagined transpires. My toes curl as his hand slips inside my panties, and he feels how drenched I am. The dampness between my legs hasn't lessened any since our time together in his office.

He pulls his lips away from my mouth, "You're so fucking wet," he hisses.

I don't bother answering him. Even if I wanted to grace him with a reply, I wouldn't be able to. My hands fly to lower his zipper, hating that I'm standing before him in only a meager pair of panties and he's still fully clothed. My breath hitches when I commence yanking his jeans down his thighs.

"You go commando now?"

When Hugo laughs, I realize I said my private thoughts out loud.

I gasp for a second time when his cock is freed from its tight restraints. *Jesus!* His penis is even larger than I remembered. My mouth salivates as my eyes absorb every spectacular inch of him. His cock is jutted out, thick and long. His balls are heavy and hanging on his thighs. He's man-scaped – not in a gross, weird way – in a hot, I can't wait to taste every inch of him way. I've seen a handful of naked men in my life, but none of their appendages have been as stellar as Hugo's. I'm honestly unsure if he'll fit inside me.

A hot trickle of desire floods my veins when my avid gaze of his body causes a bead of pre-cum to glisten on the end of his knob. If my pussy wasn't throbbing with eagerness, begging to be consumed by his cock, and Hawke wasn't waiting, I'd be dropping onto my knees to lick up every drop of his no doubt delicious cum, but for now, that will have to wait.

I swallow, hard, relieving my scorched throat when his jeans fall off his stout thighs and gather around his ankles. He hoists me up against the wall, holding me with ease with one hand while guiding his cock toward my ravenous womb with another. My insides clench when he pulls my panties to the side and braces the crown of his cock against the entrance of my pussy.

"You need to relax, babe, or I'll tear you in half."

My heart warms over his term of endearment. It's the first time he has called me a nickname. I unclench my vagina walls and thrust my tongue into his mouth. I kiss him with so much violence, his lips will be bruised in the morning. The wetness of my pussy increases as he guides the crown of his cock through my dripping folds, coating himself with my excitement. Sparks spasm my womb when the rim of his knob flicks my throbbing clit.

My back arches off the wall and tears prick my eyes when he bends his knees and thrusts upwards, hilting me in one fluid motion. A burning sensation shreds through my pussy, stealing my ability to breathe. Although accommodating his girth is more painful than having a root canal, there's also an element of carnal excitement to it, undoubtedly proving there's a very fine line between pleasure and pain.

"You not only have the sweetest pussy I've ever tasted, you also have the tightest," Hugo grunts, slowly gliding his shaft out of my stinging pussy.

My pussy ripples around him, coaxing him to stay, not willing to relinquish the feeling of having him so deep inside me. When every inch of his cock is out of me, I feel hollow, completely empty. Just as I'm about to protest the loss of his contact, he slams back into me. My head dips forward and my teeth gently gnaw on the skin of his shoulder, battling through a range of emotions. He pumps into me, hard and fast. The roughness of his strokes spurs on the sensuous moan purring from my parched lips.

Over time, the burning pain dampening my excitement shifts to a pleasurable tingle. The hot pants of Hugo's heavy breaths flutter my drenched neck when he mutters, "Fuck. I'm losing my fucking mind. Do you have any idea how fucking good you feel? Your tight pussy wrapped around my cock, squeezing me greedily."

The crudeness of his statement intensifies my pleasure. I lift my head from his sweat-drenched neck and brace it against the wall. He stares at me with wild, crazy eyes as he slows the tempo of his thrusts. His grip on my hips firms before he pulls me off the wall, giving him complete control of my body.

He carries me with ease, not the slightest bit impeded by my weight. A bead of sweat rolls down the side of his face as his lips seal over my budded nipple. I've never seen anything more erotic in my life than his ecstasy-riddled face as he fucks me into oblivion.

"This is better than any dream I've had of you," he grunts between pumps.

I moan a long, voluptuous moan that has every nerve in my body prickling. Any prior discomfort is a distant memory when his hand slithers from my hip to my pulsating clit. Dizziness clusters in my head, overwhelming me, when he rolls my clit with the pad of his thumb. My knees wobble as my race to climax gains momentum.

"I want you to come on my cock, Ava." He increases the quickness of his strokes. "I want to feel what my cock does to you. How it makes you feel."

When my eyes catch sight of his core-demolishing gaze, I lose all rational thought. Grunted, incoherent words tear from my throat as a climax rips through me so hard and fast, stars form in front of my eyes.

"God, yes, milk my cock, babe, show me how much you loved it."

The tightening of my pussy during orgasm sets Hugo off. His cock flexes, and he groans before his seed adds even more magnitude to my already soul-shattering climax. After a few more pumps, ensuring every drop of his cum is expelled, his movements still. He rests his sweat- drenched forehead against mine as we endeavor to get our breathing under control. The piquant aroma of sex mingled with sweating skin filters through the air, an intoxicating aroma that could be bottled up and sold for millions.

Hugo's eyes flutter open as he stares down at me. "That was. . ." He stops talking, seemingly at a loss for words.

"Perfect," I fill in, panting heavily.

An exhausted smile carves on his face before he nods.

"You're perfect." He seals his lips over mine, once again stealing my ability to breathe. His lips taste salty from the sweat running over them during our ignitable exchange.

"Everything about you is perfect," he mutters against my lips before peppering my jawline with kisses, compelling a new wave of excitement to form, but this time, it isn't in my pussy; it's in my heart.

As Hugo's attention reverts to my neck, heavy footsteps thud through my ears. Panic floods my veins when the handle on Hugo's childhood bedroom door lowers. A thankful sigh spills from my parched mouth when the intruders attempts to open the door are fruitless. Hugo must have locked the door at some stage between entering and now.

"Hugo, you better not be a-fucking-sleep," Hawke says, his abrupt tone bellowing through the door. "It's nearly midnight; hurry the fuck up."

The rattling of the door handle stops when Hugo answers, "I'll be out in a minute."

I moan when his hum vibrates through me since his cock is still inside me. My lips curve high when he places a kiss on the edge of my swollen mouth. Glancing into my eyes, he withdraws his half-masted penis. I'm not going to lie. Even knowing Hawke is outside waiting for him, and exhausted beyond comprehension, I'd happily go another round with Hugo. That was above and beyond anything I've ever experienced in my life. EVER!

When Hugo places me down onto my feet, I lean my back against the wall and close my eyes, endeavoring to fill my lungs with air before I faint. When air hisses from his parted lips, I flutter my eyes back open. My stomach tenses when I see the look on his face. Saying he has a horrified appearance would be an understatement. He looks truly mortified.

"Fuck." He runs his hand over the top of his head. "Fuck, fuck, fuck," he curses some more with his eyes arrested on something lower than my stomach.

Following his gaze, fresh tears prick my eyes. A trail of blood has run down my inner left thigh, puddling near the curve of my knee. My heart clutches as my eyes dart around the room, looking for an article of clothing I can use to cover myself. Standing before him naked while he's looking at me mortified is a brutal knock to my self-esteem. Noticing Hugo's undershirt on the ground, I bob down to pick it up. On the way, I notice Hugo's rapidly deflating cock also has a blood mark on it.

"Please tell me that's because you've only been with guys like Pencil Dick." Hugo's voice is a cross between mortified and angry.

I straighten my spine and peer into his repentant eyes before shaking my head.

"You're a virgin?"

Cringing at the loudness of his voice, my eyes shoot to his bedroom door, praying Hawke isn't still waiting behind it. As if this whole situation isn't embarrassing enough, having an additional witness would make it ten times worse. Satisfied the door handle isn't moving, I return my eyes to Hugo.

"Was," I squeak out, the hammering of my heart heard in my trembling word.

A stretch of silence crosses between us, awkward and heavy. My heart sinks to my stomach when regret forms in Hugo's eyes. I take a step toward him, wanting him to recall the affection displayed in our combustible exchange. An experience in which we shared so much emotion can't be regretted. It should be treasured and explored – not lamented. My heart crashes into the pit of my stomach when Hugo shakes his head and takes a step backward.

*I never thought I'd endure a greater pain than the rejection of my father, but this hurts ten times more.*

Ignoring the tear spilling down my cheek, I wipe the blood off my thigh. My movements are rushed as embarrassment festers in my heart.

After throwing his legs into his jeans and tucking his deflated cock into his trousers, Hugo paces into the bathroom. Hawke's frantic bangs on the door return as the grandfather clock in the hall loudly chimes through the house, advising it's midnight.

My tear-drenched eyes lift to Hugo when he ambles back into the room, holding a wash cloth in his hand. I bite the inside of my cheek, refusing to let any more tears fall from my eyes. The hot water on the cloth makes quick work of the blood smearing my leg. I flinch as my knees curve inward. Not because Hugo is being rough, but because even dying of embarrassment, my body relishes his closeness.

My neck cranks to the side when Hawke's deep voice barrels through the door. "Hugo, hurry the fuck up. I don't want my marriage cursed."

Hugo's remorse-filled eyes drift to mine when I still his hands from cleaning my leg. His hands are trembling so much, a shudder vibrates the entire length of my arm.

"Go." I nudge my head to the door. "I've got this."

My eyelids twitch as I fight to hold in my tears.

"It's fine. Hawke can fucking wait."

Gritting my teeth at the hurt projected in his tone, I snatch the washcloth out of his hand. The room shrinks in size when he stands from his crouched position, filling it with his large frame. My heart physically aches when I notice his shaking hands has spread to his entire body.

"They've waited years for this day, Hugo. Please don't ruin it for them."

Surprisingly, my tone comes out stronger than I'm expecting. Hugo stares at me as he runs his hand over the top of his head.

After a beat, he says. "Are you sure?" His tone sounds dejected.

Absorbing his clenched fist and standoffish demeanor, I nod.

"I'll see you tomorrow?" I ask, quoting the words he has said to me numerous times before.

When I hand him his shirt I collected from the floor, his brows furrow and he shakes his head. "Keep it."

His twitching mouth causes my lips to tingle when he places a kiss on the edge of my mouth. When he walks toward the door, his steps are urgent and quick, having him reach it in two heart-thrashing seconds. Hawke's loud bangs stop the instant Hugo unlatches the door lock. Just before he exits, Hugo's head cranks back, and he peers at me. His forlorn eyes are misting with fluid. I muster up the best fake smile I can, pretending the devastation in his eyes isn't shredding my heart into pieces.

Once the bedroom door closes with Hugo standing behind it, I crumble to the floor. Gathering my legs within my arms, I rest my tear-soaked cheek on my knees. Tonight was better than any fantasy I could have fathomed, but I never predicated the aftermath of finally handing in my V card.

It was never my intention to stay a virgin to the age of twenty-four. Life just happened, and sex never did. Growing up, I regularly used the excuse of my grandmother's trust for why I'd never go further than third base. When my father refused to let me to go to prom, my grandmother trusted me enough to drop me off at the dance without a single qualm. Unlike my father, she didn't believe spending time with her should overrule my need for social interaction.

Because she trusted me so much, I did everything in my power to keep her trust. When she passed away the year I began college, I thought my V card would soon expire. It never did. It was only after a third date with a guy I'd been lusting over in Bio-Chem did I realize it wasn't just my grandmother's trust I was striving to keep, it was also Hugo's. No man ever held a candle to him. Even though I've always denied it, I compared every man I dated to Hugo. When they failed to withstand my stringent Hugo test, my interest in them wavered.

This, ladies and gentlemen, is why until forty minutes ago, I was a twenty-four-year-old virgin.

## TWENTY-ONE

## AVA

I glance at Jorgie, who is eyeing me dubiously. She's been eyeing me with the same suspicious look since I entered the kitchen this morning. Her eyes have the same glimmer Chase's held when he topped off my champagne flute with a mimosa during breakfast. *Obviously, the giant stamp on your forehead announcing to the world that you're a virgin disappears the instant you hand in your purity credentials.*

"Is it good having Hawke home?" I use any tactic I can to shift the focus off myself. "It's only for a week and you won't get to go on your honeymoon until after the baby is born, but it must be nice waking up to a warm body lying next to you."

The smile Jorgie's been wearing all day widens. "Yes, you'd swear we're already on our honeymoon, if you know what I mean," she says with a wiggle of her brows.

I laugh before taking a sip of the fruity wine in my champagne flute. Even though my heart is hurting from my exchange with Hugo last night, I'm not going to let anything ruin my best friend's day. This is her day, and she deserves the focus to be solely on her.

"See, I told you all your worries wouldn't amount to anything.

Even if Hawke wasn't a fan of your basketball belly, you could have gotten on all fours, because from your backend, you can't even tell you're pregnant," I jest.

Jorgie's gorgeous giggle bounces around our elaborate surroundings. I love seeing her happy. All the worry fretting her beautiful face the past two weeks instantly vanished when Hawke walked in the door a day earlier than Jorgie was expecting.

When he was deployed, Jorgie was only a few months pregnant and wasn't showing yet, so she was petrified about Hawke's reaction when he saw her the first time with an expanded stomach. I was somewhat shocked by her admission. Jorgie and Hawke have a relationship every couple should strive to achieve. There are no two souls better matched than them.

"Are you ready?" questions Pierre, the eccentric hairdresser who has spent the last hour wrangling my unruly hair into smooth, straight locks.

Placing my champagne flute on the countertop, I chew on my lip before nodding. Only people who have African American heritage like mine would understand the complexity of maintaining my hair.

Because my hair was always a mass of ringlet curls, I never had it colored, and it most certainly never sat above my shoulders. I always envisioned that a shorter hairstyle would make it look like I stuck my finger into an electrical socket or even worse, like a poodle. Feeling daring, and with a gentle push from Pierre and Jorgie, I agreed to have my hair cut in a wispy wave design for the wedding. Pierre guarantees it will enhance my facial features while also being easier for me to maintain during the work week.

Exhaling a shaky breath, I flutter my eyes open. "Wow," is the only word I can formulate, so it's what I use.

I swivel in my chair to face Jorgie. "What do you think?" *Or better yet, what will your brother think?*

Jorgie's vibrantly painted lips twist as her eyes absorb every inch of my hair and made-up face in meticulous detail. My heart thrashes against my ribs, eagerly awaiting her reply.

"Remind me to hide a stick in my wedding dress," she says, her tone playful.

I arch my brow, clearly confused.

"To beat all the men away with," she adds on.

The first genuine smile of the day morphs onto my face.

"Are you ready?" I ask Jorgie. From the butterflies fluttering in my stomach, anyone would swear it's me about to get married, not Jorgie. I've never been more nervous.

"More ready than I've ever been," she replies, smiling broadly.

After ensuring the tulle on her dress has been ruffled and her veil is sitting right, I accept my boutique of irises and white roses from Kerri and take my spot in front of Jorgie. When "Everything" by Lighthouse filters through the air, Kirsty paces down the church aisle. Because we're hidden by a curved alcove of the church, I can't see any of the guests. A smile curves on my shaking lips when I hear Mrs. Marshall shushing them, demanding quiet as the wedding ceremony begins.

Once Kerri, bridesmaid number two, is halfway down the aisle, the wedding organizer gestures for me to go. I run my shaking hand down the purple satin material of my dress, roll my shoulders, and pace around the corner. When my eyes lift from the ground, the first person they lock onto is Hugo. My breath hitches, my strides faltering when I absorb how incredibly handsome he looks in a full black tuxedo with tails. His hair has been cut into a shorter, sexed-up style. His face is freshly shaven, and he fills out every inch of his suit perfectly. The visual of him standing at the end of a church aisle is so stimulating, the throbbing of my pussy overtakes the beating of my heart.

Hugo's lips part as his eyes vigorously assess the bridesmaid dress Jorgie selected for me to wear. Thankfully, Jorgie has remarkable style and selected a dress more suitable for a cocktail party than a wedding. It's gorgeous and more daring than anything I've ever worn before. There's a side split that's seductive but not trashy, and the back of the dress curves into a dovetail point. The silk material continues into a train that fans out behind me as I glide across the white carpeted aisle. When Hugo's eyes return to my face, an inhibited smile carves on his mouth. It isn't his normal cheeky grin; it's reserved and surprisingly shy. I return his smile before taking my spot at the side of the altar.

My eyes shift to the congregation of wedding attendees in enough time to witness Mrs. Marshall dabbing her eyes with a tissue. My heart squeezes, pleased that she's so proud. When the music switches to "Marry Me" by Train, Mrs. Marshall returns her tissues to her clutch purse and stands. Tears well in my eyes when Jorgie and Mr. Marshall step into the alcove at the end of the aisle. The crowd gasps at how beautiful Jorgie looks. I agree with their assessment. Jorgie looks exquisite in her wedding gown, but it's the joy invisibly radiating from her that makes her even more stunning. She's the happiest I've ever seen her.

Turning my head to the side, I discreetly dab my eyes with a tissue inconspicuously wrapped around my floral bouquet stem. Pierre would curse my head if all his hard work was ruined before the professional photos were taken. When I shift my gaze back to Jorgie, a flurry of blonde hair catches my eye. The veins in my neck thrum when my eyes lock in on the Queen of Bitches herself, Victoria Avenke, sitting in the second row. She's wearing a killer body-hugging teal blue dress, a seductive smirk, and a rampant spark of lust is firing her eyes. The grinding of my teeth overtakes my pulse thumping in my ears when I discover who her lust-riddled eyes are drinking in. *Hugo.* He must have invited her. It's the only logical reason as to why she would be here. I sure as hell know Jorgie would *never* invite Victoria to her wedding. She hates her even more than I do.

Anger overwhelms me when Hugo smiles at Victoria. Unlike the smile he issued me, hers isn't laced with unease and apprehension. I shift my eyes back to Jorgie, refusing to allow childish jealousy to ruin my happiness at watching my best friend marry the love of her life. The anger boiling my blood simmers when I see the love projecting out of Hawke's eyes as he looks down at Jorgie. Nothing but admiration spills from his eyes when he looks at her.

There's barely a dry eye in the house by the time the wedding ceremony is over. Placing a quick peck on Jorgie's cheek, I hand back her floral bouquet before gathering her train. Rose petals and rice float through the air as the newly wedded couple make their way outside the church. The anger hampering me evaporates when I see the happiness in Jorgie's love-sparked eyes. I stand to her side, proud as punch to be her Maid of Honor, as she greets her wedding guests.

By the time the wedding photographer finishes capturing the bridal party in a range of professional shots, my heart is hurting more than my blistered feet. I thought enduring Victoria's seductive gawking of Hugo the entire thirty minutes of the wedding ceremony was bad. She beat that tenfold when she had the audacity to follow the wedding party around the church grounds as we had professional photos taken.

*God forbid she was required to leave her* date's *side for forty minutes.*

Not only did she obviously ogle Hugo the entire time, she also openly flirted with him as well. I hope the wedding photographer has good Photoshop skills, as it's going to take him a lot of work to turn my rueful frown into a smile.

I plop into an empty chair at the side of the ballroom Jorgie's wedding reception is being held in, desperately needing a few minutes to gather my composure. Even though I've spent the past three hours in Jorgie's loved-filled bubble, nothing has doused the fury blackening my veins. My Maid of Honor title necessitates that I ensure Jorgie's every whim is taken care of, but I've been using it more as an avoidance tactic against Hugo. The closer I stand to Jorgie, the more Hugo stays away.

I jab a fork into the piece of fruit cake I'm holding, pretending the damage being inflicted is being done to certain parts of Hugo's body and not the poor, defenseless cake. Mrs. Mable, Jorgie's neighbor, sits in the spare seat next to me. After roaming her eyes over my face, she pats the top of my hand. "Too drunk to remember? Or regretting a drunk decision?"

My eyes rocket to hers. "I beg your pardon?" My loud roar gains me the attention of a handful of ladies seated across from us.

She rolls her rheumy eyes. "Young kids these days. Anyone would think you invented moonshine from the way you're acting." She leans in close to my side. "These crinkles you see on my face, they aren't wrinkles you're seeing."

"No, of course not," I confirm, shaking my head gently. Mrs. Mable would be easily in her eighties. Her face is well beyond wrinkled.

Her penciled brows hit her tight ringlets of silver hair. "They're life lines. My life map, showing I've lived my life to the fullest. Years of smiling, laughing, and crying. You won't see me prancing into a surgeon's office to get my face pumped with god-knows-what chemicals just so I can walk around looking like a sourpuss too scared to crack a smile for the fear of getting a new wrinkle."

Even in my woeful mood, I can't help but laugh at her statement.

"Life lines or not, that doesn't explain how you reached your conclusion," I say, placing the mutilated cake onto the table in front of me.

"Sheesh, I'm getting there." She waves her hand into the air as if she's swatting a fly. "Keep your panties on. You're not the one with your foot halfway in the grave."

Grinning, she places her teacup on the table. The floral china cup rattles in the saucer from her shaky movements. After dabbing her lips with a napkin to ensure she has no spilled tea on her mouth, she turns her eyes to me. I'd be lying if I said my insides weren't flipping like an Olympic gymnast. Other than Mrs. Marshall and Jorgie, I don't have any female companions I can talk to. Even though neither of the aforementioned would judge me, I can't discuss the particulars of this situation with them. That would be too awkward.

"Even with your pretty little mouth sagging downwards for a majority of the night , it can't hide the glimmer in your eyes. A glimmer that only happens after," Mrs. Mable coughs, clearing her throat. "Certain events."

I shyly smile and nod, acknowledging I understand her metaphor, while also confirming her suspicion.

"When Hugo came sauntering into the church, he looked like he'd been thrown under bus, but his eyes still had the same glimmer yours do. Putting two and two together, I gathered you two young'uns had an enjoyable night."

My cheeks get a rush of heat to them.

"I knew it!" she declares loudly when she sees my flushed expression.

Peering down at the thick gold band on her translucent-skinned hand, she spins the band around her wedding ring finger. "You should consider yourself lucky. My first too-drunk- to-remember encounter saw me waking up married to a stranger."

My eyes bulge. "Oh, wow. Did you get the marriage annulled?"

"Heavens no." Her eyes get a sheen of gloss over them. "A blessed sixty-five years of marriage I had to my darling Henry."

I smile at the adorable shimmer in her eyes.

"Don't let my happiness deceive you," she adds on, noticing my smile. "I gave my husband hell for months! Only once he proved his worth did I let him back into my bed."

The tears in her eyes dry and a new rascally glimmer forms in them. "That was a hard feat, as that boy knew how to shake the sheets, but by treating him mean, I kept him keen."

A genuine smile tugs my lips high. I don't know if you can legally adopt a grandmother, but if you can, I'm claiming this one.

She pats my knee. "Give him hell, sweetie. The meaner, the better."

My focus diverts from Mrs. Mable when a dark shadow envelopes the white cotton tablecloth. I don't need to lift my eyes to know who is standing before me. His woodsy smell gives it away.

Exhaling a nerve-eradicating breath, I raise my eyes to Hugo. He has removed his tuxedo jacket, and his bowtie has been unknotted and is hanging around his neck. Even with a heavy groove indented between his eyes, he looks scrumptiously delicious.

His eyes flick between mine for several heart-thrashing seconds before he asks, "Can we talk?" gesturing his head to the foyer at the front of the ballroom.

He tries to mask the nervousness in his voice, but the fast pace of his pulse bulging the veins in his neck hampers his tone. Although anger has never been a mood I can hold for long, today is an exception to that rule. Because it's not just anger I'm harboring, it's downright fury.

"No." My reply is swift and precise.

Hugo balks before staring at me like I've suddenly grown a second head. His eyes drift to Mrs. Mable as he crouches down in front of me. He tilts in close to my side, vainly trying to get a small skerrick of privacy in a room filled with hundreds of wedding attendees. The hairs in my nose tingle when the heavy scent of the alcohol on his breath filters through my nostril.

"Please, Ava." He stares into my eyes. "We need to talk."

Crossing my arms in front of my chest, I shake my head. "We have *nothing* to discuss."

Mrs. Mable's hand shoots out to pat my knee, encouraging my take-no-prisoners stance that's slipping from my grasp with every second I glance into Hugo's glistening baby blues.

The hairs on the nape of my neck prickle when Hugo's breath flutters my earlobe. "You either come with me willingly or I'll throw you over my shoulder and drag you out of here, kicking and screaming."

My mouth gapes. "You wouldn't dare."

My heart beats double-time when a boyish grin etches onto his sinful mouth. "I've never backed away from a dare, Ava; today is not going to be any different."

I huff and strengthen my stance. When I turn my eyes to look at anything but Hugo's sinfully gorgeous face, I realize our little spectacle has gained us the attention of a handful of eyes, including Mrs. Marshall.

"You have to the count of three, Ava," Hugo warns. "One, two--"

"What am I, five years old?" I retaliate, turning my eyes back to his.

"If you're going to act like a child, I'll treat you like one."

My mouth forms an O as my face reddens with anger. Before any response can escape my lips, the wedding MC announces it's time for the bridal waltz. I inwardly sigh, grateful for the distraction. My pleasure doesn't last long when the MC requests the attendance of the wedding party to dance alongside the bride and groom.

A grin carves on Hugo's mouth as he stands from his crouched position and cocks his elbow. "May I have this dance?"

Even with my insides quivering from the seductiveness in his tone, I don't allow my outer-shell to exhibit my excitement. The rugged grin on his face vanishes when I stand from my chair, sidestep him, and storm toward the dance floor. I only manage to hit the edge of the mahogany floor before Hugo's long strides catch up to me.

I keep my eyes on Jorgie and Hawke, remembering this day is about them. Hugo pulls me in close to his body, preparing to dance. Even fuming with anger, my body melts into his embrace. I huff when "I Don't Wanna Miss a Thing" by Aerosmith booms out of the speakers. *Of course Jorgie would pick the longest song in the history of songs to dance to.*

My eyes rocket to Hugo when he mutters, "What the fuck is wrong with you today?" only loud enough for me to hear. "Jorgie has an excuse for her erratic mood swings, but what possible excuse could you have?"

*Assholes who have sex with you and then turn up to the next day with a date.* Instead of saying what I really want to, I keep my mouth shut. Hugo's eyes shift between mine for several awkward seconds before his spine suddenly straightens.

"Are you on your period?" he brazenly questions.

Anger boils my blood. I try to pull away from him, but he strengthens his grip, foiling my quick getaway. "Nice try, but you still have *well* over four minutes before you're going anywhere."

I glare into his eyes, delivering every obscenity running through my brain without words. He returns my stare, minus my blatant fury.

By the time the song reaches halfway, I'm exhausted. Not just physically, but emotionally as well. I hardly slept a wink last night and spending the past several hours dodging Hugo is exhaustive work, but the crippled ache in my heart is more from dancing with him the past two minutes. We've danced previously, but it was to gritty club music, not a love song. Every word Steven Tyler sings has the constrictive hold on my heart firming.

"Why did you bring her?" I ask, no longer able to harbor my anger.

My nails dig into Hugo's shoulders when he says, "Who?"

Gritting my teeth, I nudge my head to Victoria entering the dance floor on the arm of an older gentleman with strands of silver hair on his temples. Fury unlike anything I've ever felt before shreds through my body when Hugo follows my direction, and he has the absurdity to laugh. *I'm glad he finds the situation amusing. I'm anything but amused.*

"You've been avoiding me because you're jealous?" He laughs.

Snarling, I slap his heaving-with-laughter chest before slipping out of his embrace. He snags my wrist and drags me back to him. My nipples bud when my breasts push up against his firm pectoral muscles. I glide my eyes around the people surrounding us, battling to keep my tears at bay.

When Hugo catches my disarrayed face, he mutters, "Vicky is Hawke's stepsister."

My eyes snap to his, seeking any untruth in his statement. The rhythm of my heartbeat recommences when I see the honesty in his eyes.

"I didn't invite her," he confirms, staring into my eyes.

*Oh.*

A bucket of water is thrown on the fire raging in the pit of my stomach, suffocating my anger in one quick swoop. I try to say something to Hugo, to apologize for my appalling behavior, but my mouth refuses to relinquish my words. Instead of kneeling and begging for clemency, I peer into his eyes, silently relaying my apologies.

When the bridal waltz is over, wedding attendees congregate onto the dance floor and the bridal party couples separate, returning to their respective partners. A dash of excitement surges through me when Hugo doesn't release me from his hold, he pulls me in deeper. Any embarrassment about last night dissipates as he stares into my eyes while swinging his hips in sync to the music. The dynamic between us is as intense as ever: fire sparking and combustible.

Two seconds later, Hugo suddenly stiffens.

"Excuse me, I'm cutting in."

Turning my eyes, I catch the amused face of Marvin. He's decked out in a full black suit with a light blue dress shirt. His hair is gelled in a side part, and his eyes are hazy, but the most notable feature of his face is the arrogant grin he's wearing.

"Back off, Marvin," Hugo mutters, annoyed at being interrupted.

Marvin scoffs. "I can't dance with my date?" he queries with his brow curved high.

A jolt of pain spasms my hip when Hugo strengthens his grip on my body. When his eyes turn down to me, I take a step backward. His eyes are crammed with irritation.

"Marvin's your date?" he questions.

His angry snarl has my heart rate racing, but it isn't in fear; it's in excitement. Cowardly, I nod. Air blasts out of Hugo's nose before he relinquishes me from his hold. A shiver courses through my body when he steps away, taking his warmth with him.

"Please, don't let me stop you from dancing with your *date*," Hugo snarls.

With that, he stalks to the bar without a backward glance. I stand frozen, unable to decide what to do in a situation like this. Yes, unfortunately, Marvin is here as my date, but in my defense, I asked him to come weeks ago, way before I knew he had too many of my father's characteristics, and way before Hugo was back in the picture. No woman in their right mind wants to attend a wedding without a plus one, so I stupidly asked Marvin to come with me. When he failed to show up to the wedding ceremony, I assumed he wasn't coming.

Marvin clasps my wrist and yanks me into his chest. "You look beautiful, Ava." He rakes his eyes over my body.

Swiftly, he lowers in and plants a kiss right on my lips before I have the chance to object. Even with the blare of the music blasting my eardrums, I swear I hear Hugo's furious growl boom across the room, quickening my pulse.

"Hi Marvin. I must have missed you at the ceremony?"

His face scrunches. "I didn't go to the ceremony. Snooze fest." His tone is arrogant and clearly shows he's intoxicated.

"I thought it was lovely service. Very romantic."

"You would say that. You have a cunt."

I balk, disgusted at his use of the C word.

When the song ends, I politely excuse myself and attempt to walk away from Marvin. I need to find Hugo and explain the circumstances of Marvin's arrival. I know what it felt like when I thought he'd brought Victoria as his date, so I can understand his angry response.

Marvin clutches onto my wrist. "Just one more dance," he requests, pleading into my eyes.

He stumbles in his inebriated state, bumping into Kerri and her dance partner.

"Sorry," he apologizes, half-chuckling.

I wrap my arms around him to steady his heavy sways. "Have you eaten anything tonight?"

Air seeps from my lips when he shakes his head. Taking my aide in keeping him on his feet as an open invitation, Marvin slithers his hand down my back and pulls my body flush against his. My skin crawls when he taps his fingers on the curve of my lower back. One inch lower and he'd be touching my backside.

"Thank you for the dance," I say, pulling away from his embrace. "But I have to go."

My brisk strides halt when Marvin says, "Did you know my dad is considering giving my partnership to Daniel?" His amused expression has changed to obfuscated.

Pain squeezes my heart. As much as Marvin irks me, we do have some similarities with our family situation, but there's one big difference between us. He still craves the approval of his dad, whereas I learned years ago I'm never going to get my dad's seal of approval.

I peer into Marvin's downcast eyes. "I'm sure he doesn't mean it, Marvin. You're his son. He'll always support you."

When he stumbles again, I re-secure my grip around his waist and guide him to the bar at the side of the kitchen, wanting to get him as far away as possible from Jorgie's guests before he makes a fool of himself, or even worse – me.

It takes several tedious minutes to assist Marvin across the expansive ballroom. Although my gaze remains planted on the floor, ensuring I don't trip over Marvin's stumbling feet, I can feel Hugo's eyes on me. When I reach the bar, I gesture for Marvin to sit on a stool before moving to the kitchen. When I first enter the industrial-sized kitchen, it appears empty.

"Hello?" I call out, pacing further inside.

A lady with a tight bun pops out of a walk-in fridge and greets me with a smile.

"Umm... I have a friend a little drunk outside. I was hoping you might have something that could help absorb the alcohol sloshing in his stomach?"

Her smiles enlarges before she moves toward a massive walk-in pantry at the side of kitchen. My stomach rumbles when the smell of cranberry sauce filters through my nose. Since I was fuming with anger, I didn't touch the confit stuffed duck leg they served at dinner. It smelled delicious, but my stomach was swirling so much that I couldn't risk placing food in there. My lips curve upwards when the lady paces back to me with a bag of bread in one hand and a plate of the confit stuffed duck leg in another.

"For your friend," she says in a thick, heavy accent, gesturing to the bread. "For you." My mouth salivates when she hands me the overflowing plate of food.

"Thank you so much," I say as graciously as possible, my insides beaming with excitement.

My eager steps back to Marvin falter when my eyes lock in on Hugo. He's sitting at the end of the bar, slamming down shots of whiskey like they're soda water. I hope it's an open bar or his bank account will be hurting in the morning from the fifteen-dollar-a-nip whiskey he's guzzling.

My hackles bristle when Victoria prances toward Hugo. Snarling at me, she leans in to Hugo's side and whispers something in his ear. Ignoring the desire to peg a roll at the back of Victoria's head, I place my plate on the countertop and plop my backside on the spare stool next to Marvin.

"Ava, you're a doll." Marvin snags the duck leg off my plate and devours it as if he's never been fed.

Rolling my eyes at his rudeness, I rip off chunks of the bread and dip it into the cranberry sauce. I endeavor to keep my eyes off Hugo, but no matter how hard I fight, my eyes incessantly peer at him. I can't help it. He's a magnet, and I'm attracted to him. Although he continues to exchange words with Victoria, his body language gives no indication that he's appreciating her attention. If anything, he looks annoyed. Once Marvin has consumed every smidgen of food on my plate, he lifts his eyes to mine. The concept of filling his belly with food instead of alcohol seems to have worked. His eyes are no longer glassy and bloodshot. They appear clearer with a slight hint of arrogance.

"Did you want to get out of here?" he questions.

I can't miss the ambiguity in his tone.

Without hesitation, I shake my head. "It's my best friend's wedding. I'm her Maid of Honor." *I also don't want to go anywhere with you.*

He shrugs. "So?"

My teeth grit. "It's rude to leave a wedding before the bride and groom." My tone is bitchy.

"So?" he replies again, chuckling.

He either can't read the signs I'm giving, or he's choosing to ignore them. Either way, my patience is wearing thin.

"How about I call you a taxi?" I suggest, slipping off the barstool.

He waggles his brows. "Sure, you can call *us* a taxi."

Inwardly gagging from the gleam in his eyes, I pace to the coatroom in the foyer to retrieve my cell phone from my handbag. Thankfully, since it's Sunday, the cab company advises a taxi should arrive within the next ten minutes. I store my phone in my clutch purse and place it under my arm before ambling out of the coatroom. Upon entering the foyer, I spot Marvin standing at the side. When he notices me approaching, he shoves his hands into his pockets and rocks on his heels. I can't miss the look of suggestion on his face. He looks like a man about to go on a hunt. Little does he know, he has his sight set on the wrong target.

My hesitant steps to Marvin freeze when Hugo charges across the room. His fists are balled at his side, and the veins in his neck are throbbing. Noticing my panicked expression, Marvin's eyes follow my gaze. When he spots Hugo's furious composure, his throat works hard to swallow. The speed of Hugo's steps are unbridled as he slams into Marvin, ramming him to the ground with a stomach-churning thud.

I stumble back, sickened by the harshness of their impact on the marble floor. My hand shoots up to cover my gaped mouth when Hugo's fist connects hard with Marvin's chin before they lower to pummel his ribs over and over again. Marvin attempts to fight back, but he's no match against a man of Hugo's size, much less his fury.

"Hugo, stop!" I scream when pain tears from Marvin's mouth and echoes in the silence of the foyer.

My panicked squeals gain the attention of the wedding attendees inside the ballroom. Tears form in my eyes when Hawke rushes out of the double wooden doors. My tears fall when Marvin's wildly flying fist connects with Hugo's right cheek. Even copping a hard blow, Hugo continues to wallop the living hell out of Marvin. He's relentless, pounding his fists into his body with so much force, I'm sure Marvin will sustain broken bones.

"What the fuck is going on?" Hawke's eyes drift between Hugo and Marvin wrestling on the floor and me.

More tears escape my eyes when I timidly shake my head, advising I'm unaware of what has caused Hugo's anger. Although he has always had an edge of jealously when it comes to me, it has never been this wrathful. Relief engulfs me when Hawke drags a red-faced Hugo off Marvin. My stomach churns when Marvin lurches onto his feet and spits on Hugo's chest. Marvin's face is as red as Hugo's. His coloring isn't caused by anger. It's from the pounding he copped from Hugo's fist.

"Stay the fuck away from her!" Hugo's angry voice reverberates off the walls. "If you go near her, I'll—"

"Get some of your crim buddies to come and teach me a lessen?" Marvin interrupts, his lips forming a vicious snarl.

Hugo balks, seemingly surprised by Marvin's taunt. I'm also taken aback. *Crims?*

"You didn't think I knew?" Marvin sneers. "I know everything."

The pompousness of his tone fuels Hugo's annoyance. He pulls out of Hawke's grasp and throws a hard right swung fist against Marvin's face before Hawke can to stop him.

"You know fucking nothing." Hugo's voice is the deepest I've ever heard. "You're that stupid, you can't even tell she isn't pure anymore," he roars as Hawke drags him away from Marvin.

My heart plummets into my swirling stomach.

A menacing grin carves on Hugo's face when he notices the shocked expression on Marvin's face.

Loving that he's wiped Marvin's arrogant smirk right off his face, Hugo continues to taunt, "I beat you to the punch. I already fucked her. Hard and fast against the wall. She loved every goddamn minute of it."

*Oh god. I think I'm going to be sick.*

My stomach swirls as my eyes shift around at the gathering of people watching the spectacle between Marvin and Hugo. I inwardly sigh, eternally grateful. Other than Mrs. Mable watching me with vigilance, no one is none the wiser that Hugo's statement refers to me; all their eyes remain on Hugo and Marvin.

Not even five seconds later, the rug is pulled out from underneath my feet when Marvin swings his narrowed gaze to me.

"Is it true?" he questions, staring straight at me. "Did you fuck Hugo?"

Every set of eyes in the foyer snap to me. I feel physically ill when I notice within the numerous pairs of eyes are Hugo and my parents. I don't need to answer Marvin's question, the evidence is exposed by my flushed cheeks and tear-welling eyes.

"Fuck," Hugo curses under his breath when his head cranks to the side and he notices me standing here, vainly trying to ignore all the people gawking at me.

When he takes a step toward me, I angrily shake my head. I've never been more mortified in my life. My chin quivers when I turn my eyes to Mrs. Marshall. Out of everyone here, she deserves my most sincerest apology. I not only ruined her daughter's wedding, I disrespected her by sleeping with her son under her roof.

"I'm sorry," I mumble, shaking.

A tear rolls down her cheek when she nods, accepting my apology. After one last glance at the hundreds of people gawking at me, I dash toward the double revolving doors of the hotel. Gratitude floods me when I spot the taxi I ordered for Marvin idling on the curb.

"The corner of Marcia and Trate," I request to the cab driver when I dive into the backseat.

Hugo charges out the hotel's double glass doors just as the taxi pulls away from the curb.

"Did you want me to stop?" asks the taxi driver with his dark eyes peering at me in the rearview mirror.

Wiping my hand under my nose, I shake my head. My heart hammers against my ribs, no doubt matching Hugo's as he chases the taxi half way down the street and around the corner. Only once his frame is nothing but a blur in the distance do I allow my first tears to fall.

## TWENTY-TWO

# HUGO

"I'm sorry, Sir. This bar has a very strict policy on limiting the drinks of intoxicated patrons."

"Are you kidding me?" I retort, standing from the wooden bar stool my half-drunk ass is precariously sitting on. "I'm not even close to drunk."

The hiccup sounding from my mouth douses the strength of my statement, and don't even get me started on my inability to stand straight. After guzzling enough whiskey to make most men slip into an alcohol-induced coma, my body is only just registering a warm buzz. Since alcohol was the only thing supporting me through the debacle of my life the past year, it takes me a lot to get drunk.

"Give him the bottle."

Turning my eyes, I spot Isaac standing in the middle of the out-of-date bar I'm drowning my sorrows in. His hand rests on the middle button of his suit jacket as his eyes glare at the bartender.

"If I'm required to voice my request again, I won't use words the second time around," he warns, ambling closer to the bar.

The bartender's eyes shift between Isaac and me before he leaves the half-empty bottle of whiskey on the counter and stands at the far end of the bar.

"Good choice." Isaac removes his black suit jacket and slings it over the countertop.

"Is this one of your clubs?" I ask, my words slurred as the alcohol I've been downing seeps into my veins.

A chuckle escapes my mouth when Isaac shakes his head.

"Then what are you doing here?" I pour myself a generous serving of scotch.

He doesn't answer my question. He just sits quietly in the vacant stool next to me and turns his eyes down to my busted knuckles.

Once his silence becomes too much for me to bear, I ask, "Wanna play a game?"

Isaac's brow etches high on his face, seemingly unimpressed by my suggestion.

"Come on. You want me to be your right hand man, don't you?" I slur.

A smirk carves on Isaac's mouth before he curtly nods.

"Well the right hand can't operate without knowing what's going on with the left hand."

After a beat, Isaac asks, "What type of game?"

I nearly vault out of my chair, shocked he finally spoke.

"Twenty questions," I reply, grinning.

Isaac's furious growl makes the bartender's thighs quake.

"Not your standard school yard game. Let's up the ante."

"I'm listening," Isaac interrupts, his tone stern.

"Every time one of us shares something *shocking*, we have to take a drink of whiskey."

Isaac's lips purse as he considers my suggestion. After a short period of silence, he gestures for the bartender to bring him a bottle of whiskey from the top shelf. When the bartender begrudgingly does as instructed, Isaac snags a shot glass from the wire rack in front of us.

Once both of our glasses are full to the brim with whiskey, he says. "You go first."

An hour later, we've consumed more liquor than a drunken sailor on shore leave.

"That guy I saw leaving your office after our first meeting, is he a mob boss?" I question, my words badly slurring.

Isaac's dark eyes drift to the bartender. When he discovers he's more interested in watching a re-run of a Red Sox game than us, his eyes turn back to me.

"Yes," he replies, his voice unwavering.

"Is that a good or a bad thing?" he adds on when neither of us reach for our shot glass.

"Fuck'd if I know, but I'm thirsty," I say before downing my nip.

He smirks before lifting the shot glass to his mouth. Glass clanging on the wooden countertop sounds over my laughter when he slams his glass onto the counter and his face grimaces. The whiskey he selected might be expensive, but it tastes like shit.

"You couldn't have gotten drunk at one of my clubs?" He cringes as the bile flavor slides down his throat to settle in his gut.

I laugh and shake my head. "Your whiskey is too expensive for my blood."

He doesn't attempt to refute the accuracy of my statement.

"Your turn," I say.

"Why haven't you cashed the check I gave you?"

My eyes snap to his. "Because you said I had to talk to a shrink."

He shakes his head. "So until I remove that stipulation from your contract, you're going to keep working for me for free?"

Air whizzes in my nose. "Dreaming," I say with a chuckle.

We both laugh, and I drink my nip. There couldn't be anything more *shocking* than finding out I have to talk to a shrink as a requirement of my employment. A grin tugs my lips high when Isaac also downs his nip.

"Not a fan of therapists?"

He shakes his head.

Once our drinks are replenished, I ask, "Why are you sitting so gingerly in your chair?"

Isaac's eyes rocket to mine. Although his exterior is one of the hardest I've ever seen, I noticed a wince cross his face when he first sat down earlier tonight.

Just when I think he isn't going to answer, he mutters, "I had an operation." He coughs, clearing his throat, "Down there."

My abrupt movement to secure my shot glass knocks over both glasses, spilling fragrant whiskey all over the bar. I recant my previous response. Having your manhood operated on would beat talking to a shrink tenfold.

"Should you be drinking if you just had an operation?" I ask when Isaac refills our glasses.

"Probably not, but do you think I care?"

After downing his latest serving, he runs the back of his hand over his mouth. "Why are you getting drunk in this shitty ass pub instead of celebrating your sister's wedding across the street?"

You'd think I'd be surprised he knows about Jorgie's wedding. I'm not. I learned early on that Isaac knows everything. If he doesn't know, he'll find someone who does.

"I snatched the virginity of the only girl I've ever cared about." .

I down my nip of whiskey, but Isaac's remains untouched.

"Come on," I say in a long drawl. "That deserves a drink."

"Not necessarily," Isaac responds. "I could think of far worse things than the woman I love only being with me."

"It's not that," I reply. "It's the fact I fucked her against the wall, in my childhood bedroom, without preparing her first. I hurt her."

Even with the thick slur impeding my voice, I can't miss the shaky rattle inhibiting my vocal cords. Although I've said I never wanted to have sex with a virgin before, I'm not upset Ava was a virgin. I'm angry that I hurt her.

Isaac peers into my eyes before he downs his nip.

"You think that's bad, wait until you hear the rest," I huff. "I announced her impurity to a room full of people that included both sets of our parents."

Isaac leans over the bar and snags two full-sized glasses off a wire rack. Remaining quiet, he fills them to the very brim, emptying the three hundred dollar bottle of whiskey.

"Is that the reason you have busted knuckles?" He returns his eyes to me.

I nod. "The guy she brought to my sister's wedding is a fucking douche. I was already struggling to keep a rational head when they were dancing. So when the bartender told me he was bragging about taking Ava home to *pop her cherry*, it fucking killed me. I didn't want him to touch her. I hate the idea of anyone touching her. I want to be the only one who gets to touch her," I slur as the heaviness on my chest turns lethal.

"Then be the only one," Isaac says, making me realize I rambled some of my quiet thoughts out loud, instead of keeping them in my head.

"If she's truly the one girl you want, don't wait. Because if you lose her, you'll regret it every day of your life."

Isaac lifts his glass of whiskey to his mouth and guzzles down a large portion of his serving. My brain signals for my hand to reach for my glass, but no matter how many times I stretch out my arm, my hand refuses to grasp the glass. Nothing Isaac said was shocking to me. Ava's always been the only woman I've wanted. She'll always be the only woman I'll ever want. Our connection is so strong, it couldn't even be broken with years of absence.

I just hope I can get her to forgive me.

## TWENTY-THREE
## HUGO

I shake my head when Hawke waves a beer in front of my face.
"I'm good." I gesture to the red plastic cup in my hand, half full of soda.

He places the bottle onto the table in front of me. "In case you change your mind." He takes the seat next to me on the double-seater love swing in his backyard. "So what's the deal? I've never seen you turn down free beer before."

My nose scrunches as I lift my shoulder into a shrug. "I learned the hard way that drinking makes you do stupid things."

"Stupid things or people?"

I barge him with my shoulder. "Do you need a reminder about the number of times I saved you from chewing your arm off in the morning? You have the worst pair of beer goggles I've ever seen a drunk man wear. When you're drunk, you think Betty White is hot."

Hawke chuckles a full-hearted laugh. "Come on, even if I wasn't drunk, I'd tap that. She's a silver fox."

"Would have tapped that. *Would have*," he adds on when he catches my furious glare.

He smirks against the rim of his beer before taking another swig. "I'm starting to wonder if I've been transported to an alternative universe."

"It's the pregnancy hormones running through her body; you'll soon adjust."

He smiles. "I'm not talking about Jorgie. I'm talking about you and Ava."

My heart freezes at the mention of Ava's name, but thankfully, my outward appearance gives no indication to my heart's betrayal. I haven't seen Ava the past week, but don't think that's from a lack of trying. After leaving Isaac in the desolate bar, I hailed a cab and headed straight to our apartment building. I don't know if Ava was inside her apartment, but she refused to open the door, even with me threatening to kick in it.

For a woman who gains the devotion of every man when she enters the room, when she wants to remain hidden, Ava becomes the invisible woman. I've stalked her apartment, her work place, and Jorgie's house numerous times the past week, and I still haven't seen her. All I want is the opportunity to apologize for my appalling behavior.

I'm man enough to admit when I make a mistake. I was in the wrong for the way I behaved at the wedding. In my drunken state, I reacted first and sought questions later. Even if Ava never wants to see me again, I still want the chance to say I'm sorry. I thought a hangover was the worst thing you could wake up with after a heavy night of drinking, but the guilt of knowing I was the cause of Ava's tears beats that tenfold.

"Is Ava coming tonight?" I grip the cup tighter, trying to ignore the tremor shaking my hand.

With Hawke returning to Iraq tomorrow, Jorgie decided to throw him an impromptu going away party. I'm hoping Ava's admiration for Hawke will entice her out of hiding.

"I wanna hope so, considering she's already here."

My eyes rocket to his. There's no chance in hell he missed the eagerness in my reaction. "Where is she?"

He smirks against the rim of his beer. "In the kitchen, slamming down tequila shots like they're lemonade."

I bound out of my chair and am halfway across the deck before the word "kitchen" fully escapes his lips. I hear Ava's laugh before I see her, a beautiful soulful giggle echoing down the hall. When I enter the kitchen, she acts like she doesn't notice my presence, but I didn't miss her posture straightening and her breathing pattern altering.

My pulse lowers, and for the first time in my life, panic grips my heart. Lifting a shot of tequila to her mouth, Ava downs it without bothering to lick the salt on her hand or suck on a wedge of lemon. My eyes shoot to the half-empty bottle sitting at the side of her hand. *I hope that wasn't a full bottle. If it was, she's going to cop it in the morning.*

Jorgie's eyes drift between Ava and me for several terrifying seconds. After making an excuse to leave, Jorgie scurries out of the kitchen, leaving me alone with Ava. It took Jorgie four days to talk to me after her wedding. That was a new record for Jorgie. If I didn't agree to give her the CD from her twenty-first birthday party, I have no doubt her radio silence would still be in effect.

When Ava realizes we're alone, she snatches the bottle of tequila off the counter and ambles to the door. My hand shoots out to seize her wrist before she can exit. Although she remains facing the door, she doesn't attempt to pull away from my embrace.

"I just want a chance to tell you how s—"

Before I can issue my apology, Hawke's cousin and ex-frat brother, Aspen, enters the kitchen. He smirks a greeting at Ava and me before walking to the fridge to help himself to a bottle of beer. My jaw ticks as I impatiently wait for him to leave, my agitation provoked by his vivacious assessment of Ava's body.

Once the kitchen door swings shut with Aspen behind it, I return my attention to Ava. Two seconds after Aspen leaves, another frat brother enters the kitchen.

*Fuck my life!*

Once we're joined in the kitchen by another body, I realize the room housing the only fridge in the entire Hawke residence isn't a suitable location for a deep and meaningful conversation. The hairs on Ava's neck prickle when I lean in close to her side. I'm not going to lie, my chest puffed high at her reaction.

"We'll finish this conversation later... in private."

"I'm not going anywhere with you," she sneers.

A soft moan spills from her lips when I flatten my palm across her stomach and pull her backward until her back is flush with the front of my body. My cock stirs, stimulated by her closeness.

"I'm sorry for what I did, Ava, but until you hear me out, I'm going to become your new best friend."

Her neck twists and she looks up at me, gauging the truth of my threat.

"Fine," she huffs, intuiting that I have every intention on following through with my threat. "But not here. Not now."

"When?"

She pats her hands down her dress. "Oh, darn it, I forgot to bring my planner with me." Her lips twist, and her shoulders rise as she inhales a dramatic breath. "I'll have my people call your people; we'll do lunch."

I smirk. Even pissed, she can still make me laugh. That's a very rare find in a woman these days. Her sassy primadonna attitude dulls when I lift my pinkie into the air.

"Promise?" I ask, knowing Ava will never renege on a pinkie promise.

Through gritted teeth, she says. "I promise."

As hard as it is for me to do, I let her go.

Hawke takes the spare seat next to me. "Don't do anything you may regret in the morning."

"Who said I'll regret it?" I respond, peering down at my swollen knuckles.

*I certainly didn't regret teaching Marvin a lesson.*

My eyes lift from my knuckles when Jorgie comes frolicking across the room to sit on Hawke's lap. When her lips seal over his mouth, I return my eyes to Ava. For the past two hours, Ava has been downing liquor like it's soda, batting her eyelashes, and openly flirting with every one of my single ex-frat brothers. As if that isn't bad enough, for the past thirty minutes, she's been dancing with Rhys Motherfucking Tagget. Yes, that's his real middle name. Well, it's what I've christened him anyway.

"You don't think you should say something to Ava?" I suggest, nudging Jorgie with my elbow.

Jorgie stops sucking face with Hawke and turns her furious eyes to me. "And what exactly should I say? Hey Ava, you're nearly twenty-five years old, you don't have to work in the morning, and you look smoking hot in that sexy little number, but can you please go home because my brother is about to burst a vein in his temple over you dancing with another guy?!"

The tick hammering my jaw the past two hours gains a new spasm. "If that will stop her from making a fool of herself, yeah, say that."

Jorgie scoffs. "I'm not going to kick her in the shins when she's finally having a little bit of fun. Besides, she could do far worse than snag a man like Rhys Tagget."

"Snag a man? She needs you to save her from his clutches not throw her toward him. She deserves better than him!"

Jorgie's brow cocks. "Keep lying to yourself, Hugo. Cause you know as well as I do, Rhys is one of the rare good guys in this town: a gifted surgeon with an extremely large heart."

"Good guy or not, he's looking at Ava like she's a dessert menu," I yell as the heaviness plaguing my chest the past week amplifies.

"She's safe with Rhys. He won't do anything to her that Ava doesn't want him to do."

Her reassuring words don't offer me any comfort. If anything, they agitate me more. "Maybe Ava doesn't want him to touch her," I interject, my jealousy building even more quickly than my temper.

Jorgie scoffs. "Get your head out of the clouds, Hugo. Every girl in this town wants a slice of the Rhys Tagget pie. Ava included."

Our heated argument ends when a growl rumbles from Hawke's stern, shut mouth. Jorgie's cheeks go a shade of pink as her eyes drift back to Hawke. She looks like a kid who got caught with her hand in the cookie jar. Hawke's jaw muscle is tense, and he glares at Rhys with the same "I want to rip your head off and stick it up your ass" look I've been giving him the past thirty minutes.

"Every girl but me, baby." Jorgie's tone is super high and girly as she tries to pacify Hawke's furious wrath. "I'll never want anyone but you." She cups his cheeks in her hands. "I'm all yours."

Hawke's gaze softens when he turns his eyes back to Jorgie's. I suppress a gag when he says, "You better come and show me then," not attempting to hide the sexual undertone in his voice.

My wish for alcohol has never been more paramount than when I see a spark of lust ignite in my baby sister's eyes. With a smile, Jorgie stands from Hawke's lap and saunters to the stairwell.

Hawke gestures to Jorgie that he'll be there in a minute before he lowers his eyes to me. "If you don't like what Ava is doing, stop her from doing it."

"How am I supposed to do that?" My words come out in quick succession as anger takes control of my vocal cords. "Drag her out of here kicking and screaming?"

Hawke smiles. "It might be the first, but it certainly won't be the last," he says before stalking to the stairwell.

When Jorgie notices him prowling toward her like a panther on the hunt, she squeals before darting up the stairs. Hawke is on her heels before she hits the second step. My gaze turns down to the plastic cup of Coca-Cola as my mind works to unjumble the riddle issued in Hawke's statement. I've heard it before, but I can't recall where.

Before my brain can contemplate what Hawke meant, Ava's husky laugh sounds through my ears. Lifting my eyes, I am met with her being dipped by Rhys. Her ponytail is loose and hanging halfway down her head, her skin is flushed and covered with the slickness of sweat, and her eyes are bloodshot and glassy from the copious amount of liquor she has drank, but she can still stop traffic. And from the gleam in Rhys' eyes, he fucking knows it.

The instant Rhys flips Ava up and her exquisite eyes lock with mine, the meaning behind Hawke's statement crashes into me hard and fast. It wasn't something I heard before. It was something I said. To him. It was the very first time he dragged Jorgie out of a sorority party kicking and wailing over his shoulder.

They weren't even a couple at that stage, but seeing him have enough gall to go up against a girl as stubborn as Jorgie, I realized in an instant Jorgie had met her match. They've been inseparable since that night. I don't know if Hawke is saying he thinks the same about Ava and me, but I'm no longer willing to stand by and watch Ava make a headless mistake all because I pissed her off.

The vein in Ava's neck thrums when I push off my chair and stride toward her. Her pupils dilate more with every stride I take. Without a word seeping from my lips, I clasp her wrist, yank her away from Rhys, and throw her over my shoulder.

The pounding of her fists on my back match the whacking of my heart as I make my way to my truck. Her wailing halts at the exact moment a garbage compactor and a washing machine going to battle sounds from her stomach. One of her hands shoots up to cover her mouth while the other secures a rigid grip on my jeans.

"I'm going to be sick," she squeaks out.

Her warning comes too late.

My teeth crunch together when the first splash of vomit spills through her fingers and is absorbed by my shirt. My shoulders stiffen and a low, dangerous growl ripples from my lips. I move to the rose bushes at the front of Mrs. Mable's house and place Ava onto her feet.

As she expels the bottle of tequila she drunk into the bushes, I comb my fingers through her sweat-drenched hair, securing it into a braid. I swear, I've never seen someone spew so much in my life. The bottle of tequila was a fifth in size, but she's puked more than double that.

Once her stomach is void of any type of liquid, I scoop her into his arms and continue walking to my truck parked half a block down. Carefully, I place her into the passenger seat and secure her belt before bolting around to the driver's side.

Grumbling to myself, I remove my vomit-stained shirt and throw it into the bed of my truck before jumping into the cab and kicking over the engine. Ava tries to be discreet, but I feel her eyes running over my body as I pull my truck into the car-lined street. After she's finished her avid assessment, she fans her cheeks and shifts her gaze to the pitch black sky.

"Don't you dare vomit in my truck," I warn, my tone deadly serious. "It's bad enough you hurled all over my favorite shirt, but if you vomit in my baby, I'll spank your ass."

My statement is not an idle threat. If she fails to adhere to my warning, I will spank her ass. It took me hours of scrubbing to get her Skittle spit marks off the leather on my dash, but at least that smelled refreshing. I'll never get rid of the smell of vomit.

When a chill runs down Ava's spine, I lean over and adjust the temperature of the air-conditioning. She flashes me a quick smirk in gratitude but remains quiet.

The short four-mile trip from Jorgie's house to our apartment building is made in complete silence, and thankfully, it's vomit-free. After throwing my key to the parking valet, I run around my truck to help Ava down. She rolls her eyes and mumbles something about her not being a child before she jumps down unaided.

Any further protests halt when the heel of her shoes gets caught in the crack of the concrete and she stumbles onto her knees. Seeing that her knees are bruised and bloody, I scoop her into my arms and walk through the double glass revolving doors. Ava hides her tear-stained face in my bare chest. When Patty absorbs my shirtless frame approaching with Ava in my arms, he rushes to the elevator bank and hits the call button. Because of the late hour, the elevator immediately dings open.

"Thanks," I say, pacing into the empty car. "Can you push the penthouse button?"

Patty's worldly eyes lock with mine. His gaze is apprehensive, his genuine concern for Ava beaming out of his eyes.

"I'll look after her."

His eyes bounce between mine for a short while before he says, "Damn straight you will."

"My security access code is 3156," I advise after he hits the P as requested.

By the time the elevator arrives to the top floor, Ava is fast asleep, cradled in my arms. My heart pounding is the only noise I hear as I move through my penthouse to the guest bedrooms located in the hall. The desire to take Ava into my room is overwhelming, but until I've had the chance to apologize, I don't need another imprudent decision added to my already long list of mistakes. I tug down the pastel pink comforter on the bed and gently lay Ava down.

The darkness of her hair is even more striking against the pale color of the sheets. She groans before rolling on her side, curling her legs up near her chest. Although I'm certain she has no liquid left in her stomach, I remove the plastic lining from the waste bin and place it beside the bed.

Once I've removed her shoes, I make my way to the bathroom, hoping my mom purchased some iodine and band aids when she stocked my fridge and pantry earlier this week. I send a quiet blessing to god for my mom when I find all the supplies I need to patch up the grazes on Ava's knees.

Her face winces when the iodine is rubbed over the gash on her knee, but other than that, she's unaware of the medical procedure being undertaken while she's asleep. After tucking her in, I switch off the light and take my position in the chair in the corner of the room, not trusting that I'd hear Ava if she woke from the other side of my apartment. As her breathing shallows, my eyes flutter shut and my memories drift.

When I wake up the next morning, Ava is gone.

## TWENTY-FOUR

## AVA

"I'm so sorry I'm late," I say, rushing into the office Patty and I have brunch at every Sunday. "I slept in."

I step into the small space, wrangling with bags of breakfast foods I picked up at the corner café. Normally, I'd prepare a majority of the food we eat, but with a horrific hangover and a pounding headache, I decided to purchase our breakfast instead. I dump the bags onto the glass desk, then move to the cupboard at the side to grab the plates and cutlery. My heart leaps out of my chest when I crash into a solid chest. Even though I don't need to lift my eyes to know who it is, I do.

"Good morning, Ava." Hugo stares down at me. "What's for breakfast?"

Snarling, I side-step him. "I didn't buy enough for three."

That' a lie. I have enough food to feed an army, but I'm not going to tell him that. Prior to my drunken spectacle, today is the first time I've seen Hugo in a week. I've gone out of my way to ensure I haven't had to associate with him. My desire was so vicious, when he turned up unannounced at Jorgie's house, I scaled the fence between Jorgie and Mrs. Mable's property just to avoid him. Mrs. Mable was both shocked and delighted by my impromptu visit.

*Although she may not be next time when she realizes I was the one who added extra fertilizer to her award winning rose garden.* I even went as far as sharing my aunt's couch with her cats so I didn't have to go back to my apartment and face him. Avoidance isn't the solution in any situation, but it's the only defense I have against Hugo and his alluring pull, so I've been using it to my full advantage.

After pinching the bridge of my nose to lessen my pounding headache, I amble to the cupboard and remove the cutlery and plates. The dishware clangs together when I aggressively throw it on the desk. Having the enormity of Hugo in this small space is too much for me to bear. There's nowhere I can escape from his familiar scent that makes my heart clutch every time I smell it.

"Where's Patty?" If he doesn't arrive soon, I need to leave. Being so close to Hugo hurts.

"It took a lot of convincing, but Patty agreed to give me five minutes alone with you."

My eyes rocket to his. "You'll need a lot more than five minutes to fix the mistakes you've made," I sneer. "Do you have any idea how embarrassed I was having my personal life broadcasted to hundreds of people? I've never been more mortified in my life!"

Hugo stands at the side of the room as I unpack the array of food. He has his arms crossed in front of his chest and his eyes are tracking my every movement, but he remains so quiet, I'd be able to hear a pin dropping. My eyes continually dart to the clock on the wall, counting down the remaining seconds I'm subjected to the torture of smelling his intoxicating scent. I suck in a big breath, endeavoring to get through the pain of having him stand so close but not being able to touch him. The crippling pain in my chest strengthens when I realize I'll probably never get to touch him again. *You can do this, Ava. Grow a back bone! Be strong!*

"Your five minutes is up," I say once the clock strikes noon.

For the briefest second, I pray he'll ignore my request and

demand to stay. Because even being furiously angry at him, my stupid body craves his attention, no matter how minute it is. My prayers are left unanswered when he smiles before ambling to the door, passing Patty on his way in. I slouch into the office chair and bury my head into my shaking hands. Patty walks over and runs his wrinkle-covered hand down my back.

"Did you give him the chance to explain?"

I raise my welling eyes. "No," I say with a shake of my head.

Patty's mature eyes peer straight through to my soul when he says, "You might want to listen to what the boy has to say. He's not a bad man, Ava. He cares for you."

"He hurt me, Patty."

"Trying to protect you."

My brows furrow, unable to grasp what he means by his statement. Hugo was fighting with Marvin because of his jealousy. *Wasn't he?*

The remainder of my brunch with Patty is eaten in silence. It's the quietest we've ever been. After placing a farewell kiss on his cheek, I walk to the elevator banks. The heaviness on my heart is weighing down my shoulders, making my steps slow and lazy.

When the elevator dings open, my wrist is suddenly seized and I'm hauled into the elevator car. My heart hammers against my chest when Hugo moves to the elevator panel and inserts a key into the lock. My earlier anger that was subsiding returns full pelt when the elevator doors snap shut tighter than a vault at a bank.

Gritting my teeth, I move to the elevator panel and push every button available. My effort is fruitless and the doors remain closed. *I knew Hugo living in my building would be a bad idea.*

Rolling my shoulders, I spin to face him. "Let me out," I demand.

He shakes his head. "No can do."

Fuming with anger, I cross my arms under my chest and pace to stand in the furthest corner of the elevator car, putting as much distance between us as possible.

"You agreed to talk to me last night."

"I lied," I sneer. "There's nothing you could say that will make me forgive you anyway. So you may as well save your breath."

"Lucky I've always believed actions speak louder than words."

He snatches my wrist and pulls me toward him. His mouth crashes into mine so furiously, my lips feel bruised. I yank away from him, pushing hard on his chest. He firms his hold on the nape of my neck, securing my mouth to his. When his tongue plunges into my mouth, I clench my teeth down, gnawing on the very thing that caused most of my pain - his vindictive tongue.

My knees shake when his deep growl rumbles through my heaving chest. My disloyal nipples pebble, turned on by the roughness of his kiss. Guilt swamps me when the bitter tang of blood mingles with the sweet cinnamon taste of Hugo's mouth. I didn't mean to intentionally hurt him; the buildup of anger was just too much for me to inhibit any longer.

Even injured, Hugo continues to kiss the living hell out of me. He kisses me like a man starved of my taste. Warm slickness coats my panties when I stop thrashing against him, no longer having the strength to fight off a man I've craved for years. My nipples tighten with pleasure as my fingers rake through his hair. Realizing I'm no longer fighting against him, Hugo adjusts the intensity of our kiss, switching it from a raw, primitive kiss to a sweet, heart-combusting one.

His tongue coaxes into my mouth, sweeping inside in slow, core-clenching strokes. He pulls me in close to his body, allowing me to feel how aroused he's by our kiss. A whimper escapes my lips when he grips my thighs to hoist me up the wall so I can grind against his thick, hard cock.

My heart clenches when he pulls his lips away from my mouth and peers into my eyes. His eyes are full of remorse and are beaming with silent apologies.

"It killed me, Ava," he breathes heavily, dropping his lips to my neck. "Hearing him say he was going to touch you fucking killed me."

My brows scrunch, confused by his statement. The crinkle of my brows smooths when he sucks on the skin of my neck, marking me with his mouth.

"He was bragging to anyone who would listen that he only turned up to the wedding to take you home." He pulls his wicked mouth away from my tingling neck. "To fuck you and make you his."

He stops talking to inspect the mark he created on my skin. His cock twitches, seemingly pleased with his effort. A violent shiver of arousal tingles down my spine when he sucks my erect nipple into his mouth through my shirt. I grip his hair as a jolt of pleasure rockets through my pleading pussy. My cotton shirt clings to my chest when he releases my nipple from his gifted mouth with a loud pop. The hardness of my nipples peaks more when he blows air onto the moist material. My breath hitches as he lifts his scandalous eyes to mine.

"When I saw you gathering your coat, preparing to leave with him, I lost it. I didn't want him to touch you. I *hated* the idea of him touching. I want to be the only man who gets to touch you."

I gasp in a sharp breath as I stare into his wild eyes. Even with his heart hammering against his ribs so fast, I can feel it pulsating through my body. His eyes are open and raw, exposing the cyclone of emotions surging through him. Hugo's always been a communicator, but his eyes are relaying way more than his words ever could.

I cup the edge of his jaw. "I wasn't leaving with Marvin. I was calling him a taxi," I explain, staring into a pair of eyes that have captured my soul. "There was only one man I wanted to leave with that night. That man was you."

A hiss of air seeps from his lips, fanning my heated cheeks. As I stare into his eyes, the ice that formed around my heart the past week thaws. The past seven days has been one of the hardest weeks of my life. I've barely functioned.

It's scary how quickly I've allowed Hugo to steal my heart. I shouldn't be surprised, though. He's been the only man occupying my heart the past ten years, so it was easy for me to relinquish its care to him. I've always said my crush on Hugo was childish and immature, but in all honesty, I loved him from the moment I tackled him to the ground and straddled his hips.

"Do you have time to talk now?"

Smiling, I nod. My heart stutters when he puts me back down onto my feet before he places the key into the elevator panel, selecting the penthouse button.

"How did you get a key for the elevator?" I ask, my voice croaky from the roughness of our kiss.

"My boss owns the building."

I gasp. Now I know why I'd thought I'd seen him before. He was the young man sitting in the corner of the room when I entrusted my money to the company building my apartment.

"Does your boss have a name, or are you just going to keep calling him 'Boss?'"

My pulse flutters when a broad grin stretches across Hugo's sinfully handsome face. "I might just call him Boss. It has a nice ring to it."

I roll my eyes, pretending I'm not loving his playfulness. When the elevator arrives at Hugo's floor, he encircles his hand around mine. The erratic pounding of my heart starts up again as we pace toward his door. When we reach the door, he expands onto his tippy toes and gathers a key from the top lip of the door. No matter how many times I advised the Marshall family that it isn't a safe practice, they continue to store their keys on the lip of the door frame.

Hugo opens his apartment door and gestures for me to enter before him.

"Why did it make you angry?" I question, kicking off my shoes and placing them at the side of the entranceway table.

He throws his keys and cell phone into a crystal bowl on the table. "Did what make me angry?" he replies, spinning to secure the deadbolt on the door.

I lick my tingling lips. "That I was a virgin," I squeak out.

Hugo stops frozen, dead in his tracks. I mimic his frozen posture as a frenzy of emotions twist my stomach. When he turns on his heels and looks down at me, I'm taken aback. I was expecting to see anger reflecting out of his eyes, not remorse.

"It didn't make me angry, Ava. I just wish you would have told me."

"And how exactly should I have done that? Had business cards made up to hand out on dates, warning them they were in the presence of a naïve virgin?"

I try to keep the bitchiness out of my tone. I fail miserably. Why is it anytime someone mentions the word virgin, guys run for the hill? I could think of far worse words that could be used when referring to a women's sexual experience.

Hugo smirks at my witty comment, but his heart isn't fully into it. "I would have happily accepted a card if it avoided me hurting you."

My eyes snap to his. "You didn't hurt me."

His appearance pales. "You bled, Ava."

I take a step toward him. "That's normal. That happens all the time." I stare into his remorseful eyes. "Have you never slept with a virgin before?"

His eyes widen before he shakes his head. I smile, loving that although I'm not the first woman he has slept with, I am his first something.

"Well, I guess you'll just have to take my word for it. You didn't hurt me. I'm perfectly fine."

My pulse strums the veins in my neck when he takes a step closer to me. "I don't have to take your word. You can prove it to me."

"How?" My overly girly voice echoes in the foyer of his apartment.

Agitated excitement spurs through me when I see the look of hunger forming in his eyes. "You can show me."

Eagerness builds as he places his hand on the small of my back and leads me through his residence. Because his apartment is the exact replica of mine, only ten times bigger, I know where he's leading me. My aching muscles from lack of sleep the past week loosen, surrendering to the gentleness of his touch as he guides me toward the master suite of his penthouse.

An array of emotions hit me at once when he swings open his bedroom door. Standing on shaky legs, my eyes absorb the grandeur of the room. A king-size bed covered in dark, rich material sits in the middle, a walk-in closet Carrie from *Sex and the City* would die for is on my right, and rich material covers the floor-to-ceiling windows on my left. The room is impressive and very manly. Overwhelming desire runs rampantly through my veins when the scent of Hugo's aftershave hits my senses, closely followed by the smell of his skin.

I swallow hard when he walks me to the side of the bed, unbuttoning my blouse on the way. The material sags off my shoulders before toppling to the floor. I inhale a quick, sharp breath when his gaze drops to absorb my body. His gaze is predatory and hungry, and it has my pulse thrumming. His hands make quick work of my jeans, yanking them down my quaking thighs in no time at all until I am once again standing before him in nothing but a pair of panties and a lace bra.

"Lay down on the bed," Hugo instructs, nudging his head to the monstrous bed.

My unease about following his instructions fades when he pulls his shirt over his head, exposing inches of his delicious skin. I scoot across his king-size bed as my eyes absorb every hard ridge of his muscles. It won't matter how many times I see his perfect body, it will never be enough. Wide, broad shoulders bulked with muscles, droolworthy biceps, a tight, lean waist and legs that go for miles. His body has been the cause of many self-induced orgasms in my life the last eight years.

Unfortunately, his seductive strip tease doesn't take long, since he only has two articles of clothing to remove. *I can't wait for winter.* The muscles in his arms flex when he grasps my wrist and yanks me down the bed. Any laughter preparing to escape my lips halts when his heated eyes burn into mine. Kneeling at the edge of the bed, he hooks his thumbs into my panties and glides them down my quivering thighs, exposing me to his rapacious gaze. He stares unashamedly at my bare mound. My pussy aches, begging to be consumed by him. Excitement scorches my veins when he places his hands on my inner thighs and gently pries open my legs.

"Keep them there."

I bite my lip and nod, unable to secure an entire breath. My thighs shake when he runs his index finger down my labia.

"Does it hurt here?"

I shake my head. "No."

My breathing excites when he spreads my vagina open with his fingers, fully exposing me.

"Here?" He touches my inner labia.

*God no!* My entire body is thrumming with excitement.

"No," I shake out huskily.

I snap my eyes shut when he rubs the pad of his thumb over the hood of my clit.

"Here?"

I try to force the word "no" out of my mouth, but my brain is too occupied with my rampant horniness to relinquish any words.

Taking my silence as a yes, Hugo mutters, "I better kiss it better then."

I gulp loudly when his lips press a soft, gentle kiss on my throbbing clit. I swivel my hips, shamelessly begging for more contact. My pleas fall on deaf ears when he lifts his voracious eyes to mine.

"Is it better?"

Embarrassingly, I shake my head. I've never been one for deceit, but if a little lie will force him to touch me, I'm willing to bend my rules. Hugo smiles, knowing I'm lying, but thankfully, he lets my little white lie slip. My back arches when his mouth encloses over my aching-with-desire clit. I gasp when he tongues my clit with quick fire hits, spiraling both my mind and my coil. My eyes squeeze shut, my body shutters, overwhelmed by how quickly my release is building.

"Fuck, you taste sweet. I've never eaten a sweeter pussy."

His words send a tidal wave of desire gushing through my body.

Hugo's never had any trouble communicating, and I love that even in the bedroom is no exception. I weave my fingers through his hair as my race to climax hits momentum. He continues to lick, suck, and devour every inch of me, slurping up every drop of my excitement with a thirst of a man lost in the Sahara. When the intensity becomes too much for me to bear, I grip his hair and yank him away from me.

"No, Ava," he murmurs against my clit. "That was dinner. Now give me my dessert."

My grip on his hair tightens. "I can't. I've never..." *climaxed on a man's face before.*

Although I was a virgin, I've participated in other sexual activities. My primary goal during those exchanges was to ensure my partner's every whim was taken care of. I learned early on if they were exhausted and thoroughly satisfied, they never cared that we didn't have sexual intercourse. All they cared about was getting off. So even though I have experience in this aspect of sexual encounters, I've never done *that* directly on a man's face.

"Then I'll once again be your first, babe, because I'm going to eat your pussy until you come on my face."

My body shakes, aroused by his determination. His big hand slithers up my stomach and gropes my breasts, twisting my tight buds. With the combination of his tongue lavishing my clit and his talented fingers tweaking my nipples, all concerns vanish and exhilaration takes over. I groan and rock against him, my whole body coiled and ready to release.

"That's it, babe, give it to me."

His voice vibrating through my core sets me off. My whole body quakes when I splinter into a glass-shattering orgasm. He increases the speed of his lashes, forcing me to ride the wave of intensity of my climax instead of fighting against it. The ride is crazy and wild, an out-of-body experience.

I've barely recovered from the earth-shattering aftermath when a condom wrapper being torn open sounds through my ears. I moan when the crown of his cock braces against the entrance of my pussy.

Anticipation for being filled to the brim by his large cock heats my blood. My anticipation turns to frustration when a delay stretches between us. Surprised by the holdup, my head lifts off the bed, wondering why he hasn't plunged his thick cock inside me.

Hugo's eyes are drifting around the room, seeking something. Noticing my curious glance, he says, "We need to change positions or I'll hurt you again."

Before I can protest that he didn't hurt me the first time, he leaps off the bed. I crank my elbows, watching as his naked frame retreats from the room. Taking the opportunity during the pause, I run my hands down my hair, de-fluffing the crazy mess. I can imagine how much of a nightmare I look right now. My hands drop when Hugo ambles back into the room, carrying a dining room chair. My mouth waters when my eyes zoom in on his rock-hard condom-covered cock.

He places the chair in the middle of the room before lifting his eyes to me. The raw, primal look in his eyes spears me in place. With a lift of his chin, he requests for me to join him. Through shaking legs, I slide across the bed and pace toward him. His eyes run over my body with just as much eagerness as my eyes are absorbing him. When I reach him, he sits down on the chair and offers me his hand. Excitement dashes through me when his thick shafts brushes against my drenched folds when I straddle his lap.

"This way you can guide the pace, only taking as much of my cock as you can handle."

I lick my lips and nod. He places his hands on my hips and guides me upwards until the entrance of my pussy is hovering over his thick, throbbing crown. The sting of both pleasure and pain jolts through my womb when I lower down, taking in the first inch of his cock.

"Go slower, Ava. You may be wet but your body needs time to adjust."

My breathing stops when he raises his eyes from watching our fire-combusting connection to me. No apprehension. No concern. Nothing but admiration is sparked in his eyes. He groans, and a swear words seeps from his lips when I slam down hard, taking every inch of his cock in one quick motion.

"Fuck, Ava," he growls, his fingertips bending as he obtains a tight grip on my hips, securing me to his pelvis. "I said to take it slow."

I shake my head. "You said to only take as much of your cock as I can handle." My words are breathless, my body relishing being stretched so wide.

"Because I didn't want to hurt you."

I stare into his narrowed eyes. "There's a very fine line between pleasure and pain."

Pleasure rockets through my body when he slaps my backside with enough force, fiery heat spreads across both cheeks. He stares into my eyes while soothing the sting of his slap with a gentle rub of his hand.

"There's a very fine line between pleasure and pain, but there are other ways you can achieve that thrill than using my cock."

"But I like your cock," I breathe out heavily.

A meow purrs through my lips when his cock twitches, stretching me even wider.

"I take that back. I *love* your cock." I've never felt so whole.

The smile stretching across his face is nearly enough to make me come. My god he is beautiful, a flawless specimen hand-crafted by god himself. I could stay here like this forever: our bodies connected in the most intimate way, his heartbeat felt through my palms resting on his chest as I stare dotingly into his eyes. It's perfect. Better than any dream I've ever had. It's a memory I'll cherish forever – until the end of eternity.

## TWENTY-FIVE

## AVA

My eyes snap open when a tormented moan ripples through my ears. A strange unknown environment surrounds me. Rich, dark coloring and a manly feel to the space make my concern even more noticeable. When another pained sound resonates through the quiet, I suddenly realize why I've awoken. It wasn't the thumping of my head from a lack of sleep or the thrumming of my pulse from experiencing countless orgasms overnight. It's someone in the midst of a nightmare.

I gingerly rise from the bed just as Hugo screams, "Get off!" at the top of his lungs. His leg kicks out in front of him and his fists curl into tight, constricted balls. His face contorts with pain as he thrashes against the mattress.

"Stop it! Stop it! Get off!" he screams before a tormented cry shreds from his throat.

I scamper across the bed and crawl onto my knees. My hands shake as I lift them to offer him comfort. Before I can get my hands anywhere near him, his hands shoot out and snatch my wrists. My face winces when a sharp pain jolts up my arm from his rigid hold.

"Get off!" he screams again.

Ice-cold fear chills my veins when he tightens his grip on my wrist. An animalistic groan tears from his stern, shut lips as he shoves me away from him. From the brutal force of his throw, I sail off the bed and land halfway across the room. Tears prick my eyes. Not from the pain of my wrist jarring against the carpeted floor, but from the terrified mask hampering Hugo's face. His eyes rapidly move under his eyelids as his nightmare continues to wreak havoc on his usually cheeky nature. He needs to wake up. I need to wake him up.

"Hugo, wake up!" I shout from a distance, too scared to go near him but still wanting to ease him out of his nightmare.

His violent thrashing stills, but his face remains contorted with pain.

"Wake up!" I scream again as the first lot of tears spill from my eyes.

Abruptly, his eyes pop open. His chest is heaving up and down; his pupils are the size of dinner plates, and his body is covered with a dense layer of sweat. Panting hard, his panicked eyes dart around the room. When he notices me sprawled on the ground, the sternness on his face dissipates and a new, unreadable shield slips in its place.

"Ava?" His voice is extra hoarse from the tormented screams released during his nightmare.

I can tell the instant the reality of the situation hits him, as the pain in his eyes firms. He climbs off the bed and kneels to stand in front of me. Because of how much he's sweating, his woodsy scent is even more alluring than normal.

"Did I hurt you? Are you hurt?" he asks as his eyes assess every inch of my face and body.

The rapid shake of my head sends tears flying off my cheeks.

"Then why are you crying?" His eyes drift to the bed several feet from me. "And why are you on the floor?"

I try to construct a response, but with the combination of the events that just transpired and my restless night, I'm at a loss for words.

"Fuck." He sits on the balls of his feet and runs his trembling hand over the top of his head. His body is rigid, and the aftermath of his nightmare reflects in his clouded eyes.

After a short stretch of silence, he stands from his crouched position and stalks out of the room. I want to go after him, but stay kneeling, my brain too fried to force my legs to move as a surge of chaotic emotions crash into me.

Once I've gathered my composure, I scamper off the floor and take off after him. My heart races as I make my way out of the main bedroom and down the hall. The trickling of freshly brewed coffee into a percolator changes the course of my direction. The strong, heavenly scent hits my senses as I enter the kitchen, waking me more from my agitated state. As tempting as a hot brew is right now, I exit the kitchen when I discover it's void of Hugo. After checking the den, dining room, and living areas, I make my way to the master bathroom on the other side of the apartment.

The sound of the shower running amplifies the further I walk down the hall. I knock on the partially cracked-open door before pushing it fully open. Through the billowing of steam, I see Hugo standing under the double shower. His feet are planted wide, his head bowed, the heavy pressure of the shower head blasting hot water onto the nape of his neck.

Sensing my presence, he slants his head to the side. My heart cracks when I see the bleakness in his eyes. They appear almost lifeless. Utterly broken. When his eyes return to the dark gray tiles, I strip out of my clothes, leaving them where they fall.

Cold sweat clings to my skin when I open the glass door and slip into the steam-filled space. The muscles in Hugo's back flex when I run my hand down his spine, soothing him, using my touch to free him of the aftermath of his nightmare.

"I'm sorry if I hurt you, Ava." The brokenness in his eyes breaks my heart.

"You didn't hurt me."

He angles his head to the side and stares into my eyes, calling my deceit.

My heart slithers into my gut. "You scared me, but you didn't hurt me."

I slip under his arm bracing against the wall and wrap my arms around his waist. His racing heart pounds through my ear when I rest my head on his chest.

"You're not capable of physically hurting me," I mumble against his chest.

He runs his trembling hand down my back before pulling me in close to him. I pop my head off his torso and peer into his downcast eyes. The furious beat of his heart pulverizes my hand.

"This is the only thing that can hurt me. Not you," I say with my hand over his chest.

"That's the most fucked up part of me," he says with his heavily pupiled eyes dancing between mine.

Lifting my hand, I cradle his sweat-drenched jaw. The blood coursing through his veins throbs against my palm. "Why? Because you had nightmare?"

His eyes relay the words his mouth fails to speak. He feels ashamed.

"Don't be ashamed of something you can't help. Nightmares in adults are generally caused by a psychological trigger. You have no control over them."

A rumble escapes Hugo's parted lips. "You sound like my therapist."

My eyes rocket to his. "You're seeing a therapist?"

"Not exactly," he grumbles. "My boss included it as a requirement of my employment, but I haven't turned up to a session yet."

My brows scrunch, wondering why such a stipulation would be included in an employment contract. I've never heard of such a requirement before. Hugo watches me, gauging my reaction to his confession of needing to see a therapist. I'm not at all concerned. There's no shame in seeking help during a crisis. A lot of men are embarrassed to admit they're struggling, but to me, acknowledging that you need help is one of the strongest things you can do.

I place a quick kiss on the edge of his mouth before pressing my cheek against his chest, not wanting him to feel forced to share personal information he isn't willing to divulge yet. Although his heart is still pounding forcefully, it isn't as intense as earlier.

A stretch of silences passes between us, long enough that the water cools. It hasn't been uncomfortable or weird. It just feels right. I run my hand over the small of his back, supporting him while his index finger traces the curves of my neck. With the heat of the water and the closeness of his body, any agitation hampering my mind soothes. I can only hope it's the same for Hugo.

"I reacted the way I did because when I saw the blood running down your leg, I thought I'd hurt you," he eventually murmurs a short time later.

I shake my head, denying his statement, but remain quiet, happy he's chosen to talk to me.

"I wasn't angry at you. I was furious at myself. If I'd known you were a virgin, I would have ensured your body was prepared, that you were prepared. I wouldn't have done it the way I did."

"I'm glad you didn't know then." I lift my head off his chest and look into his eyes. "That night was better than anything I could have dreamed. Because you didn't know I was a virgin, it was void of the awkwardness I'd been prepared for. The fact you didn't treat me like porcelain made it so much better. I couldn't have entrusted a better man with the task. Not many virgins get knocked-it-out-of-the-park sex on their first try. I not only got that, I orgasmed too."

I become light-headed from the broad grin etching on Hugo's face. "That just proves I fucked up."

My brow arches high into the air. "How?"

He waggles his brows. "You can't get any better than a home run, so I've got no chance of topping that."

I laugh. "I'm sure you'll find a way," I say, stretching onto my tippy toes and sealing my mouth over his.

He found a way to beat it. Not once, but twice.

## TWENTY-SIX

# HUGO

### TWO WEEKS LATER...

"Come on in, Hugo."

My eyes lift from the outdated magazine to where the voice is coming from. A lady with short brown hair offers me a reassuring smile while gesturing for me join her at the end of the hall.

"Avery Clarke. It's a pleasure to finally meet you in person, Hugo," she introduces herself before gesturing for me to enter her cramped office with a wave of her hand.

I run my sweaty palms down my trousers before entering the space. Bland, whitewashed walls, a cream shrink couch and a large blind-covered window makes her new office one of the most boring spaces I've ever encountered.

"A little bit of color wouldn't go astray," I mumble under my breath, my mood surly at being forced to attend therapy against my wishes.

"Sorry? What did you say?" Avery questions, closing the door behind her.

I shrug my shoulders. "I didn't say anything."

She smiles a tight smile before gesturing for me to sit. My eyes drift around the room. Other than a clinical-looking shrink bed in the middle of the space, there's a wooden desk and a leather chair squashed in the far corner of the room.

"I'll be back in a minute," I say, rushing to the door.

Not giving her the chance to reply, I dash into the even more outdated foyer of her office building to collect an empty chair. Avery's brow arches when I walk back into the room carrying the chair in my arms. Placing the chair down at the side of the space, I drag her faded leather chair to sit across from it. Once I have the space set up in a less depressing configuration, I take a seat. Air whizzes out of Avery's nostrils before she gathers a yellow-lined notepad from her briefcase and sits in the leather chair.

"Are you comfortable?" She stares into my eyes.

"I am now."

I cross my arms in front of my chest. I'm not trying to intimidate her. I just want to ensure she knows I'm not here of my own free will.

"Before we get started, I want you to be fully aware that anything you say within these four walls..."

"Will remain in these four walls," I interrupt, not needing the same rundown I'd been given in Afghanistan.

She smiles, seemingly pleased by my response.

"Is there anything you'd like to discuss today?"

She tries to keep the optimism out of her voice, but I didn't miss the increase of huskiness in her tone. I turn my gaze to the large window displaying the sun hanging high in the sky. It's very rare for me to see the midday sun anymore. With my new job, I'm normally arriving home as the sun is rising. I wake Ava up with a mug of coffee and a few kisses, see her off to work, then I crawl into bed, where I stay until the sun is setting.

The past few weeks with Ava has been staggering. The best weeks of my life. I've never felt as content as I have the past few weeks. I always said I wasn't interested in a relationship, but knowing

Ava is waiting for me when I come home is the only thing keeping me going. We have a vigorous sexually-sparked relationship, but it's the quiet times when I watch her sleeping do I realize that isn't the only connection we have. She's the anchor tethering me down during a storm. She's the yin to my yang. And as much as this makes it sound like I've awoken with a vagina, she has stolen my heart.

To be honest, after our first weekend together, I was worried my nightmare would have scared her away, but surprisingly, the twinkle her eyes get every time she looks at me didn't dampen at all; if anything, it grew stronger. Although I knew my nightmares would eventually return, I hadn't had one in months, so I was unprepared for how hard they would rattle me once they did return. That nightmare was by far the worst one I've endured, as no matter how much Ava denies it, I didn't just scare her that night, I hurt her.

My nightmares are the reason I've stuck to my exhausting schedule, working sundown to sun-up seven days a week. Although Isaac is adamant I can choose my own schedule, I can't run the risk of falling asleep with Ava next to me. That nightmare wasn't the only one I've had the past two weeks. I've had them numerous times, some more violent than the first. By sticking with my current working arrangement, I'll be able to see Ava while also keeping her safe. I'll do everything in my power to keep her safe.

I shift my eyes back to Avery. She's watching me cautiously, but stays quiet. The fact she doesn't push me to talk eases my agitation.

"Is there anything I can do to stop nightmares?"

Although my arrangement with Ava is working fine as it's now, I eventually want to wake up with her sleeping in my arms.

Avery's brows furrow. "Are you having nightmares?"

Gritting my teeth, I nod. There's no harm in seeking help during a crisis, but this is different. My nightmares are based on real life events, not because I watched a scary movie before going to bed.

"Are your nightmares about what happened in Afghanistan?"

My eyes snap to her. "You know about what happened there?"

Her throat works hard to swallow. "Yes." Her eyes are void of the judgement I was expecting to see. "Isaac supplied me with your details in the hope that I could help you through this, Hugo."

Unable to maintain her eye contact, my eyes shift around the room.

"How long have you been having nightmares?" She angles her head to the side, requesting my focus.

She has eyes like Ava. Inviting and warm.

"They stopped a few months after the incident, but they returned stronger than ever three weeks ago," I reply, my tone short.

Avery sits on the edge of her chair and peers deeply into my eyes. "Was there a significant change in your life that triggered their return?"

A grin twitches my lips. "I have a girlfriend," I say with a laugh, mortified by using a term only middle school kids should use.

A genuine smile spreads across Avery's face. "That's pretty significant."

I chuckle and uncross my arms, loosening my arrogant stance. I know if I gave Avery the chance, I'd like her. She also doesn't deserve to cop the wrath of the anger I've shown her the past six weeks when she calls trying to do phone consultations with me. Although her career path is horrible, so is Ava's and I *really* like Ava. Even if she's the equivalent of every child's worst nightmare.

Avery's smile sags when I say, "I also stopped drinking."

She stares at me while nodding. "Alcohol can seem like an easy fix, but eventually, it isn't even enough anymore. Until you work through the underlying issue causing your nightmares, they will never fully disappear."

I nod before turning my eyes back to the window. I'll never forget what happened in Afghanistan, so I guess I'll never stop having nightmares.

Avery encloses her hand on my clenched fist. "Something may have happened that triggered the return of your nightmares. Do you know what that may have been?"

My heartbeat turns wild as an influx of guilt smashes into me hard and fast. I turn my eyes back to Avery. When I peer into her eyes, I could pretend I was looking straight into Ava's. Avery's arm shudders as the shake on my hand vibrates up her arm.

"Ava had blood. So did Gemma."

## TWENTY-SEVEN

## AVA

I dump my purse in the drawer of my desk and amble out of my office. With summer arriving early, I'm wearing a free-flowing cotton sleeveless dress, accentuated by the pair of rosy cheeks I've been wearing the past three weeks. There's no doubt, my V card has been well and truly handed in. I've had more sex the past few weeks than most women achieve by the time they're thirty. My sex life is so vigorous, I'm rarely seen without an aroused appearance. Even with my excitement being embarrassingly exposed, I wouldn't change a single thing.

My relationship with Hugo has been going great. Almost too perfectly. He greets me every morning with a hot brew of coffee before seeing me off with a kiss on the lips, then I arrive at his office every evening for an early dinner. We've had sex at nearly every location we've visited. His truck. His office. The storeroom at a bustling nightclub. The den at Jorgie's house. Unsurprisingly, the only place we haven't slept together is at my work. Hugo is adamant he'll never step foot inside my office, let alone sit in the dentist chair.

Smiling at the mortified look on Hugo's face when I suggested he should drop in for a quick check-up today, I pace into the reception area to call in my first patient of the day. My eager steps falter when Marvin exits his office. Although his fight with Hugo was weeks ago, his face is still sporting some faded bruises from their exchange. He has spent the past few weeks ignoring me, which suits me just fine. I never had the intention of talking to him anyway.

When sidestepping Marvin, the cell phone in my white coat vibrates. Quickly, I slip it out of my pocket and peer down at the screen.

**Jorgie:** *Lunch?*

I smile while typing a reply.

**Me:** *Sound greats. I'll meet you at Capers at noon?*

Ellipses trickle across the screen as Jorgie types a response.

**Jorgie:** *Yes! I was hoping you'd say Capers. I'm dying for their Caesar salad... and cheeseburgers. See you at twelve.*

Smiling at her excitement, I return my phone to my pocket and call in Mrs. Roach and her son, Xavier.

By the time midday rolls around, I'm beyond starving. Not just for food, but Hugo as well. He's my addiction and I'm beyond saving when it comes to him. Slinging off my coat, I hang it on the coatrack in my office then dash down the corridor. Mrs. Gardner says farewell with a nod of her head as I rush past her to the parking lot at the back of the office. A blast of hot, humid air smashes my face when I exit the back door. It's only mid-May, but the temperature has been hovering around the mid-eighties.

Jorgie greets me with a large smile and numerous plates of food when I enter the restaurant.

"Hey, sorry I'm late. A mother's paranoia about a cleaning stretched my schedule thin," I say, leaning in and placing a kiss on her warm cheek.

"That's okay. It's not like I have anything better to do," she replies, her tone cheeky.

"How is the maternity leave going?" I steal a couple of French fries off her plate before signaling for a waiter.

Jorgie waits for the waiter to take my order for two iced raspberry teas before replying. "It's as boring as hell. It's only been a week. I've no clue how I'm going to survive the next six months."

I place my hand on her forearm. "You won't be saying that when you're juggling diapers, bottles and a screaming baby in five weeks' time."

A large grin stretches across her face. "He'll be worth it," she mumbles, rubbing her expanded stomach.

"Yes, he will." Tears well in my eyes.

Jorgie huffs dramatically while adjusting her position so she sits more comfortably with her expanded belly before lifting her eyes to me. "Well enough about me and my watermelon. How are things with you... and Hugo?"

I bite the inside of my cheek, internally battling to hide my excitement. Just one look into Jorgie's mist-filled eyes tells me she isn't buying my attempts at candor.

"It's really good. I wake up every morning and pinch myself just to make sure I'm not dreaming."

I try to keep my tone neutral but miserably fail. I've never been more happy. Hugo and I may have only been together officially as a couple for weeks but we have a lifetime of memories we share.

"I'm hardly sleeping because I don't want to wake up and find out it was all a dream. I also don't want to miss a single moment."

Now it's Jorgie's turn to have tears prick in her eyes. "Oh, stop it," she demands, using a napkin to dab away a few rogue tears escaping her eyes.

Seeing her happiness for Hugo and me trickling from her eyes make my own tears shed. I lower my hand down to my bare thigh and give it a gentle pinch. I sigh, relieved I don't wake up from the dream I'm living. Flinging my immature tears off my cheeks, I lean in close to Jorgie's side.

"The rumors are true," I whisper into her ear. "Hugo's nickname you try to pretend doesn't exist. It's one hundred percent true!"

My excited squeal gains us the attention of a handful of patrons. Jorgie gags. I laugh at the repulsed expression etched on her face before taking a large bite out of one of the many cheeseburgers in front of me.

After devouring enough food to feed a small community, I signal for the waiter to bring us the bill.

"I'm paying," I declare when Jorgie collects her purse from her handbag. "It's the least I can do."

She looks at me, confused by my statement.

"If it weren't for you, I'd still be fighting fate," I explain.

When a large grin stretches across her face, my heart skips a beat. She and Hugo have many similarities. A heart-stopping smile is one of them. After paying the bill, Jorgie and I walk out the restaurant arm in arm. My eyes shoot to hers when she fails to suppress a large yawn.

"Are you not sleeping?"

She shakes her head. "If having a water melon attached to my belly isn't bad enough, I can't sleep without Hawke next to me."

My heart squeezes painfully. I pull Jorgie in close to my chest. The flutter of her pulse runs the length of my arm.

"He'll be home soon," I say as a surge of emotions pummels into me.

I miss Hugo when I'm away from him for a few hours, so I can understand Jorgie's dilemma of not seeing Hawke for months. Thankfully, their absence this time around is only a matter of weeks with Hawke's squadron returning home the week Jorgie is due.

"Did you want to join Hugo and me for dinner tonight?" I offer.

Her nose scrunches as her face whitens.

"I promise I'll keep my hands to myself at all times," I say, crossing my finger behind my back.

She eyes me dubiously. "Alright, but if I see one thing that makes me gag, your lunch schedule for the next five weeks is fully booked out." She bumps me with her hip. "I've missed you a lot the past few weeks."

My heart warms. I've missed her too. More than she'll ever know.

"Deal," I say, raising my pinkie into the air.

Giggling, she accepts my pinkie promise.

"Where are you parked?" I ask, seeking her little beat-up Honda.

She peers past my shoulder. "Across the street."

I gasp when I spot Jorgie's *Baby* parked across the street. "You got *Baby* on the road?"

Jorgie smiles. "Yep." The "P" pops from her mouth. "She still needs a bit of work, but she's drivable."

Her head cranks to the right before shifting to the left. "Where are you parked?"

"Halfway down the block," I grumble. "I went around the block three times, and I still couldn't find an empty spot."

Smiling, Jorgie wraps her arms around my neck and hugs me goodbye.

"Bye," I whisper into her ear.

"You don't say goodbye, you say, I'll see you later," she reminds me.

I pull away from her embrace and peer into her glistening eyes. "And that I will," I reply. "I'll see you tonight."

She nods her head and smiles. I run my hand down the side of her arm before pivoting on my heels, my happiness clearly evident on my face. The sun warms my arms as I briskly stroll to my car. The smile on my face enlarges when I dig my hand into my handbag, searching for my keys and I notice my cell has one new text message.

My heart races when I read the message.

**Hugo:** *I've cleaned up the storeroom in anticipation of your visit. I can't wait to see you.*

Grinning like the cat watching the canary, I press the speed dial for his number and lift my phone to my ear. My smile fades when my call is directed to his voicemail.

"Hey, you've reached Hugo; leave a message."

"Hey," I say breathlessly, my excitement for his message heard in my voice. "We have a special guest for dinn--"

I stop talking when brakes squeaking and tires bouncing across asphalt pummels my ears. An overwhelming fear clutches my heart from the awful sound. When my neck cranks toward the noise, distress surges through my blood, turning it potent. My phone slips from my hand, tumbling to the ground. The screen on my cell cracks when it connects with the sidewalk, shattering into a million pieces, just like my heart.

## TWENTY-EIGHT
## HUGO

"Mark, can you give Dante a hand unloading the supply truck please?" I request, leaning over the bar at The Chapel.

Mark waggles his brows before bolting out the back entrance of the club.

"And don't break anything today," I yell, rolling my eyes.

Mark is the newest bartender at The Chapel. If it weren't for his GQ magazine cover good looks, I would have let him go his very first night, but even with him spilling more drinks than he serves, the female clientele love him. Whenever he's on duty, the women flock to the club in droves. He's good for business and staff morale.

"We're not open for a few more hours," I say when the entrance bell on the front door chimes.

I finish signing my signature at the bottom of a receipt before turning my eyes to the door. I'm shocked when I notice Ava standing there, staring at me wide-eyed. It won't matter how many times I see her, my eyes drink her in every single time.

"Hey," I greet her, pacing closer, wanting less space between us before my eyes ravish her skin. "You're early." I lean in to press a kiss on the edge of her mouth.

Normally Ava doesn't arrive at the club until a little after six PM. We have dinner together in my office before she occupies the remaining hour of my self-prescribed two hour lunch. *Obviously, she got a little excited about my teasing message.*

My brows scrunch at how cold her cheek feels when my lips press against it. Although we haven't hit summer yet, the temperatures the past week have been setting record highs. I pull her to arm's length and run my eyes over her face. Her pupils are massive, filling her entire cornea. Her face is white and covered with a dense layer of sweat, but the most concerning feature to me is the devastation reflecting out of her beautiful eyes. Her terrified look sets me on edge.

"Ava, babe, are you okay?"

"Y-your phone," she stutters.

My confused eyes bounce between hers, baffled by what my phone has to do with her frantic state. My stomach cramps with dread when her eyes erratically dance between mine and she says, "Y-y-you didn't answer your phone."

I run my hand down the front of my jeans, discovering my pockets are empty. "I must have left it in my truck after my appointment with Avery."

A heavy weight of despair slams my chest when fresh tears spill down Ava's pale cheeks. A rock settles into my stomach, subjugated with confusion. My eyes dart from Ava to Isaac when he pushes off the doorframe of my office and paces to stand next to me.

"Ava, what's going on?"

I lower my eyes to the rest of her body. The air is forcefully sucked from my lungs when I notice a blood stain on the front of her dress. My fists clench as my back molars smack together.

"Did someone hurt you? Are you hurt?" I question, my words coming out in a frantic rush. Fury blackens my veins, heating my body. "Who did this to you? Did Marvin do this?"

Tears fling off Ava's cheeks when she rapidly shakes her head. She runs her hand under her nose, wiping away the contents of her nose spilling over her lip. Her chest thrusts up and down as she strives to regain a sense of composure. I stare at her, wild-eyed and spiraling out of control.

My heart thrashes against my ribs when she whimpers, "There was an accident."

Her eyes are facing to the side of me. She looks like she's in a trance.

I grip her chin and slant her head upwards. "You were in an accident? Is that why you have blood on your dress?"

I try to keep my tone neutral, but panic and fury are making my tone come out as abrupt. I'm spiraling out of control, unable to grip the reality of the situation. I turn my bewildered eyes to Isaac when Ava shakes her head. I stare at him, wordlessly questioning if he has any better understanding of the situation. He looks just as lost as I feel.

My eyes rocket back to Ava when she says, "Not me. Jorgie," through a barrage of hiccups.

Fear grips my heart. "Jorgie was in an accident?"

A painful sob tears from Ava's mouth as she nods.

"Where?"

Her pupils widen even more, but she remains silent.

"Where, Ava!" I yell, projecting my voice over the ringing of my pulse in my ears. "Where is she?"

When Ava stays quiet, Isaac grips the top of her arms and shakes her hard enough, her teeth clang together. Normally, his type of response would cause my blood to turn potent with violent rage, but I can tell from the look in his eyes, he isn't trying to hurt Ava. He's doing everything in his power to snap Ava from her trance.

"Where is Jorgie, Ava?" Isaac's tone is demanding and clipped. "Tell Hugo where Jorgie is!"

Ava's massively dilated eyes lock with mine. "She's at the hospital."

I'm running out the double wooden door before the entire sentence escapes her lips.

## TWENTY-NINE

## AVA

I flinch when Hugo's boss wraps his arms unexpectedly around my shoulders.

"It's okay," he mutters, his voice shifting from the angry roar that pulled me out of my state of stupor, switching to a soothing purr. He wraps his arms around my shoulders and guides me toward the door Hugo just bolted out. "I'm going to take you to the hospital."

Suddenly, he stops walking and looks down at me. The sincerity in his unique gray eyes causes new tears to fall from my mine.

"Do you want to go to the hospital?"

My chin quivers as I nod. He smirks, attempting to ease the haze of fear clouding my mind, trapping me in a trance-like state.

"Roger, bring my car around." He peers over my shoulder.

The ten minute trip to the hospital is made in silence. Hugo's boss offers silent support the entire way. He grips my clammy hand in his and runs his thumb over the veins profusely bulging in my hand. Due to Roger breaking every possible traffic law, we enter the hospital emergency bay not long after Hugo.

A crippling pain twists my stomach when he throws open his truck door and rushes through the automatic glass doors. I unclasp my seatbelt, throwing it off my body before taking off after him. I shake my head, begging for the images that are going to haunt my dreams to stop playing through my mind. Once the fog hampering my brain is clear, I increase my pace. My urgent steps are guided by the need to ensure both Jorgie and Hugo are safe. When she was carried off in an ambulance, she turned her inert eyes to me.

"I'll see you soon," she whispered faintly before they slammed the ambulance doors shut.

When I round the corner of the emergency department, I spot Hugo standing at the nurses' station in the middle, frantically requesting information from the only nurse at the station. He runs his trembling hand through his hair, frustrated by the nurse's lack of knowledge. His posture shows his first emotion is fear, closely followed by anger.

Suddenly, his head cranks to the side when Rhys walks out a set of doors in scrubs. Hugo charges for him, reaching him in two heart-thrashing seconds. The concerned mask on Rhys' face causes my stomach to churn. He only began his surgeon internship three weeks ago, and he already looks exhausted.

I can't hear any words they speak to each other, but their conversation looks heated. Hugo's clenched fists firm with every second that passes. My hand darts up to clutch my neck when Hugo grabs Rhys by the neck and throws him against the wall. I stand still, frozen in shock. Two security guards race across the room and attempt to drag Hugo off Rhys. Their effort is pointless. Hugo is too strong and too angry.

Rhys is only released from Hugo's death clutch when Hugo's boss bolts across the room and drags Hugo away. Rhys falls to his knees, gasping for air. Hugo pulls away from his boss and storms toward the emergency department exit doors. My heart is torn into shreds when I see the devastation on his face. The broken look in his eyes after his nightmare was nothing compared to the soulless look his eyes have now.

Air wafts my face when Hugo storms past, tossing over a medical equipment cart on the way by. Unable to secure a breath, I crumble to the floor. When my devastation becomes too much for me to bear, I give permission for my tears to fall. Loud, howling sobs bounce off the hospital walls and jingle in my ears. My distressed cries become even louder when I realize the howling is coming from me.

When a pair of black polished shoes appears in my field of vision, I lift my tear-drenched face. The scent of expensive cologne engulfs my senses when Hugo's boss crouches down in front of me. Accepting the handkerchief he is offering, I wipe my tears and blow my nose.

A pain I've never experienced before in my life tears through my heart when his gray eyes stare into mine and he says. "You need to get Jorgie's family here. She isn't going to make it."

My eyes lift from draining lettuce leaves in the sink to the tree house in the backyard. A handful of the kids from the neighborhood, too young to understand the complexity of the situation, are climbing up the rickety wooden ladder. Their bright smiles are amplified by the sun hanging in the sky.

That was the treehouse I sat in, quivering like a bag of nerves, when I confessed my crush on Hugo to Jorgie. I'd expected her to take the news a lot worse than she did. Although she said it was "totally gross" that I'd ever find Hugo attractive, she also said she'd support me no matter what.

*I'm going to miss her every day of my life.*

Against doctors' advice, the Marshall family kept Jorgie on life support for three days, giving Hawke the opportunity to say a proper goodbye to the love of his life. Three hours after Hawke returned home, they switched off Jorgie's life support. She passed away a few hours after that, surrounded by her family and friends. She was buried this morning with her son, Malcolm, resting in her arms.

It was a beautiful service, packed with attendees as far as the eye could see. The Marshall family has always been a well-respected and much-loved entity in the Rochdale community and that shone through at Jorgie's funeral. No expense was spared to give her the heartfelt sendoff she deserved.

I run my hands down the front of my black sheath dress, smoothing out the invisible crinkles I believe are there before pouring the washed lettuce into the salad bowl. Once Mrs. Mable has placed the cherry tomatoes and cucumber slices on top of the lettuce, I walk the bowl into the dining room.

Keeping the food table stocked is helping to keep my mind off my grief. Mrs. Hamilton, Jorgie's fourth grade teacher, watches me as I pace across the room. She doesn't speak, but her eyes relay her silent sympathies. After placing the tossed salad onto the table, I roam my eyes around the space. Everyone here had some significant part in Jorgie's life. Either a family member, teacher, friend or work colleague. I was the only one lucky enough to class her as both my family and friend.

As I pace back into the kitchen, I stop frozen in my tracks, believing I saw Hugo's profile. Although I saw him at the funeral, I haven't *seen* him since the night they switched off Jorgie's life support. I don't have solid evidence, but I'm fairly certain he's sleeping at his office. I want to help him through his grief, but I'm at a loss on how to do that while also coping with my own anguish. Through shaky steps, I move to the direction of where I thought I saw him. Several eyes stray to mine to issue silent sympathies as I pace by.

Although I can't see Hugo, I know he's here somewhere. I can feel it in my bones. When I turn down the hallway, I spot him… and a flurry of blonde. I shake my head, certain I haven't seen who I thought I'd seen.

My heart thrashes against my chest as I walk down the hall and take a left at the end. I freeze at the back screen door of the Marshall residence, giving my eyes a chance to assess the situation, ensuring I don't make an irrational decision.

Once I'm certain I have the facts right, I storm out the screen door. Hearing the creak of the door, Hugo's eyes lift to mine. He tries to speak, but his words stay entombed in his throat. I sidestep him and stand in front of the bitch who deserves the severity of my wrath.

My palm sets on fire when I slap Victoria so viciously, her head flings to the side.

"You're a piece of shit! Using his grief as a way to dig your claws back into him," I sneer, my tone dangerously low as an absurd amount of anger crashes into me so hard and fast, I'm nearly sprawled onto my ass. "You're nothing but a motherfucking whore!"

An arm wraps around my waist and yanks me back. I thrash and kick wildly, fighting against Hugo's hold. I dig my nails into his arm so hard, I draw blood.

I've never been a violent person, but that doesn't stop me from inflicting as much damage as I can to Hugo's shins and arms as he carries me down the stairs of the deck and further into the backyard. I violently yank away from him when he places me onto my feet in the garage at the side of the Marshall residence.

"Calm the fuck down." He stares at me with wild eyes. "That wasn't what it looked like."

I laugh, a scary menacing laugh that displays what I'd been suspecting the last five days: I no longer have a beating heart in my chest.

"It wasn't?" I ask, my pitch smeared with bitchiness.

When he shakes his head, I yell, "Then why do you have lipstick smeared on your mouth!?"

Hugo's eyes widen before he runs the back of his hand over his lips, removing Victoria's fire engine red lipstick from his mouth. A curse word sweeps from his lips when his eyes absorb the red stain marking his hand. When he takes a step closer to me, I violently shake my head.

"Stay away from me," I sneer through clenched teeth. "I don't want you to touch me!"

My words have more of an effect on him than any slap I could have inflicted. He stands across from me, staring but not speaking.

Other than his jaw twitching, he stays perfectly still. My gaze turns to Victoria standing at the side entrance of the house. Her eyes are drifting around the surroundings, no doubt seeking Hugo.

I can barely breathe as anger envelopes every fiber in my body. I'm not just angry at them kissing. I'm angry that Hugo left me to deal with my grief alone. No support. No backup. Just left to battle through my grief one tear at a time. He wasn't the only one who lost Jorgie. I lost her too.

I straighten my shoulders before returning my eyes to Hugo. His fists are clenched, his chest rising and falling with every breath he takes.

"You can have her," I say, nudging my head to Victoria. "Because I deserve way more than you could ever give me."

With that, I pivot on my heels and exit the garage. He lets me go without a single protest.

# THIRTY

# HUGO

FOUR WEEKS LATER...

"Are you sure you want to pack it all away? He may change his mind."

My mom's eyes lift from the box she's packing to peer at me. The normal spark of life that fires her eyes has been snuffed, replaced with a pair of eyes I don't recognize. They're full to the brim with turmoil and loss. Even though it's been four weeks since Jorgie passed away, my family is still in the process of grieving. I honestly don't know if we'll ever come to terms with our loss.

"Hawke is never coming back, Hugo. I could see it in his eyes when he said goodbye," she whispers faintly.

No matter how much I tried to convince Hawke to take some time to properly formulate a rational decision, he re-enlisted in the military the day after Jorgie's funeral. He left for Iraq two days after that. It almost killed me seeing the devastation of his loss in his eyes. I was struggling losing my baby sister and nephew, but he lost his wife and son in one devastatingly cruel blow. That's more than any man should *ever* have to go through.

I shadowed Hawke from afar the days following Jorgie's death, making sure he didn't do anything to harm himself or anyone around him. Most of his time was spent at the bar on the outskirts of town that refused to hire me several months ago, stating there was no suitable positions for a man like me. I wanted to talk to Hawke, to offer him my support, but when I looked into his eyes, I knew solitude was the only thing he wanted. *Silence is the one true friend that never betrays you.*

I fold down the flap on a brown moving box and seal it with a large strip of tape before placing it on the stack of boxes at my side. I've spent the last several hours aiding my mom in packing up Jorgie's house. It's not a task I wanted to complete, but someone had to do it, and I couldn't leave that burden resting solely on my mom's shoulders.

Noticing the kitchen and living room have been packed, I move to the main bedroom. Jorgie's room is untouched, left as it was the day she died. Her perfume bottle is sitting open on her dresser, alongside a collection of sovereigns she amassed over the years.

A smile tugs on my lips when I spot a button pin for Lake George. Jorgie loved visiting that lake as much as I did. Every school break, my parents would rent the same cabin on the water's edge. From the age of ten, Ava joined a majority of our family vacations. Like every young boy, I taunted my crush for the entire break. Ava kept me thoroughly entertained.

Lake George is also where Jorgie met Hawke. If you asked Jorgie to explain how they met, she would say he was an angel who fell from heaven and landed in her canoe. It sounded a lot more extravagant than it actually was. In reality, he was climbing a tree to get his clothes I'd thrown up their after he decided on an impromptu skinny dip with a group of college girls.

When a branch cracked under his heavy weight, he assumed the water would soften his fall. He never expected to crash into a wooden canoe. He missed four games over the summer waiting for the bruises on his back to heal and even more weeks than that chasing Jorgie.

I slip out of Jorgie's room, closing the door behind me. I've done more packing than I can handle today.

"Do you think Ava would want this?" my mom asks when I pace back into the living room.

The first genuine smile in weeks crosses my face. Nodding, I remove the friendship rock from my mom's grasp. My smile enlarges when I see the difference in the size of the hands painted on the rock. Ava's hand print is much smaller than Jorgie's.

I haven't seen Ava since Jorgie's funeral. As much as what she said to me hurt, it was true. I've always known she deserved a man much better than me. I was just hoping she was foolish enough not to care.

What she stumbled on at the back patio with Vicky wasn't as it seemed. Yes, I did have Victoria's lipstick smeared on my mouth, but that was only because she dove at me before I can register what she was doing. I pulled away from her in an instant, fuming with anger.

I'd just buried my sister and nephew; the last thing I was interested in was a quick fuck in the coatroom. Even if I weren't attending a wake, I still wouldn't have been interested in what Victoria is offering. You can't spend weeks devouring a prime steak, then go back to eating a pork chop.

I was in the process of removing Victoria from Jorgie's wake when Ava discovered us. I'm going to be honest, seeing Ava finally stand up to Victoria was one of the most visually satisfying sights I've ever seen. Victoria taunted both Ava and Jorgie for years, so witnessing her being put in her place was a gratifying experience.

My eyes turn to my mom when a loud gasp escapes her lips. She has one hand covering her mouth and the other is clutching a piece of paper. She's trembling so much, the paper shakes like a leaf. When her eyes drift to mine, my steps falter. It's only the smallest spark, but it's the first time I've seen it in her eyes in weeks. Happiness.

"What is it?"

When my mom remains quiet, I remove the piece of paper from

her hand. My brows scrunch as my eyes roam over the document, speed reading the letter from the bank Jorgie worked at.

"Jorgie and Hawke's mortgage was paid in full?"

A tear rolls down my mom's cheek as she nods her head. "Do you think it's from the same company who paid Jorgie's medical expenses and funeral?"

My eyes rocket from the letter to my mom. I was unaware someone had paid for Jorgie's expenses. In all honesty, I didn't even consider how my parents were going to afford those type of expenses. I was too focused on my grief to worry about those details.

"What was the name of the company?" I query, even though I'm fairly certain I already know the answer to my question.

"Holt enterprises," my mom replies.

Perceiving my presence, Isaac's gray eyes lift from his desk, which is covered in papers.

"Did you pay my sister's mortgage?" I question, pacing further into his office.

He buttons his suit jacket as he stands from his chair. "Yes."

"Why?"

His eyes bore into mine as he scratches his brow. Most men would be quaking in their boots from the fierce look he's directing at me, but I can see that behind the furious mask he wears is a man struggling just as much as I am.

His eyes drift to the open door of his office before turning them back to me. "I understand what Hawke is going through."

My brows furrow, but I remain silent, waiting for him to decide if he wishes to elaborate on his reply.

"Seven months ago, my girlfriend was killed in a traffic accident. She was pregnant with my baby."

I suck in a big breath, shocked by his response. *How is he functioning so well in such a short period of time?*

"Everyone handles grief differently. I threw myself into building my empire."

I nod, finally understanding why Hawke left so quickly. If he didn't occupy his mind, he would have gone mad.

"Although your stories are similar, it doesn't explain why you were so generous. You don't even know Hawke. He's a stranger to you."

"But I know you," Isaac interrupts. "When you joined my empire, you became my family. I take care of my family." Even though his tone is stern, his eyes reflect genuine remorse.

I once again nod. I spent my entire life protecting my sister, but the one time she needed me the most, I failed.

A cell phone shrilling echoes in the silence that had encroached Isaac's office. I shove my hand into my pocket when its vibrating tone jingles through my thigh. I'm surprised when I notice it's my mom calling. I only left her ten minutes ago. Hitting the connect button, I press the phone to my ear.

"He's getting away with killing my baby," she yells down the line before I get the chance to issue a greeting. "The DA just called. He was released this morning. All charges have been dropped."

"What?" I reply, my mind spiraling.

The man driving the car that struck Jorgie was three times over the limit. He was arrested at the scene and charged with vehicular manslaughter. How could he get away with this? It doesn't make any sense.

"There must be a mistake. It can't be true. He was arrested at the scene."

"The only mistake is that the bastard who killed my baby now gets to walk free," my mom sobs.

I clutch the phone so tightly, my knuckles go white when my mom's howling sobs sound down the line.

"I'll fix this. I'll make it right," I promise before disconnecting the call.

My brisk strides out of Isaac's office slow when he calls my name. Cranking my neck, I stare into his stern eyes.

"Haste decisions will cause unforgiving mistakes," he warns.

"And sitting around doing nothing will make me a coward." My jaw ticks as the wave of emotions hits me at once.

"I may have failed to protect Jorgie, but I'm not going to let her murderer walk free."

# THIRTY-ONE

## AVA

TWO WEEKS LATER...

"Good boy, Jarrod, just one last swish of water and you're good to go."

Jarrod's excited eyes dart to his mom sitting in the corner of the room, seeking praise for the bravery he showed while having his first filling done. I slide my swivel chair over to my desk to collect a roll of stickers I keep in the bottom drawer. A smile tugs on the corners of my mouth when I notice the first sticker is a gold sheriff's badge with "Sheriff Brave" printed on it. Jarrod squeals excitably when I hand him the sticker and assist him down from the dental chair.

"Now remember, no more yogurt before bed. Yogurt has calcium in it, but it also has a lot of nasty sugars your teeth don't want to sleep in," I say, rising from my chair.

Jarrod eagerly nods his head before joining his mother. The fake smile on my face slips the instant they exit my office. I slump into my chair and swivel around to peer out the small office window. The room is completely silent. I've never felt more alone. I not only lost my best friend when Jorgie passed away, I also lost part of my soul.

The devastation of her loss has been even more shattering with losing Hugo as well.

Suffering the loss of two very important people in my life within days of each other was nearly more than I could bear. I barely functioned the days following Jorgie's death. If it wasn't for Patty bringing me food and forcing me to eat, I would have perished on my bed I refused to leave. I only returned to the land of the living when the two weeks' bereavement leave Mrs. Gardner kindly granted expired.

For the past four weeks, I've thrown myself into my job. Arriving before the sun rises and leaving once the sky is pitch black. Occupying my mind has been the only godsend in this horrible situation. Work is truly the only thing keeping my head above water.

Running the back of my hand over my cheeks, I remove a few stray tears that fell from my eyes before gathering my belongings from my desk, preparing to go to lunch. My stomach is swirling with how hungry I am. I inhale a quick, sharp breath when my cell phone displays I have one new voicemail. My shock isn't because no one has called my phone in weeks, it's because the voicemail is from Hugo.

I've missed Hugo more than any words can express, but I'm also angry at him... *and myself.* I'd give anything to see Jorgie again, but Hugo lives in my apartment building, and I still haven't worked up the courage to see him. Jorgie's death should have brought us closer. It should have made us realize that life is too short and we should cherish every moment, but instead of doing that, I'm letting stupid jealousy rule my heart.

My heart hammers against my ribs when I dial my voicemail and press my phone to my ear. Seconds feel like hours as I wait for the call to connect.

"Hey, Ava. It's Hugo."

Tears prick in my eyes from the dejected tone in his voice.

They roll down my face when he says, "I've missed you so much, babe, more than you'll ever realize."

I push the phone in close to my ear, ensuring I can hear his message over the furious pounding of my heart.

He releases a deep breath. "I didn't kiss Victoria at Jorgie's wake... I know what it looked like, but I swear on Jorgie's grave, it wasn't as it seemed. I'd never betray you like that, Ava. I could never... I love you. I have for years. Ever since you dove over the couch and tackled me to the ground."

A loud sob tears from my parted lips.

"I hope one day you'll find it in your heart to forgive me for what I've done."

When the line goes silent, I press the phone in tightly to my ear, assuming the line has gone dead. It's only when I hear Hugo's pants of breath do I realize he hasn't hung up.

"Goodbye, Ava," he says a short time later before he disconnects the calls.

My finger shakes as I redial my voicemail and listen to his message again, and again, and again, only stopping when a commotion outside of my office draws my attention.

"Sir, you can't go in there," Belinda, the office receptionist, says as my office door swings open.

I stand from my chair, shocked when Hugo's boss enters my office, unannounced. I haven't seen him since the afternoon at the hospital.

"Where would Hugo go if he didn't want anyone to find him?" he questions me, his words hurried and abrupt.

"What? I don't know. I haven't seen Hugo in weeks."

I pace toward him. My brisk strides halt, cut off by the furious glare Hugo's boss inflicts on me.

"An isolated place he could go where no one would find him? He wouldn't have any fear of being seen?" he interrogates.

"I don't know." I shake my head, my voice gaining an edge of fury behind it.

"Think, Ava, think!" he demands, stepping closer to me. "There has to be somewhere he could go for privacy?"

The concern in his eyes causes my stomach to twist in panic. He stares at me, his eyes begging for me to answer him.

"Lake George?"

The suit-clad gentleman shakes his head. "No, it has to be closer. Somewhere local."

A range of addresses flurry my mind, adding to the giddiness clustering my brain. There's nowhere Hugo could go that he'd be alone. Every residence I can think of is occupied. Suddenly, I freeze. My eyes snap to Hugo's boss. He's watching me with a pleading look in his eyes.

"Jorgie's house?" I suggest, my tone flat.

His eyes widen, and his shoulders square. "Yes. Where did she live?"

"Umm... I don't know?" My eyes widen.

"Please, Ava, this is very important."

"I don't know," I reply, my eyes relaying to him that I'm telling the truth. "I've only ever driven there."

His hand delves into his pocket to remove an ancient-looking cell phone. The urgency of his movements sets me on edge.

"I could show you where she lives?" I suggest.

He nods before returning his cell phone to this pocket.

"We need to hurry." He pivots on his heels and exits my office.

I grab my handbag from my desk drawer and follow him out of my office. Halfway down, Marvin steps into the hallway, checking what all the commotion is about. His eyes flick between me and Hugo's boss.

"If you leave, Ava, you'll risk your career. You'll lose everything," he threatens, his tone intimidating.

Without a hesitation, I reply, "I don't care. He's worth it."

I sidestep Marvin with my head held high, pretending my heart isn't racing a million miles an hour. I slide into the back seat of a Lexus town car parked at the curb. Hugo's boss holds a conversation on a large brick cell phone as Roger drives frantically through the streets of Rochdale. I don't hear any of the words he's speaking, the ringing of my pulse is too loud to hear anything. We arrive at Jorgie's house in record time. Relief overwhelms me when I spot Hugo's truck parked half a block down. My relief doesn't last long. *Why would Hugo not park his truck in Jorgie's driveway?*

When I attempt to follow Hugo's boss out of the car and down the sidewalk, he pivots around to face me. The sternness in his eyes causes my steps to falter and has my thighs quaking. Once he realizes I'm frozen in fear, he lifts his eyes to Roger, who is still exiting the car.

"Make sure she stays here," he instructs, his tone firm.

My stomach swirls as I watch his quickly retreating frame enter the front door of Jorgie's house. I swallow several times in a row, fighting to keep the bile in my stomach from surging into my mouth. Even in the humid, suffocating air, a cold chill of fear runs down my spine. I clutch my stomach when its churning kicks up a gear.

No longer able to hold in my fear, I lurch over and vomit into the gutter, narrowly missing Roger's polished shoes. Since I skipped lunch, my body only expels small portions of green bile. Accepting a handkerchief from Roger, I dab my mouth, removing any leftover smears of vomit before straightening my spine.

After what feels like a lifetime, Hugo exits Jorgie's front door. His face is gaunt and pale, his shirt has flecks of blood on it, and his eyes are dark and lifeless. He takes a step backward, hesitating when he notices me standing on the sidewalk.

Brushing away a tear tracking down my face, I stare at him. The pain in his eyes amplifies as he returns my stare. So many unspoken words drift between us as we stand across from each other staring, but not speaking. Our intensely searing stare down only stops when Hugo's boss emerges from Jorgie's house. His dark eyes drift between Hugo and me for several heart-clutching seconds before they lock with Hugo.

Hugo's eyes snap to mine when his boss mutters something in his ear. Although I can't hear what his boss is saying, I know the news he's delivering isn't good, because Hugo has the same look in his eyes he did when I stumbled out that Jorgie had been in an accident.

My mind spirals, reeling out of control from too many emotions hammering it at once. My breathing stills when Hugo commences walking down the concrete sidewalk. I clutch my chest when he takes a left at the end of the path. I'm standing at his right. He walks three paces away before he suddenly stops. His shoulders rise and fall with every breath he takes, but he stays frozen with his back facing me.

My heart wildly beats as I pray for him to turn around, to have the courage to face me, the courage to fight for us. The twisting of my heart amplifies from his slumped, defeated posture. My mind scrambles, trying to think of something to force a reaction out of him, to stimulate him to remember our powerful connection.

Recalling his earlier voicemail message, I yell out, "You don't say goodbye, you say, 'I'll see you later.'"

For once, my prayers are answered when he pivots on his heels and charges for me. His lips crash into mine with so much force, my feet lift from the ground. He braces my back against the car as he kisses the living hell out of me. I kiss him back with just as much passion, expressing everything I wanted to say to him the past six weeks. My sorrow, my apologies, my regret for hurting him with my cruel words. His tongue strokes into my mouth, tasting and absorbing every inch.

He steps closer, pinning me between his imposing body and the car door. A rush of heat pools in my nether regions when the thickness of his cock braces against my pussy and halfway up my stomach. Tears well in my eyes, overwhelmed by how much passion is displayed in our kiss. Every stroke, gentle nip, and soft caress of his lips has my heart enlarging more. He kisses me like a man who owns me. And he does.

By the time he pulls away, my lips are nearly as swollen as my heart. Hugo's fire-sparked eyes dance between mine as he carefully places me down onto my feet. He lifts his hands to remove the tears dripping down my cheeks, rubbing them away with a sense of urgency. Once he's satisfied all my tear stains have been cleared, he cups my face with his hands.

Air whistles out of my mouth when he stares lovingly into my eyes and says, "Goodbye, Ava."

He turns around and races down the sidewalk even quicker than earlier. I can't take my eyes off him as he urgently strides to his truck and jumps inside. His tires squeal from his heavy compression on the accelerator. The look on his face when he whizzes past me places a constrictive hold on my heart.

Once the smell of burning rubber is no longer mingling in the air, Roger guides me into the back seat of the town car I'm standing next to. When Roger pulls the Lexus away from the curb, I turn my head in enough time to see Hugo's boss re-entering Jorgie's house.

I walk into the foyer of my office building, more confused than ever. Mrs. Gardner's dark eyes drift to mine when I enter.

My voice rattles when I blurt out the first excuse that enters my brain. "I'm back from lunch."

I don't know how I did it, but I manage to fulfill all my patients' appointments and even took in an emergency case of a little boy whose front tooth was chipped by his brother's fast curveball. By the time I'm leaving my office, it's a little after nine PM.

Patty greets me with an apprehensive smile when I walk into the foyer of my apartment building. "Good evening, Ms. Westcott."

"Hi, Patty."

"Rough day?" he asks, already intuiting what my answer will be.

"I could really go a glass of wine right now."

He chuckles before pushing the elevator button for me. I stare at the elevator doors, recalling the time the doors opened and I discovered Hugo standing behind them. *I'd give anything for him to be standing behind them now, waiting for me.* I release the breath I'm holding in when the elevator doors ding open and I discover the car is empty.

I turn my eyes to Patty. "Could you please put in the penthouse floor code for me?" I shrug nonchalantly. "I...umm... left my coat in Hugo's apartment."

I cringe at my pathetic excuse. It's nearly ten PM, and the temperature is still hovering around eighty degrees.

After a beat, Patty says, "I did hear we were supposed to have rain tomorrow."

My fingernails dig into my palms when Patty pushes the P button on the elevator dashboard and inserts the four digit security code for the penthouse floor.

"I'd hate for you to catch a cold if a cool change comes through with the rain."

I issue my gratitude with a smile. When the elevator doors snap shut, I check my face in the mirror. I look as horrific as I feel. The thrumming of my pulse increases with every floor the elevator climbs. By the time I reach Hugo's floor, I'm perspiring profusely. My hand rattles when I lift it to bang on his door.

When Hugo fails to answer my knocks, I stand on my tippy toes and run my hand along the top seal of the door. A grin lifts my lips high when my fingers grasp the spare key the Marshall family members always hide there. After placing the key into the lock, I swing open the front door. My breath hitches halfway between my lungs and my throat.

Moving deeper into the space, my eyes frantically dart around, absorbing the enormity of the situation. The entire apartment is empty. Not partially empty. Empty, empty. Like no one has ever lived here empty.

An overwhelming sense of fear envelopes me as I make my way out of Hugo's apartment and back down the hall. My mind is hazed, confused as to why Hugo would move out of his apartment only months after moving in. My eyes lift when heavy footsteps boom through my ears. Two gentleman dressed in dark suits are briskly walking down the hall.

"Sorry," I apologize when I scoot past them.

My eyes rocket to the side when the gentleman's brisk movements reveal a black revolver holstered on his waist. *Maybe they're detectives working Jorgie's case?*

I push the elevator button before turning my eyes back down the hall. My interest is piqued when they stop at the front of Hugo's apartment. I lean into the elevator doors, concealing myself in the nook. My heart leaps out of my chest when the gentleman carrying a gun kicks in Hugo's door. I fall forward, tumbling into the elevator when its doors suddenly open. I didn't hear it ding, announcing its arrival over the erratic beating of my heart. I lean out of the elevator in just enough time to see the gun-carrying man exit Hugo's apartment.

"I'm sorry Mr. Petretti; he's gone."

A man with a heavy set of wrinkles angrily snarls. "Find him and anyone associated with him. Find them NOW!" he shouts.

I jump when his thunderous roar echoes down the corridor. My heart stops beating when his head suddenly flings to the side and he spots me spying on him. A squeal parts my lips as I stumble backward, landing onto my backside with a sickening thud.

"The elevator!" he shouts.

I scamper off the floor and rush to the dashboard. The tremor of my hand shakes my arm as I frantically push the door close button. Feet stomping on a tiled ground overtakes the mad beat of my heart. Relief engulfs me when the doors start to shut. I squeal when a man lunges for the door.

Thankfully, he's too late to stop the doors from fully closing.

I step backward and lean my damp, slicked skin on the back wall of the car. Closing my eyes, I gulp in air as the signs of a panic attack overcome me. I've never been more petrified in my life. Nothing but evil reflected from Mr. Petretti's eyes when he stared at me. His eyes belong to the devil.

My eyes snap open when the elevator dings announcing it has arrived at my floor. I exhale a shaky breath before stepping out of the elevator car. Digging my hand into my purse, I frantically search for my keys as I pace to my apartment. My brisk strides halt when I'm suddenly grabbed from the side.

"You need to come with me," says a raspy voice, dragging me further down the hall.

## THE END...

Don't fret, Hugo's second book is already available!
Beneath the Sheets

**Have you read Isaac and Izzy's book yet? The first is FREE. You can find it here: Enigma**

If you want to hear updates on my stories and the man of Ravenshoe, be sure to like my Facebook author page.
www.facebook.com/authorshandi

**Join my newsletter to remain informed:**
http://eepurl.com/cyEzNv

**Join my READER's group:**
https://www.facebook.com/groups/1740600836169853/
Hunter, Hugo, Hawke, Ryan, Enrique & Brax stories have already been released, but Brandon, Regan and all the other great characters of Ravenshoe will be getting their own stories at some point during 2019 & 2020.

# ALSO BY SHANDI BOYES

### **Perception Series:**

Saving Noah

Fighting Jacob

Taming Nick

Redeeming Slater

Saving Emily (*Novella*)

Wrapped up with Rise Up (*Novella - should be read after Bound*)

### **Enigma:**

Enigma of Life

Unraveling an Enigma

Enigma: The Mystery Unmasked

Enigma: The Final Chapter

Beneath the Secrets

Beneath the Sheets

Spy Thy Neighbor

The Opposite Effect

I Married a Mob Boss

Second Shot

The Way We Are

The Way We Were

Sugar and Spice

Lady in Waiting

Man in Queue

Couple on Hold

Enigma: The Wedding

Silent Vigilante

**Bound Series:**

Chains

Links

Bound

Restrained

Psycho

**Russian Mob Chronicles:**

Nikolai: A Mafia Prince Romance

Nikolai: Taking Back What's Mine

Nikolai: What's Left of Me

Nikolai: Mine to Protect

Asher: My Russian Revenge

Nikolai: Through the Devil's Eyes

**RomCom Standalones:**

Just Playin'

The Drop Zone

Ain't Happenin'

Christmas Trio

Falling for a Stranger

## **Coming Soon:**

Skitzo

Trey

Printed in Great Britain
by Amazon